M000032425

A KILLER SECRET

JEFF BERNEY

BAQJAC ENTERTAINMENT

COPYRIGHT

Published: December 27, 2019
www.jeffberney.com

ISBN: 978-1-7343921-0-4

To my incredible wife, Christy.
Without whom I'd still be adrift.

ACT ONE

"He that has eyes to see and ears to hear may convince himself that no mortal can keep a secret. If his lips are silent, he chatters with his fingertips; betrayal oozes out of him at every pore."

— SIGMUND FREUD

1

"Why are you doing this to me?" Edie screamed as her fists punched at the air, connecting with the emptiness around her. The strap at her neck chafed as she jerked against it.

Steam billowed up from under the hood of her car as it crept towards the side of the street, no longer under the control of its driver. "Typical," Edie muttered. She seldom felt in control of anything in her life. The seatbelt strap cut into her neck again as the tires hit the curb and the car came to a stop. She shivered as she touched her neck. What a lovely start to date night.

Date night. Good lord, she felt like a teenager whose secret plans to meet her lover had just fallen apart. The streetlight above her hummed a menacing tune that echoed down the block of the deserted street.

She rummaged around in her purse for her phone, though she knew it was a waste of time. She tapped Adrian's name and listened to it ring. And ring. Of course he wouldn't answer. He never did. She couldn't wait to hear tonight's excuse. Would he go for the classic *I didn't hear it ring* or maybe a variation like *I never felt it vibrate*? Maybe he'd use her favorite, *I was enjoying an electronic-free moment of zen.* The only thing zen-like about

Adrian was his unabashed ability to live in the moment, consequences be damned.

She grabbed her bag, jerked her keys out of the ignition, and
slammed the car door shut behind her as she stepped out into
the otherwise pleasant night. She contemplated calling a car
service, but the restaurant was just a half mile away. She could
find it on her own. She didn't need a man's help, but as she
looked around into the darkness another shiver snaked up her
spine. She wondered why she had even agreed to this date, to
this life.

She walked away from her crippled car. Every few steps, she
looked over her shoulder. Her eyes examining every shadow for
any sign of movement. Her mind conjuring up dark, long-buried
demons. She laughed at the irony that even psychologists could
succumb to illogical fears and made-up monsters.

Don't be silly, Edie, she told herself as she picked up the pace.
"You're alone," she mumbled to the benign darkness. *You're
always alone.* She looked down at the phone in her hand. Adrian
hadn't tried to call her back or even text to check on her.

He really wasn't very good at being her...what would she call
Adrian? Boyfriend? No. That word reminded her of high school,
heavy petting, and heartbreak. One out of three, sure, but still
not right. Lover? Only if being inside her, huffing and puffing
from behind qualified, and she reluctantly agreed it must. She
hadn't had much luck with men at all beginning with her first
love and heartbreak. It was middle school. She was totally infatuated and completely wrapped up in this boy only to find out he
was using her for sex and called her 'Eat Me' behind her back.

So maybe she deserved Adrian. Adrian was her mentor, her
business partner, her roommate. He was the reason she ended
up wasting her talents and her life in Kansas City.

Ah, Kansas City. After living in America's heartland for three
years, Edie was convinced that the area's original settlers must

have happened upon this part of the country in either the early spring or early fall. For a few glorious weeks twice a year, Kansas City seemed like paradise. Blue skies, cool weather, light breezes and either the brilliant greens of spring's rebirth or the fiery reds, oranges, and yellows of fall's rapturous decline into winter. The rest of the year you could expect heat and humidity so thick it felt like you were walking underwater in a hot bath, or cold so bitter it felt as though you were being cut by a thousand tiny razor blades every time the angry winds blew. The idea of all those cuts sent a chill down her spine. Edie tried to imagine how someone could survive without central air conditioning or heat. Our ancestors had clearly been tougher than we are now.

Luckily, it was currently early spring. So, despite the fact that she had left her car almost a half-mile back and was wandering the city streets alone at night, Edie was almost enjoying her little impromptu evening walk.

She looked up at the stars, barely visible beyond the buildings and the light pollution of the city. Her mind drifted back to her love life. Not for the first time, she wondered why her life felt so cursed. She hadn't believed in god since she was a young girl. If he did exist, he clearly had a grudge against her.

She thought about the men she'd been with. It was a small, unremarkable group. Some had deserved her love. Others just tried to take it. She hated the very idea of romance. In her opinion, love was the biggest lie of them all. And lovers were just fooling themselves. And, based on Edie's experience, usually fooling around, which brought her right back to her first point. Love was a lie, and the whole world was in on it.

This cheery idea rattled around her head as she turned the corner onto a much darker, dingier street. Her footsteps echoed off the walls around her. The street seemed to close in on her. The air, which had just felt refreshing, now felt stifling on this part of the block. Her breath turned shallow and ragged. *Just keep walking*, she told herself. Just a few more blocks.

Something crashed behind her. The hairs on the back of her neck tingled, and goosebumps raised in waves over her bare arms. It sounded like someone tripped over a garbage can in the alleyway she had just passed. She stopped. Unable to move. When it came to the fight, flight or freeze reflex, Edie's body inevitably chose to freeze every time. The quick tempo of her heart pulsed in her head. She tried to unlock herself, to will her body to obey her desire to get the hell out of there. Finally, after several deep breaths, she was able to move.

She ran so fast she kicked out of her heels, ripping her nylons on the rough sidewalk. She always wore hose or leggings. Even in the humid heat of Kansas City's summers. They were like a protective layer. Armor almost. But even they couldn't make her feel safe now.

Edie dared a glance behind her as she ran. A man and his little dog emerged from the alley. *He wasn't a threat, right?* Still, she didn't like the way he stared at her. And it wasn't necessarily a coincidence that he was walking the same way she was.

Out of breath, Edie finally arrived at the restaurant. She was spooked, disheveled, and late. She was always late. Adrian would accuse her of doing it on purpose. Which of course she usually did.

2

A drian stood as Edie approached. He had been sitting with his chair turned away from the table because Edie always insisted on sitting with her back to the wall. That was fine with him, but it meant he inevitably had to sit facing away from their table until she showed up, late as always. But she was worth the wait.

She was even more breathtaking than usual tonight. Her cheeks were rosy, her eyes shiny. She seemed almost out of breath with the anticipation of their night out. He loved that about her. She was a small woman, not emaciated like a model at all but almost with a certain boyish quality about her that he found both endearing and attractive. Her body was compact and as reserved as her nature. She didn't need big breasts (although he frequently offered to pay for them should she change her mind). She had no butt to speak of, which meant she didn't enjoy the occasional spanking that just slipped out of him in the heat of the moment. Secretly, it thrilled him to know he inflicted a little pain during their most passionate moments. He believed she liked it too, deep down. The most womanly thing about her was her long, straight jet black hair. It seemed even longer when she combed it out because of her short stature. But he preferred it in pigtails. She only obliged him on special occasions, but that was okay with him because it made those times all the more titillating. Tonight it was straight. A bit disheveled even, which was sexy as well.

"You look ravishing, my love," Adrian said as he leaned in to deliver a double tap of air kisses near both her flushed cheeks, careful not to touch her.

"You're crazy. I'm a mess. I came straight from work. I tried calling you. My car broke down, and I had to walk. I ran half the way," Edie replied.

"In our profession, it is rather cavalier to use the word 'crazy,' don't you think my darling?"

"I use it when it seems appropriate, Adrian, as always."

Adrian dismissed her aloofness as he pulled out her chair and waved at the waiter to bring the food he'd previously ordered for the two of them. Edie ordered a glass of wine as the waiter sat a plate in front of her.

"More water, sir," the waiter asked, looking sideways at Edie as he spoke.

"Yes, my good man, and keep them coming," Adrian joked.

Adrian loved dining out. He enjoyed the witty repartee with the wait staff, knowing that the vast majority of his jokes soared well above their heads. Most of all, though, he enjoyed basking in the beauty of his much younger lover, partner, and best friend. No matter the occasion or her mood, being seen with Edie invigorated him. She was no mere arm candy, although she was quite striking. She made him look and feel better. He knew that age and the circumstances of the last several years hadn't been kind to him. He knew that some of his associates called him Grimace, a reference to the portly purple McDonald's character. Others called him Friar Tuck, again because of his size, but also because of his thick beard and his thinning hair, which formed the classic Monk's ring. All of that melted away when he was in her presence. All that remained were the two of them. Edie and Adrian against the world.

People say love is all grand gestures and heartache. For Adrian, who considered himself somewhat of an authority on the matter, love was actually the little moments, the quick glances, the space between the action. That is why, as they sat through a mostly wordless dinner, he felt completely at ease. Completely in the moment.

ADRIAN'S QUIET CALM TURNED INTO A RAGING STORM WHEN THE waiter returned with the bill and his credit card. As Adrian downed the last of his drink, the waiter smiled and handed everything to Edie. He felt his face flush even before Edie raised her head to look at him with bemusement in her eyes.

"What do you think you're doing?" Adrian spat at the waiter.

The waiter jumped and stammered an apology that seemed to Adrian to be more of an auto response without any understanding of the indignity he'd just heaped upon his diner.

"How dare you hand her the bill when it is I who gave you our dinner order, I who have done all the talking to you and I who placed my credit card in the folio that you so obtusely picked up and returned to the wrong person," Adrian barked.

"I'm sorry, sir," the waiter stammered. "I just assumed..."

Adrian didn't allow him to finish. He stormed out of his chair, upending it loudly on the restaurant's wooden floor, grabbed Edie and pulled her behind him towards the door.

"I will be having my bank dispute this bill," Adrian yelled as he continued to march toward the exit. "And you will never have the honor of my patronage again. I have half a mind to sue."

Edie, whose face was even more flush now than when she had arrived, giggled under her breath but loud enough for

Adrian to hear. He ignored her, refusing to hold the door open for her as he rounded the front of his car and fell into the seat.

"Don't forget about my car," Edie said after she'd given Adrian a few minutes to relax as they drove towards home.

"I'll call a service tomorrow. It's too late and too dark for me to do anything about it tonight anyway," Adrian responded through clenched teeth. He wouldn't have done anything even if it were daylight. Although he enjoyed smoking cigars, golfing, playing racquetball and riding his Harley on the weekends, he had never seen anything manly about manual labor. He was simply too evolved to be a grease monkey.

"How could that waiter make such a moronic mistake?" Adrian fumed. "Hadn't he seen me put my card on the table? And even if he hadn't, why just assume?"

"Darling, we've been through this so many times I feel like I'm talking to one of our patients," Edie responded as she stared at the stars through the passenger window. "It's not the waiter's fault. It never is. If anything, your parents are to blame. 'Adrian Hillary' is quite the effeminate name. One can't help but wonder if they knew what they were doing."

Edie's insult hung in the air between them like an angry, low-hanging storm cloud as they rode the rest of the way in silence.

Adrian climbed into bed next to Edie. She had already showered and was reading a book. She had changed into her 'don't even try it' sleepwear, which consisted of baggy jogger pants and an oversized sleep shirt. He nudged his chin into her arm. She yanked it away from him and curled it across her chest without seeming to lose her place in whatever trashy romance novel she was currently enjoying.

"I have something for you," he said.

Edie didn't look up. *Why was she so upset?* He was the one whose honor, whose manhood, that weaselly waiter called into question tonight. He felt his face flush again, but he wouldn't let anger ruin this moment. He set a small pink bag on her lap.

"Open it. Please."

Edie finally looked at him and sighed. She never accepted his gifts well. She was the center of his life, his rock, his only friend. He loved to spoil her by giving her little reminders of his love and devotion. She loved to torture him by making him work for it. Luckily, he enjoyed the give and take. Especially when she pretended that she had no interest in giving so that he had to take.

She grabbed the bag and upended it onto her lap.

"Gee, more lingerie. What a surprise."

"You don't like it? I can get you something different? Another necklace maybe? I know you liked that ring we saw the other day. I could get it for you in the morning," Adrian said.

"No. I don't want any jewelry. I don't want anything, Adrian. We've talked about this. It all comes with strings."

"No strings," Adrian said. "Just my love. I'm going to go smoke. Have it on when I get back."

Adrian slipped out of bed and into the hallway before she could protest. He knew she'd do what he asked. She always came around.

ADRIAN MELTED INTO HIS WORN, OVERSTUFFED LEATHER CHAIR AT the center of his cellar. This was his favorite room in the house. The home was originally built in 1895 by J.J. Heim, one of Kansas City's first beer barons. Mr. Heim had used the cellar to store his private stock. When they first moved in, Edie had refused to go down to the cellar because it was dark and dingy. But Adrian had had it completely remodeled into an old world wine cellar with dark woods to accompany the existing stonework. The cellar now had a full bar, a pool table, and a walk-in humidor. Still, Edie hated it down there.

A ring of smoke floated around his head from his Romeo Y Julieta. They reminded him of his love for Shakespeare and for Edie. He only smoked Cuban cigars. It made him feel manly, rebellious. The pleasure wasn't quite as naughty since the US relaxed the ban on Cuban cigars and anyone could bring the vaunted sticks into the country for personal use, but Cubans were still scarce enough to appeal to his elitist sensibilities. Especially here in the backwater, backwoods of Missouri. God, every time one of the yokels pronounced it 'Missouruh,' Adrian wanted to beat them over the head. No wonder this was a flyover state. You risked the loss of several IQ points every time you landed.

How had he landed here? It was an accident really. Once a renowned academic, Adrian had traveled constantly giving lectures and signing copies of his book like an aging rockstar in a tweed jacket. He had had his choice of tenured professorships at all the best universities in the country. And yet, for her, he had given up everything. Lately, he was second-guessing his decision and wondering if it wasn't time for his second coming. After all, his royalty checks had run out years ago. It wouldn't take much for him to get back on the radar and back on top where he belonged.

The thought of his come back calmed him a bit. He reached over to the record player perched on the small mahogany table next to his chair and gently lifted the needle onto the record. Normally he only played jazz. The wall across from his impressive wine collection was filled with vinyl treasures. The real stuff, not Kenny G elevator schlock. But nights like tonight called for something different. Soon Johnny Cash began to sing-talk about growing up as a boy named Sue. Adrian never understood why his parents gave him the name that made him an instant target to every bully throughout his academic career. It wasn't a family name. All his dad ever told him was that Adrian was a man who meant a great deal to his mother, but he never said why. And his mother never wanted to talk about his namesake.

He glanced at the clock as he snuffed out the remains of his cigar. It was time.

EDIE WAS A BEAUTIFUL WOMAN, BUT EVEN MORE SO WHEN SHE pretended to be asleep. The wrinkles around her eyes dissolved, making her look younger. Her breathing was slow and deep, pushing her small but well-rounded breasts out as if she were offering them up to him, just to him. And the slight part of her lips invited him in.

She had changed into her new outfit. He crawled in bed behind her, pushed the panties to the side and pushed himself into her with one quick thrust. She moaned softly into the pillow. He grabbed her shoulder and pushed into her over and over until he could hold back no longer. Afterward, he let himself slowly shrink until he fell out of her, arranged her panties, wiped himself on the back of her lingerie and pulled her onto her back.

He leaned in for a kiss and was greeted with a smack as Edie pushed him away. He smiled as he rolled over onto his own pillow. He loved their love. Rough at the edges, just like Edie.

3

The graveyard shift. What an interesting name. Depending on your point of view, graveyards are either always open or always closed. So how did the late night work schedule come to be called the 'graveyard shift?'

Timothy had heard once that the name came from 1500s England. People were so afraid of being buried alive that the bourgeois and aristocracy arranged for bells to be attached to their loved ones' coffins. A watchman was assigned to roam the graveyard at night listening for the muffled sound of the bells, ready to dig out those who weren't quite ready to shuffle off this mortal coil. Apparently, this was where the terms 'dead ringer' and 'saved by the bell' came from as well.

Whether true or not, Timothy liked the romance of this story. He could almost picture himself as the little night watchman wandering around the graveyard. What power he'd wield. He alone could decide if the living remained dead. Alas, he was born too late. Instead of watching over the dead and not-yet-dead, here he was shuffling through the cobwebs (real and fake), wandering the crooked halls and exploring the dungeons, torture chambers, and lobby at The Edge of Hell, Kansas City's oldest haunted house.

The security company Timothy worked for sent him all over the city at all hours. He rotated locations throughout the week, but the haunted houses in the West Bottoms were always his favorite assignment. He liked the quietness. He knew every creaky floorboard, every fluttering cobweb, and every costumed mannequin. Sometimes he'd stay after his shift in the offseason and sleep for a few hours in one of the coffins or in the large, elaborately carved Victorian bed in the zombie brothel room. The red silk sheets felt cool against his bare skin, and he liked that the female zombie mannequins watched over him. He usually dreamed of being with them.

He flipped his flashlight as he wandered through the maze of passageways, pointing it into the dark corners as he passed by each room. Nothing moved. Nothing was ever out of place. As much as he enjoyed the ambiance, he couldn't escape the fact that his was a lonely, boring job.

Timothy slowly crept down the house's majestic staircase. He liked to practice sneaking around, moving with catlike precision and stealth through the dark. He stopped on the massive landing and shone his flashlight at the two-story mirror that covered the wall there. His reflection looked so small, though he was average height. His dusty blond hair looked like a mop flowing out from under his Yeti trucker's cap, and the scar on his cheek looked even redder than normal though he was sure that was just a trick of his mind and the surroundings. Sighing, he continued down the stairs even slower now.

Finished with his rounds, Timothy collapsed onto a folding chair in the storage room/office on the main floor. He loved the graveyard shift, but it really took its toll on him when he wasn't able to sleep during the day. Too much to do. Too many plans in the works. He couldn't slow down. He felt the old familiar tug, the shakiness and the nagging buzzing in his brain that grew slowly louder every day he hesitated. He knew he had to do something. But not yet. Soon. For now, he hunched over in his chair, pulled his hat further down on his head, and pulled the nudie magazine from his back pocket. Sure, porn was easy to get and free online, but he liked the feel of the pages between his fingers and the glint of the light as it reflected on the models' bodies. It made it more real for him.

THE MAGAZINE FELL TO THE GROUND AS TIMOTHY'S HEAD HIT THE wall behind him. Damn. He hadn't realized he was falling asleep. He stood and stretched. A few jumping jacks helped him push the sleep from his brain. He gathered his magazine, rolled it up and shoved it back into his pocket. His watch taunted him with the fact that it was just four in the morning. Two more hours before his shift ended. Better do some rounds to help wake himself up and get his mind right.

He quietly walked to the back of the building. He enjoyed starting at the loading docks. A little fresh air and a pull on a joint would help to keep his mind right until the end of his shift.

He tipped his cap to the majestic vampire and the lady wolf. They sat motionless in a dark corner of the room off the office. Timothy always felt like he was walking through photographs. Like a time traveler in an alternate, haunted universe. It made him feel powerful but alone. Like he didn't belong.

A cold draft pushed all thoughts from his mind. The back door was open. Shit. Unless the asshole who broke in disabled it, that meant he had triggered the silent alarm.

Timothy pulled the door shut and scrambled to the office. Damn exhaustion. He should have seen the red lights on the alarm panel when he woke up. He never should have fallen asleep in the first place. He punched in the code but could see it was too late. A patrol car was most likely already on the way. He stashed his magazine with the others and the gun in the hidden drawer under the surface of the desk and leaped up the stairs, taking them three at a time. He just had time to make sure everything was in order in the zombie brothel room before he heard the cop. A woman.

"Hello?" Her voice bounced around the vast emptiness of the haunted house. "KCPD. We got a two-eleven-S...shit."

Timothy froze on his way to the top of the staircase.

"We got a call about a possible burglary in progress. We're looking for the guard on duty. Hello?"

"Hi. I'm here. I'm coming down," Timothy called out but didn't move.

"Come out slowly. I want to see your hands," the officer yelled.

Timothy held his arms stiffly in front of him as he slowly walked down the stairs. He couldn't help but smile at his reflection in the mirror. "It's okay, officer. This happens all the time. There's a homeless guy who comes in on chilly nights when he can't find any other place to hole up. Sorry about the alarm." Timothy looked directly at the woman as he spoke.

When he finally reached the bottom of the stairs, she asked for his ID. She scanned it and passed it to the other cop and was about to frisk Timothy when her partner, an older paunchy dude with a pocked face and snow white mustache, put his hand on her shoulder.

"That won't be necessary, Mr. Ridle," he said as he handed his ID back. "We'll just need to take a look around. Is the gentleman still on the premises?"

Timothy kept his eyes on the woman as he responded to the male cop. "I don't know. I didn't see him tonight."

"What do you mean? How do you even know who broke in then?" The woman cop's eyes darted around and her grip tightened on the butt of her holstered gun. She was kind of cute. Her curly dirty blonde hair barely reached her shoulders. Her uniform and body armor left a lot to the imagination, but that didn't stop Timothy from making some assumptions. She was his type. He might have to explore this budding relationship further.

"I fell asleep," he admitted without dropping his gaze or his voice. "I know it's Hank because nobody else would be stupid enough to sneak into this place. There's nothing to steal."

"Nonetheless, we'll have a look around. I need you to stay behind us." She needn't have worried. Timothy wasn't going to leave her.

THE CRISP MORNING AIR WHISTLED THROUGH THE VAN'S WINDOWS as Timothy drove aimlessly around the city, too amped up to go home. She was invigorating. He had braved a sniff of her hair when she had stopped abruptly in front of him. He had pretended he couldn't stop in time, though he was careful not to touch her. She was edgy. That might have resulted in a bit too much touching and maybe even a broken arm. Her partner explained after he sent her to the car to report in that she was a new transfer and was filling in from homicide. This little tidbit intrigued Timothy even more. A homicide cop. How fun. And she was gorgeous.

His fingers tapped loudly on the steering wheel. His breath fogged the windows. His eyes darted from side to side. Seeing everything but taking in nothing. He had been searching. For something. Anything. To make him feel alive. To be part of something. And then she was delivered to him. Right to his fucking door. He didn't know if he believed in fate or a higher power, but he did believe in taking advantage of the things right in front of you. He had a mission now. It'd been a long time.

Their chance encounter was the first time he felt powerful since leaving the military.

He was chasing it now. And yet he was crashing. The adrenaline was dissipating. He could feel the power, the happiness slowly slipping from his grip. He'd go home. He'd plan. He'd get it back. He always got it back.

4

"The last thing he said to me was that the bananas were rotten. He always hated an overly ripe banana, my Henry."

The elderly woman sat ramrod straight on the front edge of the couch. Her hands like knotted talons as she gripped the tarnished brass enclosure of her massive avocado green macramé bag. Edie wondered if she had made it herself before the arthritis set in.

She liked Ruthie. Edie saw the soft reflections of tears at the corners of her tender eyes as she spoke about her husband. What must it feel like to love someone so much that your mind conjured them up even after their death?

"We all hope the last words of our loved ones will be some profound proclamation of their love for us," she said as she folded her hands on the notepad in her lap and looked Ruthie in the eyes. "The mind works in ways scientists still can't fathom. When those last synapses fire, there's no telling what memory or emotion they'll jog loose and shoot to our lips. From what you've told me, I know he loved you very much."

Ruthie's eyes narrowed, and her grip tightened around her

bag. She seemed to shrink into herself as she shook her head. "Oh no, dear, my Henry went in his sleep after we had, you know," she leaned forward and tilted her head as if she could transmit the inference to Edie. "No. I mean it was the last thing he told me this morning as we ate breakfast before I got on the bus to come here."

"Oh, I see." Edie slumped back into her chair. Was she a psychologist or an exorcist?

"I told him, not for the first time mind you, that I always buy in bulk. Even when he was alive and it was just the two of us. It's so much cheaper. Even with the membership fee at that fancy warehouse place with the man's name." Ruthie unlatched her bag and dug around until she found a tissue. She dabbed at her eyes as she continued. "He always hated having so many bananas around. Too much of a good thing, I guess. He complained about wasting money because we couldn't eat them fast enough."

Edie nodded and smiled at the lonely widow. Love has the power to make you crazy. When you're in it, and when it leaves.

"Now he visits me, in the mornings mostly," Ruthie continued. "All he ever wants to talk about are those darned bananas and how they've gone bad. What do you think it means, dear?"

The woman looked at Edie as if she held the answers to life's biggest mysteries. Edie pursed her lips and looked at the doodles on her notepad. Normally, she drew little ribbons, but today her page was filled with bananas. She said the first thing that came to her mind. "It sounds like it's time to make banana bread, Ruthie." She put her hand to her mouth to stifle a laugh.

CAN YOUR EYES BE WATERY AND DRY AT THE SAME TIME? EDIE strained to keep them open. Lord knows what she looked like. The Davidsons didn't seem to notice, but then they'd been engaged in a heated argument for nearly 45 minutes. Edie's elbows dug into her thighs. She hoped the pain would keep her awake. A part of her prayed for sleep.

If she dropped onto the floor and started snoring, would these puerile lovers even notice? Would they walk over her body without so much as a look down while they argued their way to the door at the end of their session? Edie coughed to cover the laughter that had been building in her throat.

"Let's ask doctor McEvoy what she thinks we should do," Mrs. Davidson said as she turned from her red-faced husband to Edie. Her own face was almost perfectly round. Her eyes, too small for her face and too wide apart, bore into Edie as she waited for words of wisdom.

"About what?" Edie didn't even pretend she knew what their argument was about, but she hoped it might sound to her patients like a brilliant psychological maneuver to force them to answer their own questions.

"Exactly," Mr. Davidson said as he slapped his hands on his thighs and pointed to Edie as if she had just delivered some profound decree. "This whole argument is a waste of time. We should get a cat."

His wife's tiny eyes turned on him. He leaned away as if the heat of her gaze might melt his face. "I'm allergic to cats. You know that, Harold. We are getting a dog. Unless you want me to die."

When Harold didn't answer quickly enough, Mrs. Davidson smacked him across the face. Edie, who had been trying to regain her composure and control of the situation, shot out of her chair. She stood over the couple, hands on her hips like a disappointed mom, and glared at the two of them before melting into laughter.

"You two are fighting like cats and dogs about cats and dogs."

Neither Davidson joined in her laughter, but at least they'd stopped fighting. "Look. Your time's up, and my next appointment is here. Just have a kid. It fixes every relationship," Edie said through a painted-on smile.

EDIE SAT BEHIND HER DESK DURING HER NEXT SESSION. SHE FELT Kevin's eyes drift up and down her body even from across the room. Could he see through her desk?

"So last time we talked, you said you had something important to get off your chest," Edie began. She cursed her choice of words as the teenager's eyes wandered south of her eye line.

"Yes," he said after a long pause. "I think I'm in love with my aunt. I know that makes me a freak, but I just can't help thinking about her. I imagine kissing her during school. I hope she'll come over to my house when my parents are at work. She'd pretend she didn't know they were gone at first, but then…"

Edie smacked the cold leather blotter on her desk to stop Kevin before he got too worked up. "You're not a freak. Having a crush on an aunt is perfectly normal, in fact."

"Yeah, but I think this is more than a crush. I mean the only porn I can watch are the videos of the horny aunts who want to seduce their nephews."

"Nothing unusual there either. Although I'd try to limit your porn intake."

Kevin's face turned crimson. "Okay, I will," he whispered as he stared at the floor. Or maybe he was looking at her feet under the desk. "So you're saying I should quit watching it, quit thinking about it and just do it?"

He smiled so wide Edie could see his tonsils. She shook her head and scribbled a note on his chart. "Freud would love you," she said.

"Thanks," Kevin said, still smiling. "But I'm only interested in one woman."

. . .

EDIE'S HEAD THROBBED IN TUNE TO THE YOUNG WOMAN'S tantrum. "Jesus, dad! I'm not a kid. Stop smothering me. If this is how you treated mom, I don't blame her for leaving you."

The rumpled old man in an equally rumpled suit sitting next to his daughter erupted into a fit of crying. He placed a calloused hand to his face. Edie thought for a moment he might use it to erase his own features. Tears as big as raindrops flung from his eyeballs in every direction, showering his daughter. Edie scooted her chair back to avoid the spray.

"I just want things to go back to the way they were when we were a happy family," he sobbed. "I cook, I clean, I do everything for you. And you still don't love me."

The young woman eyed the door. Edie silently counted down from ten and wondered if she'd leap over her dad or run around Edie's chair as she made her escape.

"This is what I mean, dad. I don't want a damn butler. I want a father. You've spent my whole life trying to be my friend when all I wanted was for you to tell me when I've screwed up, give me consequences, give me examples to live by. As far as I'm concerned, I never had a father."

Edie stared at the two of them. They shared her couch but nothing else. And yet here they sat every other week. The same fight. The same tears. The same abandoned escape plot.

All she had for them was a spot on her calendar and a box of tissues.

WHEN THE THIRD TOENAIL LANDED ON HER NOTEPAD, EDIE decided to end Randy's session early. That he felt comfortable plopping down on her couch, kicking out of his shoes, and tossing his socks over his shoulder had intrigued her at first.

But then he had pulled out the clippers and spoke to her about his childhood while casually clipping his thick, yellowed nails. And the smell. Edie gagged and nearly threw up, but she was afraid if she opened her mouth one of his toenails would fly into it.

"I'm sorry, Randy," she said from behind her hand. "I can't do this. It's just too much for me."

Randy stopped in mid-clip. He stared at her for a second and then put his socks and shoes back on. As he stood to leave, he paused and fidgeted. His right hand hovered in the air in front of him. His fingers twitching and twirling around each other. "Can I get those back please?" He asked, pointing at the remnants of his nails sitting on her top page.

"MY HUSBAND IS ABUSING MY SON. THEY BOTH DENY IT, BUT I HAVE proof this time." The woman's eyes darted about the room, never alighting on anything for more than a millisecond. Her hands wrestled with each other in her lap, clasped so tightly that her skin glowed white and the blue veins in her knuckles pulsated. Her accusations barely elicited an acknowledgment from Edie who had learned it was better to let the woman rant than to suffer her withering accusations of bias and medical malpractice.

Dorothy had been a patient for a couple years. A portly woman, she seemed even heavier due to the weight of her psychological burdens, of which she had many. Her main ailment centered on the sexual proclivities of her husband. Earl, ten years her junior, was actually husband number four. Her son was 32 years old. And, as far as Edie could ascertain, the men were either engaged in a completely legal and consensual relationship or the entire thing was a figment of Dorothy's imagination.

"So what should I do?"

Edie looked up from her notepad at her patient's sudden question. She smiled and looked back down at the page for any helpful notes she might have subconsciously scribbled down. All she saw were ribbons. A reminder of the only skill that survived from her tenth-grade art class. Edie could sketch three-dimensional ribbons in all shapes, and she often absentmindedly doodled ribbons when she was deep in thought. Not very helpful, but pretty. That's how she felt about herself lately.

"Dorothy, you know that's not a fair question. It's not my job to give you advice. I can only listen and ask the questions you might not be willing to ask yourself."

"Like what?" Dorothy's face reddened, her eyes widened in a wild frenzy and the veins in her neck and forehead threatened to burst, painting Edie's ribbons with a spray of red polka dots. "What question could I possibly not want to ask? Because I've done a lot of questioning of the men in my life, and I don't think any of it has helped. Not one damn bit!" Dorothy seemed startled by her own outburst. "Why are you smiling? Is my pain funny to you?"

"Not at all, dear," Edie said. "Do you realize that this is the first time I've seen you yell? The first time you've allowed yourself to lose control."

"Why is that good?"

"Because you, like all of us I'm afraid, are not in control. That's just an illusion we use to make ourselves feel better. And, in your case like so many others, to beat yourself up over. So, yes, seeing you lose control does make me smile. I'm delighted, in fact. I think this is a big breakthrough, Dorothy. Don't be afraid of emotion. Embrace it."

"That sounds like a lot of horse manure if you ask me," Dorothy responded as she forcibly smoothed the front of her slacks. "I can't afford to feel. Feelings lead to pain, and I have had enough pain. I simply want to know why the men in my life do what they do and how I can put a stop to it before it drives me insane."

"I don't have all the answers for you, Miss Dorothy," Edie began.

"You don't seem to have any answers for me, Doctor McEvoy," Dorothy interrupted. "That's the problem. I've been coming to see you twice a week for 28 months. In that time, I've lost two husbands and am on my way to losing a third and my only son. I'm not saying it's your fault, but if I'm being honest it sure doesn't seem like you've been much help either."

"I'm going to be honest with you, Dorothy. Coming here, seeing me, talking isn't going to magically fix your life. You can't just show up. You have to do the work. At therapy and at life. You have to be willing to take a hard look in the mirror and judge yourself as honestly and as critically as you judge the people in your life. That's when breakthroughs happen. That's when you can learn to stop bottling everything up and actually feel things. Sure some of those feelings will hurt, but not as bad as you'll hurt yourself when all those bottled up emotions finally, suddenly and without warning burst and lead to a breakdown or worse."

"I don't think this is working out," Dorothy frantically gathered her things as she spoke, not once looking at her therapist. "I've given you a chance. I've given you my time. I've poured my heart out. And, like everyone else in my life, you have let me down." With that, she stood and left.

Edie sat in stunned silence for a moment. She thought of the advice she'd just given Dorothy, but her mind quickly drifted further and further from her tidy little office and Dorothy's messy life. She thought instead of her own mess. Wouldn't life be so much easier if you could change the people you love? She knew better than to indulge this question, but like Dorothy, she sure wished she could.

SILENCE. NOT AWKWARD OR TENSE OR EXPECTANT. JUST QUIET reflection. That's what Edie and her sixth patient of the day had been sitting in for the last 45 minutes. Sometimes that was all a patient needed, to sit in a safe space with no judgment. Unfortunately, the peace did not accompany the quiet for Edie.

It had been several hours since Dorothy walked out, but Edie still couldn't shake the feeling of failure. Was she really that bad at her job? Being a psychologist was frustrating. Sometimes the answers to people's problems were so simple you just wanted to scream them at your patients. As Edie tried to analyze her feelings, she frowned. Being the doctor and the patient was even more maddening. It put your personality, your intelligence, your very being at odds with itself. You felt self-doubt, even self-disgust. You searched for meaning everywhere.

Edie looked up from her doodles. Her patient, Maria, seemed to have nodded off. Edie sighed. She was putting her patients to sleep now. That had to be some kind of new low. She knew all about depression, but raw knowledge was useless. And a depressed therapist was the worst kind of depression. You knew what was wrong with you and what you should do, but that just made you hate yourself more. You knew it was a disease, but you also saw it as a personal weakness. And certainly, one that someone with your level of education, training, and expertise should be able to overcome easily. So when you can't, when you don't, your failure just fuels your downward spiral.

"How are you feeling today, Maria?" Edie asked just to break the monotony that let the darkness of her mind take over.

"Depends on who you ask," Maria responded without opening her eyes.

"Well, I'm asking you."

"But I'm bipolar, so there's never one easy answer is there?"

Edie smiled as she remembered one of her first patients when she was a graduate student. "You know I asked one of my first patients once how he would describe himself. He was bipolar, too. You know what he said?"

Maria didn't take the bait. Edie continued anyway unfazed.

"He said he was a benevolent lover of life, women and French cheeses."

When Maria continued to ignore her, Edie continued. "I thought that was interesting, so I asked him how others would describe him. His answer was pretty spot on. He said 'I think they'd say I'm a bit of a dick actually.'"

Edie smiled. Her attempt at lightening the mood and engaging her patient may have failed, but she liked that story. It reminded her that we all think of ourselves very differently than others do.

"Okay. I think our time is up. See you next week."

Adrian's voice blended with Sonny Rollins' saxophone riffs coming through the aftermarket Bose surround sound speakers that accentuated his old car's natural shimmying. *He liked to surround himself with beauty*, Edie thought. The best car. The finest cigars and wine. A killer sound system. She, too, was just another status symbol, just another outward trophy on display for all to see that he was a worthy man living an exemplary life.

He rambled on about his day. He always did. And she seldom listened. Luckily he didn't expect a response. He was never looking for a conversation so much as an audience. If she had known that years earlier, maybe things would have worked out differently.

She thought about the first time she saw him. He was in his element. He was beaming. He was engaging. He was damn transcendent. She fell in love with him then. Like so many before her. Taken in by the myth of the man. She wished someone had slapped the stars from her eyes and showed her the cracks in his facade. Maybe it wouldn't have happened. Maybe it still would have, but she could have walked away and returned to her life. Instead, here she was, driving in an out-of-date luxury car, her life speeding out of control.

5

The sand burned Edie's feet so badly they pulsated a bright red in the fleshiest parts and a brilliant white around her toes and heels. The wetness clung to her, and the biting coastal winds cut at her eyes and exposed skin. She forgot her bag. She laughed at how many more times she forgot it than brought it on her nightly walks. No bag meant she had no cover-up. Her favorite snow white bikini did little to protect her.

Still, she loved the solitude of Ocean Beach late at night. The tourists, locals, surfers, and even most of the homeless had long departed. When the sun disappeared from this part of California's coast the heat quickly evaporated like the mist of the waves in their endless cycle. The throngs of sun worshipers disappeared as well. Swapping their wetsuits, books, towels, and sunscreen for mixed drinks and mingling at the many bars, clubs, and restaurants that made San Francisco such an electric place to live.

Edie loved the sound of the waves at any time of day. They drowned out the cacophony of this noisy world and even helped to silence her restless mind, which seemed to never quiet while she was awake. Her day was filled with an endless string of half-formed, fleeting thoughts that branched out and splintered off into path after path of random, scattered directions. Usually, her introspection darkened with the waning of the day. She dreaded the night when she was alone with her thoughts. A prisoner in her own mind. That's when the many paths of thought converged into one frightening direction, which forced her to relive and reanalyze the worst moments of her life. But the hypnotic beating of the waves seemed to wash away these thoughts. The beach at night was the only place Edie felt safe.

She laughed at herself. If she were one of her patients, she would force herself to find the deeper meaning in this. But like many of her patients, she was good at hiding from her own shadows. She thought again about her lack of focus. It had never come easy for her, which didn't help in her line of work. Doodling and word association helped, but she feared she would never be a great therapist.

A calm washed over her as she walked. Even the coldness couldn't dampen her growing euphoria. She walked without a destination in mind. She let the wind guide her. She shivered but wasn't sure if it was from fear, the chill, or the excitement of her solitary late night adventure. She walked up to a beautiful rock bridge cut into the deep cliffs that formed the coastline. As she walked under the natural archway, the slowly spinning light of a nearby lighthouse winked suggestively at the sea in a never-ending dance of light and dark. Was she lost? She was familiar with these two landmarks but they didn't belong here and definitely didn't belong together. Each should be further down the Pacific Coast Highway, well south of San Francisco.

She stopped as a shadowy figure stumbled out of the lighthouse keep and limped towards her. A sudden lightning strike ripped open the sky and a rush of rain threatened to wash away the sand beneath Edie's feet, pulling her into the sea where her sudden wave of panic would be drowned out forever. Her stomach clenched. Her breath stuck in her throat. The sand felt like shackles around her ankles. As the shadowy figure tottered toward her, Edie frantically searched the shore for something, anything, to ward off the impending apparition. She spied a charred branch sticking out from an abandoned fire pit that was probably once surrounded by smiling beachcombers enjoying a freedom Edie would never understand or enjoy herself. She pulled the branch from the pit and dragged it behind her as her feet inexplicably carried her towards what she knew would be a deadly confrontation.

Each step seemed to cover the distance of ten, and in a blink, Edie was face to face with a woman in a torn and bloodied nightgown that must have once been as white as her skin. An almost perfect bloody handprint covered the material over the woman's left breast. The rest of the full-length cotton gown looked like an abstract expressionist's painting full of splatters, strokes, and smears in a random pattern that left Edie mesmerized, unable to meet the ghostly woman's gaze.

Edie tightened her grip on the rain-slick branch, which suddenly felt like no more than a twig in her unsure hand. Slowly she forced her eyes to meet the woman's. As they did, the woman let out a deathly wail and a moan that seemed to shake the sand beneath them and drown out the storm and the sea. She looked so sad Edie thought. And familiar in the way strangers often do. She couldn't be much older than Edie. They both had eyes like opals with flecks of luminous greens and blues.

"Are you okay," Edie whispered, still trying to find her voice.

"He's dead," the woman shuddered. "I had to do it. I had to."

"I understand. Can I help? Can I call someone for you?" Edie once again cursed her forgetfulness as she realized her phone was in her bag.

"I had no choice."

"Everything is going to be okay," Edie said even though the pounding in her chest and the churning of her stomach told her that was a lie.

She reached out to take the woman's hand, but before she could the confessed murderess lunged at her, grabbing her by the shoulders. She shook her violently, and the wildness in those eyes terrified Edie.

"You believe me, don't you? I need you to believe me. Nobody matters but you."

Edie struggled to free herself from the woman's steely grip. Her hands seemed larger than they should have been.

"Nobody matters but you. It's okay. It will be okay. It's just an episode. I won't leave you. I won't leave you," the woman repeated in a rage.

"Get off of me. You can't touch me like that! I'm not yours," Edie screamed as she continued to struggle.

"It's okay. It's okay. Shh. Quiet now. Let's get you home. Nobody matters but you...Edie," the woman whispered in her ear.

Edie froze. Her muscles tensed. Then she saw the knife in the woman's hand. She nodded slightly to herself. Her decision made, she shoved the woman, grabbed the branch with both hands and swung it in a wild arc with all her might. The thunder and the surf seemed to crash in time with the blow across the woman's face. She fell backward and shrieked with pain and rage.

"You bitch," the woman spat in a low growl that seemed to come more from the sky above her than from her mouth. "I'm doing this for you. I'm trying to save you from yourself. Damn it, Edie, wake up!"

Edie stared in disbelief as the woman melted in front of her, leaving Adrian hunched, his hands cupping his face. She dropped the now broken branch and fell to the snow with a wail. Why did this keep happening?

"Jesus, Edie," Adrian muttered as he spat a tooth into the snowbank of the dimly lit park in their Columbus Square neighborhood. "I'm just trying to save you. You know this isn't a safe place after dark. Especially dressed like that."

Edie looked down at her hands. They trembled in the cold she hadn't felt until he woke her. The park was more than a mile from their house. It was a lovely place during the day with tree-lined sidewalks and a large wading pool.

"You know I don't like to be touched." Edie's response floated softly into the night in a puff of breathy condensation.

"What in the world were you doing with that branch?" Adrian said as he took off one of his gloves and pressed his hand hard against his cheek to slow the bleeding. "You nearly took my head off. I've never seen you like that. I think I may need stitches."

Edie concentrated on her breathing. Breathe in for 10 seconds. Hold it for 10. Breathe out for 10 seconds. Her head hurt. Her feet burned. Every muscle in her body tensed against the cold.

"I told you I don't like to be touched," she exhaled as she looked around to get her bearings then walked toward home not caring whether Adrian followed. She felt bad about her reaction. He probably thought he was riding in on his white horse to once again save his helpless heroine from the darkest depths of the night and of her own mind. The sound of his boots crunching in the light dusting of early spring snow grated on her. Their relationship was so complicated. Things had been so much easier when she was in school.

"Wait up, E," Adrian called out as he jogged up next to her. He placed his sweater around her shoulders, pulled her into him tightly, and rested his non-injured cheek on the top of her head as they walked. "You know I worry about you. I wish you'd let me in again. I don't know what has happened to us."

"You don't know what happened?" she yelled and twisted herself from his grip. "Maybe you should point your analytical genius inward for once. I don't think you've ever bothered to really look at yourself. If you saw what I do, you'd know what you have to do."

"What do I have to do? Tell me, Edie. You want me to let you go, is that it?"

"Yes. I do sometimes think that would be better. For both of us."

"Never going to happen," he huffed. "How many times do I need to tell you you're mine? I'm yours. We belong together. It's as simple as that. And I don't need to be a genius to know that. It's obvious. You know that, too, when you're in your right mind. You haven't been taking your meds again, have you?"

"You're such an ass, Adrian. This has nothing to do with my state of mind or whether I do or don't take my pills."

"That sounds like an answer to me. And if you were worth anything as a psychologist, you'd know it's a shitty one."

"Go to hell," Edie screamed as she reached their doorstep, threw the door open and stomped to their room.

EDIE WAS DRYING OFF AFTER A HOT SHOWER WHEN SHE SAW HIM standing in the bathroom doorway. If her senses hadn't been dulled by the trauma of her waking dream, the cold, and their fight she would have jumped. Instead, she barely acknowledged him.

She walked coldly around him and got into bed with her back to him. The bed creaked under his weight as he sat down on his side. The prick of the needle was followed by the sensation of ice water flowing through her veins.

As the sedative quickly worked its magic, Edie once again wondered at how she'd arrived here.

6

A drian looked around the room. It was true his practice was growing, which was no surprise under his leadership, but he just couldn't shake the feeling it could be bigger. He should be bigger. Adrian's dreams of being one of the greatest psychological minds in history waned with each passing day in this pedestrian town. Well, that wasn't completely true. He was inarguably one of the greatest psychological minds. But, stuck in this flyover cow town playing dress up as a real city made it impossible to prove his prowess to the people who really mattered. For all the disdain this dumbed-down nation of nose picking, beer guzzling, illiterate inbreds had for coastal elites, Adrian knew the truth. Coastal elites earned their status because they were better than everyone else. One day he'd reclaim his rightful place among them. Just not today.

Today, he fiddled with the bandage he had carefully applied a few hours ago. The injury was deep but fairly straight. He had already been to the dentist and had called a plastic surgeon on his way into the office to schedule a consultation in an hour. First, he had to pretend to be excited for the news he was about to share with his mediocre peers.

"Good morning, everyone!" Adrian smiled widely. What was the point of spending the money for perfect caps if you didn't share their gleaming perfection with the world? "I'm excited to share our latest class of pro bono patients. As you know, this is something important to Edie and me."

He glanced over at his lover who just stared at the floor. He shook his head slightly. Edie, it seemed to him, slept walked through life. She had shown so much promise. He wondered what happened to the spark that first attracted him to her. The wonder at life, the thrill of digging deeper. Now she just went through the motions. He'd have to have a hard talk with her. He chuckled softly as he mentally reminded himself to check her for weapons first.

"We have a fairly large class this time," Adrian continued as he scanned the rest of the small but cozy break room he had designed to mimic his favorite old English pubs. His other three associates leaned forward in their overstuffed brown leather seats. There was Ruby Fisher, Kimberly Ito, and Chloe Booth. All young, attractive and eager. Just like Edie had been when he had plucked her from obscurity. They hung on his every word.

"I've assigned you each two cases. Except you, Edie. I feel you can probably only handle one right now. When you get back on track, we will talk about maybe taking one of the four patients I've assigned myself to pick up the slack." Edie's face reddened, but she refused to meet his gaze. No matter, his point had been made.

Adrian passed out the patient files, and the group spent the next thirty minutes reviewing each case, making notes and consulting one another on how to approach the important first session. Everyone that is but Edie. She slipped out as Adrian leaned over Ruby's shoulder to get a better glimpse of the file and of her ample breasts. Although he was rightfully distracted, he saw Edie leave out of the corner of his eye. He sighed and continued with the work at hand. He lowered his head and rested his chin on Ruby's shoulder. She didn't move. Good sign. Perhaps he could share the seeds of his greatness with her in some one-on-one mentoring sessions.

EDIE SHUT HER OFFICE DOOR, LEANED AGAINST THE WALL AND closed her eyes. Just breathe in. Ten seconds. Hold. Breathe out ten seconds. Her hands clenched and unclenched as she tried to will the pain back down into the pit of her stomach and shoo the anger out through her pores. She refused to lose control. Not while she was awake anyway.

She walked with measured steps to her desk and placed her single patient file at a ninety-degree angle on her blotter. As she sat down, she tried not to think about her partner, both in life and in practice, drooling over Ruby's breasts. It hadn't been lost on her that Ruby's outfits had become increasingly more revealing. Edie didn't want Adrian's behavior to bother her. Hell, it'd be an easy out, an escape she desperately wanted. But jealousy was human nature, and no amount of education or reason made you safe from its evil whispers in the back of your brain.

She stared at the file, not yet able to open it. It's not that she didn't like pro bono work. She enjoyed helping those who wouldn't normally be able to examine their own lives. But she knew that wasn't why Adrian created the pro bono project. For him, it served two purposes. The first was to look good to the handful of colleagues he still kept in contact with at Columbia, though the number of faculty members who still spoke with their disgraced former department chair dwindled each year. The second was more personal. Edie believed these cases were a form of personal penance for Adrian, though she doubted he would acknowledge or even understand that rationale. Sometimes Edie believed this vaunted psychologist was incapable of aiming his sharp observations at his own behavior.

The folder on her desk taunted her. It was fairly thin, and she had to admit she felt that sense of curiosity that had compelled her into this field in the first place. Of course, that curiosity was the reason she ended up with Adrian, so why should she continue to feed it?

Adrian was a genius. His Mensa membership certificate and a printout of his IQ score hung in mahogany frames in his dungeon of a study at home.. Copies of them also hung in less garish frames in his office. She smiled to herself as she remembered her first day in one of his introductory courses. He opened the class with a slide of his credentials. She had immediately loathed his boorishness. There were only two required textbooks in that class. Both still sat on her bookshelf behind her. One was the works of Freud. The other was Adrian's own book. It had been a modest hit as modern psychology books go. He coined the term 'coastal crazies' for the seemingly endless supply of psych cases on both coasts of the United States. It got him on a number of talk shows and had reporters calling him on occasion to appear on this and that news panel as an expert in his field. Oh how he loved those calls. Nobody called anymore.

Edie slapped her hand over her mouth to quiet the laugh she hadn't meant to let escape. Why was Adrian's hardship such a joyous thought? Maybe because she, more than anyone else, knew that it was both self inflicted and deserved.

Pushing those memories aside, she finally picked up the folder and read about her new patient. *Oh, this ought to be interesting* she thought and wondered if she was up to the challenge.

BEFORE ADRIAN COULD GO CHECK ON EDIE, HIS FIRST PRO BONO case, a man by the name of Chuck, arrived. Twenty minutes early. That told Arian a lot about Chuck. He was a middle-aged, middle manager at a local grocery store. His tan, his hair, his white teeth were all too perfect. When they introduced themselves, the man's handshake was too aggressive and threatened to pull Adrian into him. His smile was too big. His eyes too dead. Classic case of over-compensation.

"Have a seat, Chuck, and tell me what's on your mind," Adrian said as he pointed to a couch that looked like it belonged in a hunting lodge.

"Well, I don't know where to begin," Chuck admitted as he sank into the couch.

"Why don't you tell me what you're hiding and why you don't think you're worthy of love or admiration."

Chuck fidgeted in his seat, suddenly very interested in a loose thread on his trousers. Adrian loved this part of the dance, in which he quickly established that he was in the lead. Actually, he thought of therapy more as a boxing match. Two opponents squaring off, their guard up, foot work dancing them around the ring. He found that a few well-placed jabs in the beginning often helped to drop his patients' guard.

"I'm actually here because I'm not happy, and I don't know why," Chuck recovered while still avoiding Adrian's gaze.

"That's a good start, but let's go deeper. Why aren't you happy?"

"I don't know," Chuck said. "Some days I'm fine and others I find myself wishing I'd never been born and thinking everyone in my life would be better off without me. I guess I'm here to find out why and to stop before..." He trailed off there and finally met Adrian's eyes.

"Oh, but I'm just here as a sounding board," Adrian said, "someone to guide you along on your journey of self-discovery. I can't stop you from hurting yourself or anyone else. And that's not what I'm here for. But you don't really need me. I think you already know what's wrong."

The two men stared at each other. The silence filled the room. The scent of sweat slowly soaked into the walls around them. Walls, Adrian knew, that would feel to Chuck as if they were closing in on him, ready to squeeze the truth from his chewed up lips.

"I'm worthless. A fraud. I may look like I have it all together, but inside I'm constantly freaking out and feel like one small thing might send me into a downward spiral," Chuck whispered to the floor.

"Exactly," Adrian said as he swiveled around and reached for one of the copies of his book that lined the expansive walnut bookshelf behind his desk. He gave all his new patients an auto-graphed copy. At a slight discount, of course.

"Read this," he said as he surveyed the shell of a man in front of him where a cocky fraud had once sat. Adrian loved taking his patients down to the studs so he could rebuild them. "And don't worry, Chuck. I can fix you."

7

The man's cough startled Edie from her reading. She looked up to find him standing next to her closed door. What the hell?

"What are you doing in here," she said in a tone she hoped sounded more patronizing than panicky.

"I have an appointment," the man said as he flashed her a smile. "But I think I'm in the wrong room. Either that or your boss is out?"

"Mr. Ridle?" Edie asked as she checked the name on the file she'd been engrossed in. "It's customary for my patients to wait until I've either called for them or come and received them from our waiting room. And I am the boss."

"Oh? I thought you were a man."

Edie sighed and forced herself not to roll her eyes. This was already coming off the rails. "I am Dr. Edie McEvoy," she said, pronouncing her name correctly for him to help with the confusion. "And you are Timothy Ridle. It looks like we're both in the right place. So, if you're ready, please have a seat."

But he didn't sit down. He shuffled from foot to foot, his smile slowly fading along with his gaze.

"What is it, Mr. Ridle? This is a safe space, so please speak up."

"Well, ma'am, it's just that your name is confusing. They told me I could choose who I talked with when I called, and my choices seemed pretty clear. Some woman doctor named Adrian Hillary and some man doctor named Eddy McEvoy."

"Sorry to disappoint you, Mr. Ridle," Edie said as she leaned back in her chair. "There is a male and a female choice here for sure. But Adrian is the man. Would you like to see him instead?" Edie secretly hoped he would decide for her because she was already prepared to drop this case.

"Well, I don't know," Timothy said. "I don't really like talking to women. I mean, it's more like I can't talk to them. I want to, it's just..." His voice trailed off but Edie noticed his smile had returned at the corner of his lips.

"You seem to be doing a decent job, or is it that you can only talk to women about your inability to talk to women?"

That seemed to work. Her new patient looked around, still avoiding her gaze and sat down. First on the corner of the over-stuffed white couch then, after crossing and uncrossing his legs several times, he moved to the armchair Edie normally sat in during her sessions. No bother, she would remain behind her desk. She felt that was the best option with this particular patient, anyway.

"So I've been studying your file, Timothy."

"Read anything interesting, doc?"

"You tell me? Do you find life interesting?"

"Interesting? No. Life is life. It's just the space between our nonexistence and our death."

Edie looked at the cover sheet in the file. "Are you fascinated with death? Is that why you work at a haunted house?"

Timothy smiled again. He had a brilliant smile; she had to

admit that. He was a handsome man but a crazy one. She unfortunately knew his kind all too well.

"I'm not so much fascinated with death as I am disinterested in life," Timothy responded while staring at an interesting corner of Edie's coffee table. "The way I see it, there's grinders and there's gods. And I sure as shit ain't going to live my life grinding out one forgettable day after another."

"So you don't consider a nine-to-five security gig grinding?" Edie asked.

"First of all, I work at night. Everything worth experiencing happens at night."

"I apologize if I offended you, Mr. Ridle, I'm just trying to get a feel for the man you are. Am I to surmise that you believe you're a god then?"

Her new patient stifled a laugh in his hand and pretended it was just a cough. "You know. They say your life is what you pay attention to. I wonder what you pay attention to, doc?"

"Thankfully, I'm not the one answering the questions here." Edie smirked despite herself.

"I'm not sure I like this system. It seems kind of one sided. I mean I can't get better if I don't trust you, can I? And how can I trust you if I don't get to know you?"

"That's not how therapy works, Mr. Ridle. I think you know that given the vast list of psychologists and therapists you've seen in the last two years," Edie said. "And our times up."

Timothy didn't move. "I like you, lady doc," he said, finally meeting her eyes for a brief second before studying her bookshelf. "Despite what the voices in my head think."

"Oh, Mr. Ridle. I've heard that one before. You will have to be more original if we're going to make this work."

"Really? I slayed my last doctor."

"Then why move?"

Timothy suddenly stood up. His smile quickly faded. He seemed to hesitate, unsure of his next move. "He stopped practicing," he muttered as he opened the door. "See you next time, lady doc," he called from the hallway.

EDIE'S MIND WANDERED AS SHE PLAYED WITH THE TEA BAG IN HER oversized mug. Her day had flown by. After Timothy, her other six patients seemed dull and pedestrian. She sat in the breakroom enjoying her tea when she felt the gravity of Adrian's presence near the door. What is it with men sneaking up on her lately?

"How was your day?" he asked as he poured himself a cup of coffee.

"It was interesting," she responded over the top of her mug to hide her smile. "My new pro bono case apparently specifically chose me because he thought I was the only male therapist in the practice."

"Well, he clearly has issues," Adrian said as he turned away, grabbing a stale bagel from the kitchenette as he walked out without another word, which was the best outcome Edie could have hoped for.

"I'll see you at home later," she called after him as her way of telling him she wouldn't be leaving with him. He hated when she worked late.

ADRIAN PACED UP AND DOWN THE MIDDLE OF HIS BELOVED CELLAR. Smoke emanated from the Montecristo he gnashed between his teeth. A thick cloud floated in the air, marking where he had walked.

He had tried to hide his feelings earlier when Edie once

again brought up the effeminate nature of his name. She knew it was one of his triggers and yet she insisted on bringing it up again and again. It's like she derived some pleasure from his pain. The one person he cared about most, whose opinion mattered most, was the same person who relished his rare moments of self-doubt. If he really thought about it, he might come to believe she didn't love him. But that was crazy. He was her life. And she his.

A sudden thought occurred to him. He could use this. His life. Edie's. An exploration of the pleasures and pain of an intellectual coupling. It would be a love story to the practice of psychology, and more importantly, it could be his way back. He excitedly flicked the ashes of his cigar into the cranium of his custom ashtray, a bust of Sigmund Freud.

He sat down at the bar. His Desk was just six feet away, but Adrian feared his excitement and motivation to begin this new scholarly endeavor might wane between here and there. Instead, he grabbed a legal pad and a pen. All of history's masters did their best work with just the simple tools and their own complex thoughts.

He scratched out the first few lines of his thesis. He already envisaged his new life. Faculty chair once more at Columbia. Penthouse apartment overlooking Central Park. Edie's renewed adoration. The looks on his detractors' faces as they were forced to fawn all over him and swear they never supported the actions against him.

The excitement coursed through him. A celebration! That's what a moment like this called for. He rummaged through the fridge and grabbed a bottle of Dom Pérignon. Never one to wait until a project was complete to celebrate, Adrian popped the cork and took a long pull directly from the bottle.

He looked at the half page of prose and decided it was a

proper start. You can't rush genius. A good night's rest would allow his brain to percolate on the topic. He poured the rest of the champagne down the drain, left the burgeoning manuscript on the bar, and headed up to lie down with his muse.

8

E die wandered aimlessly through the empty house. She wore only a simple black slip. She worked from home most Wednesdays because she had no patient appointments. She called these days her office hours. They were supposed to be spent transcribing notes and making observations and connections from one appointment to the next with each of her patients. In truth, she just needed a break and seldom bothered working at all on Wednesdays. It hadn't always been that way. A smile teased at the corner of her lips as she remembered a time when she felt a sense of honor and pride in her elite calling. Now she rarely got dressed on these off days. She told herself everyone needed a day to regroup.

As she walked down the winding stairs from the turret that connected the main floor to the upstairs bedrooms and then the attic, she thought about how much she hated this house. Adrian loved to tell anyone who visited him here about its history as the home of Kansas City's first beer mogul. Curiously, he always left out the part where it briefly served as a mental asylum after the beer baron's mysterious death, though she secretly believed that was the real reason he bought the place. What these walls must

have seen, she thought as her fingertips floated lightly across the
Victorian wallpaper. What they're seeing now. If she had lived
during the house's time as an asylum, would she have been a
patient or a psychologist here? Could she be both? She felt like a
patient now, committed against her will with no way to escape.

Well, she had one way, which was why she always scheduled
these private office hours. The work she did here was psychological she reasoned, forcing her darkest thoughts back into the
shadowy corner of her mind before their ugly tendrils could
wrap themselves around her consciousness and take control
again.

Sappy classic rock softly whispered to her from the whole-
house sound system. Billy Joel reminded her he loves her just
the way she is. *He's the only one*, she thought. And as her bare
feet plodded softly across the hardwood floors, Simon and
Garfunkel's "The Sound of Silence" let her know she wasn't
alone. An idea that turned on her when she got to the entrance
to Adrian's cellar.

She paused at the thick rough oak door. The driving tempo
of her heart drowned out all sound. Her hand hesitated as she
reached for the knob, as if it knew the dangerous task she asked
of it. Her fingers twitched. She glanced over her shoulder, sure
Adrian had somehow materialized. She blinked away his
apparition and forced herself to breathe so she could descend
into the one area in the house explicitly off limits to her. It had
been so important to Adrian that he have his 'own space,' he had
made his lawyer add it to their roommate agreement. That two
reputed lovers needed such an agreement apparently felt odd
only to her.

She pressed her ear to the door and listened. Adrian left for
work two hours ago, and there was no other entrance but this
door between their fancy three story foyer and the sunken living
room. Edie remembered how she had burst into tears when the

realtor showing them the decrepit old house's potential had called it a family room. Adrian had shooed her back out to the car and left her shaking there while he finished the tour.

Satisfied that nobody was waiting on the other side to attack her, she slowly turned the knob and looked down into the forbidden, far reaches of Adrian's inner sanctum. As she reached the bottom, the room's totems of masculinity assaulted her senses. The worn brown leather, deep mahoganies, and blood-red decor belied a man in deep denial and unfathomable levels of overcompensation.

The smell of dank basement mixed with stale cigars to create an aromatic arsenal that smelled like a mix of locker room and ashtray with a hint of mold.

She pulled a facial tissue from a box next to Adrian's recliner to cover the powerful olfactory assault and pressed deeper into the darkness of the room and of Adrian's mind. She headed to the bar where an empty bottle of champagne sat next to a beat up legal pad. Tears welled in her eyes as she read the familiar handwriting. Her whole body trembled, and she couldn't help but be instantly transported back to those cold days at Columbia when she first met the man she would come to idolize and then despise. Hadn't he put her through enough?

Her instincts kicked in, causing every muscle in her body to freeze. Every time she couldn't handle life, her body retreated into itself. She hated that about herself. She wanted to fight, but her body betrayed her every time. Breathe in for ten seconds. Hold. Breathe out for ten. Determination slowly pushed the fear from her body, and she finally turned and raced up the stairs and through the house to the master bathroom.

AS SHE GRABBED THE BOX OF RAZOR BLADES HIDDEN IN THE bottom of her box of tampons, Edie thought of Timothy. She had seen him two more times since their first strange encounter. She and her colleagues all agreed he exhibited all the signs of a classic doc hopper, someone who sees a doctor just to score pills. And when that doctor cuts him off, he moves on to the next and the next.

Still, he was interesting, and she had to admit that not much in her life fit that description lately. He spoke in riddles and clichés and never looked her in the eye. She sensed something deeper lurked just under the surface of the mask he wore. She could feel it. Maybe she would help uncover it and fix him. Wouldn't that prove she deserved Adrian's respect?

She looked down to see the three neat lines of blood flowing across her left inner thigh. God it felt almost orgasmic, better than the sweaty, mechanical oscillations of her impotent lover.

After blotting the newest cuts that would soon become beautiful scars, she smiled at herself in the mirror. Each scar was like a prisoner's calendar of captivity, surreptitiously scratched into their cell walls. She had been cutting herself since her second semester of graduate school. It started as a cry to herself to get out before it was too late. The scars soon turned into silent witnesses to the dark turn her life made.

She forced herself to stop thinking about what happened back then. Otherwise she'd have to cut again, and Adrian might notice. She only cut herself on the front of her inner thighs and pelvis. Adrian only paid attention to that part of her body from behind. He hadn't noticed them yet, which meant he never would.

9

E die sat at the dining room table. She had long ago hidden her cutting supplies, showered and applied ointment to her new scars. They puffed up nicely and made excellent additions to her collection. Her thighs tingled and stomach clenched as she thought about her secret therapy. She'd had plenty of time to prepare for the evening. The grandfather clock in the parlor announced the seven o'clock hour. Adrian, ever the picture of predictability, would arrive home in about half an hour.

The antiquated gong of the doorbell shook her from her thoughts. Dinner, right on time. She opened the door and reveled in the delivery boy's response. He looked about 18 or 19. His mop of brown hair hid half his face, but the half Edie saw quickly turned crimson as he slowly took in her body before trying to look away.

"Do you like it?" Edie asked. "It was a gift from my lover." Edie twirled to give the boy a complete view of her ensemble. She'd chosen a relatively tame number by Adrian's standards. A white floor length silk sleeping gown clung to her body. The neck line plunged nearly to her belly, and the hem split up to her mid-thigh. She wished she had the boobs to really give the boy a show, but a quick look at his pants told her it definitely did the trick.

"Um, here's your food," the boy stuttered without looking at her. Edie felt ashamed that she had subjected such an innocent thing to her own whims. She knew what that felt like. She pulled her thin matching robe around her in a sudden burst of modesty and took the bags from the struggling boy. Neither of them said another word as she signed the receipt, giving him a two-hundred dollar tip. He deserved it, and it was Adrian's credit card, anyway.

While she felt bad about the boy, she was glad to know her outfit worked. She had just finished setting the table and was lighting the candles when she heard Adrian's car pull into the drive. The sound of the late 70s Mercedes convertible was unmistakable. It was loud and rough, just like its owner. Edie still didn't know what Adrian saw in that car. It was in the shop more than on the road and every little thing cost a small fortune.

For a man who had no idea how to handle himself in a garage, he sure liked the status he attached to that money pit on wheels. Edie could say the same for his abilities in the bedroom and his affinity for her. The sound of the front door slamming shut cut her self analysis short, but she promised herself she'd reexamine that line of thinking soon.

"Hello, darling," Edie purred as Adrian rounded the corner from the foyer and stopped in his tracks. "How was your day?"

"What the hell is all this?" Adrian asked as he looked over the scene in front of him.

"Can't a woman properly welcome her man home once in a while?" Edie asked as her fingers slid down the front of her nightgown, knowing full well why he was so surprised. She never attempted to have dinner waiting for him when he got home. "Come sit down. I've made you an Old Fashioned and have all your favorites laid out for you." As she spoke, she spread her legs, allowing the gown to fall away from her left leg in a not-so-subtle attempt to keep him off his game.

Adrian set his briefcase on the table, sank into his chair and finished his drink in one swig. Edie leaned in, tracing little circles lightly across his knuckles. "Uh oh," she whispered. "Are you all...tense?"

"I got an email from Alistair," Adrian said as he moved his hand from Edie's and dug into the sushi she had artfully arranged on a platter between them. After devouring four pieces of sashimi and a third of a firecracker roll, he continued, "They filled my old chair position."

Edie smiled into her napkin and coughed to cover her laughter. "What happened to Charles? I know he was just interim chair, but he'd been a member of the department even longer than you, right? I thought he made a great replacement."

"Old Charlie?" Adrian asked, his voice rising an octave letting Edie know her shot had had its intended effect. "That old codger could barely carry my briefcase, let alone carry on my legacy. Besides, he apparently decided to retire and start his own practice somewhere out in the country. I pity the poor souls who intrust their minds to that man." He got up and poured himself another drink. Straight bourbon. "No. They brought in some young hotshot from Princeton. It's a disgrace if you ask me."

"Well, you know about disgraces," Edie said as she folded her napkin across her plate. Time to take off the gloves and have some fun.

"What on earth has come over you?" Adrian spoke in the measured tones he only used when trying to control the anger that bubbled just under the surface. Edie loved this side of Adrian. It was his true self. When he got angry, he couldn't keep up the facade of the genteel, erudite professor.

"You know exactly what I mean." Edie smiled. "The reason

we're here. The reason I'm here. The reason neither of us is going anywhere in life or in our careers." She sat back in her chair and crossed her arms. "It's bad enough you screwed up your own life, but you killed my career and destroyed my soul at the same time. And if you think writing about whatever twisted version of our relationship you believe to be true and analyzing it to death as some kind of psychology revenge porn on your old colleagues will change what happened or the fact that everyone now knows the real you, then you, my dear, are quite frankly crazier than any of our patients."

Silence hung in the air between them for several minutes. They stared at each other. Edie could almost see the flames behind his beady eyes. The wrinkles in his forehead looked deeper than normal, he had put on more weight, and she noticed more grey in his beard and surviving hair. She refused to look away from her fallen mentor.

Finally, he broke their stare, drained his glass, and walked with measured steps to his chair. Leaning on its back, he quietly responded. "How dare you invade the sanctity of my private space."

Edie threw her head back as the belt of laughter escaped her lips before she could stifle it. It seemed to form deep in her belly and shook her whole body. "That's what bothers you the most?" She asked, wiping a tear from her eye. "That I invaded your privacy? I haven't had any privacy since you took over my life. And I sure as hell will not allow you to put what's left of it on display so you can feel better about yourself and prove that you are still worthy of worship for your analytical genius."

"Edie, baby, where is this coming from," Adrian said with a sigh. "I thought we were happy. I thought you were happy."

"Oh Jesus. You really are stupid. I am not happy. You do not make me happy. I even try to get away from you in my sleep." Edie laughed again.

"Darling, this is just a phase. You know that," he responded in a tone that told Edie he was about to enter his lecture mode. "Your sleepwalking is merely a manifestation of pent up pain from your childhood. Nothing more. Seeing what you saw, dealing with what you had to deal with at such a young age. Those psychological scars run deep. I wish you would let me help."

"Help? You have no clue how to help me. You know waking someone in that state is the worst thing you can do, but what do you do?" she mocked him. "And we both know that my issues extend beyond my childhood."

"Do you want the truth?" he asked in an equally mocking tone. "I do know better, but your continued issues and failure to confront them bore me. I no longer have the patience to play along with your dream-state delusions."

"What a pedestrian diagnosis and lazy response." Edie chided. "Not surprising. Yours generally are."

"How dare you attack me in such a personal way!" Adrian cried as he pushed his chair over.

"Seriously?" Edie asked, the smile widening on her face. "That's how you respond? That's what you respond to? You're a selfish, egotistical child, Adrian. A spoiled ass who believes, incorrectly I might add, that he is better than everyone. You're not better than me. You're not better than your patients. And, oh, in case you didn't get the hint, you're not better than your former colleagues who have so easily, quickly and completely moved on as if you had never been in their lives. They're better off now that you're gone. I think I probably would be too."

Adrian's face turned red and a vein in his forehead pulsated. Without another word, he downed his drink, calmly righted the chair, picked up his briefcase, and walked out the front door. Edie waited for the sound of it slamming shut, but all she heard was the soft click of the latch connecting with the doorjamb, followed a moment later by the obnoxious ignition of the Mercedes.

ADRIAN PUSHED AND PULLED ON THE GEAR SHIFT UNTIL THE Mercedes ground into reverse. He punched the gas but let off the clutch too fast and the high-priced heap lurched backward before dying. While Adrian firmly believed that nothing was as manly as a manual transmission, he admitted, to himself anyway, that his carefully crafted machismo evaporated every time he stalled out.

He took a deep breath, started the car again and over-revved the engine to ensure he'd keep it in gear. As the car flew backwards down the driveway, he didn't bother turning around. He knew the twists and turns of his driveway by heart, and nobody was ever on their sleepy street this late in the evening.

Just as he bounced over the dip at the end of their drive, a van appeared out of nowhere. He slammed on the breaks. The van never swerved, and the driver didn't even apply the brakes. What an asshole. Adrian had half a mind to follow the punk to get his license plate number. The thought of what might happen if the van stopped made him think twice.

Instead, he carefully looked up and down the street for any other cars or pedestrians before finally taking off. What an anti-climactic departure. He couldn't even storm out of his own house right.

He banged on his steering wheel as he drove, and the whole car shook. He hated the thing and had contemplated selling it, trading it in or pushing it off a cliff at least once every year for the fifteen years he had owned the cursed machine. It leaked oil so quickly he often joked that pouring a bottle directly on the driveway would be more efficient. And he was sure he had replaced enough vacuum hoses, motor mounts and hydraulic cylinder rods for a fleet of Mercedes. But the damn thing was his fathers, who had loved it more than he loved his own son.

"This is the Mercedes 450SL," his dad had told a young Adrian as he sat on his father's lap in the driver's seat the night he brought the car home. "It's the last model year. The last of its kind. That makes it special. And you are never to touch it."

It was only fitting that Adrian took it after having his father institutionalized. It was a great responsibility. And had his dad been coherent, he would have enjoyed the rite of passage that saw Adrian deliver his father to the hospital in his beloved car and then drive off with it, neither to be seen by him again.

Families are unduly complicated, Adrian thought, as he pulled into the parking lot of his office. He'd sleep on the couch and make things right tomorrow.

10

E die arrived at the office after Adrian had already straightened the couch, shaved and freshened up with the spare toiletries he kept there. He had just tucked in the tails of a brand new dress shirt, one of several he kept stashed in his desk drawer, when Edie breezed past his door without so much as a glance in his direction. He could be hanging from the rafters for all she knew. And yet she walked by, holding a single cup of coffee and looking quite rested. Typical.

Adrian spent the night tossing and turning. It had probably just been from the stiffness and squeakiness of the leather couch. But he had to admit that despite her rage, he worried about her all night. What if she had another sleepwalking episode and walked in front of an inattentive driver or into a crowd of thugs who gang raped her repeatedly before discarding her on the sidewalk like a bag of trash? That last thought had played on a loop in minute detail all night.

His first patient would arrive within the next hour, so that gave Adrian enough time to make things right with Edie. He couldn't stand their little tiffs. He knew with a bit of effort she would come to see things his way. She always did. That's one of the things he loved about her.

Her office door was closed, standard practice for most of the psychologists in the office. As he reached her door and was about to open it, he noticed the discreet light in the top corner of the door. It signaled to fellow practitioners and office staff that a session was in progress. Adrian hesitated with his hand on the knob. He hadn't seen anyone else walk by his office. Perhaps she was just trying to avoid him. Why was she always putting him into these predicaments?

He pressed his ear to the door.

"YOU'RE QUIET AGAIN," EDIE SAID, BREAKING THE SILENCE THAT had begun immediately after their perfunctory greeting. "I don't think I have to tell you this works better if you talk to me."

"How so?" Timothy asked, his first words since he sat down fifteen minutes ago. Only his mouth moved. He sat with perfect posture. His hands rested easily on his lap. His eyes were closed. Edie found his stillness curious, envious even.

"Well," Edie responded. "I'm not your first therapist. I won't be your last. You're here to score. Once you do, you'll do the minimum you can to keep the pills coming. And when that stops working, when I finally wise up, you may change your behavior for a bit to see if that gets things back on track. But ultimately you'll move on."

"Is that what you're afraid of, doc?"

"What's that supposed to mean?"

"Are you afraid I'll leave you?" Timothy asked through a smile which Edie quickly recognized as both patronizing and sarcastic, a blend with which she was far too familiar. He opened his eyes to look at her briefly before lowering them to the floor and studying the carpet. "Do people always leave you, doc?"

Edie looked up from her page full of ribbon doodles and tapped her pen rapidly on her legal pad. She stared at him for a moment even though he never met her gaze again. "I'm not sure what you are implying, but these sessions are about you not me."

"That doesn't seem fair. Or fun. I mean I can tell by looking at you I hit a nerve. It might make you feel better to share. Or don't you practice what you preach, doc? Maybe you're above getting help?"

Edie felt her face flush. She gripped her pen so hard her knuckles turned white, but she hid them behind her pad so he wouldn't notice. "We're not here to have fun."

"That's too bad, doc. I think we could have a lot of fun."

"I think this session is over," Edie slammed the paper on the coffee table and stood up.

"Hang on, doc," Timothy said, still sitting. "You wanted me to talk. Now that I am, you want to cut me off?"

"You know very well why I am cutting you off," Edie said as she looked down at him. "It's been a month. You're not taking this seriously, so why should I? And why should I continue if you so clearly just want to play games?"

"Okay, okay. I'm sorry. I'm not good at this. Despite all my practice. But you know I have to be here."

"Yes, I understand what 'court ordered' means, Mr. Ridle. But it doesn't mean I have to be the one whose time you waste. You are under the order of the court, not I."

"You're right. I'll try." He reached for her hand but she whipped it behind her and out of reach. "Hey. I'm sorry. You're right. Please don't cut this short."

Edie hesitated. He looked sincere, but she suspected he could put on whatever face he felt necessary to get his way. Still, she had an obligation to help. Dammit, why was she even in this position? This should be Adrian's case. They'd be great together. Two narcissists with potential sociopathic tendencies. Odd. That was the first time she'd tried out a diagnosis on Adrian. Maybe she belonged in this job after all. She sat back down and gathered her pen and paper.

"Fine. You have one more shot," she said without looking up.

"What do you want to know?"

Edie sighed and dropped her pen onto her legal pad with a dramatic thud. "It's not what I want to know, Mr. Ridle. It's what you want to share. What is on your mind? What is bothering you? I want you to dig below the surface. Otherwise we won't get anywhere, you won't get any better, and we will both have wasted a lot of time. And I don't like to waste my time, Mr. Ridle."

Timothy looked off into the distance over Edie's shoulder. The wall there was bare. She had purposefully not hung anything on that wall so patients wouldn't get distracted. And yet this particular patient stared at that blank, off-white wall as if he were examining a great work of art in a museum.

"There's this woman I'm seeing. Well, that's not right. It's just…I saw her. We met. And I'm interested in pursuing her." He trailed off, and after a few moments Edie realized he wouldn't give her more without some prodding.

"That's a good start," she said as she jotted down some notes amongst the ribbons. "What's her name? How'd you meet?"

"She stopped by my work the other morning. We didn't talk much but there was a spark, you know? I've felt it before. Sort of an itch you need to scratch. You ever felt like that, doc?"

Edie continued to probe. "If you didn't talk much, what drew you to her?"

Timothy smiled and looked directly at Edie. "She's stacked, doc. And she's like you. She's bossy and authoritarian and shit…

Oops. Sorry." Timothy's apology seemed reflexive rather than sincere, but Edie didn't interrupt him. This was the most he had spoken in any session. "She's perfect. I bet she was a cheerleader in high school. I bet she was the type of girl who could bat her eyelashes and get any boy in school to do whatever she wanted. She was probably one of the popular kids. You know the type. Bunch of stuck up pricks who think they rule the world, only to get a rude awakening after graduation. I bet nothing ever satisfied her. Know what I mean, doc?"

"It's interesting you relate this grown woman to a teenager. Is that how you see all women?"

Timothy's face hardened, and he sank into the cushion behind him. Edie didn't want to lose their momentum, so she said the first thing that came to mind, breaking one of the cardinal rules of her profession. "I went to high school in Northern California. I know the kind of kids you're talking about. The privileged elite. The girls whose fathers bought their love, and sometimes their silence..."

"California? I wouldn't have guessed that."

"Not all California girls have big boobs and blonde hair, Mr. Ridle." The comeback slipped out before Edie could stop it.

"That's true, I guess, but I just meant you seem smarter than some rich, liberal, valley girl type."

"Where did you go to high school?"

"Fine. I'll answer your question, doc, but we'll come back to you," Timothy said with a wink. "I went to Eisenhower High. It was a typical small town school. Most of my class spent their four-to-five-year high school careers in a drug-induced fog. Then there were the farm kids. They were another big group. They didn't so much go to high school as they took a break once in awhile from helping run their family farms."

"Which group did you belong to?"

Timothy stared at the floor. "Me? Well I was more of a loner than a joiner. At least until I graduated. The ink was still wet on my diploma when I enlisted."

"Do you want to talk about your military service?" Edie asked.

"No. I want to talk about my girlfriend."

"I thought you said you've only met her once?"

Timothy sighed, but Edie sensed it was more theatrics for her benefit. "She will be mine, doc. That's all that matters. She just doesn't know it yet. I told you. I have an itch, and it won't be satisfied until I scratch it."

"So what's your plan? How do you intend to woo this woman?"

"First, who says 'woo' anymore? You're not an eighty-year-old nun, are you? And second, I'm not going to woo her. I will take her. She will submit to me. She's going to be mine. I promise you that. Nice little itch I plan to scratch over and over..."

"That's enough," Edie interrupted.

"Getting a little hot, doc?"

"No. I just don't want us to wander too far into this when we are running out of time for now." Edie's skin felt hot, and she was sure he could see the red blotches that always crept across her neck when she got flustered. "Let's leave things here for today. I think we should talk more about your childhood and your military service next time."

"Oh, doc, but we are just getting started," Timothy said as he stood up and walked to the door, not waiting for Edie to respond or to say goodbye. *What a creepy guy*, Edie thought before admonishing herself for putting such an unprofessional label on a patient.

ADRIAN DRUMMED HIS FINGERS ON HIS PERFECTLY CENTERED DESK

blotter. His eyes flitting between the open doorway and the clock made of elaborately positioned and slightly rusted oversized gears that hung on the wall behind his couch. He usually enjoyed watching the gears make their halting circles as the time slipped past. He loved getting lost in the precise movements and constant forward progress of his timepiece as his most boring patients rambled on. Today, however, he just wanted those gears to speed up.

Finally, Edie's charity case walked by and out the front door. A creature of habit, Edie followed closely behind, headed to the kitchen to grab her lunch and eat in her office.

"Edie, would you step in here please?" he asked, hoping he sounded casual.

"What is it, Adrian? I'm on lunch and don't have much time before my next patient."

Adrian frowned and trudged forward. "I want to talk about last night. Come in and close the door."

Edie remained just outside his doorway. "What's there to talk about? You're using me, our life, to further your career. I'm not surprised. If anything, I'm shocked it took you this long to make that choice."

"What choice? And come in here and shut the door." Adrian spoke through gritted teeth.

"The choice between your career or your...whatever the hell I am."

Edie was getting too riled up, but Adrian couldn't stop himself from asking his next question. "What do you mean 'whatever the hell I am'?"

Edie laughed loudly and continued in a more vociferous manner as she walked in, leaned over his desk, and stared coldly into his eyes. "What am I, Adrian? Your student, worthy of getting special attention and private tutelage at the feet of the master? Your employee? Someone with such little self-confidence and self-esteem she'll follow you wherever you go? Or maybe I'm just a hole for your underwhelming penis?"

Adrian stood up, kicking his chair out behind him. "How dare you speak to me like that in my office. I built this place. It's my reputation that brings in the patients. You were a mediocre student, and you are an unexceptional psychologist. And as for our love life, I never hear you complain."

"You never hear me at all. You're such an ass. Everything is about you and your precious career."

"Need I remind you that if it weren't for you, I would still have a distinguished career in academia. You were broken when I found you. You're broken now. And you've torn my life to shreds."

Edie slowly straightened up and tugged at the bottom hem of her blouse. "I may have been broken, but you shattered me. You, the genius psychoanalyst. Instead of helping me, you preyed on me. You're more broken than I ever was. And some cut-rate new book from a psychologist who couldn't cut it won't change a thing. Not one damn thing." Her words reverberated around him though her voice, cold and measured, barely rose above a whisper.

"You have no idea what you're talking about," Adrian said. He knew the entire office could hear their argument. What must they think of Edie? "I am working on a thesis that involves my own personal narrative. You just happen to be in it."

"Well, I have news for you, Adrian. I can change that."

Adrian felt the sting of her words as sharply as if they'd been her hand striking his cheek. He struggled to find the words to calm her. Instead, he fell into his chair and waved his hand as if he were half-heartedly swatting at a fly. "That will be all, Edie. You have lunch, and I have an appointment waiting."

Edie smiled. Adrian expected her to laugh or perhaps actually smack him. But she took a slow breath, and walked out of his office without another word.

THE SOUND OF A VACUUM STARTLED EDIE FROM HER READING. THE cleaning crew came at nine like clockwork. Adrian must have left hours ago. He hadn't knocked. Or maybe he had.

As she looked up from the pile of paper scattered across her desk, the lateness of the hour surprised her. She had been so engrossed in the new paperwork she had completely missed dinner, an act her stomach now loudly admonished her for.

The package had arrived right after lunch. She had forgotten her call with Master Sargent Brian Chapman a couple weeks ago. Master Sargent Chapman served as the army psychologist at Fort Leonard Wood. Edie called the base commander's office the day she received Timothy's file. She had noticed he served in the army but no further information was included in her file. She had a hunch, given Timothy's history and the number of doctors, therapists, social workers, and psychologists who had examined him over the years, that there would also be a record from his years in the military.

She knew there had to be something, but she never imagined just what one little phone call would uncover. Their next session would be an enlightening one.

11

"I have this dream," Timothy said after several minutes of silence. Edie had long ago learned to wait him out. "I'm walking in the middle of a deserted city street. Barefoot. There's broken glass everywhere. It crunches below my feet. Every new step gets slipperier and more painful as the cuts grind deeper into my skin. But I keep walking. I don't slow down." He paused as he rubbed a scar on his left cheek.

"What drives you to keep moving?"

"I don't know. That's not true. It's the hunger. I'm hunting. She knows I'm following her now, and we both know I will catch up to her, eventually. Her scent is in the air. It's a mixture of vanilla, sweat, and fear. You know the kind of intense animal smell you get when your adrenaline is on overdrive? The air is filled with that, too."

"Where are you? Why is the city so empty?"

"It's a goddamn war zone, doc. You'd leave too if you could. She tried. So did I. Everyone left eventually. One way or another."

"Why aren't you wearing any shoes?" Edie found herself taking real notes. Her ribbons deserted like Timothy's city.

"I don't know that either. I just know I need to keep marching. Her scent is driving me crazy. It hangs in the air between the
acrid odor of smoke and burnt bodies. I can feel the crunching
of my feet. It's almost like I can hear it, even though I know I
can't. I can't hear a goddamn thing except the high-pitched tone
ringing loudly in my ears. No amount of shaking my head or
digging into my ears with a numb finger can stop it. So I ignore
it. I ignore everything and just keep marching."

"Marching? You've said that twice. Why that word?"

"My story more interesting than your little doodles today,
doc?" Timothy flashed a rare smile that set Edie's skin on fire.

"I always pay attention," Edie said too fast. "Let's keep this
about you, shall we? Why do you think you said 'march' instead
of walk or stumble or any number of other words?"

"You think that's significant? Maybe I just don't have much of
a vocabulary. Maybe I just like the poetry of it. Or maybe I've
done so much marching in my life it's the only way I know how
to move."

Edie saw her opening. "That's right. You were in the military.
Afghanistan, right? Tell me about that."

"Oh, doc. No, no, no." Timothy shook his head like Edie's
mom used to when she had disappointed her. The gesture made
every muscle in Edie's body tense. Her pulse throbbed in her
ears. "We were doing so well, doc. I was sharing; you were asking
just the right amount of questions to keep it going. Can't we just
enjoy the good thing we've got here?"

"You're right." Edie said as she looked down at her scrawling
notes to gather her thoughts. "You have that dream a lot, don't
you?"

"Every damn night, doc. Like a movie I've seen and don't
want to see again, but it's on, and I can't find the fucking
remote."

"Do you ever catch up to her?"

"Haven't yet. What would it mean if I did?"

"Well," Edie began slowly, which she hoped came across as contemplation rather than stalling. "I think that would mean you finally found resolution. That whatever it is you're chasing finally worked out. Or maybe a dream is just a dream. A distraction your mind needs during a stressful time in your life."

"A dream is just a dream, huh?" Timothy scoffed. "Is that like the guy who said sometimes a cigar is just a cigar?"

"That was Freud, and I've never been one to hold him up as the god some psychologists still believe him to be."

"Oh really? I thought he was the father of all this quackery," Timothy said. She knew he was teasing, egging her on, though his tone and face betrayed nothing.

"This 'quackery' as you call it is about listening and introspection. Dr. Freud, in my humble opinion, only listened for one thing and therefore heard that one thing in every patient. He was obsessed with sex. If you ask me, he was the one with an oppressed sex life and just projected his own eccentricities in that area onto his patients."

"Oh," Timothy said flatly.

"Oh what?"

"Oh nothing. I just didn't realize you didn't like sex, that's all."

"That's out of bounds," Edie said as she bolted from her chair and paced the room.

"Sorry, doc," Timothy said in a mostly convincing tone of contrition. "Do you ever have recurring dreams?"

Edie sighed. She could admonish him again and risk him shutting down again or answer his question. She knew what she should do, what Adrian would do, but she felt she had finally gotten somewhere with Timothy in their last couple sessions. Besides, she thought, she needed to gain his trust before springing her next question on him.

"Yes. I do. I think many people do. Like I said, dreams are just your brain's way of working through things your conscious mind isn't able to for whatever reason."

"So what's your dream, doc." Timothy leaned forward.

"I'm a girl. Well, not a little girl, but I'm much younger. Maybe a pre-teen. I'm back on the beach in California. I like to walk to clear my head. The ocean is my home, my safe place. But..." Edie trails off as the images come crashing down around her.

"But what, doc?"

"I stumble upon a woman all bloody and holding a knife." Edie whispered.

"Oh, that's good. That's almost better than mine." Timothy seemed like he might jump out of his seat. "Do you fight? Do you kill her? How does it end?"

"It doesn't end. It never does." Edie shook her head to clear the visions she had been running from for so long. "Now, I've indulged you long enough, Mr. Ridle. Why don't you tell me about your military service?"

Timothy sank back into the couch as he shook his head. "Come on, doc. I thought we were beyond this. Just because a guy says 'march' doesn't mean he is dreaming of his days in the service."

"I'm not talking about your dream. I'm talking about your service. Service to this country. You know there is no shame in having trouble dealing with things that happened during war or re-assimilating into society afterwards."

Timothy laughed. "Oh, doc, you sound like a movie. Is this the part where I tell you you can't handle the truth?"

"Timothy," Edie said gently as she took her seat again. "I spoke with one of your former therapists. He told me some of the stories you shared. It must have been horrible. I can't imagine how I'd deal with it if I were you."

"That's right, doc," Timothy spat, and Edie felt a sudden chill in the room. "You can't imagine it. You have no idea what I've seen. What I've done. Weren't we having a good time? Talking about our dreams? Why do you always ruin everything? Why do you try to outsmart me? You all try to outsmart me, but you can't. Nobody has yet, and nobody will. I do what I do because I want to. Not because war made me. I'm not some whiny ass using PTSD as an excuse or security blanket. I'm a man, doc. I know how to handle my own shit."

"I'm sorry," Edie said as Timothy jumped up and paced around the office. "Calm down, I only want to help."

"Help? You have no clue what you're doing here, doc. We both know that, with your textbook questions and fake empathy."

"Calm down," Edie said more sternly. "This isn't helping anything. You're mad, and that's a good thing. That means I hit a nerve, something raw you want to keep buried but that wants to come out. The more you keep pushing it back down the more it's going to keep owning you."

Timothy stopped and doubled over with laughter. "God, do you even hear yourself? You sound like the crazy one, doc. You're all high and mighty. I bet you think you're better than me. But we have the same dreams, don't we?"

"If you don't want to deal with this, I don't think I can help you. You need to calm down or leave," Edie stood up and hoped he couldn't see her trembling. She wasn't sure if it was from fear or anger, but she knew they'd crossed a line and it would either lead to a breakthrough or an end to their sessions.

"You're right. You can't help me," Timothy said as he headed for the door. "I doubt you've ever helped anyone. Especially yourself."

He slammed the door behind him before Edie could respond. She sank back into her chair, her muscles giving out underneath her as the adrenaline pulsed through her body and filled the air with its acrid smell.

"WHERE IS MY CAR?" ADRIAN ASKED AS HE STORMED INTO EDIE'S office that evening at seven o'clock. Edie couldn't believe it had gotten so late again. She had spent the hours after her session with Timothy reviewing her notes and making a list of questions and assumptions about his case. She hadn't been this engaged with a patient before and the thrill of it had made the day fly.

"Oh, I almost forgot," she said without looking up from her notes. "I had it towed."

"You what?" Adrian exploded. "You had no right. What gives you the idea you can just get rid of my car?"

Edie burst into a fit of laughter. She didn't even know it was in her. It was a deep gut laugh that shook her whole body. And then, just as suddenly, turned to a torrent of tears. Two men had yelled at her today. Two men she was just trying to help.

Adrian's eyes widened and his features softened at her outburst. He looked like a statue. Or a little boy unsure of what he happened upon or how to get out of it. She composed herself and put him out of his misery.

"I didn't get rid of it. It should be delivered within the next half an hour. I had it towed to the shop. It was running rough, and I didn't want you to get into an accident."

ADRIAN SLOWLY MELTED INTO THE CHAIR ACROSS FROM HER DESK. He studied her face. She had been acting so odd lately he wasn't sure what to expect. But this, this he never would have foreseen. She hated that car, and yet she had it taken to a mechanic because she worried about him. His face flushed, and he felt the tears welling in his own eyes. He quickly rubbed his hands over his face to cover his moment of weakness.

"Thank you, Edie. I thought you despised that car."

"I do, but I wanted to show you that even though I was mad, I still care for you, and that deathtrap is your most prized possession, so I thought you'd appreciate if it ran better."

"I certainly do," Adrian said through a wide smile. "Why don't I go make a reservation for us, so I can drive you to dinner when my car gets here?"

"I'd like that."

Adrian hopped out of the chair and ran to his office to call their favorite restaurant. He didn't even care if that nasty little waiter was working tonight. He knew she would come around. Everything was finally back to normal, finally as it should be.

12

E die looked up at the clock for the fourth time in the past ten minutes. Timothy's file lay closed in front of her on her desk. She flipped open the folder but immediately slammed it closed again. There was nothing new to review. Nothing she hadn't already read and reread, committing to memory.

She and Timothy hadn't made as much progress as she first thought. When she pushed him to open up about his military career, she knew it would be a difficult conversation. She couldn't have anticipated the depth of his repressed feelings surrounding that area of his life. And she certainly couldn't have foreseen the outburst that ensued.

She felt like a fool waiting for a patient who obviously didn't intend to show up. She wanted to apologize for moving too fast. A memory flitted across her mind of a lecture Adrian used to give. One of her favorites. He believed therapy was a dance. The patient and psychologist had to be in sync, moving to the same beat. It involved a lot of back and forth and unspoken communication to choreograph something special, something more than the sum of the two parts. The two dancers. But she forgot the one critical ingredient to success. The patient leads. Her move in their last session had tripped them up.

Twenty minutes past their start time, Edie shoved Timothy's file back into her filing cabinet. He would have been her last session of the day, so instead she planned to go home early while she still had the house to herself and could administer some of her own private therapy. Her inner thighs tingled at the thought of the blade's kiss.

Her heart raced as she hurried to the door and turned off the lights. She looked back into her office as she opened the door to make sure she had everything and bumped into a very disheveled Timothy as she stepped through the threshold.

"What's up, doc," Timothy deadpanned as Edie recoiled, pushing herself off of him and propelling herself back into her office. Her eyes wide, she held her purse between her patient and herself as if it could shield her from whatever he intended to do after skulking around outside her office door.

He meandered in and hit the light switch without turning to look for it. After blinking a few times, he sat down casually in his customary spot on her couch and stared directly at the wall. Edie slowly lowered her purse.

"What are you doing here, Mr. Ridle."

"We have an appointment, doc."

"Correction. We had an appointment. One that should have started nearly thirty minutes ago. One that you failed to show up to. And one that I have now canceled." She stood there. The silence building between them. He didn't seem to mind the quiet or the wait. She could stand neither. "Fine," she sighed as she closed the door and gathered her pen, paper and wits.

The silence fell over them once again. "Look, you're down to twenty minutes now. I'm not sure what you think you're accomplishing here other than wasting my time. Maybe that has been the game all along." Her barbs didn't move Timothy to speak. She took a breath and continued more contritely. "I want to apologize for pushing too hard last time. I realize your years in the military are a source of great discomfort. I would like to get to a place where you feel comfortable working through that discomfort. However, we have not yet arrived at that place."

"So why don't you?"

"Why don't I what, Mr. Ridle?"

"Apologize."

Edie slapped her pen down on the blank page of her legal pad and sighed for what felt like the hundredth time during their abbreviated session. "If you had been listening, you would have heard that I did just apologize."

"I was listening," Timothy said, still without looking at her. "And I heard you say you want to apologize, but I didn't hear you apologize."

Edie looked at the ceiling and breathed into her impending frustration. After several controlled breaths, she looked at her patient. "I'm sorry."

"Don't worry about it, doc. Water under the bridge."

"Great," Edie said through a glued on smile as she picked up her pen. "Now, what would you like to talk about for the next fifteen minutes?"

"Well, you say you want me to dig deeper," Timothy said. "So I'd like to talk about a girl I've been thinking about a lot lately." He paused, probably to see if Edie would object to another story about his bizarre relationships with women. When she just sat there, arms crossed and foot tapping, he continued.

"It was middle school," Timothy said with a wispy voice as he recalled a distant memory. "I was in love with this girl, but she barely knew I existed. I was the kid in second-hand clothes who sat alone in the cafeteria eating my bagged lunch and spent the time between classes evading the school bullies. She was the popular, rich cheerleader who was always in the middle of a group of friends and hangers on."

Edie jotted down a few notes as he continued. "I watched her all the time. Her name was Stephanie. I would practice conversations in the bathroom mirror at home but never got up the nerve to approach her in real life. I sat behind her in math, but it might as well have been an empty chair for all she knew or cared. But I knew her. I knew what route she walked to and from school. I knew her favorite school lunch. I knew the name of her dogs and her younger sister. I knew the scent of her hair."

"How did it make you feel that she never talked to you?" Edie interjected.

"Invisible. I like that feeling now. I'm used to it. But back then? It crushed me, doc. I used to sit at my desk in math class and write her love notes I'd never give her. One day, though, a note I'd crumpled up before the start of class somehow fell next to her chair. She found it after class when she was gathering her books." Timothy's voice trailed off as he sat lost in that faraway moment.

"What'd she do?"

"Well, on that particular note I'd simply written 'I love you' over and over in what you might call the frantic scrawling of a lovesick, testosterone-ridden pre-teen. We're talking all different sizes and in all directions. The page was just covered with my love."

"And?" Edie prompted.

"She asked if it was mine. I said no, so of course she uncrumpled it. You should have seen the look on her face. She was disgusted, doc. Her face turned red, and she kept shaking her head. When she showed it to her friends, they all laughed hysterically. It was like my life was crumpling up like that paper.

I just wanted to reach out and grab it and run. But that'd be admitting I wrote that crazy shit. So I just sat there and listened to them talk about how creepy it was."

"Did you ever tell her it was you?"

"Hell no. But one day, I think it was the next semester, she wrote something cruel about the teacher on the chalkboard before class. That teacher, Mrs. Powers, was really hard on her. Just rode her all semester. So I think she was just blowing off steam, you know?"

"What did she write?"

"Something about how if Mrs. Powers was all that, how come her husband was powerless to stop himself from sleeping with her sister."

"I can imagine that probably didn't go over well."

"Not for me it didn't. When Mrs. Powers walked in and saw what Stephanie had written, she started crying and yelling. Demanding to know who did it. So I looked around and then calmly raised my hand."

"You took the blame?"

"Yep. I got suspended for a month, too. But the kicker is that Stephanie never said thank you. Never said anything to me at all. Not in class. Not in the halls. Not at lunch. Never a note even. That's when I learned that all the bullshit in the movies about the hero riding off into the sunset with the girl is just a bunch of crap. Probably written by a bunch of dudes who never got a girl in real life. How's that for deep?"

"That's a fascinating story, Mr. Ridle, but what does it have to do with why you are here?" Edie asked as she examined the progress of her latest ribbon.

"Isn't it obvious? I fall in love too quickly. I fall in love all the time. Still do. But it never works out. And it never will."

Edie rolled her eyes. "While I find your budding love life

interesting, I'm not sure it behooves us to make that the focus of our time together, speaking of which we are now well over this week's time." Edie stood before he could object and walked back to her desk to sit down. "I want you to think about what you want to get out of these sessions and if you even want to continue our work together. If you do, next time I don't want any more of these random stories that just pop into your head. Therapy is hard work, Mr. Ridle. Not some game. Let's stop playing, shall we?"

Edie stared at him in what she hoped appeared to be a calm and authoritarian manner. She felt neither. To her surprise, he stared right back. Their gaze remained locked for several seconds before he stood and left without another word. *Such an odd man*, Edie thought and doubted she'd see him again.

EDIE LOOKED UP FROM THE NOTES SHE HAD BEEN TRANSCRIBING. The clock in the shadows across the room read ten. She had gotten lost in her work in a way she hadn't in a long time. It wasn't just Timothy's case either. Suddenly she found herself doodling less and writing more. She had spent the last several hours furiously making notes about each of her patients, posing hypotheses and writing probing questions for future sessions to fill in the occasional holes or clear up things that just didn't add up in her mind yet.

Rubbing her eyes as she locked up the office and walked to her car, she thought about Timothy's story today. Was there something lurking deeper there or was he just playing with her? Life seemed to be one big joke to him. Lord knows he never seemed to worry about anything, especially women.

The hair on the back of her neck stood up as she got to her car, the only one in the parking lot. She looked around and didn't see anyone. But she couldn't shake the feeling. She quickly unlocked her car, threw her bag in, jumped into the driver's seat, and locked the door behind her.

She needed some serious stress relief. Maybe Adrian would be asleep so she could have a little therapy time before bed.

13

Timothy sat ramrod straight on the couch. If nothing else, the military had impressed upon him the importance of good posture. 'Good posture is the sign of a good soldier,' his drill instructor would yell at him, his face so close to Timothy's he could smell the rotten remains of the man's most recent meal. Spittle flew in every direction, falling like a light rain drizzle on Timothy's face. He hated that man, but he sure as shit sat up straight now.

"Have you thought about our last session, Mr. Ridle?" Dr. McEvoy asked after several quietly comfortable minutes had passed.

She seemed edgy today. Maybe that old fuck she lived with wasn't giving it to her on the regular. He seemed like a pompous ass. Wonder what she saw in him. The doc wasn't a 10 on any scale, but wasn't a dog either. And she was nice. Personality went a long way with Timothy. He hated sexy women with that blank stare that told you they had nothing going on between their ears. You might as well be fucking a department store mannequin.

"Mr. Ridle? If you're just going to sit there with that goofy grin, perhaps we should decide this isn't working. You can move on to your next therapist or just squander whatever opportunity you have left to face your past."

He looked at her for the first time since he arrived. He liked the effect his looks had on her. She tried to play it off, to play it cool. But he saw it. Her face flushed just a little. Her eyes dilated. One corner of her mouth curled into a half smile before she caught herself and pursed her lips. She had a natural beauty. Not like a model. Not even close. But her look was sweet. Almost innocent. And she had a sadness behind her eyes that drew him to her.

"Remember when I told you I joined the army right after high school? Well I mean it was the same day I got my diploma. I marched right off the stage and into the recruiter's office, conveniently located on the same block as the school. We didn't have much in our little town, but we had an army recruiter. I bet they do that all over these United States. Set up shop in Podunk, dead end towns. We were like flies trying to escape a jar before we suffocated. And there they were like a dot of honey. Something sweet to distract us, draw us out."

Timothy swallowed hard. He hadn't thought about this part of his life in a long while. He preferred to look ahead rather than dwell on the shit he'd crawled through to get there.

"I think serving your country is a noble calling, Mr. Ridle," Doctor McEvoy said. "Are you from a long line of veterans?"

Timothy laughed. "I'm from a long line of fuck ups and retards, doc. So joining the army seemed like a family reunion."

"Tell me what high school was like for you?"

Timothy contemplated for a moment. That question caught him off guard. "Well, you may not believe this, but I was awfully quiet in high school. All school, actually. I wasn't a nerd or a stoner or a jock. Like I've said. I was more of a loner. But by choice, you know?"

"That must have been hard in such a small town," Dr. McEvoy said in a way that sounded more like a statement of solidarity than a question.

"You from a small town, too, doc?"

Dr. McEvoy laughed. She had a beautiful laugh. It sounded genuine. Not the laugh of his mother or most women he met. "Not at all," she said. "I'm from San Francisco. So I'm really interested in the dynamics of small town life on your development."

"I don't know about my development, but small towns aren't much different from big ones. Groups of people who think they're better than other groups. People who have and people who have not. There's crime, too. In fact, several kids went missing in my high school while I was there. Mostly jocks. A few girls, too. From the popular cliques. But I didn't miss them, any of them. They were mostly from the groups who sometimes teased me about my second-hand outfits or my smell or my general weirdness. I couldn't wait to get the hell out of that town."

"Did you find a better fit in the marines?"

"The army, doc. The marines are pussies. And yeah, I did. The guys in my platoon were mean mother fuckers. Rapists. Killers. Bastards, all. You had to be tough to make it through basic. And even tougher to make it through a tour or two in Afghanistan."

"You did two tours, didn't you?"

"Yes." Timothy stiffened his back, not realizing he had curled into himself as he'd been talking.

"Was it difficult? Combat, I mean?"

What a naïve question, Timothy thought. "Combat drove a lot of men crazy. The good and the bad. Killing people is the great equalizer. A bullet doesn't care what's in your heart. And out there in the desert it was kill or be killed. I liked it. And I was good at it. So much so that I was highly decorated. If the brass knew what really went on during those patrols, well maybe I would have been court-martialed instead. But then again, maybe they did know. I was eventually discharged because I think they figured out I liked it too much."

"I saw nothing in your file that indicated anyone felt that way," Dr. McEvoy said. "I can't imagine the enormous pressure you must have felt. Being asked to kill for your country is a hard thing to reconcile in your heart."

"I'm not surprised there's nothing like that in my file, doc. The military is great at shining a light on its heroes so it can hide its darker edges in the shadows. The government doesn't want to admit they create monsters."

"You think you're a monster, Mr. Ridle?"

"After the army, I was back to being a nobody. From nowhere. So I became a drifter. Living in a van. I moved fluidly, invisibly between cities, small towns. State to state."

"You didn't answer my question," the doc pressed him.

"The army set me up with psych evaluations after I got back to the states," Timothy said as he stared at his feet. He'd missed a spot near the toe of his right boot. His drill instructor would yell at him for becoming so lax. "But I quickly fell through the rather large cracks in the VA system. For a while I continued to look for therapy, mostly out of boredom. But then I got into some trouble with the sheriff when I went home. That's when the courts decided therapy wasn't a choice anymore. So here I am."

"So you're only here because of the courts?" Doctor McEvoy asked, and he sensed her disappointment.

"Well, that and curiosity."

"Curiosity?"

"Yeah. About whether anyone would correctly identify me for the monster I am."

. . .

EDIE TOYED WITH HER PEN. SHE HAD FILLED HER PAGE WITH NOTES instead of ribbons. She felt on the edge of a breakthrough. She didn't want to ruin the momentum, but she feared Timothy was about to lead her into a dark place. If she went with him, let him guide her, she would be doing exactly what she was supposed to and exactly what she had asked him to do. But if she were honest with herself, she believed less than half of Timothy's stories.

She decided to trust the process if not the patient. "I've known you for nearly two months now, and I don't think you're a monster. What exactly is it that makes you a monster, Mr. Ridle?"

Timothy moved forward on the couch and leveled a rare steady gaze at her. After a few seconds he finally spoke. "We're all just chasing the next high. Even you, doc. I bet you have a few secrets you hope are never discovered. Something that might make you a monster to others, even those who supposedly know you the best."

Edie gasped and rocked back in her chair. "As I've said many times, Mr. Ridle, these sessions are not about me."

"Oh but they are, doc. We are both here, so how could these little moments we share not be about both of us?" Timothy continued, watching her as he spoke. She felt her skin blush under this strange new scrutiny. "Any way, my point is we are all addicts. I'm not just talking about drink or drugs. Some of us are addicted to adventure. Others to work or winning. Shit, doc, happiness is the most elusive high of all, and we're all chasing that one. Trouble is, like all great drugs, the next hit of happiness is never as good as that very first one. What's your drug of choice?"

"I'm more interested in what you're chasing. What is that elusive high for you?"

"Well, contrary to your expert opinion, it's not drugs. But

that's okay, doc, we all make mistakes."

Timothy finally turned away from Edie and turned his gaze back to his favorite corner of her coffee table. Edie watched him closely. He rubbed his hands on his knees. His legs bounced slightly. A bead of sweat slowly formed on his brow.

"There's something different about me, doc. Something I've never said out loud. I'm not sure I'm ready to." Timothy's voice faltered, and Edie sensed real hesitation.

"Sometimes the best way to tell someone something is to just close your eyes, take a deep breath, and say it," Edie said in what she hoped sounded like a calm and comforting tone.

Timothy continued to stare down at the most fascinating coffee table in the world. After a moment, he took a deep breath and continued. "When I'm listening to people, I often drift off and my mind wanders."

"I do that all the time."

"Do you wonder things like what it would take to pop one of their eyeballs out of its socket?" Timothy asked as he looked up and deep into her eyes. "Because I do. And it doesn't stop there. I wonder if I could do it before they even noticed. I see the whole thing in my mind, and it's more like a memory or a vision of the future rather than some daydream." Timothy paused again but continued before Edie had time to understand what he was saying and respond. "Sometimes I feel my face being drawn like a magnet towards men as they talk," he continued. "Like I'm going to kiss them. I don't want to, mind you. I never have. I'm not gay, doc. But it's like the pull of gravity on the ocean. The tide threatens to wash me ashore on the salty sweetness of their lips, and I don't know what that means."

Edie sat back. Setting her pen down and folding her hands together. "It's normal for your mind to wander. We all do it. Sometimes boredom makes your brain go into overdrive. But really, it can happen at any time. Some studies even suggest that our minds wander for nearly half of all our waking hours. And it can be worse if we have unresolved issues that are worrying us."

"So I shouldn't worry about my mind wandering into these dark areas?"

"Not at all. Thinking something isn't the same as doing it," Edie responded and felt satisfied that she was helping a patient in desperate need of a breakthrough.

"And what if it's not just thinking about it?"

"What do you mean, Mr. Ridle?"

"We talked about how easily I fall in love. Remember that?"

Edie smiled. She had been expecting some dark revelation, but as mundane as a lovesick patient might be, she knew love could cause as much pain as a knife. It could be wielded as a weapon just as easily as it could be used as a shield. "I do," she said.

"I think I should tell you about some of my lovers. I don't usually share such details of my intimate life, but I think I can trust you. I can trust you, can't I, doc?"

"Of course, Mr. Ridle. I'm here to provide you with a safe place to share."

"Okay," Timothy sighed. "I don't know where to start, but here goes. There was a woman I met at the gym. She was hot, and we would catch ourselves checking each other out. I changed my routine to make sure I worked out whenever she was in the gym."

Edie flipped to a new page. Her pen flew across the paper as she took furious notes.

"We became regular racquetball partners. We made out in the middle of a match once until we were fucking right there in the racquetball court. She broke my heart, though, when I snuck in a workout on one of my off days only to find out she played with other guys."

"You mean you walked in on her fooling around with

another racquetball partner?"

"No. She was just playing a match, but it didn't matter. I thought what we had was special. She didn't."

"Did you talk to her about it?"

"Oh, we had long conversations about it. But eventually they became one sided, and she just vanished."

"I'm sorry to hear that," Edie said. "Relationships are always hard, no matter how much you have in common. It takes compromise and communication."

"I don't believe that's true, doc. At least when it's true love." Timothy's eyes felt as if they could bore into her brain and unlock her own secrets.

"And have you found true love?" Edie asked mostly to take his attention away from her.

"Maybe. I'm not sure yet. I mean there's a woman who has real potential for sure," Timothy replied as he looked away again. "Other than that, though, there have been your garden variety hookers, waitresses, hairstylists, and store clerks. You know, the kind of women one easily meets on the road and can strike up a conversation with. They all showed such promise. Until they didn't live up to my standards for the fairer sex."

"Oh really," Edie said through a smile. "And what does it mean to not live up to your standards?"

"It can be small things. In fact, most are," Timothy said. "In my experience, perfection is just the right mix of little habits. Unfortunately, one of my former lovers was a farter. One cussed like a sailor. Another insisted I open every door for her and bring her flowers every time we went out. So I left some daisies on her shallow grave."

"Grave?" Edie blurted out as the hairs on the back of her neck stood up and her stomach tightened.

"I'm sorry," Timothy smiled. "I think I buried the lead. Remember how I told you I've drifted around since I got back to the states? Well, I've been leaving a string of missing women in every town and city I've visited. But the thing is, they're not missing. Well, not just missing. They're dead. And it's all because, like you said, I fall in love too easily."

Edie froze as his words washed over her. She was alone in a room with a patient who just confessed to being a murderer. What an incredible breakthrough.

ACT TWO

"No one who, like me, conjures up the most evil of those half-tamed demons that inhabit the human breast, and seeks to wrestle with them, can expect to come through the struggle unscathed."

— SIGMUND FREUD

14

Timothy smiled. He hated the word 'giddy,' but it perfectly described his feelings as he watched Dr. McEvoy's response. He saw signs of her inner struggle roll like thunderclouds across her eyes. Did her patient just admit to being a murderer?

He had planned to blow off today's appointment, drift along a while until the urges resurfaced and once again he could no longer control them, and then he'd find another doctor to help just enough for the cycle to repeat itself.

But he liked Dr. McEvoy. She was vulnerable. Sincere. Not like most psychologists he'd met, and he'd met a lot of them. And, unlike any of his other doctors, she was a woman. He had a rule about that. It was quite clearly listed in his file. And yet here he sat, on the couch of a beautiful woman to whom he'd just told a dark, ugly story about himself.

"If it helps, I only kill women who deserve it. Women who aren't capable of love," he said, if only to break the silence he normally relished.

Edie slowly raised her head, and her 30,000 foot stare focused once again on Timothy. The storm clouds in her eyes seemed to dissipate. He started to smile but realized he stood in the eye of the storm. He braced himself.

"I find your excuse rather cavalier and thin," she scolded. "But then I'm not sure I even believe you at all. I think this is just another diversion for you. Something to ensure we continue to see each other, to save you the trouble of shopping for yet another therapist."

She studied him, and he could feel the daggers shooting from her eyes. Still, he met her gaze. "When I came back from active duty, I tried to get help," he said. "I told you that. You've seen that for yourself in my files. I didn't feel comfortable anywhere, probably because I didn't feel comfortable in my own skin. That's why I drifted around the country. I ended up here to take care of my mom when she had a stroke."

He paused to make sure Dr. McEvoy was paying attention. She continued looking at him, but she didn't seem to be there, and she was no longer drawing those silly ribbons all over the pages of her notepad. "You still with me, doc?"

"So you're taking care of your mom at the same time you're killing women?"

"Sure. But don't worry, doc, I'm not Norman Bates crazy." He laughed. It felt good to laugh so freely, to have someone to connect with again.

Edie picked up her pen. "How long have you lived in Kansas City?"

"About two-and-a-half years," Timothy replied. "How about you, doc?"

"About the same," Edie said as she started doodling. "What part of town do you and your mom live in?"

"Her house is in the West Plaza area on Belleview between 47th and 48th," Timothy said. "Belleview is fitting, right?"

"That's a nice part of town." Dr. McEvoy ignored his question. He didn't like that little habit but recognized it as one most psychologists shared. They all thought they were in charge of the conversation. In his experience, though, they never were. Eventually that irony would sink in with Dr. McEvoy as well.

"Well, it's close to a nice part, I guess. My mom's neighborhood gets the riffraff who can't afford to live in the more hoity-toity apartments and neighborhoods. There's a lot of stupid crime like breaking and entry and theft. But people know not to mess with me and mine. It's really the perfect place for someone like me to live. Just a block or two from all those rich jerks shopping at their ritzy stores and drinking their overpriced beers in their quiet, uptight bars."

Edie shook her head as if she believed she could shake away everything Timothy was telling her like a dog shedding water.

"I'm just kidding, doc," Timothy chuckled. He relished the look of relief in her face. She looked cute when her guard was down.

"Oh, thank God. Why in the world would you tell me a story like that?"

Timothy looked at the corner of the table for a long while. He wasn't quite ready for their conversation to end. Their sessions were the highlight of his week. It took a lot for him to trust someone, and he felt Dr. McEvoy might be able to help him. Hell, maybe he could even help her. Wasn't he always being told that relationships were a two-way street?

"I think you misunderstand," he teased. "I just mean I don't shit where I eat. At least not with the more serious stuff. I'm not going to sit here and say that if I happened upon a blackout drunk college sorority girl that I wouldn't indulge. Know what I mean? I am a man after all. You put that stuff in front of me, and I will dive in every time."

Edie's face flushed. *Damn*, Timothy thought, *maybe she was more than just pretty.* "Wait," she said in a weird high-pitched falsetto before taking a breath and continuing in hushed tones. "Just wait. What are you saying? That this is all true?"

Timothy laughed until tears blurred his vision. "I'm just opening up like you wanted, doc."

"Mr. Ridle, quit playing with me. Are you or are you not a murderer?"

Timothy stood up, and Edie must have thought he was about to leave because she jumped up, too. He walked over and casually looked at her diplomas on the wall. He'd studied them many times from the couch, but he enjoyed the suspense of the moment. He had her completely enthralled with his story, with him.

He turned around. She stood behind her chair. Her legal pad and pen on the floor. The desperation clung to her body like a thin coat against a harsh winter wind. He could smell her fear, and he liked the scent.

"Everything I've told you is true, doc. Every. Single. Word."

EDIE FELT LIKE A MOUSE BEING TOYED WITH BY A CAT IN NO RUSH to put her out of her misery. Her feet felt nailed to the floor. Cool sweat coated her skin like a thin shield. Her heart beat so fast she couldn't catch her breath.

Timothy made a move toward her but stopped when she flinched. Edie refused to believe this was happening. So many thoughts filled her head that none of them could come in clearly. She knew she could scream for help. Adrian was in the office. So were many of her other colleagues. But she could barely talk let alone scream. And what could this man do to her in the time it would take someone to rush in?

A realization washed over her like the ocean waves of her childhood and nearly pulled her under.

"Just...just give me a minute," Edie stuttered, her mouth

suddenly dry. "Stay right there. I don't want you to move. I don't want you to talk. I...I have to process this."

Timothy respected her instructions. He nodded slightly and leaned against her desk, studying the carpet as if some hidden message might soon emerge there.

Okay, Edie, she thought to herself. *Get it together*. She forced herself to take a few deep breaths, but she remained standing. It'd be easier to rush to the door if things came to that.

One of three scenarios was true. Her patient could actually be a serial rapist and murderer, which meant she had a legal obligation to contact the authorities. Or he could really believe his stories, but in reality they were just elaborate delusions to help him deal with and escape from all the pain and killing he experienced growing up, in the military, or both. Or he was a sociopath with a talent for reading people and situations and drawing on what he learned to get under a person's skin.

She didn't believe Timothy was delusional. So either he was a rapist and murderer or he was a sociopath. Neither was something she had dealt with before or even felt equipped to handle. And if he was just toying with her, how did he know her weak spot? How had he managed to make it so personal? Had he been targeting her? Maybe it wasn't a coincidence he showed up at her practice and on her couch.

She took a final, ragged breath, her mind made up. "Come sit down, Mr. Ridle," she said as she gathered her pen and paper. "We have a lot to talk about."

Timothy smiled. He had thought he'd miscalculated, misjudged her. *Atta boy, doc*, he thought.

"So, let's talk about what you just shared," Edie said as Timothy settled back onto the couch.

"Anything for you." He smiled and held her eyes with his. "I'm an open book."

"I think you're anything but an open book, Mr. Ridle," Edie said as she broke their staring contest and talked instead to the couch cushion next to him. "And, anyway, I'm most curious about what kind of book you are."

Timothy laughed. "Do we still need to be so formal, doc? I feel like we're starting to get to know each other, share some things, grow this relationship of ours. You can call me Timothy."

"What I call you shouldn't matter or affect our sessions," Edie said as she worked on a particularly elaborate ribbon doodle. "And, for the record, our relationship is nothing more than therapist-patient. I don't want you reading anything else into it or believing it is anything more."

Timothy laughed. Dr. McEvoy, Edie, visibly flinched. He enjoyed that. She tried to hide it, but he was getting under her skin. He bet she thought about him between their times together, wondering where he was and what he was doing.

"My mom never won mother of the year," Timothy began as he once again found his favorite corner of the coffee table. "Hell, she was never even in the running. I always wanted a pet, but she didn't think I could handle the responsibility. There's something about a boy and a dog, isn't there, doc? That first pure relationship. There are no games. No manipulations. But I never had a dog. Never even had a cat or a hamster. Closest I came were the cockroaches in our trailer. I'd name them before I squished the life out of them. But you know cockroaches. I eventually ran out of names."

"Are you suggesting you became a rapist and murderer because mommy wouldn't let you get a dog?" Edie huffed.

"I think my mom thought of me as her pet," Timothy continued. "She loved me in her special way. But she just wasn't equipped to raise a child. She could barely take care of herself.

Looking back on it now, I think maybe she was a little slow. Even at a young age, I was more of a parent to her than she was to me. Did you have both parents, doc? Did you get along?"

Dr. McEvoy ignored the question. "Did your mom hit you?"

Timothy smiled at the thought. "Oh god no. She couldn't hurt a fly. And besides, she was much too busy most of the time to bother with me. You see, her only goal in life was to find Mr. Right. I used to think she was looking for a good dad, but the guys she brought home weren't the fatherly type. She never found Mr. Right. She kissed a lot of toads though. Well, she did a lot more than kiss. The walls of our trailer weren't exactly thick, and there wasn't anywhere I could go except outside to escape the animal sounds that came from my mom's room when she had a man over. And she always had a man over."

"How did that make you feel? Did you and your mother ever talk about it?"

"She didn't allow me to comment on her 'gentlemen friends.' That's what she called them."

"Did she ever tell you she loved you, show affection in any way?"

Timothy thought about that for a long time. "I remember when I found out mom was the tooth fairy. I was seven. Every time one of my teeth wiggled even a little, I'd start working at it. I would dig at it with my pocket knife. I even tried to hammer one out one time. Whatever I could do to speed up the process so the tooth fairy would leave me money. I always got two shiny quarters. Like they just came from the bank vault, all polished and shining like the treasure they were to me. One night I caught her digging under my pillow when she thought I was asleep. I kept my eyes closed until she walked out of the room, but I knew it was her. The air smelled of cheap perfume, cheap cigarettes, and cheap sex. I was disappointed at first that it wasn't some beautiful fairy visiting my room that night. But after that, I cherished those quarters every time I lost another tooth. And I kept them all. Still have the collection. They were the only signs in our otherwise cold relationship that proved she loved me."

"That's a sad story, Mr. Ridle," Edie said. "But lots of kids grow up with distant parents or no parents at all. Why is it this story is the one that came to mind, that it's your mom you want to talk about, when I asked you whether you truly are a rapist and murderer? A question, by the way, you still haven't answered."

"Sorry, doc," Timothy said as he stood up, careful not to spook her. "Times up. I'll see you next week." And with that, he walked out before she could protest.

15

The night slowly slid past Edie's windshield as she drove aimlessly through the city. She had stayed late at the office again over Adrian's protests. He wanted to take her to dinner. She thought about telling him about her session, about Timothy's confession, but she needed to digest it all for herself first. She knew Adrian would fly off the handle. He'd insist that they call the police or worse, he'd take over the case.

While she didn't yet trust that Timothy was telling her the truth, she hadn't felt this alive in a long time. It felt like the walls she had put up years ago to keep the world out were starting to crack. She wasn't as numb anymore. Wasn't sleepwalking through life at the moment. And she couldn't risk Adrian taking that away from her.

More than that, though, she wanted to keep seeing Timothy to spite Adrian. She would tell him eventually but only when the time was right. After what happened at Columbia, she secretly hoped she could confront and bring down a rapist. Adrian thought he was protecting her by limiting her number of cases and handpicking her patients, but his plan had backfired. Timothy's file contained several holes and superficial evaluations, but nothing indicated the bombshell he had revealed today.

Edie looked around as she drove slowly through the city. Kansas City was a nice place for a middle of America metropolis. It struck her as a large town playing the part of a city. That was evidenced by the fact that most businesses were closed and the streets dark and deserted even though it was only eleven o'clock. She wondered what Timothy was up to and hoped he was at home or work and not out chasing the woman he'd told her about, the one that in his mind he was already dating. That's when she realized she had subconsciously steered herself towards Timothy's neighborhood.

Without thinking, she drove to the intersection he had described. Condos lined the block. They all looked either new or well maintained. Nothing about the neighborhood seemed to match the hard knocks, ruffian description Timothy had given her. After circling the cluster of condos a few times, Edie chastised herself and drove off. She wasn't sure what she had expected to find. Although she wouldn't have been surprised to find him sitting out on his stoop waiting to wave as she passed.

On a whim, Edie drove to Loose Park. It was one of the first parks she visited when she and Adrian moved to Kansas City. The rose garden was understandably the site of many weddings, even in KC's stifling summer months. But on this unusually crisp end-of-spring night, Edie found herself all alone as she wandered through the roses, stopping occasionally to take in their intoxicating perfume. Roses reminded her of her childhood. She and her mom would buy a rose bush for her grandma every year on Mother's Day. It was a tradition that Edie had hoped to continue with her own children.

A familiar urge swept over her, and Edie knew immediately what she had to do. She jogged back to her car, cutting through the neat circular rows of rose bushes to forge her own, more direct path. Once at her car, she popped the trunk and fumbled to remove the emergency spare. As soon as the assembly mechanism that kept the tire in place was loose enough, she shoved her hand under the tire and felt for her stash.

She looked around to make sure she was still alone and then walked back to the center of the rose garden with a small bundle under her arm. She sat down under the large fountain and took out a fresh razor from the canvas pouch. It shone brightly in the moonlight. She played with the angle so the light reflection danced across her skin. She slowly lifted the hem of her skirt with her other hand. Her fingertips causing a wave of goosebumps to crash over her inner thigh. She let her fingers explore the perfectly straight rows of raised scar tissue from her previous handiwork. Then she gently brought the razor to her skin and held it there. One corner poking at her inner thigh. She took a breath, arched her back and cut. Her legs quivered, her eyes rolled back in her head, and she bit her lip to silence her moaning. It was the first time she'd climaxed in a long time, and the first while cutting.

16

E die played with the papers on her desk. Lining everything up in a neat ninety-degree angle to the left corner then shuffling them around and lining them up equally square to the corner on the right side of the desk. She crossed and uncrossed her legs. Looked at her watch and then at the wall clock.

Timothy wasn't late, but Edie's last appointment had canceled at the last second, which meant she'd spent the last forty-five minutes pacing, nibbling at a lunch she couldn't taste, re-reading Timothy's file and her notes, and willing time to speed up.

At two past the hour, Timothy sauntered into her office and sat at his normal place on her couch. Neither acknowledged the other. Edie supposed he was waiting to gauge her mood. She knew he was an emotional chameleon. When she could stand the thick silence no longer she began their session from her desk.

"Has anything...changed with you in the last week?" she asked.

Timothy laughed, and turned away to avoid returning his smile or blushing from its effects.

"I assume you are asking if I've either decided to admit I made everything up or, if it is true, have I killed anyone new," he said in an unfaltering voice that both intrigued and scared her.

She nodded, and he continued. "Well, doc, the answer to both is no." He let it hang in the air, appearing to dare her to make her next move.

Edie tried to think. Her stomach hurt from the guilt and anxiety over keeping this secret from Adrian. She knew she couldn't continue without help. She wasn't sleeping, which on the upside meant she wasn't sleep walking or suffering from her normal nightmares. Instead, she had become trapped in this waking nightmare.

Glancing at her notes, she spotted a half-formed thought jotted down inside a ribbon from their second meeting. "Tell me about the woman you're seeing. Does she know what you...are?" She asked while staring at her desk.

Timothy didn't answer. She felt the heat of his gaze, and she couldn't help but slowly lift her head and look at him. She expected a smug smile, but he seemed genuinely confused.

"You told me you had serendipitously met a homicide detective. I believe you said you were looking forward to getting to know her better. I can only assume now you weren't talking about dating."

His thousand-watt smile made her blush. "Oh yeah, her. I suppose you're wondering if she's alive and well. Truth is, I've moved on. Love is fickle that way isn't it, doc?"

"Moved on?"

"Yep," Timothy said with a casual nod. "I might see how she's doing some other time. You know how it is. 'If neither of us are seeing anyone in a few years, we should get together' kind of thing."

Without warning, Edie threw up on her desk. Timothy jumped up and stepped toward her, but she motioned him away with both hands. Her vomit tasted of bile and chicken caesar salad. When she could finally compose herself, she smoothed back her hair, ran the back of her hand across her mouth and took some slow breaths.

"I'm afraid we're going to have to stop this," she whispered. Her throat burned, and her stomach warned her that the storm hadn't yet subsided.

Timothy stood rooted in the middle of the room. He seemed unsure of what to do. She thought it an odd look for him. Everything about him had been so controlled until now.

"Stop?" he asked. "You mean today or for good?"

"Just go," Edie managed to say before cupping her mouth and jumping up to push by him as she rushed to the bathroom.

17

Timothy drummed his fingers on the steering wheel and fussed with the seatbelt. He had spent the last few hours parked on the street under an oak tree across from Dr. McEvoy's office. He thought it strange that she hadn't gone home after he left.

Officially he was on duty, but today was a roving day. He should be across town monitoring two buildings that were about to be demolished as the city continued to knock down its history to make way for the latest and greatest in urban loft living. The assignment was pretty cush. All he had to do was drive by every hour to check for vandals then do a walk through every four hours. None of which he'd gotten around to doing in days.

The phone on the seat next to him vibrated. He ignored it, his eyes glued to the front door of Edie's building. He knew it was his boss calling to check in. Nobody mattered but the doc. His body buzzed with that old familiar sensation. He couldn't sit still. He needed to see her again. She shouldn't have let anything take away from their precious time together.

His phone went off again. Whoever was trying to get ahold of him wouldn't stop until he answered.

"What is it?" he asked before he'd even raised the phone to his ear.

"Hey, Timmy, where you at, man?" his boss asked. He was a weak man who avoided conflict with practiced passive aggressive ease.

"I'm roaming, Daniel," Timothy replied tersely. "What do you need? I'm on the job."

"Well," Daniel said, drawing the word out. "That's the thing. I've got your vehicle pulled up on the GPS, and you've been parked for most of the day. Everything all right?"

"The damn van broke down," Timothy lied without hesitation. "I had to use my own vehicle today. You've got to keep up with the maintenance on these things, man. It's getting ridiculous. That thing is a deathtrap."

"Oh no," Daniel said without a hint of mistrust. "I'll have one of the guys tow it back to HQ right now."

As his boss rambled on, Dr. McEvoy finally emerged. Her fat lover walked with her, his arm around her. They passed her car and got into his.

"Don't bother, Danny boy. I've been working on it for the last hour and think I've finally got it up and running. I'll bring it in tomorrow."

Timothy hung up before his boss could protest and pulled into traffic several cars behind the doc.

TIMOTHY DIDN'T WORRY ABOUT STAYING TOO CLOSE BEHIND THE Mercedes. He knew the route to the house by heart. If that wasn't their destination, they'd end up there eventually. But the fat slob drove Edie directly home.

Timothy parked down the street. What a shitty neighborhood, he thought as he flipped on his police scanner. He liked the squawks of the radio. For him, they were like what ocean sounds must be to some people. And the straightforward delivery of the dispatchers always comforted him, quieting his thoughts.

There was a lot of crime on this side of town. It might have been one of the ritzy neighborhoods in the 30s and 40s, but that was a long time ago. All the good people had died off. The money moved to the south of Kansas City. The houses that were lived in now were occupied by low rent lowlifes. And the ones that weren't were filled with crack heads, prostitutes and drifters. Still, old mansions and historic homes dotted every block, and the new rich were slowly rediscovering the area.

It wasn't safe yet, and it'd be a shame to lose his new therapist prematurely. Not after they'd shared so much. So he sat in his van, watching over her until the street lamps came on. Reluctantly, he finally drove away for the night.

18

Adrian uncorked a second bottle of wine. When Edie moved her glass out of pouring range, he hesitated for a second before shrugging and pouring himself a generous portion. Edie watched as he slid his hand over the base of the glass, his index and middle fingers clamping around the stem, and swirled to aerate the wine.

Edie couldn't remember the last time she'd seen him drink more than a single glass of wine in one sitting. Lately he had been drinking a splash of whiskey if anything at all. She hated his drinking, and he knew it. Too much red wine helped the real Adrian, the one he so adeptly kept hidden, slip to the surface.

The smell of it on his breath made her want to vomit. It reminded her of their university days. She tried to push such thoughts from her mind as she leaned against the kitchen island for support and stared out the window at the darkness. She lived in the darkness now. More so than ever before. She shivered at memories that wouldn't be suppressed. Some distant. Some fresh. All of them dark.

Half of her reflection stared back at her in the window. A strange trick of the light. It, too, seemed fitting. She wasn't whole. She hadn't been in years. Not since her parents. And not since another stormy night when a younger, more naïve version of herself knocked on her professor's door.

The sudden flash of lights from a car as it turned around in front of the driveway pulled Edie from the darkness. She turned back towards Adrian, thankful for the push of a stranger's lights. Adrian had been oddly quiet for as many glasses of wine as he'd had. On a good day, he could drone on whether or not his audience was paying attention. Fueled with a bit of drink, he would often recite whole passages from one of Freud's studies, switching in and out between English and German without even noticing. This eccentricity always amused Edie the most. Adrian had studied German as an undergraduate. He said it made him feel closer to Freud. But now, so many years later, he couldn't speak a word. Unless he was drunk. When Adrian went full-on German, Edie knew it was time to cut him off.

But he wasn't speaking much tonight, in either language. He just stood across the kitchen from her, watching the wine swirl around his glass with a distant, hollow expression on his face. Edie recognized that look. It was the look he got when he was deep in thought, and it usually only happened when he was writing.

The thought of Adrian's current pet project caused Edie a lot of conflict. She considered it a personal affront. An assault on top of an assault. But, on the other hand, as long as he was preoccupied with a project, he'd leave her alone. In fact, she suddenly realized that this was probably the best time to inform him about Timothy.

Edie reached across the kitchen island and grabbed the nearly empty bottle of wine. She took a deep breath as she poured the liquid courage into her glass. After a sip, she looked up at Adrian. He was still in his own world. She might as well have not been in the room at all. But she was, and she knew this was the best time to tell him about her patient.

"So, I need your help," Edie began, having learned long ago to play to his ego. "You know that pro bono case you gave me?"

Adrian blinked and she could tell he was back with her. She continued before he could interject. "At first I thought he was a doctor hopper just looking for a quick fix before moving on," she said before pausing to make sure she still had Adrian's attention and to steel herself for his reaction. Sure that he was still with her, she finally let it out. "He told me recently that he is a serial rapist and murderer."

Edie nearly jumped out of her skin at the sound of Adrian's laugh. It was deep and mocking. His whole body shook, and he threw his head back as if laughing at the gods for the stupidity he had to live with.

"Oh, you poor little girl," Adrian chuckled. "Can't you see this idiot is just playing you?"

"I don't think so," Edie said quieter than she wished she had.

"Edie, Edie, Edie." Adrian shook his head as he spoke. "You radiate emotions, baby. Even a low-functioning sociopath could find your hot buttons."

"You speaking from experience?"

Adrian flinched as if the weight of her words slapped him across the face. Edie saw the anger pulsing in the vein on his forehead and in his eyes that closed into narrow slits. His jaw clinched. She knew this dance well. Adrian's greatest weapon, his mind, was shutting down. Rage was taking over. He was like some dime store version of Jekyll and Hyde.

Edie couldn't help but laugh. Even in anger, especially in anger, the man she once admired was impotent. He didn't have the balls to strike her physically, and now that his emotions had taken over he couldn't use his rapier wit against her.

"You stupid little cunt," Adrian hissed. "You're being played.

You're a child playing dress up. This man is no more a serial killer than I am."

Now it was Edie's turn to be shocked. She had counted on his anger shorting out his tongue. His words felt like a gut punch.

"He's more than an alleged serial killer," Edie said haltingly. "But I guess you didn't want to bring up the rapist part to avoid an uncomfortable comparison. Right, my darling?"

Edie threw her half full glass of wine into the sink where it shattered, sending wine and glass shards across the counter and window.

The color had drained from Adrian's face. His eyes wouldn't meet hers. Edie took a deep breath then left him standing there to lick his wounds.

ADRIAN STOMPED DOWN THE STAIRS TO HIS CELLAR. HE NEEDED room to think. As he poured a healthy dram of whiskey, he thought about Edie's last biting words. What an ungrateful little brat. When he found her she was nothing. He plucked her from the obscurity of a 400 person classroom and gave her private lectures and insights that nobody else in her class received. He was her mentor. Not her, her...Goddamnit how could she say that about him? How could she think it?

He downed his whiskey and paced furiously in front of his humidor. Sure, he had vices. They surrounded him down here in the safety of his den, and the darker ones oozed just under the surface of his daily life. But he loved her, for god's sake.

And this nonsense about a serial killer patient? How many times had he seen this in his career? He could write a book about it. He paused. That's an interesting thought. He dug around for a pen and searched for the manuscript he'd been working on for weeks. He found it in the bottom drawer of his desk. Odd, he would have sworn he'd left it on the blotter. Oh well, he thought as he scribbled a note on the top sheet. His idea might be a bit tangential but it could be an interesting subplot. Frankly, it could warrant its own book. He might have a series on his hands now.

His adrenaline fading, Adrian slumped into his favorite leather chair. For the second time in as many minutes he felt a twinge of frustration. He never moved his furniture, and yet his chair was at a slightly different angle and a tad farther away from his table than usual. He'd have to talk to Edie about invading his private space.

He thought about her flight of fancy as he adjusted his chair. What if she was right? Could he have accidentally assigned her such a significant case? He struggled to remember why he had given her that particular patient. For one, he recalled the patient asked for her by name. Strange, but not all that unusual in this day and age of LinkedIn profiles, social media and professional association websites. That paired with his normal criteria for which cases Edie received must have made his decision easy. Still, if she had stumbled upon a case of such magnitude, by all rights he should take over.

He shook his head at the empty room. His mind made up, he selected a cigar from his sizable stash and turned his attention to his manuscript. No matter which way Edie's little case went from here on out, the dissection of it would make excellent material.

EDIE SANK BACK INTO THE CLAW-FOOT TUB. A SMALL CANDLE flickered, throwing dancing shadows across the dark walls and ceiling of the bathroom.

The washcloth draped over her face acted as a calming shield from the craziness her life had become. Her fingertips traced light circles over the careful lines etched into her inner

thighs. Touching these secret, forbidden pleasures had a meditative effect on her. She couldn't explain it, nor did she care to. It
was her private pleasure.

Her mind drifted between the two men in her life. One an
apparent rapist and murderer. The other....

She smiled at how they'd both yelled at and belittled her on
the same day. The only difference between the two men was that
Timothy not only knew who and what he was but also had the
fortitude to admit it not just to himself but to her.

Would he change? Could he? Could she help him? She shivered. Perhaps at the danger those questions posed, but it was
probably just that the bathwater had cooled.

She turned the hot water on with her foot and sank deeper
into the water. Despite the day she'd had, she couldn't shake the
feeling she was on to something. This could be big. For her
career for sure, but it was deeper than that. It had been a long
time, but she finally felt she had a purpose. A mission.

The newly heated water reinvigorated her, and when she
finally pulled the plug, she had a plan.

ADRIAN JUMPED UP SCREAMING AND FLAILING HIS ARMS. HE BEAT
at his chest furiously. The smell of burnt cotton, singed hair, and
stale cigar hung around him like the smoke that clung to his
face, stinging his eyes.

He had fallen asleep on the leather couch in his cellar as he
wrote notes longhand on a legal pad. His book, he was sure,
would be even more influential than his last.

The cigar he had been chewing on while taking small, intoxicating puffs that fueled his words must have dropped to his
chest as he slept. Luckily, his legal pad had fallen to the ground.
How the world would have mourned such a loss in such a tragic,
yet befitting, way. A genius spending his last moments on earth

unveiling dark psychological issues, imparting wisdom and hope for all who come after him.

Comforted by the thought his death would not have been in vain, Adrian gathered his notes, stubbed out the remains of his near-death cigar, and jogged upstairs, eagerly anticipating the fresh air. The moon shone through the floor-to-ceiling windows that framed the front door of his mid-century estate. The twin beams created natural directional beacons, crossing paths right outside the kitchen door. His mouth dry from the wine and smoke and his head pounding, Adrian instinctually followed the light.

"Oh." Adrian jumped for the second time in as many minutes. "I'm sorry, my darling. You startled me."

Edie didn't turn towards him or even acknowledge his presence. Adrian's blood boiled. What an ungrateful tagalong she was revealing herself to be. He suddenly realized the situation. Embarrassment flickered across the innermost depths of his brain. He shook his head and rolled his shoulders before cracking his neck. His eyes narrowed and his heart quickened.

She was asleep, standing in the kitchen, mindlessly scooping up handfuls of gummy bears, and slowly chewing on them like a cow on its cud. They were her one vice. He thought he had hidden them, but even in her sleep she could uncover his secrets.

She stood at the kitchen island. Her eyes stared out the window without seeing. She looked like some enchanted princess caught in a loop. Her jet black hair absorbed what little light the night gave up.

His heart skipped when he realized she was wearing her hair in pigtails. He loved how that made her look even younger. It reminded him of the first time he saw her. She was a student in one of his experimental psychology classes, and although the attendance record would show she had been present at each of his twice-weekly lectures that semester, he never noticed her until she visited his office one late afternoon. Her hair was in pigtails then, too. Her smile melted his heart and turned him to putty, ready for her to mold him into something new. She asked him for help, but it was she who would help him.

He blinked, and the memory faded, but the embers of that first encounter still burned somewhere deep. How could they have fallen this far?

He shrugged away his self pity as he crept behind her and bent his head to her shoulder. She wore one of his dress shirts. He always encouraged her, but she rarely acquiesced. And yet, here she was in a fugue state looking exactly as he pictured her in every dream he'd had of her since their first encounter.

He slowly slid his hands up her outer thighs. They felt smooth and warm against his light caresses. He breathed in the intoxicating scent that always made him lose control. Not tonight, he promised himself. Tonight would unravel slowly so as to linger in their minds and loins for a long time.

His fingers reached the hem of her borrowed night shirt. He hesitated for a breath to see if his attention had awoken his lover. Satisfied she was still entranced, his hands pushed upward and inward. The weight of his chest on her back pushed her upper body down, pinning her to the countertop. She stopped eating her candy but otherwise seemed oblivious to the change in her situation.

He smiled as he discovered she wasn't wearing panties. Good girl. He smiled again to find her warm and ready. He had a newfound appreciation for her sleepwalking episodes.

Ever so slowly, he shifted his weight to push into her. She moaned slightly under her breath but did not stop him, nor did she appear to awaken. Emboldened, he pushed on, increasing his pace and vigor despite his intention to hold back. She always had that effect on him. He couldn't get enough of her, be close enough to her, love her more.

Lost in his own ecstasy and ready to explode, he didn't notice when his lover's limp body hardened. As he finished, he finally heard her screams.

"I knew you were loving this, too," he said between gulps of breath.

He pushed off from her and backed away slightly as she turned to embrace him.

He felt the pain before he saw the blood. She struck like lightning. The knife must have been left on the counter from their dinner. It did little more than lightly scratch his exposed chest through the burn hole in his shirt, but he instinctually struck back with a backhand across her cheek.

The force of his blow turned Edie's whole body. Her knife hand swung wildly, causing her impromptu weapon to slice her own forearm before slipping from her hand and clattering to the floor.

Adrian pushed her into the counter with enough force that he heard something crack.

"Look what you've done, you little cow," he bellowed, holding his chest if not his temper.

She collapsed in a bloody, whimpering heap before him. He spat on her and went to clean himself up.

19

"You ready to tell me what's going on now?"

"I already told you, Mr. Ridle," Edie said with all the patience of a kindergarten teacher explaining for the hundredth time why one doesn't stick crayons up one's nose. "It's nothing, and it's none of your business."

He'd been trying to get her to open up about the bandage on her forearm and the reason for her slow movements for nearly the first half of their appointment. She found it annoying but flattering. She fully understood how crazy that was, but she couldn't help it. Of the two men in her life, wouldn't you know it was the serial killer who treated her with the most respect.

She winced as she crossed then re-crossed her legs. Every little movement shot spasms of hot pain up her spine. It felt like jolts of electricity; each one making her wince, which caused more jolts. She was stuck in a pain spiral. She needed something stronger than ibuprofen, but she worried a doctor might question her injuries. She couldn't afford to have the police poking around her life right now. Adrian would tell them everything about Timothy the second he thought it would help him out of a jam. With a sigh, Edie turned her attention back to her patient and tried to will the pain away.

"I'd really like to try to focus on you now if you don't mind," she said. "I don't feel like we've made any headway since you told me you're a brutal serial killer who hunts women for sport."

"Why, doc, I'm shocked at your directness," Timothy said, his trademark perfect white teeth on full display. "And here I was worried we'd have another puking incident. I brought these just in case." As he spoke, he pulled out several carefully folded trash bags and some black rubber gloves.

Edie's loud burst of laughter escaped before she could clamp her hand to her mouth to stifle herself. Tears pooled in the corner of her eyes as she blinked through the pain in her back. Then she noticed Timothy's gloves looked well used with several spots covered in dark stains.

"I've done a lot of soul searching since our last couple of sessions," Edie said as she slowly composed herself. "I think I can help you, Mr. Ridle. Anyway, I'd like to try. But I can't do anything if you don't stop joking around and start opening up. You can trust me, you know."

"I can?" Timothy asked in a falsetto voice. His smile faded, and he sank back into the couch. "So you're saying whatever I say in here is between us?"

"That is generally how it works."

Timothy sighed. "I know how it works, doc. First you tell that bloated buffoon you work for then you tell the cops."

Edie shook her head. This was shaping up to be another disappointing and fruitless session. "Yes, I can tell the police if I believe you are a danger to yourself or others. We're not there yet. In the meantime, I'd like to help you."

"Help me what, doc? You weigh less than most of the bodies I might need help with."

"I find your jokes to be quite distracting."

Timothy smacked the couch cushions with such force that Edie let out a little scream followed by a slow, painful moan.

"Look, doc," he said, all hints of humor suddenly gone like a switch had been flipped in his head. "We're talking in circles here. I'm not saying another word until you tell me about your goddamn injuries."

They stared at each other for several moments.

"I simply don't see where it is any of your business," Edie said, unable to meet his eyes. "So why don't we change the subject. Tell me more about your military life."

Timothy stared at her quietly as he put his hands behind his head, reclined further into the couch and slid his feet up on the table.

After several minutes of silent staring, Edie threw down her pen, too mad to feel the pain. Staring at her notepad, she wove together an explanation. "It's stupid. I was chopping vegetables for dinner. I didn't hear my roommate when they walked in, so when I turned around, I jumped, cutting myself and falling back into the counter. That's all. I'm embarrassed by my own lack of dexterity and for being startled so easily."

She deliberately looked up from her notes. Timothy's eyes seemed to bore right into her brain, but he didn't say a word. "Can we please drop this ridiculous sideshow now? We only have twenty minutes left, and I'd very much like to talk about your military service."

"I'D RATHER TALK ABOUT SOMETHING ELSE," TIMOTHY SAID AS HE obsessively brushed the lint from his black t-shirt.

"What else would you like to talk about?" she asked without looking up from her notes. He could sense her disappointment.

"Anything. The army is boring. It really has no basis for why I'm here or how you can help me."

"Thank you for your very thorough professional opinion, Dr. Ridle, but in my considered opinion, I happen to disagree. So let's just see where it takes us, shall we?"

"That's just it," he sighed. "It won't take us anywhere." He studied her as she doodled on her notepad. She was always doodling. It seemed like she constantly zoned out during their conversations. Somebody really should teach her some manners.

Edie slowly looked up at him. Her lips tightened into a thin line. Her eyes showed no emotion or hint of what was going on inside her head, but he knew she was analyzing him. She set her pen down and absent-mindedly scratched at her bandage.

"I've talked to your army psychologist," she said. The words hit him like a slap across the face, but he refused to show it. The good doctor had just issued a direct challenge. She had called him out, called him on his lie. He hated being cornered, but he enjoyed playing with such a worthy adversary.

"Not Old Ward the 'Tard?" He asked through a pasted-on smile. "How is that career idiot? Still jerking boys off, filling them with happy pills, and sending them off to die?"

He laughed. Edie did not. She looked down at her notes and, after a pause, picked up her pen and wrote something among her page of ribbons. He snickered as she kept writing. Surely his little inside joke wasn't worth so much prose. She emphasized her point with a period she stamped into the paper with enough force he could tell she'd pierced a hole through the page. It might as well have been his heart.

"Fine," he said. "What do you want to know?"

"Thank you," Edie said as she looked up at him. He could see the compassion in her eyes. "Why don't you start by telling me about why you enlisted?"

"Oh, that's easy," Timothy said as he relaxed into his story. "Did I ever tell you about my hometown?"

"No, but I think you know that."

Timothy smiled. "Well, you see, doc, it all started in my hometown of Eden, Missouri. Ever heard of it?"

"No. Tell me about it."

"Not much to tell, really. It's no magical garden paradise, that's for sure. Just a faded dot on the map. If you head south of Kansas City towards Arkansas, you'll eventually pass by Eden. Although if you're like most people, you won't even notice. The town has a population of about 200 people. Six hundred if you count the citizens of the cemetery, and the local politicians usually do. There are wind turbines all over. The fields are full of them. Might as well be since the only viable crop these days is meth. That started when I was in elementary school, I think. In fact, the town's only exports are wind and meth. And maybe killers."

Timothy let Edie catch up on her writing. She furiously scribbled even more intensely than normal. He thought he could see a slight curl at the side of her mouth. He liked that she was enjoying the show so far. As her writing slowed, he plunged back into his story.

"I already told you I was the only child of a lonely woman whose only goal in life was to find a man." He stopped until Edie looked up at him, then continued. "Remember how I said we had thin walls? I mean you could practically see the light through them. And you could definitely hear everything. Now that I think about it, sitting in my bed staring at that thin wall and listening to my mom and her constant parade of lovers enjoying their fifteen minutes of fame was like trying to watch porn on a TV channel you can't quite tune in. Know what I mean?"

Edie sighed, which made Timothy smile. "Do you think your mom loved you?"

"Oh, I think she loved me the best she could, she was just ill-equipped for a child. And she was so busy trying to make a man love her she didn't have any extra love left over for me. I also think she was a little slow. I suspect it was from her head hitting the headboard too many times. All those guys may not have stuck around, but they really did stick it to her good." Timothy paused again for effect. "Who knows. Anyway, most days I was more of a parent to her."

"So you joined the army to get away from your mom?" Edie asked. To Timothy's disappointment, she refused to acknowledge the humor of his childhood predicament.

"I guess that might have played a small part in the decision," he said. "I mean, you have to understand, I was the dirtiest, poorest kid in a town full of dirty poor kids. I was small, too. But I was fast. Every day was a race. I could outrun most of those backwoods, backwards bastards. But I couldn't outrun their BB guns. They picked on me constantly. "Do you know what it's like to hide your whole life?" He blinked and realized he'd had his eyes closed.

Edie cleared her throat. He thought he saw tears at the corner of her eyes. He had to lean forward to hear her. "As a matter of fact I do understand."

He willed her to continue, but she just sat there across from him, her eyes drifting downward and glazing over as her vision went inward and into the past. He wished he could see what she was looking at.

She shook her head as if coming out of a trance. "Still, though, lots of people grow up poor and picked on. Surely you don't expect me to tell you everything is all right, and all is forgiven?"

Timothy shifted his feet and rolled his shoulders at her rebuke. He hadn't expected such a cold reaction to a story that still made his own stomach plummet.

"And besides," Edie said, breaking the silence. "I asked you why you decided to join the army. Or am I to believe you ran away and enlisted at six years old?"

Timothy sniffed and shook his head. There's a layer of ice under that hotness. He wondered how deep it ran. If sweetness did nothing for her, he could certainly switch to sickness.

"Ok, doc. But you first," he said as he sat forward and rested his arms on his knees.

"OH, MR. RIDLE, YOU EXHAUST ME," EDIE EXHALED. SHE CLICKED her pen a few times then set it on her notepad. She couldn't remember another session in which she'd taken so many notes. The ratio of words to doodles was unusual for her.

"I mean it, doc," Timothy insisted. "You want the good stuff, you gotta give me something good in return."

Edie weighed her words carefully before continuing. Interviewing an admitted rapist and serial killer could make her career, if that's what she wanted. But talking about herself made this personal. She shouldn't cross that line any more than she already had. Not with Timothy.

"Look. You've been to enough psychologists and logged enough time on a therapist's couch to know that's not how this works," she said while studying her nails. "If you want my help, I'm here for you. If you want to play games, well you can do what you're best at and find another therapist." She nodded her head with finality as she finished but didn't look up.

"Nice monologue, doc. Did you rehearse that one?" Timothy chuckled.

"I'm serious, Mr. Ridle," Edie whispered.

"I am too, doc. If you want to keep seeing me, you need to show me I can trust you by trusting me with some stories of your own," Timothy said. "I'm not asking for your deepest, darkest sexual fantasies. Just help me know who you are."

How did she allow herself to be so easily cornered? She looked up and was greeted by Timothy's brilliant smile. Did he always look so smug? Everything in her training, everything in her gut told her she shouldn't play his game. Giving him personal information gave him power. But wasn't their power dynamic already messed up? And if she didn't play along, there was nothing stopping him from following through on his threat and leaving her for another therapist just when she was finding renewed meaning in her life's work.

She closed her eyes and inhaled. In her mind's eye, she saw the waves crashing along the beach. She could smell the salty air. She opened her eyes and stared into his.

"I grew up in Los Angeles," she hesitated. "My dad was a police officer." Tears welled up in her eyes. "He was my best friend. The best man I've ever known," she continued. "He always wanted to be a detective. That's where all the fun is, he used to say. He told me once that being a cop was like being a babysitter, a house sitter, a marriage counselor, and a party chaperone all in one. But being a detective, well he thought that was his destiny. He could really help people then."

Her throat closed up and her tears ran freely down her face, but she didn't look away from her patient. He wanted to know, and hearing her own story brought back memories she'd locked away long ago.

She wiped away a few tears, but they were quickly replaced by dozens more. "He died in the line of duty when I was ten," she sobbed. "He was responding to a domestic violence call. When he got to the address, the neighbor who had called 911 pointed to the house where my dad discovered a man raping his wife. In the struggle, the man got ahold of my dad's gun..."

Timothy handed her the box of tissues she kept out on the table for patients who were criers. She finally broke their gaze and grabbed a few, quickly blotting at her eyes.

Edie's hands dropped to her lap. Her notebook, long forgotten, fell to the floor. She didn't notice. One of her thumbs traced urgent circles along the nail of the other as she continued almost absentmindedly now. A floodgate had been opened and her memories came crashing through. She was helpless to stop them.

"My mother and I were never really close while my dad was alive," she croaked. "I always assumed she knew I loved him best. And maybe she thought he loved me best, too. Instead of bringing us closer, my dad's death just drove the wedge between us deeper. Maybe it was my fault. I retreated from the world. Dad was my world, so why wouldn't I? My mom eventually got married again. I was sixteen. He was not like my father at all."

Edie closed her eyes and inhaled again slowly. When she opened them, she exhaled, tucked her tissues in her pocket, picked up her notebook, and looked expectantly at Timothy.

"Now, Mr. Ridle, it's your turn. I want to hear about your military career."

Timothy shook his head. He hadn't expected the doc to spill her guts, and definitely not in such a raw way.

"Wow, doc," he said. "How do I follow that?"

"With your own truth, Mr. Ridle. Please."

"Well, like I said before, I joined the army to escape the small town hell my life had become. It was the best decision I've ever made." He looked at her. She'd gone back to doodling, but he decided to cut her a little slack.

"I felt like I had finally found my people. My tribe or my family, whatever you want to call it," he continued. "Rapists. Killers. Bastards all. I fit right in."

The doc looked up at this remark. He'd figured she would. "Are you suggesting everyone in the military is a rapist and killer like you, Mr. Ridle? Or are you simply using the army as an excuse for your current criminal behavior?"

Her eyes sparkled. He admired her passion and enjoyed finding new ways to bring it to the surface.

"No, doc," he laughed. "I'm not saying everyone in the army is like me. But enough are that I felt at home for the first time in my life."

He could tell she wasn't convinced, but he continued anyway, glad to have captured her complete attention again. "Unlike a lot of the guys, combat didn't drive me crazy. Maybe it was because I was already so shellshocked from childhood. Or maybe it was because I was already crazy. All I know is that I liked it. I was good at it. And the army recognized that. I earned a lot of combat commendations." He chuckled to himself. "Man, if the brass knew what really went on during our patrols, maybe we would have been given a court martial instead of so many medals. Or maybe they did know."

"What did go on?" the doc asked as she leaned forward, her pen poised above her tablet.

"Oh, all kinds of things, doc."

She sighed. He enjoyed her little silent tantrums. He liked how open she was becoming to him. They grew closer and closer with every session.

"Let's just say I didn't suddenly start to rape and kill people after I left the military," he said with a wink.

"According to your army psychologist, you suffered from delusions of grandeur," Edie declared as if she were reading. "Far from seeing you as a threat to yourself or others, he believed you made things up to be accepted by your fellow soldiers."

"I already told you, doc," Timothy sighed. "Ol' Ward the 'Tard was a quack. You have more analytical talent in your little pinky toe than that guy does in his whole body. I told him what he wanted to hear. Nothing more. Nothing less."

"You told him you raped all the women in a village because he wanted to hear it?"

"You bet he did, doc. And I bet he beat off to that story all night," Timothy spat.

"Are you telling me you made that up?"

"I didn't say that now did I?" Timothy teased. "I had a lot of relations with civilians when I was deployed. That's military talk for rape, by the way. But then all sex in the army is rape if you think about it. Nobody consents to being sent to the desert for years on end with no real mission. Nobody consents to having strangers from a strange country roaming around their streets, searching their houses, taking their men away in the dead of night. You do what you have to do to numb yourself. But you know what I mean by that, don't you, doc?"

"WHAT THE HELL DO YOU MEAN BY THAT?" EDIE'S HANDS AND NECK seemed to spontaneously bleed sweat from every pore. She grabbed at her pen as it threatened to slip from her numb fingers, hoping her patient didn't notice. Her eyes blinked rapidly, but not as rapidly as the thoughts now circling in wild jumbles in her brain.

"Oh, come on, doc." Timothy snorted. "I see you and that fat fuck. I know you're partners in every sense of the word. I mean, Jesus, you'd have to be blind not to see it. And you, doc, you'd have to be numb to continue to take it."

Edie's arms went limp and fell to her sides. She slid down in her chair. Her head hung into her chest, bobbing up and down with each labored breath. She could feel her heart racing as if trying to escape her chest and her office.

"I really don't know what you're talking about, Mr. Ridle,"

she whispered through a too dry mouth. She couldn't meet his eyes but could feel them on her, seeking the truth and not finding it in her voice.

Timothy let out a slow sigh. She thought it sounded almost comforting, not like his normal sarcastic sigh but one of knowing, understanding, caring even.

"Jesus, doc," he said. "Get your head out of your ass. You sit here week after week and tell me this process only works if we can trust each other, if we're honest with each other. Is that all a load of crap? Or do you really mean the rules only apply to me? Because if that's the case, I'm out of here, and you'll never see me again because I can't trust someone who expects me to be honest but then so obviously lies to my face. To my goddam face."

The room spun around Edie. Her stomach, already knotted and tight, threatened to expel her lunch. Her eyes wobbled. Waves of goosebumps tingled across her skin.

"Doc?" Timothy's voice sounded far away and muffled. Like he was yelling at her under water. She felt the hot sting of tears return.

"Doc? You're scaring me. I'm sorry. Let's just talk about something else. Please."

Edie sobbed uncontrollably. Her arms, useless just a moment ago, cradled her heavy head. How had she fallen so far? How could she let a patient, this patient, penetrate her defenses, and why did she feel so compelled to tell him her truth?

She wiped the tears away with the back of her hand and finally looked at Timothy. He returned her gaze. His features had softened a little, or perhaps that was just her imagination. She took a slow, deep breath. She needed to regain control of herself and the conversation.

"Rape is not something I take lightly, Mr. Ridle," her voice wavered between shouts and whispers. "I can no longer sit here week after week and listen to you make light of something that turns a woman's world upside down and changes her forever."

She felt dizzy, like she might pass out, but she refused to break their eye contact. He swam in front of her through her tear-soaked vision. She willed Timothy to feel the pain he'd inflicted on who knew how many women.

He seemed to be about to say something when the door to her office flung open wildly.

ADRAIN COULDN'T BELIEVE WHAT HE'D WALKED INTO. EDIE'S office smelled of sweat and tears. It felt like walking into a strip club but without the beautiful, nearly naked women eager to do whatever he wanted.

Edie appeared more like the patient, and Thomas or whatever his name was, like the therapist. She looked like she'd just confessed all her sins.

"Jesus Christ, Edie," he barked. "Get ahold of yourself. Everyone can hear you blathering on and crying. This isn't some ladies' auxiliary meeting. It's serious therapy for people with real problems. Or at least it used to be."

Adrian turned his gaze to Edie's patient as he spoke these last words. He could see the man's face flush. Good, maybe he'd stand up and try something. He looked pretty fit, but Adrian definitely had a weight advantage. And the cops were always quick in these situations. It'd be a great anecdote for his book. Instead, the man winked at him and turned back to Edie. Had she seen that? She had to have seen that.

"What are you doing in here," she hissed.

Adrian turned. He hadn't expected such venom. He'd come in to save her from making a further fool of herself. He took a step back before recovering.

"You have a patient waiting," he said. "This session has gone on long enough. In fact, I think this whole thing has run its course. It reeks of unprofessionalism. Our practice has a reputation for helping deserving patients. If you can't do what's right, I will."

He stomped out, slamming the door behind him before she could make a scene. He had lied about the waiting patient, but he had to do something. People would talk. She was becoming an embarrassment.

20

"You had no right to interrupt one of my sessions," Edie screamed. She shoved a stack of neatly arranged papers off the corner of Adrian's desk. They flew across the room, fueled by Adrian's desk fan, fluttering softy to the floor. She looked around for something heavy to throw that would make more of a fitting statement, but Adrian's office was as sparse as his emotions.

"I have every right, my dear," Adrian calmly replied without looking up from the notes he had been taking before she stormed into his office. "Your current actions are simply reinforcing my decision and demonstrating to me that you have lost yourself in this case. This made up, silly delusion that you've found the next Bob Berdella or Fredrick Coe."

It took every ounce of Edie's strength to stop herself from spitting in his face when he finally looked up at her.

"You are a pompous ass," she hissed through clenched teeth, but she could already feel the power draining from her body. His words were like a gut punch. He always knew how to get into her head.

Adrian laughed under his breath in that perfectly condescending way of his. "I may be," he said. "But that doesn't change the fact that you've lost yourself in this foolhardy search for some kind of self redemption."

Edie slowly sank into the nearest chair.

ADRIAN PUT ASIDE THE DRAFT OF HIS LATEST CHAPTER, BUT NOT before making a note to add in the part about his papers being flung from his desk. *That'd make a nice moment*, he thought. They slowly sank to the floor like his colleague's hopes for a successful career.

He looked down at Edie, his poor confused Edie. He shook his head, stroked his beard, and measured his words before continuing. "Look, my darling. This profession isn't for everyone. It takes a certain intellect, a particular understanding of the motivations of the human heart and mind." He paused before concluding. "And a keen sense of one's self so you don't drown in the sorrow of others and your mind doesn't start exploring its own dark recesses just as some patient express their own darkness."

She sat there, her gaze turned to the floor. He saw a petulant child where he'd once seen so much potential. She had once been a lump of bright clay he thought he could mold in his own image. What a pity. She had so much promise. He couldn't understand what could have changed her in such a radical fashion. Surely if she would just pay attention and follow his example, she would not only be a better therapist but would be much happier.

"I have an idea," he said, breaking the silence, and he hoped, breaking the ice. "I don't believe your patient is the serial killer he claims to be," he rushed to continue before the fresh new fire in her eyes threatened to derail their adult conversation. "But I believe you believe he is. So why don't we treat him together?

That way I can observe your sessions to get a better understanding of what makes this man tick. After all, you said yourself you thought he was just looking for a quick score. And if it turns out he is as dangerous as he imagines, wouldn't it be better, safer if I were involved?"

"I don't believe you," Edie huffed without meeting his eyes.

Adrian shook his head. Maybe she was indeed a lost cause. He had a fleeting thought about how to introduce this twist into his book. It'd make for a good cautionary tale for future colleagues.

"I think I'm being generous here," he said. "I haven't yet instructed you to drop your patient, I have offered to give up my time with my own patients and studies to provide a substantial consultation, and I am telling you I believe that you believe you are on to something real here."

Edie smacked her hand onto the now-clean corner of his desk. Her passion startled him, but he managed to keep his composure through her tantrum.

"So let me see if I understand your generous offer," Edie hissed. "You don't believe me, so you would like to interrupt any progress Mr. Ridle and I have made so you can gather evidence of how wrong I am. On top of that, if it turns out that, god forbid, the great Dr. Adrian Hillary is wrong, you want to be involved so you can take all the glory? You amaze me, Adrian."

She stood and leaned on his desk, looking down on him in a way that made him squirm in his seat. He wasn't used to such a show of unrestrained brattiness.

"You can go to hell," she said.

The fire in her eyes threatened to burn into Adrian's soul. He pounded the desk with both his hands to hide the shudder that snaked its way up his spine.

"Just remember, my darling," he spat. "I tried to help you. I tried to reason with you. I tried to keep you from making a mockery of yourself, this office, and our profession. But as you have repeatedly made clear with such passion, I do not control you. Therefore, I will allow you to keep seeing this patient for the time being. But if you don't find concrete evidence to back up his wild stories, then I will shut this down. For your own good."

21

Timothy fluffed the lumpy red pillow and meticulously smoothed out the crusty bedspread with his hands, reflexively checking his military corners. As he made his final adjustments, the clock down in the office rang out in its slightly off-key macabre tone. Two in the morning. His little project had taken him four hours. He stepped back to admire his handiwork and smiled at the thought of the fun he'd soon have here.

He stood in the center of The Edge of Hell's zombie brothel room. His heart raced with anticipation. He had snuck in supplies over the last week, hiding them under the bed. The offseason gave him plenty of time to remake this room as his own. The owners didn't bother coming around unless there was an emergency. They paid him to keep the druggies, the thrill seekers and the bums away. Luckily the cool spring weather had given way to the muggy hell of a Kansas City summer, so the bums had stopped breaking in to escape the chill. He'd hate to have his little side project interrupted by another visit from the police. Although he liked the idea of seeing that perky detective again.

He lined up all but one of the zombie hooker mannequins

against the walls of the small bedroom. Each mannequin's hand was duct taped to the one next to it in what he thought of as his sexy seance circle. He didn't want to communicate with the dead so much as to bring his little fantasy to life. In the middle of this circle stood the oversized canopy bed that he'd pushed to the center of the room. It was much heavier than it looked. The whole thing was made of iron. Even the box springs. He'd nearly given himself a hernia.

He slipped off his uniform, carefully folding each piece, and set them on the bedside table next to a small lamp with its scarf-draped shade that cast a shimmering red shadow onto the underside of the bed's canopy. Then he climbed into bed next to the mannequin he'd dressed with a black pigtail wig he'd found at Goodwill. The wig was a little short and well used, but it was close enough as long as he didn't focus on it. The mannequin wore a brand new white silk dress shirt, a stylish light gray herringbone blazer, and a matching skirt. A shiver jolted though his body as he smiled at his conservative but provocative companion.

He propped himself up on his elbow and stared into the beady black dots that substituted for eyes. He'd have to get a pair of sunglasses or figure out a way to paint a better pair of eyes that would draw him in like the real ones did. He ran his hands lightly along her cold, plastic arm. He tried to imagine, to suspend reality as he often had in the desert. But it was too much. After all his work, this just wasn't anything like the real thing.

An idea struck him, rocking him back against his pillow. A lump formed in his throat. His cheeks burned, and a chill shuddered down his spine as he reached for his phone.

It had been an easy thing to get her number. It's amazing the kinds of things people throw away. One coffee-stained phone bill was all it took. And figuring out which of the two mobile numbers on the bill was hers didn't take a lot of work either. He simply called a few of the numbers that had placed incoming calls to each. One received calls from the local race-track, a casino, a cigar shop, and even an Asian massage parlor. The other's incoming call list was short. It had received calls from a pharmacy, the office, and the other mobile extension.

He punched in the number he'd already memorized. His thumb hovered above the send button. He held his breath. And connected the call. It rang six times.

"Hello," a man's sleepy voice answered.

Timothy hesitated. How had he guessed wrong?

"Hello? Who is this?"

Determined, Timothy finally answered. "Hi. This is the Jackson County Sheriff's Department. I'm trying to reach Dr. McEvoy. This is an urgent call regarding one of her patients. I'm sorry. Have I dialed incorrectly?"

"No, no, this is her number. Hang on a sec."

There was a shuffling on the other end of the line, and Timothy could hear Adrian trying to coax the doc awake. This was already not going according to plan. Timothy hated the idea that she shared a bed with that fat loser. He shut his eyes, trying to concentrate on his next move. He had no idea what he was going to say. The lie about the sheriff had just come out with no thought.

"Hello?" Her voice was thick with sleep, which gave her a sultry quality. She sounded like one of those phone sex opera-tors he and his fellow soldiers used to call using the pre-paid phone cards their families would send in their monthly care packages. He wondered what she was wearing.

"Hey, doc."

He heard her sharp intake of breath. Then silence. But she didn't hang up. That must mean something.

"Mr. Ridle, what do you think you're doing? How did you get this number? Are you okay?"

Her voice quickly changed from arousing to angry. But she had asked if he was okay. She did care. He knew it.

"I'm good, doc. I was just lying here thinking of you." He looked over at his Edie mannequin. "I thought I'd call and chat. I mean you're the only one I really talk to anyway, so why wait until our next session. Did I wake you up?"

"Mr. Ridle, I think you should know you are now on speaker," she said, rudely ignoring his question. "Furthermore, it is unprofessional and out of bounds for you to be calling me on my private line at this hour or any other. Do you understand?" She sounded scared. Old what's his name must have more power over her than Timothy had thought.

Timothy sighed. He had thought she might be mad at his little intrusion, but he never expected her to so easily break the sanctity of their private conversation.

"Tim," the fat fuck said. "This is Dr. Adrian Hillary. This is a serious breech of etiquette, my friend. Invading your therapist's privacy, not to mention impersonating law enforcement, is a matter for the police, whom I will be calling as soon as we finish this call."

Timothy broke into a stage laugh. "First, I didn't impersonate law enforcement," he said. "I simply said this call was from the sheriff's department. I never said I was the sheriff. And I didn't call to talk to you, so you can just shove your empty threats up your fat ass. I'm calling because I'm having an emergency and need my therapist. Second, 'Dr. Adrian Hillary'? What the hell? Your parents gave you not one but two chick's names? What's your middle name, oh great and mighty doctor? Gloria?"

"You son of a…" Adrian began before the doc interrupted.

"What's your emergency, Mr. Ridle?"

"I'm having some urges, doc," Timothy winked at

mannequin Edie as he spoke. "I just needed someone to help talk me through it." His hand slid down his stomach as he breathed heavily into the phone.

She ignored his theatrics as usual. "Is this about the woman you've been following?" she asked. She seemed genuinely concerned.

"Look, Tim, this is highly irregular," the asshole interrupted. "I insist you leave Edie, I mean Dr. McEvoy, alone. If this is an emergency, you need to call 911. If it isn't, you can talk about it in your next session, which if I have my way, will be your last."

"Shut up and get off this call," Timothy barked.

"I will not shut up, nor will I leave you to talk to Edie in your present state. You're a menace. You're a drain on her time and on our practice's resources. And furthermore, you and I both know you're a fraud, a charlatan who is just looking to score a quick fix or indulge in some sick fantasy about your female therapist. Either way, I'm cutting you off."

"Cutting me off?" It took all Timothy's concentration to keep his voice calm. "If anyone is going to do any cutting, it will be me. Of course the piece of you I would cut off is tiny and useless, but I guarantee you'll feel it. I can already picture all the ways I can prolong your pain, my friend. So why don't you back the fuck off and let me get on with my therapy so I can get better. For both our sakes."

It sounded like someone covered the phone. Timothy could hear the two talking heatedly. When Edie came back on the line, her voice was louder. She was talking directly into the phone. He could no longer hear the blowhard she lived with.

"Look, Mr. Ridle," she whispered, again sounding very seductive. "I know you enjoy playing games, but I can't have you calling me like this. It doesn't help either of us. Now, do you have a legitimate problem? Are you in danger, or do you feel you're an immediate danger to others?"

"Oh, doc," Timothy said. "You know the answers already. I need you to help me with these urges."

"Hang up right now and call the police, Mr. Ridle."

"You're the only one I want to talk to, doc. You're the only one who can help me." He closed his eyes, buried his head in the mannequin's hair and inhaled the scent of the perfume he'd matched to Edie's.

"What are you doing, Mr. Ridle? Who is there with you?"

"Oh no, doc," Timothy said as his hand drifted under the covers. "You don't get to know that. Not yet. Just know I wish it was you."

The line went dead before he could talk his way out of the creepiness even he felt from his answer. He hadn't meant to say it, not out loud at least. He buried his head deeper into mannequin Edie's hair and imagined what he'd do if she were really lying next to him.

22

E die stared out the window. She couldn't remember the last time she'd been awake to watch the sunrise. The first rays of the sun erased her reflection as she leaned against the sink. Her mind wandered to a faraway time and place. To a much younger version of herself. To the smell of copper, smoke, and burnt meat. She shook her head and blinked away the memories that were always there at the edge of her mind, threatening to crash down upon her and pull her under.

"I think it's clear what we have to do, don't you?"

Edie jumped at the sound of Adrian's voice. She hoped he hadn't noticed. She took a moment to collect herself before she spoke. She was already on edge, and Adrian's tone threatened an impending shouting match.

"I know what you want to do, and I admit it is probably the right decision," she said after taking a deep breath. "But think about what this would do for our practice, for your exposure, if he really is what he says."

She could see the wheels turning in that egomaniacal brain of his. How could she have ever admired him so? How did she allow him such total control over her life? She vowed to herself that things would change, and soon.

"You know, you may have a point," he conceded. "But I don't want this to go on forever. I'll give you the weekend. Do some research. See if any part of his story checks out. I tell you what, I'll even join you. Who knows? It could be good for us."

Edie sipped her coffee, hiding her smile behind her mug. She knew exactly what she wanted to do first.

"This is ridiculous even for you," Adrian complained. They'd been sitting in Edie's car for an hour. He hated her car. It had no character. No style. No creature comforts that would make a prolonged outing more pleasant, especially on a particularly nice Saturday like this one.

"Oh, shut up. You're just looking for an excuse to close the file on Mr. Ridle and continue on with your book," Edie responded without taking her eyes from the entrance to the haunted house she was sure Timothy had mentioned in one of their sessions.

She was so testy lately, Adrian thought. Perhaps he should suggest a little side-of-the-road tryst right there in her car. This part of the city was certainly secluded enough. The whole time they'd been parked, they had only seen three people, all of them homeless. He looked back at the cramped backseat and quickly changed his mind. Later. He'd help her take the edge off at home. Maybe she'd even forget all about this exercise in futility afterwards. He smiled at the thought.

"Look," he said trying to keep the peace as he imagined their future lovemaking. "I understand your passion. I even admire it. And while this little pet project is not nearly as important as my latest academic works, I am willing to indulge you. To an extent. But, Edie my love, we are not some dime store detectives in a cheap novel. Do you really think this pseudo stakeout will yield any results beyond a bad back and a crooked neck?"

She sighed and turned to meet his eyes for the first time in the last hour. "You told me this morning I had the weekend. I don't expect you to be enthusiastic or even supportive, but if you're just going to complain the whole time, I would be happy to drop you at the house."

Her eyes dared him to push her. He knew she was angry, which aroused him more. His mind flickered back to an evening in his office at Columbia. He had almost gone home early. Luckily for him, and for her, he had lost track of time as he was deep into research for an article.

"I just had an idea," he said with a distant smile. "Wouldn't it be more efficient if we spent our time doing what we've trained to do?"

"What are you talking about?"

"I mean we need to do our research," he exclaimed. "Until now you have taken your patient at his word. Let's dig into his story, look at the timeline, and see if we can poke holes in anything he's told you. I think you'll see then that his fantasy doesn't hold together."

"What are you suggesting exactly?" Edie asked, but he could see she was already realizing his idea was better than hers.

"I mean, my dear, let's go to the office and see what we can find out."

EDIE MASSAGED HER NECK AS SHE TYPED YET ANOTHER SEARCH query into her browser. She absentmindedly plucked a piece of prosciutto and scooped it into the last remaining bit of Winnimere cheese before tossing it into her mouth without taking her eyes off her search results.

Adrian wandered over to her desk from the coffee table

where he had set up his laptop. "How's it coming?" he asked as he poured more red wine into the glass she had been ignoring.

She pushed herself away from her desk, looked up at him and rubbed her eyes. "I'm not sure how you believe this is more exciting than my stakeout," she sighed. "Two hours of clicking from one heartbreaking story to the next, and I still don't have a better picture of Timothy's past or even a good idea of what I should be looking for."

"Well, I thought a good meal and some wine would smooth things along at least." Adrian had insisted they stop at The Cellar Rat, a local upscale liquor store, on their way to the office. It was the only place in town he could custom order his pretentious, albeit delicious, cheese.

"Thanks for that," she said, giving him at least the cursory compliment he had been searching for. "But everything I've read makes my stomach and my heart ache."

"Let's go over what we've discovered so far," Adrian said as he grabbed his notepad. "The nearest estimate I can find claims there have been 220,000 unsolved murders in the United States since 1980. That's roughly fifty-six-hundred a year or over 400 a month. That's a lot of pent up anger and mommy issues."

"I don't like what your calculations say about you," Edie said as she flipped through her own notes.

"Well, I don't like what they say about the competence of our police," he shot back. "You find anything good?"

"Good? No. I've been focusing on reports of missing women. The numbers are just as grim. Right now, there are about 41,000 missing women in the US. The only good news is that most of them are not local. There are 251 missing women in Missouri, 13 in Kansas and just 24 in the Kansas City area."

"Of course those numbers only include the women who had someone who cared enough to report them missing," Adrian reminded her, as if that were at all helpful. "I'd venture your pet patient is smart enough to hunt at the margins of society where his victims are more like feral animals."

Edie slumped back in her chair. She hated that she hadn't made more progress, but she couldn't help but notice Adrian's phrasing. "How can so many people just disappear?" she wondered aloud. "It's like the entire population of Lubbock, Texas, or Buffalo, New York, just evaporated one day. Why don't we see it? How could we have let it get this bad?"

"It's not all that bad, really," Adrian said. "If you think about it, that's just eight tenths of one percent of the population of our country. If I drank eight tenths of one percent of your wine, you'd never notice. Even if you were looking right at your glass the whole time."

He took a drink from her untouched glass for dramatic effect and ended up downing the entire glass. "Well, you get my point," he smirked. "But that's not our worst problem."

"What do you mean?" Edie asked, though she was beyond ready to end their conversation.

"I've been digging into American serial killers," he said. "It's quite fascinating, really. I may have the genesis of my next book."

Edie rolled her eyes. "Good. I'd prefer you concentrate on the lives of strange killers rather than mine for your works."

"I don't see why I need to discriminate, my dear."

"Just tell me what you found," she said as she closed her eyes and rubbed her temples to soothe the headache that threatened to crush her head with its vice-like tendrils.

"Well, basically the government has absolutely no idea how many serial killers are currently active in this country. Another supporting argument about the ineptitude of our police forces if you ask me. Anyway, estimates vary wildly from 115 to 2,000 serial killers who are roaming our streets, checking us out in the grocery store, serving us cocktails, or sleeping next to us."

Adrian wiggled his eyebrows to emphasize his last point. Edie once again ignored his infantile gestures.

"So where does this leave us?" she asked, looking up at the ceiling as if to open the question up to whatever higher power might exist.

"Well, it means we simply don't have enough to corroborate ol' Timmy's story," Adrian said. "It also means your patient is smart enough to know that a story like his can't be disproved without a great deal of time and resources."

Edie knew he was right, which just angered her more. She needed time to think. More than anything, though, she needed sleep. She'd figure out a new approach in the morning.

Timothy inhaled the air around him, his head moving side to side as he tried to pick up her scent from the competing smells of the house. No luck. He sat on the island in the middle of Edie's kitchen. His palms flat on the cold surface of the countertop, his legs dangling over the edge.

He tried to imagine her here. Did she cook? What was her favorite dish to make? He felt like she'd be the kind of home chef who would begin each dish with the intention of following the recipe exactly only to mess something up and decide she might as well roll with it and improvise the rest.

He hopped off the counter. His hands had left sweat prints where they'd pressed hard against the surface, but he knew they'd disappear without a trace. Just like him. He eyed the tidy kitchen one last time before walking out, his left hand sweeping absently against the butt of the knives neatly arranged in their mahogany butcher block.

At the doorway he paused and looked down both ends of the hallway. The security panel on the wall to the left near the front door blinked a slow green as if to assure the homeowners that all was well. It had almost been too easy to disable the alarm. He smiled to himself. The benefits of a life in the military and security industry were few, but boy did they come in handy.

He headed toward the front door but veered to the right and slowly climbed the winding staircase to the second floor. The stairs continued up, but he knew from watching the house at night that the master bedroom occupied most of the second floor on the front side of the house. He crept along the narrow hallway and stopped at the first door on his right. He took a deep breath then turned the knob and let the door swing away from him, as if it were inviting him in to discover its secrets.

He stood at the edge of the king sized bed then walked around to the side that must be Edie's. The bedside table was neat and sparsely populated with an ocean breeze scented candle and a single wallet-sized photo in a tarnished brass frame of a cop holding a young girl. They were both smiling. They had the same eyes. He set the frame down and kneeled down beside the bed. He lowered his head and breathed in the scent of her body. He knew she didn't sleep in the nude, but he imagined his face pressed against her thigh.

Angered by his weakness, he stood and wandered out of the room, careful to close the door behind him. His fingertips glided along the bumps of the wallpaper as he sulked through the hall and down the stairs. He felt like a ghost doomed to wander the earth. He could watch, but he would never be a part of the world again. Or maybe he was more like some reflection in a photograph. He was there but just beyond the frame. No matter how much you squinted or changed the angle, you could never really bring him into focus.

He wandered over to another closed door near the base of the stairs. He stared down at the darkness for several minutes, half expecting it to stare back. Then, oblivious of the hour, he rambled down the stairs into the depths of the basement.

.   .   .

ADRIAN LIGHTLY CARESSED EDIE'S BARE SHOULDER. SHE HAD
quickly turned down his advances as soon as they'd gotten into
bed. He'd spent the entire day indulging her fantasies; he
thought it only fair that she should spend a half hour indulging
his. But, as with most women, she needed a bit more encouragement and gentle prodding. He liked that.

Edie jabbed her shoulder at his hand to push it away. Adrian
smiled. *And so the game begins*, he thought. He continued to rub
her shoulder until she made a tactical error and turned fully on
her stomach, completely exposing her back to him. Maybe that
was her plan? She could be more into this than she was
letting on.

Emboldened, Adrian scooted closer to her, pressing himself
against her. Her arm lay between them, her hand nearly
touching his thigh. He repositioned himself and began rubbing
against her hand.

"Are you serious?" she asked without turning her head
to him.

"Come on, baby," he coaxed. "We've spent all day doing what
you want to do. Let's do something I want."

She shot up, jumped out of bed and paced around the room.
"I can't believe you're actually turned on after what we learned
today," she yelled. "What is wrong with you? Women are being
taken, being raped and brutalized, being killed. And you want to
have sex? Would you like to tie me up? Is that it? Do you get off
thinking about choking me to death as you penetrate me?"

"Oh calm down, Edie," Adrian huffed. "If you're not in the
mood, you're not in the mood. But don't psychoanalyze me for
desiring my lover. I don't think we need Freud to understand
that I'm not the one with the problem here."

Edie laughed. "I think your precious Freud would have a

field day in your head, babe. You're not as well adjusted as you'd like to think. In fact, you can be a sick fuck. You want to do it? Let's do it."

Edie pushed her panties down and kicked them at his face. Then she climbed onto the bed, her eyes never leaving his, until she turned and presented herself to Adrian on her hands and knees.

"Come on," she said in a sensual tone. "You want to take me? Take me."

Needing no further encouragement, Adrian entered her, delighting in her eagerness and gasps of pleasure. He knew what she wanted even when she didn't.

EDIE STARED AT THE SHADOWS ACROSS THE CEILING WHILE ADRIAN snored softly next to her. He had continued to thrust into her even as her tears fell onto the sheets, even as her groans of pain and anger grew louder. He had taken her as he always did, with no regard for her at all. She was just a means to an end for him. Luckily for her, his end came quickly.

She closed her eyes and thought about all they'd learned today. She was more convinced than ever she needed to keep seeing Timothy. Something about him cried out to her for help. Maybe she needed him as much as he needed her.

As she drifted to sleep, she pictured him in her office. On her couch. He stood and slowly walked over to her chair. She sat frozen, rooted in place, as he took her notepad and tossed it onto the floor. He grabbed her by the shoulders and pulled her up. His breath was hot on her neck. He nibbled there, and she felt a chill shoot through her body.

His lips were at her ear now. She smiled and shuddered with anticipation at his plans for her.

23

Adrian tapped his index finger repeatedly on the J key of his laptop. It was a physical tic he picked up in grad school. Something about the tactile bump of that particular key and the way the subtle vibrations fluttered through his knuckle helped him stay focused. Only rarely did he look up to find a line of Js neatly in a row at the end of whatever he had been typing. Today, that line had grown into three pages before he came back to the present.

Dammit. *Why can't Edie grow up*, he thought as he held down the backspace bar. If she had been a better student, he wouldn't feel compelled to carry her weight, to coddle her, to give her a job when no one else would. If she were a better psychologist, he wouldn't constantly have to check her work. She would know men like this current patient of hers got off on manipulating naïve young women to get what they wanted.

Adrian had to admit he didn't yet know what her patient wanted. He had believed it to be drugs, but if that were the case, the guy was not very good at it. *Highly unlikely at this point*, he thought. He was equally inept if he was trying to get Edie into bed. That little feat was actually quite easy.

Adrian's finger once again bounced mechanically against the J key as his mind wandered back to a dark office in a deserted wing of the psychology building at Columbia. What began as an attempt to explain a rather complex lecture he had delivered earlier that day on Freud's research into the oedipal complex had turned into the first of many wine-fueled, intimate encounters with Edie.

He remembered her unbridled passion for the topic. Adrian always loved that lecture. The controversy alone was enough to inspire a rousing classroom debate, which inevitably reinforced Adrian's admiration for the founding father of his profession. Edie had wanted to know if the oedipal complex applied to women. Of course it can, but it manifests itself differently for the fairer sex. In women, he explained, they typically experience penis envy and risk homosexuality or other neurosis if their situation remains unresolved. After their tryst, he assured her she was okay. Father issues were normal, and he would happily oblige her fantasies.

"Adrian?"

Edie's voice startled him. He thought it was part of his memory, but when he looked up, she was standing across his desk looking down on him.

"Yes?" he responded as he blinked away the last of their long-ago encounter.

"We were supposed to go to lunch, remember?" She seemed frustrated. "I've got a session in 45 minutes, so if we're going, we better hurry."

"It's with him, right?" Adrian could hear the contempt in his own voice, so it didn't surprise him that Edie's posture suddenly went ridged as she crossed her arms and tilted her head like a bull tilting into a banderillero's red cape.

"If by 'him' you mean Mr. Ridle, then yes." Edie said as she leaned down placing her hands on his desk as if she were a teacher about to berate an insolent student.

"I thought we decided our discoveries over the weekend would decide whether he remains a patient of this practice?" Adrian leaned in to match her posture.

Edie slammed her fist onto his desk then threw herself into the nearest chair, her eyes never leaving his. "We agreed I could have the weekend to determine if it would be prudent to keep Mr. Ridle's business. We found nothing to conclude his story is real, so while you won't be able to write the next great American psychological study on the underlying neuroses of an active serial killer, you can rest easy knowing I will be safe with our dime store sociopathic liar with narcissistic tendencies."

Adrian's laugh bellowed through his office and echoed beyond the walls. He stood up and sat on the edge of his desk, looking down on his belligerent protege. "While I don't believe we found any conclusive evidence that supports the assumption your patient is a serial killer, we also discovered nothing that proves he is not. What I take away from our little weekend adventure is that there may be thousands of as-yet-discovered serial killers in our midst, and contrary to your view of me, I would prefer to err on the side of keeping you safe."

"That's just it. I don't care about your preference," Edie said as she ran her fists along the arms of the chair. "Mr. Ridle is my patient. I am the one who will decide if his treatment here is finished. I am the one to determine his state of mind and whether I believe I can help him. Not you. This case, my case, has nothing to do with you. I think that's been your problem from the beginning." She stood up and paced like a caged tiger, putting the chair between Adrian and herself.

Adrian shook his head in disbelief. Edie had always been fiery, but never had she defied him like this. "Oh, what little you must think of me." He looked at her, knowing that even as she avoided his eyes, she would feel the weight of his stare. "This man, this fraud, has turned you against me, against us. I don't know what hold he has on you, my dear, but I am telling you now, you are not safe. One way or another, you are going to get hurt. And I can't bear to see that happen to you. I love you, Edie."

His words hung in the air between them, he hoped they would bring her back to him, to give her the strength to shake off this charlatan and remember what they shared.

"You love only yourself, Adrian." Edie said as she retreated from his office.

24

The doc seemed antsier than usual. She remained behind her desk even as their session started and only occasionally looked up from her doodling when Timothy stopped talking for more than a few minutes, which he began doing a lot just to get a reaction from her.

Bored, he switched tactics. "So, did you have an exciting weekend, doc?"

She cocked her head and stopped doodling for the first time in the last 30 minutes. "Why do you ask?"

"Ooh! Somebody had an adventurous weekend. Tell me, doc, did you and the old fatso do it? Oh, I know. Did you get into a heated argument after I called you and end up having hate sex? That's the best kind, isn't it?" He leaned his arms on his thighs and rubbed his hands together as he awaited her answer.

She gave him one of her patented stage sighs to show her displeasure in his line of questioning. He ignored it. Normally, if he waited long enough, she broke the silence first.

"As I've told you many times, Mr. Ridle, my sex life is none of your concern," she began slowly, as if she were measuring each word for its weight. "But I do want to talk to you about your call now that you bring it up."

"Does that mean you wouldn't want to talk to me about it if I hadn't brought it up?" Timothy sat back in the couch and placed his feet on her coffee table. He knew she didn't like people to put their feet on her table, but he thought he might as well get comfortable for the tongue lashing he knew he was about to receive. And, he enjoyed getting under her skin.

She ignored both his question and his gesture. "Calling your psychologist outside of business hours is highly irregular, much less calling them at home. How did you get my number, anyway?"

"Are you upset I called or that the blubber boob you live with caught us?"

As if on cue, she sighed again. "Let's keep this about the two of us please."

"Gladly, doc," he interrupted with a smile.

She closed her eyes and pinched the bridge of her nose. He must have hit a nerve. He wondered if he should cut her some slack or keep pushing on it.

"Look, Mr. Ridle, I am doing all I can to help you. I truly am. But I'm not sure this will work if we don't have boundaries, if you don't respect our doctor-patient relationship. Because that's all this is and ever will be. I'm not one of the women you allegedly hunt and make your own. I'm not your mother either. You don't have to fight for my affection or attention. I am not here to love you, to worship you, to be controlled or manipulated by you. Do you understand?"

Timothy stood and paced the room, being mindful to keep the coffee table, chairs and the doc's desk between them so he didn't startle her.

"I know you're not my mother," he flung the words out as wildly as his arms flailed through the air. "We'd have some serious issues if you were, trust me, doc. And what do you mean 'allegedly'? Are you saying you don't believe me now? Why are you suddenly turning on me? I trusted you, doc. You're the only one I've told this to, and you just decide I'm full of shit?"

He flung himself into the chair she usually sat in during their sessions. His head fell back, and he stared at the ceiling. "Are you saying this is over? You don't want to see me anymore? Is that it?"

Edie stood and moved one of the visitor's chairs at her desk so she could sit next to him. She sat there, looking at him, almost daring him to look at her. He wouldn't. She didn't get that satisfaction.

"I'm not saying I don't want to treat you any more. Far from it. I'm also not saying I don't believe you. I just don't know that I do yet, but I am determined to help you. I just can't do that if you insist on playing games with me. I need you to respect me, to respect my privacy and my space. I think we can make this work. Don't you?"

He blinked slowly and turned to face her. "It's about time, doc. I thought you'd never come around to seeing things my way."

EDIE SHOOK HER HEAD AND TRIED TO HIDE HER SMILE. WERE ALL the men in her life so messed up? That thought quickly caused a random scrap of a memory about the beach and the blood to flash across her mind like a movie she couldn't turn off or turn away from. She bolted out of her chair and busied herself with putting her furniture back in its proper place. Timothy didn't seem to notice her change in temperament and dutifully moved back to the couch so she could take her normal spot across the table from him.

"Okay," she said. "Now that we got that out of our systems, it looks like we only have about fifteen minutes left. Let's talk about you."

Timothy smiled. "Sure thing, doc."

"I feel like we've been hopping around in your history and not really getting anywhere," she said, talking to her pages of notes as she leafed through them. "You claim you had a tragic childhood. That you began raping women while deployed. And that you are now stalking a homicide detective."

"Check your facts there, doc," Timothy interjected. "First, I don't claim anything. I tell it like it is. Second, I never said I was stalking a homicide detective, just that I'd met her and was looking forward to getting to know her better. She smelled good."

Timothy looked genuinely hurt. Edie shook her head at the idea someone so calculating and cold could feel such a benign emotion. How strange the human mind is. Even a murderer could feel the small emotions though the larger ones escaped their grasp.

"Fine," she said. "I stand corrected. But as I recall, the detective interested you but something changed. Is that because you're afraid she might get too close and uncover your secret? Or because you found an easier target?"

Timothy looked at her for a long moment before finally running his hand across the light scruff on his chin. That was new, Edie thought. He was normally meticulously groomed. Maybe he was just trying to hide the scar on his cheek they had yet to talk about. Edie thought the slightly scruffy look was a good one for him but immediately chastised herself for such an unprofessional thought.

"Let's just say I found a deeper connection with someone new."

Edie felt flushed and suddenly wanted to change the subject. "I see. Let's, um, set that aside for a second. I, uh, notice you haven't shaved. Does it have something to do with that scar? Would you like to tell me about how you got it?"

"This?" Timothy asked as he ran his hand along the smooth white skin barely obscured by his light beard. "Not much of a story there, doc. Just the result of a drunken bar fight in some backwater town in Mexico. A guy didn't appreciate his girl giving some gringo her attention. I generally try to stay calm in such situations but that time I about lost my head."

Timothy's smile told Edie all she needed. The story was a lie, and he was quite proud of it. She had wanted to focus their conversation today. If they kept talking in circles, she would never help him nor learn something that would hold Adrian off from either kicking him off their patient roster or calling the police.

"Mr. Ridle, I don't expect you to be forthright with me about everything. I really don't. But I would appreciate some common decency. I'm trying to help you. How can I do that if I don't believe you?"

Without missing a beat, Timothy fired back. "Believe me or don't, doc. But don't lecture me on the truth. What is the truth anyway? Your truth about what we're doing here, about our relationship, isn't the same as mine. Is one a lie? Your truth about who I am and what I do isn't the same as mine. Your truth about your past is just a much a fantasy as mine. So don't sit there with your fancy Ivy League diploma and challenge my truth. You don't know me. You know only what I show you."

"That's just my point," Edie interjected. "What you show me isn't true."

"Nobody shows their full truth, doc. Not me. Not the pope. Not even you."

Edie let this last barb hang in the air for a minute, giving Timothy a chance to cool off. She had wanted to evoke a reaction, to pull him from his shell, but she hadn't anticipated such a strong response. She made a mental note to go back over their conversation later to pinpoint what nerve she might have exposed. Perhaps it would prove to be the key to helping him.

"Let's move on," she said with all the subtlety of a parent who didn't quite believe their child but knew any further discussion would just escalate and intensify their argument. "I want to come back to the dream we discussed earlier. Can we do that?"

Timothy seemed more than willing to change the subject, so Edie flipped back though her notes to refresh her memory. "You said you were following a girl, marching after her. Have you had that dream again since we talked about it?"

"Every night, doc, like I told you before." Timothy ran his hand across his stubble, one finger tracing his scar.

"We didn't have time to dive in before. Why do you think you were chasing this woman through a war zone?"

Timothy leaned forward, resting his forearms on his thighs and spoke to the ground. "I wasn't chasing her. I was hunting her. It was primal."

"Did you want to hurt her? Were you trying to help her?" Edie whispered.

"Both, I think. I catch her some nights, but not always. When I do, I grab her in my arms and kiss her."

"What does she do?"

"She stabs me in the heart. Every time." Timothy slapped has hands to his chest and collapsed back into the couch. "She stabs me with a shard of glass, the same glass I'd been marching over, that'd been bloodying my feet during the whole dream."

Edie shifted uncomfortably in her seat. "So you were chasing her, trying to hurt her. How does that make you feel?"

"That's just it. I don't think I was. I think I just wanted her to notice me, to want to be with me. I thought she did, but then she attacked me. I just wanted to love her....Doc, what's wrong? I'm not lying, I swear."

Edie didn't realize she'd been crying. Balling really. The kind of ugly, guttural cry that comes from deep within from a pain long hidden but never really forgotten. She tried to breathe, to turn off the torrential downpour and the low groans that shook her whole body, rocking it back and forth.

"I was raped," she gasped between sobbing breaths. "I was raped," she repeated softly as she wrapped her arms around her shoulders and shrank into herself.

Her patient was on his feet and at her side before she saw him coming. His hand felt like a hot poker on her shoulders. She shrugged away from him and ran to the nearest corner, hysteria overwhelming her and threatening to pull her under. Her screams sounded muffled, as if they came from someone in a distant room.

"What the hell is going on in here," Adrian boomed as he burst into the room.

ADRIAN QUICKLY TOOK IN THE SITUATION BEFORE HIM. ONCE again, Edie seemed more like the patient than the psychologist in the room. She looked like a petulant child who had been scolded by her patient. Meanwhile, her patient, the one with the fake rape fantasy, stood near her like a predator about to pounce.

Without thinking, Adrian lunged at Timothy, grabbing him by the collar and yanking him through the door into the lobby where a small crowd of colleagues and patients had gathered to watch the soap opera unfold.

"You are no longer a patient here, sir," he screamed as he threw Timothy to the ground.

As Timothy hit the floor, he seemed to come to his senses. Adrian was shocked at how quickly he leapt to a standing position and assumed a fighter's crouch. "I don't think that's your decision, asshole," he spat as the two began slowly circling each other.

Adrian, operating on long-forgotten reflexes, raised his hands into a boxer's stance he hadn't used since his college days. "The hell it isn't." Without taking his eyes off the louse, he called over his shoulder. "Someone call the police. We need to have this man escorted from the building immediately."

"There's no need for the cops," Timothy said, holding up his hands in surrender. He must have known he was outclassed. "I just want to be able to come back and work through my issues. Just like everyone else here," he spoke to the crowd.

Adrian dared look around and saw men and women entranced by the cheap theatrics of the moment. A couple held their phones in front of them, capturing the moment for posterity. He'd have to remember to get copies and then have them delete the originals. Patient-doctor confidentiality and all that.

He looked back at his opponent, who had dropped his arms and lowered his eyes. Adrian saw his opening. He pushed off with his back foot, lowered his shoulder and slammed into Timothy, driving the smaller man into the wall.

"What the hell is going on?" Edie yelled as the two men pushed and pulled at each other, each trying to gain the advantage.

"Stay out of this," Adrian bellowed as he worked to break the headlock Timothy had maneuvered him into. "You've caused enough distraction. I'm handling this now."

"For god's sake," she yelled again. "You're grown men acting like little boys on a playground. Mr. Ridle, stop this right now."

Surprisingly, her patient released Adrian and once again held his hands up in supplication. Adrian took a half step back, weighing his next move. Edie walked over and glared up at both men. "Honestly," she said. "Adrian, what kind of example are you setting for our colleagues and their patients? And, Mr. Ridle, I expect more from you as well. This is ridiculous."

Adrian couldn't believe the impact her words had on her patient. The guy actually leaned back against the wall and hung his head in what appeared to be shame.

"I'm sorry, doc," the man whined.

Adrian struggled to keep his voice calm. "This is not appropriate, Edie. You need to get out of the way. I'll handle this piece of trash."

"You're the trash," Timothy whispered so that only Adrian could hear.

Without thinking, Adrian swung at Timothy. The younger man's eyes widened then narrowed to slits as he ducked the blow. Adrian's momentum threw off his balance. His fist connected with Edie's cheek, making a loud cracking sound. Her scream muffled by his body hitting hers as they fell to the floor in a heap.

25

A drian paced the length of his cellar. He hated physical altercations. Fighting represented the lowest form of masculinity. Primates charging at each other to establish dominance, to gain the best mate. And yet Edie's moronic patient, Mr. Ridle, had pulled Adrian down to his level. Worse yet, it had happened in front of his colleagues and employees.

His face reddened as he thought of the repercussions a single moment would have on his moral authority at the office. It reminded him of his ordeal at Columbia. One bad decision, a solitary lapse in judgment after a lifetime of toeing the line, had cost him his reputation, his career, his life.

He poured himself a dram of whiskey and swirled it absent-mindedly while selecting the night's cigar. His mind traveled back to the precipice of his academic demise. He'd become an instant pariah in all the preeminent academic circles. Every university he called had refused to meet with him, politely of course, even though his credentials were impeccable. Word travels fast at the highest echelons of academia.

He snipped the cap of his cigar and lit the foot, puffing vigorously as he rotated it in the flame of his torch to ensure an even burn. He held the thick spicy smoke in his mouth. He exhaled, and could already feel himself relaxing. He resumed his pacing as he remembered the growing shame he felt when he realized that the elitism he had once reveled in had turned on him. He found no solace and no prospects at any top school, so he had embarked on his current self-imposed exile in the middle of the country, equidistant from either coast. He never would have survived without Edie. And now, it seemed, she was turning on him as well.

He drained his glass and poured another. He felt restless, powerless. He collapsed into his desk chair. As he set his cigar in the ashtray, he noticed his laptop was askew. He reached into his top drawer and pulled out his manuscript. Immediately, he saw that the pages were out of order. Edie had been snooping again. He'd really have to speak with her this time.

What if she had broken into his laptop? He quickly flipped it open and pecked at the keys to enter his password. He clicked around the screen and scrolled to a folder, hidden deep within his hard drive. He entered another password, and unlocked his illicit photo collection. Everything seemed to be in order. He clicked slowly through the pictures. His breath quickened, he looked back And up towards the door at the top of the stairs before shifting in his chair, one hand slipping into his lap.

No! He closed the folder and shutdown his laptop. He was not a low-form primate with no discipline, no impulse control. He wandered over to his record player and put on something to sooth his inner savage beast. Then he gathered up his manuscript and pulled out his pen. He'd put his passion into his work where it belonged.

HOURS LATER, ADRIAN SCRATCHED ANOTHER LINE THROUGH AN errant word. His pages and his fingers were stained red from his latest round of aggressive cuts. He had nearly finished the second draft and hoped to share it with a few select colleagues in the next week or two. But even though he knew he was writing a seminal work in the field of psychology, that would place him in the same rarified air as Freud, he currently found it hard to concentrate on this latest revision.

He set his marker aside with a sigh. His cellar was unusually quiet. The only sounds were the soft pops from his speakers. They vibrated and ricocheted around the cellar as the arm of his record player hopped up and down in a perpetual dance at the center of a limited pressing of Coltrane's "Blue Train."

What was he going to do about Edie? He'd only ever taken an interest in her in the beginning because she seemed so vulnerable, so innocent. But lately he found it impossible to have even the simplest of conversations with her. She seemed to be building up walls between them. Isolating herself from the life they had enjoyed together, built together.

He puffed absentmindedly on his cigar, twirling it between his finger and thumb as he thought about their first time together. It was a tender moment. He missed it. He missed them. He loved her. Of that he was sure. He just wondered if she still felt the same.

He felt he was pushing her away. But only because she was so standoffish. Was she using this new patient as a foible for his jealousy? She knew what it'd do to him. She knew his passion wouldn't allow him to just idly watch her leave him behind. How could he break through? Even though he didn't know the answer, he was determined to fight for her.

A thought occurred to him. He set down his cigar, picked up his pen and wrote furiously as the words, bottled up for so long, spilled from his heart onto the page.

. . .

ADRIAN STOOD QUIETLY NEXT TO THE BED HE SHARED WITH EDIE. The soft glow of the lamp on her side table provided the only light in the room and cast his long shadow across her body. Though her eye was bruised and her nose swollen where her patient had caused Adrian to hit her, she looked at peace. For once not tormented by the battered dreams and fragmented memories that caused her to wander restlessly in her sleep.

Her past was pain. Her present unstable. But her future was his, and he wanted nothing more than to make her happy. He just needed her to do her part. He could make her happy if she would just make herself listen to him.

He leaned his letter against her lamp, then leaned over and gave her a light kiss on the forehead before softly joining her in what he one day hoped would be their marital bed. As he drifted off to sleep, with thoughts of their future together cementing a smile on his face, Edie began tossing and turning as was her normal nightly routine. He was about to wake her with a soft nudge when a single word escaped her lips that caused his hand to recoil before he could awaken her. Surely he'd misheard her. There it was again. Two words now. *Oh, Timothy.*

His heart sank. He had heard her correctly. She was moaning her patient's name. Not in fear. Not in pain. But the slow, tender moans of a woman in the gentle throes of passion. He knew those sounds from her. They were distant memories, a fact that made her current cries of another man's name even more hurtful.

What should he do? If he woke her and confronted her, she'd just laugh at him. His eyes filled with tears as he got out of bed, and careful not to disturb her, shoved his letter into the pocket of his robe and shuffled off to sleep on the couch in his den.

26

"What's wrong with you?" Edie had grown tired of Adrian's games. He had punched her, yet this morning he was the one acting like he'd been wronged. Like she had bruised his cheekbone, blackened his eye, and nearly broken his nose. She took measured breaths, partly to keep herself calm but also because anything deeper made her whole face pulse.

"Nothing," Adrian huffed as he heaped a spoonful of sugar into his second cup of coffee. He rarely drank more than half a cup before heading to the office. He seemed to enjoy coffee more if someone else prepared it for him, and his secretary had been trained long ago to keep the cups coming throughout the day.

Edie shook her head and smiled at his obvious evasion. She could see the truth in his eyes and on his red stained fingers. "You were up all night working on your book again, weren't you?"

Adrian grunted and stared at his cup as he spoke. Come to think of it, Edie realized he hadn't looked her in the eyes all morning.

"As a matter of fact, it's finished," he snorted. "But I don't think it's something we should talk about. You have made your displeasure about my academic return perfectly clear. I wouldn't dream of boring you with my work when you have such an important case of your own that so obviously consumes your every waking moment and then some."

He spoke the last three words softly, practically spitting them as if trying to expel a bad taste from his mouth. Edie recognized his contemptuous mood and decided not to question his delivery or push him for more details about his book.

She felt exhausted. She had slept little the night before. She had yet to process her personal admission to Timothy or Adrian's violent response to her most critical patient. She felt on the brink of something. Perhaps a breakthrough. Or just as likely a breakdown.

She sipped her coffee, which had cooled as rapidly as her relationship with Adrian. They sat in silence until it was time to head to the office then rode in more silence until they separated at the lobby without a word.

"No. I won't let it go, doc." Timothy paced around the office. It felt smaller than normal, like the walls were slowly moving in on the two of them. Nervous energy kept him in constant motion, circling his confines like a caged animal. The doc, his doc, was a rape survivor. Fate surely had to have brought them together. He wanted, no needed, to know more.

"As I've already told you many times," she said, "I shouldn't have shared that with you. It was a breach of decorum on my part, and I refuse to go into it. We are here for you. Not me."

He could sense the desperation in her voice. "The lady doth protest too much, methinks."

She smiled. A crack in her armor. He pressed on. "Look. I get it. You have a professional code, but haven't we moved beyond the purely professional, doc?"

"First, Mr. Ridle, we most certainly do have a purely professional relationship. Your growing belief otherwise is partly responsible for recent unfortunate events."

"Your flatulent boyfriend is the reason for that shit," Timothy interrupted. "But I'm sorry that happened to you. You still look real good to me, doc. Luckily, your man has tiny delicate hands."

She ignored his disruption. "And second, I said what I said in a moment of weakness. I'm human. It happens from time to time, but it is not right for me to take your time to talk about my issues. I'm here to help you. Not to use our sessions to work through my own problems."

Timothy stopped pacing. She smiled at him. He couldn't reconcile her look of bemusement with her serious lecturing tone. "What's so funny, doc?"

"I'm wondering the same thing," she said. "You're grinning like a cat who just ate the canary. I'm not sure I want to know, but what were you just thinking about?"

"You're too young for that weird cat reference. It sounds like something my grandma used to say when I was a kid. And I was just thinking of one of my favorite movies. Did you ever see 'Silence of the Lambs'?"

"Yes, and I believe you've brought it up before." Her voice was soft but took on a harsh edge as she answered. Her smile faded, and Timothy could tell she was afraid of what turn their conversation was about to take.

"It's one of my favorites," he continued, ignoring her discomfort. "They really nailed the mind of a predator. But I didn't bring it up for that reason. I just think maybe we should strike a deal like the one Hannibal and Clarice had, you know?"

She stared at him intently. He couldn't read her look, which made him more nervous than usual. He paced around the room again. Slowly her smile returned and then, out of nowhere, she laughed. Her eyes sparkled with life even as she cursed lightly in pain. "You mean their quid pro quo arrangement? Is that what you'd like? You share with me then I have to share with you?"

"Yes, that's it. That's what I want, doc." He held his breath while holding her gaze.

She absentmindedly ran a finger up and down her inner thigh as she considered his suggestion. He knew he had her. Surely that was a sign she meant him to see. It was as if she wanted him to imagine it was his finger and not hers that so lightly caressed her leg. His heart raced.

Finally, her face broke into a wide, purple and yellowed grin. "Am I to be the Hannibal Lecter to your Clarice?"

He slapped his hands together loudly and laughed at her fumbled attempt at humor. As silly as the idea was, it served to lighten the tension that had been building for most of their back and forth this session. "You can play whatever role you want, doc, as long as you play with me."

"Oh, Mr. Ridle," she scoffed. "We both know it is you who are playing with me. But regardless, I'm willing to play along. For now."

She flipped the page on her notepad and looked up at him expectantly. "You start," she said with arched eyebrows and her pen poised expectantly at the top of the page.

He plopped down onto the couch and threw his feet up on the table with a flourish of confidence that belied the tightening knot in his stomach. This was a dangerous game the two of them were playing. He could no longer be sure if he was the cat or the mouse. The idea of striking a bargain like this had come to him on a whim. He hadn't expected her to agree, but he couldn't let on. Perhaps she had known and was testing him. If so, he wouldn't give her the satisfaction. He knew what his first quid would be to her quo.

He tilted his head and smiled with the grin that had always

gotten him into as much trouble as it got him out of in his life. He locked eyes with her, telepathically reaching across the room to let her know she'd made a mistake but silently telling her it was too late for her to turn back now.

"Okay, doc," he began. "Unlike some killers, the only thing I take with me are my memories, which I revisit. A lot." He sat up and leaned forward, never breaking eye contact as he continued. "I tend to get really excited when I think of the things I've done. If you know what I mean. In fact, I usually end up masterbating. I can't help it. Before I know it, my hand is pumping away."

He paused as his smile grew bigger. She broke first, looking down at the notes she was furiously scratching into a piece of paper absent of her normal ribbon doodles. "Something weird happened the other night though," he continued. "It was the night we had our little phone conversation. I was lying in bed reliving one of my many adventures when you suddenly crashed the party in my head."

She stopped writing, and he saw her hand had turned white around her pen. Her breathing quickened but still she wouldn't look at him. "I have to tell you, doc, my climax that night was more powerful than my first kill."

He stopped and leaned back into the couch, draping his arms across its back cushions, and waited.

EDIE FOCUSED ON HER BREATHING. SHE REFUSED TO LOOK UP, TO look at him. She blinked to bring her notepad into focus, realizing that even though she had been looking at it during his entire story, she hadn't truly paid attention to what she was writing. Her handwriting was frantic. Over and over she had written "he knows, he knows, he knows" followed by "so much blood." The words confused her. She had no recollection of writing them and hadn't the faintest idea what they meant. She forced herself to loosen her grip on her pen.

She rolled her shoulders and slowly looked up at her star patient. He looked smug, like a man without a care in the world who just dropped by to chat about the weather and his plans for the weekend. Isn't it amazing, she thought, how deeply we can hide our secrets, sometimes even from ourselves? Edie shivered but quickly recovered. "That's your opener? That's the best you can do after almost six months worth of weekly sessions? Some hand-me-down knockoff from a character who had less than two minutes of air time?"

Timothy raised his hand and waved it in the air, and Edie flinched. "Oh, but what a memorable two minutes the poor Mr. Miggs had."

"Well, despite your questionable story, I will hold up my end of the bargain." She dropped her pen onto her notepad and carried them both to her desk. She thought about reciprocating by telling him she, too, had dreamed of him. But what purpose would that serve other than to stroke his ego? She needed to remain in a position of power.

When she was ready to share, she stood there, leaning against her desk as if it alone would hold her up. She spoke to the wall. "I knew my rapist. At least I thought I did. How can you know someone when they only show you what they want you to see? How can you trust them when from the moment you met they saw you only as prey, as an object to use up, a flame to stamp out?"

Tears stung her eyes, leaving warm streaks down her cheeks. She let them run free. She had never told anyone this secret before. "He was caring and gentle at first. He listened and offered advice. He was my best friend. Until he became my worst nightmare."

Her legs buckled, but her arms kept her up, bolstered by

the cold wood of her desk. She took a deep breath and continued. "When does making love become rape?" She laughed and shook her head. "I've asked myself that a thousand times. I went to bed with him willingly. I was giving myself to him. But that wasn't enough. He had to take me. He tied my hands and legs. His hand pressed on my mouth so hard I thought my jaw would break. He whispered softly in my ear as he forced himself into me. He laughed at my tears. And when he was done, which thankfully didn't take long, he left me tied there while he cleaned himself up and went to the kitchen to grab a bottle of red wine and two glasses. He was gentle again as he untied me. Loving even. It was like a switch had flipped, and he was the man I fell for. But I wasn't the same. How could I be? I tried to tell him. He just couldn't see what the problem was. I had wanted it, he said, so it wasn't really rape. More of a rape fantasy. Can you believe that? His fantasy. My internal death."

The hands on her shoulder sent a shiver through her body. She jerked away and scrambled over her desk. She hadn't heard him get up. When she looked up at him from her crouched position behind her chair, he had his hands raised and was slowly backing away.

"You don't like being touched." It wasn't a question. "I should have known. I'm sorry. I was just. I just wanted to comfort you."

"Men don't comfort, they take." She slowly stood, wiping at her tears and straightening her blouse. "They make you believe they're your knight, but their armor is always tarnished and dented from the pointless defensive punches of the damsels in distress who came before you."

He retreated to the couch. His smug look replaced with an expression of pity. Edie didn't know which made her blood boil more.

"How did it end with him," he asked. His knowing stare bore

through her, but she refused to give him the satisfaction of an answer.

"I don't even know why I'm trying to help you, Mr. Ridle. You're just like all the rest. You don't deserve help. Certainly not from a woman, not from me. Who am I to tell you what you are doing is evil? I'm not sure I know the difference between good and evil anymore. I should just turn you in, but why should other women be saved when I wasn't?"

27

Timothy's black t-shirt clung to his body like a wetsuit, which was fitting since the humidity of the summer night felt like he was walking through a sauna. The lack of a breeze made breathing difficult. He chuckled at a random thought that exploded into his head like the IEDs he and his buddies feared whenever they were on patrol in country. Breathing in this weather felt almost like being waterboarded. The pentagon could save itself from the anti-torture crowd by installing saunas in US detention centers.

He shook the stupid idea from his thoughts. Stay on mission, he told himself. He stepped out from under the tree that he'd been using for cover. No need to worry about being seen at this late hour. Everyone in the neighborhood would be fast asleep in the comfort of their air conditioned homes, falsely believing they were safe from the world outside their walls.

He looked up at the second story window. A soft glow shone from deep inside the room. Must be one of the lamps on the bedside tables. He wondered if she might be awake, maybe reading a trashy romance or studying his file for clues he knew weren't there.

One of the first Army quacks the brass had forced Timothy to see had called him a non-entity. He could disappear from the face of the earth and nobody would care. No one would notice. Timothy thought the doctor was trying to make him angry, to draw him out. He could still see the look on the poser's face when Timothy had agreed with his assessment.

But his new doc was different. As he stared up at the yellowish glow of the window, he was glad fate had brought them together. When she looked at him, he felt like she really saw him. At least the parts of him he wanted her to see. Still, that was new for him.

He thought about breaking in, watching her sleep, but the light in the kitchen evaporated the safety of the shadow he'd been standing in. He slowly backed up and, reluctantly, headed to his truck.

Catch you later, doc, he thought as he left.

THOSE DAMN GUMMY BEARS AGAIN. ADRIAN SHOOK HIS HEAD AS HE leaned against the doorframe, arms crossed, and watched his sleeping beauty shovel handfuls into her mouth like some lifeless zombie taking nourishment from a fresh kill.

She stood crouched on the countertop, her bare feet in sharp contrast to the dark granite. Her silky robe fluttering around her. He barely recognized her anymore. She was an apparition floating across his kitchen and through his life. She looked primal. Where was the lost but lovely soul he'd fallen for? Without him noticing, she had shrugged off that sweetness somewhere along the way like some outgrown layer of skin. He only now realized the extent of her metamorphosis. She appeared ready to fly from the healing sanctuary he had built for her, because of her. Those same walls that had once made her feel loved and safe now must feel like a prison.

Tears rolled down his face as he rolled up the sleeves of his robe. His hands clinched and unclenched. He had allowed this to go too far. It stopped tonight.

He lashed out suddenly. His fists beat against the walls on either side of the doorway as he spread his arms, willing Edie to awaken, both physically and emotionally. A guttural yell escaped his lips, vibrating up from deep recesses he forgot existed.

The glass canister Edie had been clinging to seemed to fall in slow motion. It looked to Adrian like it paused for a second, hovering just over the floor, before it shattered in a colorful explosion of gummies and glass. The bears bounced and scattered along the floor, advancing on him like an army. When they finally halted their approach, Edie's screams pierced his heart like one of the glass shards and threatened to blow his eardrums.

One hand clutched her chest, ripping at her nightgown as if she were trying to dig out her heart. Her other hand reached frantically for something to hold on to as her feet slipped out from under her.

Adrian ran to her, the minefield of candy and glass forgotten. He left a trail of bloody footprints across the floor. He felt no pain but that which emanated from within. He knew only that he had to catch her, to keep her from falling into the abyss. He slid the final few feet, slicing his leg, arm, and side. The force of Edie's landing on his chest knocked the wind out of him.

She immediately swung her fists into his chest and face with a blind fury Adrian hadn't expected. Her eyes were wide and wild. He grabbed her roughly into a bear hug, his face buried in her hair. He whispered, "It's ok, my baby, I love you," repeatedly in her ear. Instead of soothing her, it intensified her attack until he could no longer hold on to her or defend himself. He threw her across the floor. She slid into a counter and jumped to her feet.

"What the hell, Adrian!" The words struck him as intensely as her fists had moments before.

Adrian raised his hands as he struggled to stand. Blood ran down his arm and leg and pooled around his feet. "I'm sorry. I only meant to wake you, but after everything that's happened lately I just lost control."

"I can't do this anymore," she said as she gathered her robe around her.

"Do what?"

"This, Adrian. I can't do any of this. It isn't working. We aren't working. Maybe we never did."

The blow of her words nearly sent him reeling back to the floor. "I'm sorry I overreacted. I've done that a lot lately. I know that. But it's because I love you. We can make this work. We just need to go back to how things used to be. You'll see."

Her laugh sent a shiver down his spine. "How they used to be? Do you think I was ever happy with you? Is that why you're writing some new thesis? So you can regain your former glory and take me along for the ride?"

"I just want you to be happy."

"But you don't make me happy, Adrian. You never did. I think I need to move out. I need some space."

"No. Don't. I'll move into the guest room. We can talk about this. I'll give you some space. You'll see, we just need a little time."

"Fine, but I'm taking the guest room, and I'm not promising anything."

Edie left without another word. Adrian collapsed against the counter. All of his expertise couldn't save his own relationship. He felt helpless for the first time in his life.

. . .

EDIE SAT ON THE EDGE OF THE UNFAMILIAR QUEEN BED IN THEIR guest room. She stared at her feet as she playfully dangled them like a child who hadn't a care in the world. What she wouldn't give to be a child again. Before grad school. Before Adrian. Before her dad died. Before....She couldn't bring herself to finish the thought. Even the sanctity of her own mind wasn't safe. Not anymore.

The room felt stuffy and smelled its age. Like the rest of the house, they had updated the guest room before they moved in, but it occurred to Edie that she was about to be the first person to actually put this room to use. Despite the renovation, the lack of use seemed to have caused the room to revert to its former self. It smelled of dust and mouse droppings.

She yanked the blankets and sheets from the bed and replaced them with fresh linens. Then she lit a candle and kneeled at her bedside to pray. As she clasped her hands, she wasn't sure what caused her to resume the practice that died with her father when she was just a child. Ever since his death, she felt a loneliness. She lost her dad and her faith all at once. Maybe if she could rekindle a little piece of the religion that had kept her dad so positive despite the fact that he dealt with the worst scumbags on earth every day he put on his badge, she could find the courage to keep going. Even if she didn't have as important a purpose as her dad.

It all came back to Timothy. If she could change him, if she could turn him away from the darkness she knew would consume him if it hadn't already, then maybe she would be redeemed. Maybe then the pain she felt every day, every single day, would be lifted. If a little bedtime prayer could make that happen, why not try?

She clenched her hands tighter and squeezed her eyes shut until a few random tears escaped. She searched for the right words to send into the universe and quickly realized she had nobody to pray for except Timothy. She prayed that he would have the strength to overcome the urges she knew were making his stomach turn and his heart race. The urges, that if left unchecked, would take over. She prayed she wasn't too late to save him. Even if he had already given in, maybe she still had a chance to pull him out of the darkness. It couldn't be too late. She needed it not to be too late.

Her eyes flew open. She realized she had been holding her breath. She grasped at the fresh comforter as she gasped for air. Her head sank to the bed. She slowly calmed herself and pushed herself up. She had forgotten to pray for Adrian but decided he didn't deserve an intervention, from her or from whatever god might have been listening.

The light of a passing car drew her to the room's tiny window. The neighborhood looked both eery and peaceful from her new vantage point. The wind blew through the trees, kicking leaves and debris down the deserted street. Her room was in the house's turret, way above the rest of the roofline. For a moment she felt like a fairytale princess waiting to be rescued from her tower. But she hadn't been imprisoned by some evil witch or jealous queen. She hadn't even been locked away by Adrian. No. She was lost long before him.

She thought back to her latest conversation with Timothy as she looked down from her fairytale tower. He wasn't the knight she expected to see riding up on his glowing white steed. But was she his? Were their struggles against fate only helping to fulfill it? She felt very much like a player in a Shakespearean drama. What consequence yet hung in the stars for the two of them?

She lay her head on an unfamiliar pillow and fell asleep to those all too familiar thoughts.

· · ·

ADRIAN DRAINED HIS WHISKEY GLASS AND IMMEDIATELY POURED another. Only alcohol would erase the pain of his lover's words. He leaned against his record cabinet and gently set the needle down against a Sonny Rollins' record. A little saxophone might help as well.

As he clipped the end of his cigar, a Cuban because the toughest times call for the best cigars, he thought about his album choice. Sonny Rollins found immediate fame, but what should have been an easy ride took a sharp turn when he didn't get the respect of his peers. They told him he sounded like everyone else. That his licks were too mechanical. Too expected. He sounded too much like the greats every jazz musician emulates before finding their own voice, their own style.

So he took three years off and toured small joints in Europe. And when he got back to the United States, he would practice late at night under a bridge. It was there that he finally found the style he would become known for. And it was from there that his next record, "The Bridge," would be named.

Adrian sucked on an ice cube as the first notes of the album bounced around his man cave and through his soul. He was Sonny Rollins. In isolation. Desperately trying to find his voice again. And until just now, Edie had been his instrument.

He shuffled over to his couch and fell into its cold but welcoming embrace. All was not lost. All would be forgiven in the morning. His glass slipped from his hand and shattered into a sticky, melting mess as he melted deeper into the couch. He'd clean it up tomorrow. He'd clean everything up. His life would be tidy again.

28

Edie finally heard Adrian crashing around in the cellar as she rinsed her breakfast dishes. His snoring had echoed around the house for the last hour. His ability to sleep so well while she had spent a restless night up in her princess's turret kept the flame of last night's anger burning.

"I'm going to be late," he said as he passed by the kitchen door on his way to the master bathroom without a glance her way.

"What makes you think I care?" she yelled after him.

He returned and poked his head through the doorway. Still in yesterday's clothes, now wrinkled and soiled. His arms crossed and brow furrowed. "Look. I know last night got out of hand. And I know we have a lot to talk about, but can we please be civil? At least until after I've showered and had a cup of coffee?"

Without warning, she hurled her coffee mug at his head. He ducked behind the door frame as it whizzed by and crashed into the wall behind him. "You want some coffee? Here's a cup. Make it yourself."

"Edie, don't be a child," he said from behind the safety of the wall. "I don't know what is going on with you, but it needs to stop, and it needs to stop now. You're better than this. At least I used to think you were."

"You don't know a thing about me," she screamed. "Not one goddamn thing. You've made me up. Conjured me from your deepest fantasies. I could disappear tomorrow, and you'd easily replace me with someone else you could mold in my place."

Adrian stepped through the doorway, arms still crossed in front of himself as if to fend off any more flying dishes or other missiles of Edie's rage. "I know plenty about you, my dear. You want to believe you're mysterious, but you're just like the rest of us. A product of your childhood. Troubled by an obsession with a daddy who left you too soon and a mom who moved on quicker than you thought she should. And why is it, do you think you're so enamored by your current patient?"

Edie reached for the plate in the drying rack, but Adrian ran out the door before she got the satisfaction of flinging it at him.

"No wonder they ran you out of academia," she screamed, knowing the insult would hit him more squarely and hurt him more deeply than the plate ever could.

EDIE DRUMMED HER PEN ON HER DESK BLOTTER. HER LEGS SHOOK in time with the drumbeats. She stared at the second hand slowly sweeping around her wall clock. Its moments were unrepentant. To her it appeared as if it sliced its way around and around. Cutting deeper and deeper into the present, always cutting out the past.

Timothy was twenty-five minutes late. *Quite unlike him*, she thought. The events of the last couple of days made her feel antsy. Her body felt like it was flowing with an electric current just waiting to get out, to shock her system. The hairs on her arms and neck vibrated with a static she knew she wouldn't be able to contain for long. She'd felt it before. Before Kansas City. Before Columbia University. Before Adrian. After her father.

She threw her pen onto the desk. It scattered across the surface and bounced onto the floor as if it were escaping her mood and had decided it'd rather leap to its doom over the edge of her desk rather than witness what was to come. She stood and paced the room, unsure of what to do next. The walls slowly closed in on her. A cold sweat glistened across her skin. Her mind raced as she recognized she was no longer in control of her thoughts. They came and went at their own will. Old memories long buried crashed down around her, threatening to pull her under like the white-capped waves of her childhood.

She stopped at her door. Her fingertips rubbing together. Her eyes darting up and down the hallway. She closed it quietly and locked it. She hesitated more than once on the short walk back to her desk. Willing herself to leave, go for a walk, anything. But, like her mind, she wasn't in control of her body. It did what it wanted. It moved her closer, edging her towards her desk, to where she could feed its hunger.

She'd never done this before. Not here. She sat back down at her desk and closed her eyes. She slowly raised her skirt and bunched her stockings around her calves. Her fingers drawing little circles lightly across her skin. Goosebumps following in their wake. Ripples of pleasure rolling across her thigh. Her other hand was in her desk drawer before she knew it, grabbing the toy she'd hidden there long ago but never used.

Her whole body vibrated with anticipation. Her head rolled back as she sank deeper into her seat. She slipped out of her shoes, kicked out of her stockings, and placed one leg on her desk so she could get a better angle. Then, as her hands finally reached the apex of their journey, she bit down at the sweet release of the blade.

Her back arched, and a slight moan escaped her lips at that

first cut. In her mind, she saw her younger self on his bed. She was smiling, still thinking she was in control even though he had already bound her arms and legs with silky burgundy ribbon. The vision gave the illusion that her wrists and ankles flowed with blood.

He stood above her. His excitement evident. The look on his face was wrong. His eyes that once sparkled with intelligence and sensitivity were just two dark dead cavities now. His smile was wild and frenzied. She fought against her restraints. This wasn't what she wanted. Not anymore.

She told him to let her go, that she changed her mind. He laughed. A humorless, soulless laugh. "Silly girl," he said to her. "You can't turn back now. You're mine. I'll be playing with you for the rest of your life. You'll either learn to like it or at least learn to play along."

Then he knelt between her legs and thrust into her without warning. She screamed at him to let her go. She yelled for help. He slapped her sharply across both cheeks and pressed his hand over her mouth and nose. She struggled to breathe. Fought to remain conscious.

The last thing she saw before she blacked out was his face drawing close to her. He softly kissed her on the cheek as he roughly took her. "I love you," Adrian whispered into her ear as she passed out.

Her body jerked as she climaxed. She quickly grabbed a handful of tissues to staunch the bleeding before slowly straightening her skirt and picking up her pen.

29

The sun had long ago begun its slow decline as Edie walked to her car. A streak of orange-tinted red light hung just above the horizon as if god himself had carefully cut a thin razor slice into the sky. She quickly looked away and forced her eyes to follow her shoes even as her own new scar tingled with electric excitement at the thought her secret release might somehow be holy.

Adrian was still holed up in his office. Neither of them acknowledged each other as she had walked by on her way out. Timothy had never shown up, called with an explanation or answered any of her dozen calls.

She felt as empty as the parking lot as she got into her car. Hers and Adrian's were the only vehicles left. Everyone else had gone off to enjoy time with family and friends.

What must that be like, she thought to herself as she turned the ignition only to hear a single metallic click. She cursed under her breath as she turned the key again, this time more forcefully as if a bit more strength would convince her engine to start. The dash lights flickered and died. As she looked over at Adrian's car, so did her hope of avoiding another confrontation.

He appeared at her window as if summoned by her thoughts. She sighed and tried to roll down the window before realizing she couldn't even complete that simple task with a dead car. She opened the door a crack and spoke to him through the tiny opening.

"Can you give me a jump or something?"

She saw his smile grow and the mischievous boyish twinkle in his eye. Whatever joke was bouncing around his head, he rightly kept it to himself. "You know my expertise is in the more complicated matters of the mind, not mechanics. Even if I had jumper cables, I'd hardly know how to use them."

He opened the door and bowed, his other arm sweeping towards his car is if he were a valet ushering her to safety. *This is the knight I deserve*, Edie thought to herself as she bound out of the car and slammed the door shut. Adrian jumped back, barely pulling his fingers from the doorjamb before they were crushed.

"What the hell, Edie," he shouted, holding his hand as if she had smashed his fingers. "I'm trying to help you. All I have ever tried to do is help you. I should leave you here!"

"Maybe you should," she yelled right back. They were inches from each other, chests almost touching, a passerby might mistake them for boxers about to begin their match.

"I am tired of your self pity and lashing out," Adrian shouted to the sky. "What do I have to do to prove my love? What do I have to do to get you to come back to me?"

"Ha," Edie scoffed. "I haven't left. I can't. You've made sure of that, haven't you? And love? Really? Is that what you call it?"

Adrian's voice softened. He sounded like a scorned child. "You can leave any time you want. But I hope you don't. Because, yes, I do love you. You're the center of my universe. I'd be lost without you."

Edie threw her head back and laughed as loudly as she

could. Tears ran down her face. She leaned against her useless car so she wouldn't fall over. "You don't know what love is. I'm an interesting puzzle to you. You can't figure me out, but you want so badly to know what makes me tick. I'm a project, a research subject, a topic of scholarly conversation. You no more love me than you do that stupid car you spend so much money on."

Adrian threw his briefcase on the ground and comically kicked one of Edie's tires. "How dare you! Where would you be without me? I'll tell you exactly where you'd be, my darling. You'd be a psych patient rather than a practicing psychologist. You never would have been able to overcome your childhood. I saved you from that. I saved you! And this is what I get? The wrath of an ungrateful, petulant little girl?"

Edie recoiled as if he'd struck her. Without another word, she reached back into her car, grabbed her own briefcase, and slumped into the passenger seat of Adrian's car. She felt his stare on her cheek for several minutes, but she refused to meet his gaze. Finally he gathered his stuff and got into the car.

She stared out the window. His already small car felt downright claustrophobic with him sitting next to her. As they turned out of the parking lot, Edie thought she saw Timothy parked across the street. She strained her neck as they drove passed, just as the man pulled his ball cap down over his face.

ADRIAN SQUINTED INTO THE DEPTHS OF THE REFRIGERATOR AS IF waiting long enough would compel it, like one of his patients, to let go of its secrets. He was hunting for the mustard to top off his late-night roast beef sandwich. He despised the very idea of the late-night snack. It screamed weak conviction. If you couldn't control the little impulses, how could you expect to control the important ones? His late-night rummaging through the fridge was different, of course. His hunger had nothing to do with a weakness. He simply needed something to soak up the half-liter of whiskey he'd consumed for dinner and dessert after the vitriolic showdown he and Edie had in the parking lot after work. Thankfully, none of their employees had witnessed it.

There it was! That lovely squat jar of yellow heaven. Hidden behind a bag of spouts that smelled past their prime and a quart of plain yogurt. He missed the days of his youth when his fridge contained pizza and beer and other essentials. And always the sour goodness of yellow mustard.

As he closed the refrigerator, the mind-numbing bleating of the home alarm system startled him. The mustard jar crashed to the kitchen floor. He did his best imitation of a traditional Russian dance, but his high kicks just helped to splatter the pungent globules across the kitchen, spraying cabinets and countertops in every direction as his bare feet stomped on broken glass.

Dammit, he thought, *is nothing in this house simple?* If he were being robbed, he hoped the perpetrator would let him eat his sandwich in peace before killing him, or worse, violating him in front of Edie. Shit. Edie! He pressed his palms to both sides of his throbbing head and ran out of the kitchen knowing what he'd find.

He stopped dead in his tracks. His mustard-covered hand on the doorjamb of their wide open front door. "Oh sweet Jesus, Edie, what have you done," he cried.

Edie sat under a weeping willow. In some alternate universe where they were happy, where he made her happy, where he could fix her, she'd look beautiful and inviting. Tonight she looked cold even in the sweltering heat. Dead almost. She wore a white, flowing nightgown, one of his special gifts to her. It was covered with blood. Her head was propped back against the tree's trunk. Her eyes wide but unseeing as her hand mechanically pounded against her thigh. A small glint from the moonlight through the trees reflected off what must be a tiny blade in her hand.

Comprehension finally broke through his haze, and Adrian ran towards his lover. Drink and shock made it feel like she was a mile away instead of mere feet. He slid into her side and immediately applied pressure to her thigh. Her arm continued its robotic attack, though now his shoulder and neck were its unintended targets. He flinched as the blade ripped through his skin. He swung his arm to block her attack and inadvertently backhanded her across the face.

She awoke with wild eyes and renewed flailing. Her heels dug into the ground and his legs as they fought to push her away from him. A low primal wailing reverberated through her lungs and escaped her lips. Slowly at first, like the first whistles of a teakettle. Then more frantic as her panic reached full steam. He lunged at her, his hand clasping her mouth to keep her from alerting a nosy neighbor. What would they make of this scene? What could they? Her cries staunched momentarily, he wrestled the razor blade from her hand, nearly losing a finger in the process.

He leaned into her. His forehead touching hers. "Edie," he whispered. "Edie, you were sleepwalking again. You, you were sitting out here cutting yourself. I'm going to let you go. I'm sorry I had to restrain you." He waited for her breathing to calm and then collapsed backwards into the lawn.

She pushed herself back against the tree as if she could burrow into it or, perhaps, become a part of it. But she didn't say a word. Not one word. Couldn't she see the mess she'd made of things?

He sat up slowly, careful not to spook her. He held his hands out between them and after a few breaths he bent over to examine the damage she'd done to herself. "Oh my god, Edie, what have you done?" Her bleeding was merely superficial. Her wounds criss-crossed through her skin in a haphazard way, which made sense for someone who cut themselves in an unconscious state. But the dozens and dozens of neat rows of scars revealed a far darker problem.

She pulled the hem of her nightgown from his hands and folded her legs beneath herself. Still she didn't try to defend her actions. "How long? How long have you been doing this, Edie?"

Something seemed to snap within her. Her body stiffened. She raised her chin and met his stare with an icy glare. "Ever since you took over my life. Ever since that night you took what you wanted from me and turned me into a harlot. I'm a goddamned cliché, Adrian. You trapped me. I am stuck with you all because I needed help in a class I really loved. All because I trusted my professor, the great Adrian Hillary, the pride of Columbia. The rapist of grad students."

She trailed off into an hysterical giggle that dug like claws into Adrian's temples. "What on earth are you talking about? You came on to me! I resisted until you practically threw yourself across my desk. Are you kidding me? How can you think I would ever...is that why you have been so distant these last few months?"

He leaned in to hold her but the look in her eyes, that of a wild cornered animal, made him think twice. She needed help. "Listen, Edie. The ability to surgically remove large chunks of fact from your hippocampus and replace them with fantasy is not normal. My darling, you need help. I...I should have recognized it. I should have known. You've been sleepwalking through life, Edie. It's like you stopped living, stopped growing, stopped feeling. Every since your parents..."

"Shut up! You don't get to talk about that. I told that to someone I thought I could trust. Then you took that trust and used it to poison me. To control me. To try to make me something I'm not."

"But what have I tried to make you, Edie?" Adrian suddenly felt exhausted and old. "What have I done other than endure the scandal of our love. I was forced to resign in front of all my peers, Edie. None of whom were man enough to stand up for me, to stand with me, after you falsely accused me of rape in public. All while in private begging me to keep you around and take you with me when I left. Now look where we are, my love. Because of you. Because of this damn hold you have on me. You think you're trapped? I'm the prisoner here." He slumped to the ground again. His strength and his will tapped.

Edie scoffed. "Now who's the one with the false memories, oh great professor? You're the captive? You own this house. You own our practice. You own me."

They were both silent. Having said more to each other than they had in months, maybe they were out of words. *Perhaps*, Adrian thought, *they were out of time.* His heart broke as he realized she was beyond even his help. He had been blinded by love for so long. He saw her clearly for the first time, a bloody mess huddled against a tree in the dark. But she was no innocent, hurt puppy dog. No. She was a coiled, cold-blooded snake, no better than the psychopath patient she was infatuated with.

He stood up and wiped his hands across his pants, adding blood to the mustard stains. "I feel sorry for you, Edie. I really do. How can you hope to help your patients when you're incapable of helping yourself? It's not all your fault though. I was a fool for thinking I could help you, to save you from your past, from yourself."

His words seemed to float past her, none sinking in as she sat perfectly still, her cold eyes never even blinking. Tears erupted from him with a force he'd never experienced as he choked out his next words. "We're done. Tomorrow I'll move into a hotel until we can sort out our affairs. I will, eventually, keep the house of course. I'm sorry, Edie. I just can't do this anymore."

Her mouth contorted into a smile, but it didn't reach her eyes. He recoiled at her crazed expression. As he turned to walk away, she whispered, "You can leave, but I won't make it easy for you. I won't be the victim. Not this time. Not ever again."

30

The warmth of the morning sun slowly melted Edie's dreams away. She awoke with a smile, feeling more rested than she had in months. As she stretched, the silky sheets slipped from her naked breasts. She pulled the blankets up to her neck and blinked as she looked around the room. The wrong room.

The curtains on the master bedroom's picture window were pulled open, which explained the sunlight that only a moment ago had felt refreshing. Now it felt intrusive. Adrian always neglected to close the curtains at night. Edie had long suspected he enjoyed the idea of other people watching as the two of them made love. She always made him close them, and even though nobody else lived with them, she also insisted the bedroom door be locked before she would give herself to him for the couple of minutes it took to get it over with. But she hadn't slept with Adrian or in this bedroom since they're fighting escalated weeks ago.

She took a slow breath and tried to recall how she'd gotten there. A peek under the covers confirmed she was naked. A fresh bandage covered her inner thigh. She ran her fingers over it. She sat up, kicking the sheet aside and slowly pulled off the medical tape. A familiar tightening clenched within her stomach as she took the gauze away and saw several fresh cuts. She gasped. Unlike her normal, steady handiwork, these new scars were jagged and crisscrossed each other as well as several of her older scars. She gasped for air and frantically wiped tears from her eyes as she pushed herself further into the safety of the bed. The coldness of the headboard's metal bars burned into her back.

Slowly, she brought her breath and her mind under control. A quick glance at Adrian's side of the bed confirmed he either hadn't slept with her or had made his portion of the bed when he got up, which was not like him at all. She didn't feel like they had had sex. He must have maneuvered her into bed and then slept in her room or, more likely, his den.

She looked around the room, but there was no trace of her nightgown or any other piece of clothing. The room was immaculate except for a broken water glass near the side table. It must have been knocked over when she went (or was put) to bed.

Maybe I walked to bed in my sleep, she thought as she bent to pick up the pieces of glass, *and my mind brought me to the room it was most used to.* Lost in thought, she barely noticed she'd cut herself until she looked down to see the blood dripping onto the glass shards she was picking up. She ran to the bathroom and wrapped her hand in a towel as she threw away the broken glass. She stared at herself in the mirror as she applied pressure and waited for the cut to stop bleeding. Aside from bedhead, nothing looked out of place or off. She threw the towel in the sink. She'd make Adrian clean up the mess later. It was his fault anyway for putting her to bed in the wrong bedroom.

As she reached for the bedroom door, she was even more convinced Adrian had put her to bed and hadn't tried anything in her sleep. Maybe he was serious about trying to make things work. As she turned the knob, the familiar click of the lock springing open jolted her from her thoughts.

SHE DIDN'T FIND ADRIAN IN HER BEDROOM IN THE TURRET. NOT that she'd expected to. Surely he'd prefer the couch in his office, or rather the whiskey in his office, to her quiet bedroom. She quickly showered and dressed, thinking all the while about the opened curtains, locked door, and broken glass. What the hell happened last night? It wasn't abnormal for her to not remember a sleepwalking episode, but she always had Adrian to fill in the gaps. And he was always eager to do so, taking on his professorial tone and using each occurrence as a teaching moment.

She stopped at the top of the cellar stairs and called down to him. She waited a moment, but when she didn't hear him rustling around, she slammed the cellar door and continued to the kitchen. It was good he hadn't poked his head into the stairwell. Her blood pulsed in her temple threatening to erupt like her mood. A cup of coffee would calm her. She should know better than to talk to anyone, let alone Adrian, before she'd had her morning fix.

He wasn't sitting at his normal seat at the island. Nor was his coffee mug in the sink. *Not a good sign*, she thought, as she reached for the coffeepot. It was cold. Just like Adrian to think only about himself and decide to stop for a cup of coffee on his way in to work. Either that or he was still passed out on his couch, whiskey seeping through his pores as he slept it off.

The lack of coffee was the last straw. For all his talk lately about how much he loved her and of wanted to make things work between them, he wasn't starting off in a very convincing way. She bounded down the hallway and flew down the stairs into the cellar. Adrian's office was dark and smelled of tobacco and whiskey. Just as she'd thought. She flipped the switch as she barked his name. But, as she quickly saw, she was yelling at an empty couch. In fact, the whole room was deserted. She walked around the bar. Who knew? He might have passed out on the floor there. But he wasn't there, and the bar area was immaculately clean, as was the rest of his office. Typical Adrian. The only room he ever took care of was his own.

She slowly plodded up the stairs, leaning heavily on the railing as she climbed. Back in the kitchen, she made a fresh pot of coffee. The aroma as it brewed helped to shake the cobwebs loose in her mind, but she still couldn't remember a thing about the night before. The last thing she remembered was going to bed in the guest room after a lonely dinner.

The first hot sips calmed her nerves. She sat in the kitchen and gnawed on a piece of toast as she finished two cups of coffee. With a sigh, she decided she couldn't put off facing the world any longer. She called a car service, locked up the house, and stood on the front stoop waiting for her ride, a third cup of coffee in hand.

A feeling in the back of her mind drew her across the driveway to their garage. She typed in the code, and before the door had rolled all the way open, she saw Adrian's car. What the hell. She touched the hood, something she'd seen in a cop movie once. It was cold. Obviously, Adrian hadn't moved it since parking it there yesterday evening. She laughed to herself. She pictured Adrian trying to sneak out early that morning to avoid a confrontation only to find that his prized possession wouldn't start. Again. Karma is a woman, my dear, and she is a bitch.

. . .

As Edie watched the city slide by outside her window, she tried to clear her mind of everything. She hoped that if she relaxed she might remember something, anything, about what happened last night. The more she couldn't remember, the more frustrated she became.

She looked down at her shaking hands. She placed them in her lap and counted to ten as she inhaled. Counted to ten again as she held her breath. Then counted to ten once more as she exhaled. She continued her breathing exercise until the world around her disappeared. All she saw were her hands. All she heard was the sound of her own breathing. She emptied her mind. Whenever a stray thought wiggled its way into her consciousness, she smiled at it and sent it on its way.

Still nothing came to her. No grand revelation. No lost memory. At least she'd calmed down. A child psychologist had taught her the simple breathing technique while she briefly lived in a children's group home. After her father. After the nightmare at the beach house. He hands began to tremble again. She briefly acknowledged the memories before neatly boxing them up and stashing them back into a deep recess of her mind.

One day she might be strong enough to deal with what happened back then. But not now. Besides, she had enough to worry about. Her fights with Adrian had grown in frequency and intensity lately. Something big was about to happen. She didn't know what, but she could definitely sense it. It was like a wall of storm clouds moving towards her on the horizon. No matter which direction she turned, the storm was coming. There was no place to hide. She'd have to stand and face it.

"Ma'am?"

Edie looked up with a start to see her driver staring back at her through the rearview mirror. The car was parked in front of her office building.

"Sorry," she said with a forced smile as she gathered her stuff and stepped out of the car. She looked up at the building as the car drove slowly away. She felt alone and lost. Like everything in her life was suddenly unfamiliar and new. Like she could just walk away and never look back and nobody would know. Nobody would miss her. She hesitated then went inside.

31

"What's wrong?" Timothy ignored the doc's question as he prowled the full length of her office. He felt amped up. Electrified. Like his skin was on fire. His mind raced. His vision blurred. It felt like the pre- and post-mission adrenaline of his military days. Of course those were fueled by a healthy dose of government-supplied 'supplements.'

He paced from one corner to the next. The office seemed smaller than usual. Every knickknack, every painting, seemed to vibrate with an energy he would swear radiated from his own body, like everything in the universe was connected and he was its center.

Timothy's eyes darted constantly from one spot in the room to another, never focusing on anything but seeing everything. He was convinced something or someone might jump up from behind the desk or couch at any moment.

He stood in the middle of the office and closed his eyes. His head fell back as if he were basking in the sun rather than the hum of florescent bulbs. He forced himself to slow his breathing. Breathe in for ten seconds. Hold for ten. Breathe out for ten seconds. Just as the doc had taught him. He felt her eyes on him, but thankfully she remained silent. After ten rounds of this breathing exercise, he opened his eyes. The room still vibrated around him, but it had dimmed to a subtle hum.

He walked over and took his place on the couch. "Are you wearing a wire?"

Her hand, which had been in mid-motion flowing across the page, stopped. She slowly looked up at him. Her eyes told him immediately he'd mis-stepped. He couldn't afford to lose her. He forced a laugh. It came out much louder than he'd meant it to. Noticing the bandages on her hand, he tried to move on, hoping she'd come along with him.

"What happened to your hand? You sure are getting banged up a lot lately. You and the ogre get into a fight? I bet you won, didn't you?"

She sighed on cue. "Mr. Ridle," she began, and he knew his deflection had worked, "how many times do we have to have this conversation?"

"Actually, doc, I thought we had settled it. I thought we trusted each other. Don't we?" He held her gaze until she looked down at her ribbon-filled notepad.

She looked off to a blank space on the wall over his shoulder, and he prepared for a more forceful rebuke. Instead, when she looked back, her eyes welled with tears. A single tear fell onto her paper, smudging her latest distracted doodle. He watched it fall as if in slow motion, as if, if he wanted to, he could slow it down, stop it, even reverse its course. The floodgate now open, more tears slid down her cheeks unchecked as she let out a great sob, followed by a slow moan that seemed like the escaping gasp of a child who'd been locked away, lost and long forgotten.

She looked at him with an intensity and a loneliness she'd never shown before. "He's gone," she whispered, as if she had no breath left with which to speak.

"That fatheaded fatso? What a relief. What happened?"

Her head dropped into her hands, and he could see the wince she tried to hide when the weight was too much for her damaged hand. "I don't know, really. We must have had a fight."

"What do you mean, doc? Feels like you'd probably know if you had a fight. You saying you hurt your hand because things got physical? Did you call the cops?"

"I sometimes sleepwalk," she admitted, her eyes shut tight. She was finally giving in and giving up her secrets. "All I know is that I woke up this morning, and he was gone. I assume he was out all night carousing and boozing it up like he used to. He can't stand to deal with things head on, but..."

"But what, doc? And how does that explain your hand?"

She raised her hand as if shaking her fist at the gods. "My hand is fine, dammit. It has nothing to do with Adrian or any of this. I cut it picking up a broken glass."

"So what's wrong? What aren't you telling me? Is there another woman?"

"There's always another woman, Mr. Ridle." Her eyes scanned his face with a look that was weary but wise. He felt her examining him, searching for a chink in his armor. "The thing is, his car was in the garage this morning, but he was still gone. We don't live close to anything he could walk to, not a bar, not even a liquor store."

Timothy sank back into the couch with a deep breath. "Is that all? Hell, doc, he probably just called a car service. How can you be so sure he's out getting wasted?"

"It's just what he does, Timothy." She sighed and sank back into her own chair. "He never could handle conflict. Especially when his own manhood is called into question. We used to fight a lot when our affair had lost its luster, when the excitement and naughtiness of it wasn't enough anymore to keep his attention."

Timothy leaned forward and reached for her damaged hand. She pulled it back before he made contact. "I'm sure he'll be back when you get home tonight. Either that or he'll come stumbling in here this afternoon, in the same rumpled clothes as yesterday, wreaking of booze and pretending nothing has happened."

She shook her head, and he couldn't tell if it was with resolve or sadness. "You don't know him. You have never seen him at his worst. He lost everything when he was forced to resign. He was a king on that campus, but then he had to tuck his tail between his legs and leave in disgrace, dragging me with him like some ill-gotten consolation prize."

The intercom on her desk buzzed, and the receptionist let her know her next appointment had arrived.

"I'm so sorry I took up all of our time, Mr. Ridle. Tell me, how are you?"

"It's okay, doc. I'm better than I've been in a while. Nothing to share really. I'll see you next week. Things will be better. You'll see."

He left before she could respond, nearly bumping into her next appointment in the hallway. He slowed outside of the asshole's office but didn't look inside.

32

The brightness and heat of the morning light shining through the living room window woke Edie from a dreamless sleep. She'd fallen asleep on the couch waiting for Adrian. She sat up with a start. She felt rested, like she'd slept, really slept, for the first time in years. What a time to overcome her nightly issues.

She checked the security system control panel by the front door. The alarm hadn't been disarmed all night. So Adrian hadn't returned. Where the hell was he? Did he retreat into the arms of another lover, someone with fewer or more interesting issues?

When she hadn't heard from him after her shower, her thoughts moved from jealous anger to the first whispers of worry. She dressed for work with little enthusiasm, all the while images of Adrian floated in and out of her mind.

First, he was with another woman. Then, he was dead in a ditch, his body all mangled and bloodied from a late night hit and run as he walked from some tawdry bar, trying to make it home to her. Then he sat, head in hand, his blazer wrinkled but neatly folded across his lap, in the drunk tank at some nearby

police station. Nursing nothing more than a pounding headache
and rueing the day he had met her.

She dumped the last of her coffee into the sink and placed
her cup neatly in the dishwasher. Her hand hovered above her
phone. What if he had been mugged or killed? Their neighborhood wasn't exactly safe. Particularly at night. Not for someone
like Adrian.

She sat back down at the counter and stared at her phone.
Willing him to call. She'd dialed his number a dozen times last
night and at least a dozen more this morning. Every call went to
voicemail, and he hadn't so much as texted her back. What a
relief a one-word missive would be right now. But he'd know
that and would refuse her even the smallest relief.

This is crazy, she told herself. He's a grown man. He'll be
back in his own good time. He'll have an excuse. He might even
have a present, a token of his love and an expression of the
promise that will accompany it. He'll change, he'll say. He can't
live without her, he'll plead.

With a sigh, she picked up her phone.

THE KNOCK ON THE DOOR STARTLED EDIE. AFTER CALLING THE
police, she put on another pot of coffee and camped out on the
barstool at the kitchen island. It was the one Adrian usually
claimed. Something about sitting where he so often did brought
her a little relief in what had become a strange couple of days.

She sat facing the window overlooking the driveway. She
could plainly see the dull Ford Taurus police cruiser sitting
there not more than twenty feet from the window. She could
even hear the ticking of the engine and the low hiss of steam as
whatever was leaking from that ancient monstrosity of tax-payer
apathy slowly trickled onto the drive. It was as if the ground
itself was rejecting the car above it.

And yet she hadn't noticed the car drive up nor heard the officer get out of the car through what was surely a creaky door. Her mind had been on sand, wind, the smell of the tide, and the faraway scent of smoke and roasting meat that drifted from campfires, food trucks, and random vendors along the boardwalk. There was a hint of something sickly sweet just under the surface. A copper smell she couldn't quite place but which made her heart beat faster and the breath catch in her lungs.

Another knock on the door finally pushed her from the past and off of the barstool. She shook her head to clear it as she shuffled to the foyer. She wished she hadn't called the police. She checked her reflection in the mirror. She looked the right amount of tired and distraught. She paused at the door to collect herself. After a deep breath, she pasted on a smile and greeted the officers.

"Hello. Thank you for coming so quickly." Edie had opened the door just enough to stick her head out.

The two police officers standing on her front porch looked like they had walked right out of central casting for a buddy cop movie that would be full of explosives, car chases, and funny quips. Surely it would be a box office smash despite being dismissed as derivative drivel by the critics.

One of the officers was older with the requisite tire around his belly that pushed the bulletproof vest under his shirt up into his neck, or rather necks. Its top straps surrounded his rather large and hairy ears, which from her vantage point seemed to be the only hair on his face or head. Edie couldn't tell immediately if he was excessively short or merely appeared so by standing next to his tall, lanky partner. His partner looked decades younger. He wore an aggressive mustache that covered his lips and seemed to mingle with his nose hair.

"Yes, ma'am. May we come in?" The younger one spoke with a nasal tone. Edie wondered if it had something to do with a hair clog in his nasal passages. She ducked her head behind the door to hide her smile. She coughed into her hand to cover the laugh she couldn't hold back, then she opened the door fully with a sweep of her hand.

"Of course, gentleman. Please."

She showed the two to the kitchen and offered them coffee while they discussed the reason she had called them. "I'm a little embarrassed to tell you the truth," she said after handing them their mugs of coffee. "Adrian doesn't do this often, but it's not the first time he has stayed away. I just….his car is still in the garage, and I...well, he's not the walking type if you know what I mean." Edie's eyes focused on the small rotund officer as she spoke these last words. *Oh where was Adrian*, she thought. He would love this show if he were here.

"What happened to your hand, ma'am?" the portly policeman asked.

Edie lifted her bandaged hand and looked at it as if noticing it for the first time herself. "I'm just a klutz I guess. I dropped a glass of water and cut myself picking up the pieces is all."

Edie's eyes narrowed as she watched the officer immortalize such a trivial fact on the pages of his tiny notebook. She shook her head and turned to his partner. "I'm worried that he got into trouble at a bar or on the way home if he decided to walk. Is it possible he's in your drunk tank?"

The young officer almost spit his coffee. He was definitely the comic relief to pudgy's straight man. Edie could almost hear the laugh track in her mind.

"No, ma'am. We don't really have a drunk tank. That's just a made up movie term. If we booked him for a drunken disorderly, he'd be in central holding until he posted bail. Then he'd still have to appear eventually in front of a judge. What's his name?"

"Adrian Hillary." She noticed the officer's face turn red as he turned to leave the kitchen, his hand reaching for the mic attached to his shoulder strap.

"I'll just call it in," he said with an off look on his face. "Be right back."

Officer Porky Pig got her attention with the incessant tapping of his pen on his note pages. "What time did you say your husband went missing, ma'am?"

"I didn't, and he's not my husband."

"Sorry, ma'am. You mean you don't know what time your, uh, boyfriend left?"

Edie rolled her eyes at the officer's high school vocabulary. "I have no idea. I didn't notice until I got up yesterday morning. So sometime between nine in the evening and seven in the morning, I guess." The gravity of her words pushed Edie backwards into the countertop. Her hands shook as they kept her from completely falling to the ground. Even when he wasn't here, Adrian could still control her, was still the center of her world.

"Do you mind showing me around, ma'am?"

"Not at all, officer."

There was no sign of Officer Nose Hair as they left the kitchen. Edie guided the other officer through the rooms of the main floor, most of them she realized they seldom used. Then she took him upstairs. She ignored the set of stairs to the guest room where it would be obvious someone was sleeping and took him directly to the master bedroom.

The officer pushed past her in the doorway, asking her to stay in the hall. *What a rude little man*, she thought. She hadn't a clue why he'd suddenly be so interested in the bedroom. Pervert.

She saw a camera flash in the ensuite bathroom where he'd disappeared to and wondered what could be so interesting that she hadn't noticed when she had gotten up that morning. He was jotting something down in that silly notebook of his as he came out of the bathroom. "Everything okay, officer? Did you find something?"

"Is there anywhere else in the house your husband spent a lot of time, ma'am?"

Edie cocked her head and studied his face as he finally looked up from his notes.

"Ma'am?"

"Yes. He spends a great deal of time in the cellar in his office. Right this way, officer." She had to stop herself from adding porky at the end.

When they got down to the cellar, Edie turned on the lights.

"Please don't touch anything else, ma'am, and would you stay right here, please?"

"Of course." Her pulse quickened. This was not at all what she'd expected.

The officer slowly made his way around the room. He paused at Adrian's desk and pushed some of his papers around with the back of his pen. He seemed to look admiringly at Adrian's walk-in humidor as he walked past it. He paused again in front of the bust of Sigmund Freud. "Some times a cigar is just a cigar."

"Excuse me?" Edie called from the doorway.

The officer ignored her. He turned away as he toggled the mic on his shoulder and spoke into it. Edie couldn't make out what he said.

The door at the top of the stairs opened. The younger officer stood in the doorway but made no movement. Edie turned back to the other officer and was startled that he was so close. She hadn't heard him approach.

"I'm afraid you'll have to come with us, ma'am," he said as he reached for his handcuffs.

33

Timothy shifted in the seat of his truck. He couldn't get comfortable. His mind raced. His ass hurt. And his doctor had stood him up.

When the receptionist had told him Edie wasn't in, he thought he had misheard her at first. The doc never missed a session. He remembered one appointment when she could barely speak and had interrupted his stories every few minutes with a hoarse cough that sounded like it was rattling around her chest, playing an off-key xylophone on the inside of her ribs before exploding across her lips. If she allowed people to touch her, he was sure he would have felt the heat of a fever. He would have sworn he could see the heatwaves radiating from her forehead.

He checked the old-school analog clock on his truck's dash. He'd been sitting outside her office for over two hours. Somewhere around hour one his ass had gone numb. A few minutes ago the feeling had suddenly returned with a vengeance and now it throbbed against the lumpy springs of the bench seat, which used to be leather but was now mostly duct tape.

He jumped out of his truck to give his cheeks a rest. He leaned against the door and wondered what could be more important than their session, this session. A lot had gone unsaid between them last time. He knew that. He was sure she did, too. Was she afraid to face him? Was she ashamed at all she had shared with him? With what she hadn't yet? He knew from experience that most psychologists keep their private lives to themselves. If they tell any anecdotes, they are generally about other patients. That always seemed weird to him. For all their talk of doctor-patient confidentiality, every one of them seemed eager to share the crazy shit they've learned from one patient in the name of helping another.

He did a couple high steps in place to get the blood flowing then leaned his elbows on the hood of his truck and stared at the front door to her office. He was parked in his favorite position across the street, although today he could have easily parked right next to the front door. It was late morning but the normally bustling lot was nearly empty. Was he forgetting some holiday? No. The slightly cute but overly annoying receptionist surely would have mentioned that. If it was a holiday, she wouldn't have been there in the first place to let him know the doc was out.

The weight of last week, how they left things, what they left unsaid, weighed on him. He knew they were at a crossroads in their relationship. They were either going to go forward together or he would go it alone from here on out. He hoped he wouldn't have to leave her. Strangely, she was his only friend. The first he'd had since he left the military. But last week showed him they may not be as close as he had imagined. They both had had an opportunity to speak and yet all he could do was pace around her office like some crazy man, and all she did was work on her little doodles with an energy and enthusiasm he'd never seen from her.

His mind made up, he scrambled back into the cab of his truck and peeled away from the curb. He knew her routines. If she wasn't at the office, nine times out of ten she was at home. She didn't seem to have a life outside of this place. He liked that about her. It was something they had in common.

34

The coffee tasted like someone had made it with stale coffee grounds that had been recycled for at least a dozen pots. Even with six teaspoons of sugar, its flavor still reminded Edie of what she imagined a gym sock would taste like if it were left in the bottom of a pot filled with tired, burnt coffee. She could see the bottom of the cheap styrofoam cup through the cloudy liquid. Still, it was hot. And she was bored. Funny how you could endure such torture in the name of boredom. The triviality of a bad cup of coffee became a welcomed thirty minute diversion, a much-needed exercise for a brain that had been worn down by hours of silly questions from stupid police officers who seemed polite on the surface but who obviously hoped she'd crack and confess to whatever it was they believed she had done to Adrian.

Adrian. This was all his fault. Any moment now he'd come waltzing in, his arm around some detective, a cigar smoldering between his fingers as he laughed like he'd just pulled the biggest and best prank in the world. He'd be ready to take her home to a new beginning. He'd smile and laugh the entire car ride, smug because she loved him enough to worry, to call the police. Then, in bed, he'd expect a little congratulatory action.

Edie prayed nothing was wrong with him so she could give him a piece of her mind and maybe a taste of his own medicine. But something in the back of her mind told her that her hope was misplaced.

The clock on the wall read midnight. It was officially Friday. She'd been at this police station for a little over fourteen hours. She had been searched, a bit overzealously, by a female officer with a five o'clock shadow and raunchy breath. She had been photographed, fingerprinted, and read her rights. Then they had taken and cataloged her shoes, purse, and phone before leading her to a holding cell. She didn't ask why she was being treated like a criminal, and so far nobody had volunteered that information.

Her cell wasn't much to look at. It felt like a shoebox compared to her home. A rusty bunk bed sat against one wall. Both mattresses were rolled up on their box springs. No sheets. No pillows. The tank of the stainless steel toilet doubled as a sink. No soap. Just a few squares of toilet paper. No mirror.

She had just unrolled the bottom mattress and sat down on the bed when the female guard Edie had nicknamed Quasimodo came and led her to a tiny interrogation room. And there, in a room even smaller than her cell, she'd been sitting in silence for most of her time at the station.

The lead detective had questioned Edie for hours without ever revealing what she thought she knew. She simply expected Edie to give up, give in, and confess to god knows what.

Edie had to be careful. She'd listened to enough true crime podcasts to know that cops, even the dumb ones, were good at getting innocent people to confess. They didn't care if they got the wrong person as long as they closed the case and could move on to the next. Assembly line justice. God bless America.

. . .

LIZ SAT AT HER DESK IN THE DESERTED DUTY PIT DEEP IN THE bowels of the Metro Patrol Station of the Kansas City Police Department. Her steel desk and matching chair radiated a coldness that befitted her mood. Even though the early fall temperature was fairly mild, inside the building it felt a good ten degrees colder. The department never kept the temperature regulated in this decrepit building. It always felt too hot in the summer and so cold in the heart of winter you could see your breath and needed gloves to touch the keys of your ancient computer. Computer was too lofty a term, really. Liz was convinced the machines they made her and her fellow detectives use were the missing evolutionary link between typewriters and computers. Criminals were getting more and more sophisticated, and yet here she was on something with less power than a Commodore 64.

She leaned back in her chair, careful not to let the back support tip her center of gravity and send her tumbling onto the floor as it so often did. She swung her weary legs up and rested her feet on her desk. The coldness of the surface threatened to creep into her toes, but this was the only position she could think in.

She flipped through the pages of the report she'd already memorized. Another rich, intelligent, professional woman who seemed to have it all. What was it with these women? By all accounts, they had worked hard to get where they were. Why put all of that in jeopardy? Why risk everything on a stupid, senseless act that was sure to ruin them? And why were they always, all of them, so bad at it? If it were her, she would know precisely what to do. Not that she'd thought about it much. Occupational hazard really. But there had been many times when her mind would wander, usually on a date with a dead-end prospect, and she could see the perfect crime formulating in her mind. It was so vivid. Like a step-by-step guide revealing itself, inviting her forward.

She shook her head. Damn late nights were killing her. She checked the clock on the wall. It was covered with a light film of dust and grease and hung crooked, but she could still make out the time. Twelve thirty. She was now officially entering hour fourteen of her twelve-hour shift.

She flipped the cover of the file closed and kicked her feet off the ice block of a desk. She'd let her uncooperative suspect chill long enough. It was time to get some answers so she could put this case and herself to bed.

LIZ POKED HER HEAD INTO THE OBSERVATION ROOM TO MAKE SURE Randy was awake and ready to start recording. "All set?"

Randy shot up from the couch Liz had spent too much time on herself. The fabric was almost transparent, and like most of the furniture in the place, duct tape adorned its many holes to help keep the springs from poking through. He rubbed his eyes and got up to sit at the equipment table. After checking to make sure a new tape was in the machine, no disks or optical drives here, he shook his head. "Yep. Sorry. Just taking advantage of the downtime."

"No worries. I've been there," Liz said as she looked through the glass at her subject. "She looks worn out. Let's see if we can finish this. Then we can all go home. Well, almost all of us."

After a final glance at her subject, Liz turned her attention back to Randy to assure herself he would stay awake. A confession wouldn't matter if he didn't do his job and immortalize it for the D.A.. As convinced as she was going to get at this time of the night, she took a deep breath, put on her game face and headed to the interrogation room.

. . .

LIZ SAT DOWN OPPOSITE YET ANOTHER SUSPECTED MURDERER. She nearly snorted as an inappropriate thought flashed through her mind. She shook her head and flipped open the file she'd brought with her, but she knew if anyone reviewed the tape closely enough they'd probably ask her what she was thinking as she sat down. The silly thought that rocketed past her mind's eye was that she had had more dates with murderers and dead people than with men in the last few years.

Luckily, her subject seemed to be dozing despite the bright lights and cold metal of the table and chair. "Good morning, Ms. McEvoy. I'm sorry it's so cold in here. I know this is the part in the movies where the friendly cop offers to have someone turn up the thermostat to gain the suspect's trust, but our HVAC is an ancient contraption that even our bomb squad guys are afraid to touch."

No response. *Tough room.* "Look. I know you want to get out of here. Maybe take a hot shower. Get a decent cup of coffee. Sleep in your own bed." Ms. McEvoy slowly raised her head and looked at Liz. *Wonder which one of those three options got her attention*, Liz thought. Maybe it was all of them. The lady's trifecta.

"Are you ready to talk now? I mean really talk?"

"About what? You've asked me the same questions over and over for hours. Do you know what the definition of insanity is, detective?"

Liz sat back in her chair and cocked her head. "Oh yes I do, Ms. McEvoy."

"It's Doctor McEvoy, actually, but call me Edie please. I hate my last name. It was my stepfather's."

Liz scribbled a note on her pad. "In my line of work it helps to know the definition, Edie. Sometimes people in your shoes like to play at it as if it'll lessen their crimes. You saying you want to talk about insanity?"

Edie shook her head and smiled. It was the tired, condescending smile of a practiced shrink. Liz had seen it many times in court. "I called you people, and I end up here. You ask me mundane questions repeatedly for hours. Then you waltz in with jokes all while calling me a suspect. I assume we are through with the mental beat down portion of your process. May we please move along to the real interview now? I really would like a shower and a real coffee."

"You want to be real now? Great. Mr. Hillary is dead, and I believe you killed him."

Edie's smile faded as she slumped back in her chair. Silent tears ran from her wide eyes down her face leaving trails through what little makeup remained. Liz studied her intently. A suspect's initial reaction when they know you know can be very telling.

"What are you talking about? How? Why are you just now telling me? I want to see him? How? Why? Why am I here? I need to be with him. I need to....Oh my god." Edie wailed into her hands.

Liz gave her a few minutes to compose herself. She'd give her an eight on her scale of believability. Not that she believed her. She just recognized a good act when she saw one. "That's a lot of questions. Let's start with what I know. The deceased..."

"Adrian. His name is Adrian," Edie interrupted.

"Adrian," Liz corrected herself as she jotted down another note and a question for later, "is dead. We know you and he fought a lot. We've already heard about an incident from earlier this year involving a patient that ended with you getting a black eye."

"Where did you hear that? That kind of thing is privileged.

And it was an accident. It happens in my line of work from time to time."

"That was a good answer, Edie. Not very original though. Let's try this one. How do you explain the screaming match between you and the deceased in the parking lot of your office the evening before he disappeared?"

There it was, Liz thought. A slight flinch and rapid blinking. Edie took a deep breath and stared directly at Liz with a look that could have melted the ice in this refrigerator of an interrogation room. "We were discussing a case. It got heated. People argue, detective. You and your boyfriend never fight?"

Liz coughed and continued on. "Sure. Sure. And the internet searches about serial killers? That all routine as well, Edie?"

EDIE DROPPED HER HANDS TO HER LAP AND SQUEEZED THEM HARD. She directed all of her emotion and effort into crushing her thoughts in her hands rather than showing them on her face. She wanted to look down. She knew they must both be bone white under the pressure. Better her hands than her face. But lowering her head would signal to this awful woman that she felt guilty, which she did not.

She took a slow, deep breath. "As you can imagine, detective, one in my line of work often has to search for things the average person might find distasteful or even suspect. I would venture that your browser history might look similar to mine, would it not?"

The detective, who had been leaning on her elbows with her face as close to Edie's as the rickety table would allow, slumped back in her chair. "Did he hit you?"

Edie smiled at the rapid change in the interview's direction. She occasionally employed the same technique with new clients. Keep them off their guard and they're more likely to tell you the truth. Lies take time to formulate, so an unnatural pause speaks volumes. And, frankly, lying becomes too tiring for most people after a while. They either give up or begin contradicting the lies they continue to tell.

"Adrian is like most men," Edie said. A slight smile curled at the edges of her lips as she held the detective's eyes with her own. "He has always had trouble controlling his basest instincts. They manifest themselves primarily when he is drinking, which he has rarely done since we moved here to Kansas City."

The detective looked up while continuing her furious note taking. "So the extensive wine collection and expensive whiskey?"

"All for show," Edie said as she shook her head slowly. "Another symbol of his status and virility. He wants desperately for the world to see him as a man's man, to view his good tastes as a measure of his good nature."

"So the whole mess of empty wine and whiskey bottles we found in the cellar, those were just for show as well?"

"I never insinuated that Adrian is a teetotaler, detective. Merely that he doesn't drink that much. The bottles are from years of accumulation. He is a brilliant but lazy man. Too self important to remember to take the glass to the recycling center."

"How long have you and Adrian lived in the city?"

"Almost four years."

"I see," the detective said as she flipped to a new page in her pad and wrote another manic note. "Would you like to know how Adrian died?" She asked in such a matter-of-fact way that the hairs on Edie's neck tingled and a shiver raced up her spine and shook her shoulders.

"Excuse me?"

"It's just that you haven't asked about the details of your boyfriend's death. Most people have a lot of questions, the most obvious being how their loved one died."

Edie and the detective looked at each other for a long time. All motion in the room seemed to stop. Edie searched the detective's eyes and demeanor for any clue of her thoughts and next steps. She could tell the detective was doing the same.

"I'm sure you know, detective, that people process grief in a number of ways. Questions or a lack thereof are no more an indication of wrongdoing than a sweaty brow or an inability to meet one's eyes. There is no one biological response to tragedy."

The detective dropped her pin and turned her head. She stared at the mirror that took up one entire wall of the interrogation room. Edie wondered if she was waiting for some telepathic sign from a supervisor or partner on the other side of the glass.

"Was your boyfriend a Freud disciple?"

Edie frowned and blinked at the oddity of the question and yet another abrupt turn in the conversation. "Yes. Like many male psychologists of his age, he holds Freud's theories in high regard."

The detective's frantic writing continued anew as she shook her head and bit her bottom lip. "Well, that explains the cigar then."

"What on earth are you talking about?"

"We found Adrian's body in the middle of the rose garden at Loose Park. He was naked and on his knees. His face in the dirt. His hands tied behind his back with a lace sash. A single rose had been placed between his teeth. And an expensive cigar, the kind we found in your cellar, was shoved up his backside."

Edie slapped a hand over her mouth to silence the laugh that had erupted from deep within her. Even as her laughter intensified, her tears flowed freely.

"Funny, huh? An elderly woman stumbled upon the display while taking her dog for an early morning walk. She nearly had a heart attack."

Despite the terrible night she'd had, despite Adrian's disappearance and brutal murder and the fact that she appeared to be the prime suspect, Edie was suddenly overwhelmed with a single question. "Tell me, detective, have you ever been to a haunted house?"

LIZ SHOOK HER HEAD. WHAT AN ODD WOMAN SHE WAS DEALING with. Probably psychotic. Clearly a sociopath. She showed no remorse for her dead boyfriend and laughed at the humiliating way his body was left to be discovered. "His throat was cut, and a single stab wound went straight through his heart," she continued, refusing to be thrown off by Ms. McEvoy's strange question. "In your professional opinion, what kind of person are we dealing with?"

Her suspect shook her head slowly and leaned back in her chair. After a moment she stretched, raising her arms over her head and arching her back. She placed her hands in her lap deliberately and slowly rolled her shoulders as she looked off to the side and stared at the mirror on the wall. It seemed to Liz as if she were looking right through it. She was sure the officer on the other side found it a little disconcerting.

"Surely you don't expect me to do your job for you, do you?" Ms. McEvoy said as she turned to look directly at Liz, cocking her head, and smiling slightly. "I mean, if this is the way you treat all your expert witnesses, I'm surprised anyone ever agrees to help you."

"Did Adrian have any enemies?"

Liz shook her head and made another note as Ms. McEvoy let out another uncontrolled burst of laughter and shifted in her chair. "Oh yes, detective. He was quite good at collecting people who found him repugnant."

"Like who? I need names."

"Whom."

"Excuse me?"

"It's like whom, not who."

Now it was Liz's turn to shift in her chair. She slowly set her pen down on her notes, happy with herself that she hadn't thrown it as was her first impulse. "Ms. McEvoy," she said through clenched teeth. "You don't seem to be taking this very seriously. Someone you supposedly loved has been murdered. Why aren't you more interested in helping us catch the person who did this?"

The suspect brought her hands up from her lap and clasped them together on the cold surface of the metal table. She took a slow breath, looked right at Liz, and cocked her head slightly. "Don't patronize me, detective. You and I both know, as do the people behind that glass, that I am the only person you are investigating for Adrian's death. And I can tell you that you are wasting your time as well as mine."

Liz stood up and walked over to the mirror. She spoke into it as she looked at Ms. McEvoy's reflection. "Then help us stop wasting your time. Help us understand your relationship. Give us some names of other potential suspects so we can clear you and move on with this investigation."

Liz watched Ms. McEvoy's reflection closely. She sat perfectly still. Her posture was impeccable for someone who had spent so much time awake and in the uncomfortable furniture in the station. She looked tired, but barely disheveled. Certainly more put together than most suspects after more than 24 hours of waiting and interrogation.

Slowly, the woman in the reflection pushed her own chair back and quietly crossed to the opposite side of the tiny windowless room. She leaned against the faded grey cinderblock wall and spoke to the floor. "What is it you want to know?"

. . .

THE DETECTIVE TURNED TO FACE EDIE FROM ACROSS THE ROOM. Edie smiled slightly at the way the detective put her hands in the pockets of her blazer and leaned against the two-way mirror. She was mimicking Edie's posture, a common psychological trick. It subconsciously relates to the patient that the two of you are on the same page, in sync. That the doctor, or in this case junior league detective, is on your side.

To test her hypothesis, Edie raised her right foot and pressed it against the wall behind her as if she needed the extra support to maintain her balance after such a harrowing ordeal as the death of her lover and nearly thirty hours of police custody and questioning.

"Do you know why there is a knife missing from your kitchen?" the detective asked in what Edie was sure was meant to be a nonchalant way. She didn't move. Didn't mirror Edie's new stance.

"And how exactly do you know that?" Edie asked.

"Quite simple, really," the detective said as she raised her right foot and rested it against the wall behind her shin. "We counted them. Not only do you have an odd number, but there is a spot in your butcher block where a knife should go, but it's missing."

"Maybe it's just in the dishwasher."

"We looked."

"Maybe it broke, and we hadn't gotten around to buying a new one."

"It's a chef's knife."

"I don't know what that means, but we probably just used a different one."

"You don't have another chef's knife."

"And you know this how?"

"As I stated, we inspected and counted all of your knives, Ms. McEvoy."

"Oh."

"So would you mind telling me where it might be?"

Edie smiled. She was beginning to like this detective. She couldn't control how long she would be a guest of the KCPD or what insipid questions she'd have to endure, but that didn't mean she couldn't have a little fun. It might even help the time go by faster. "I think you have the wrong idea of Adrian and me."

"I do? Please enlighten me." The detective sauntered to the table, sat down and poised her pen to capture Edie's explanation even though every word was being recorded.

Edie walked over and took the detective's place at the mirror. She tried to make out the person or persons she knew were mere feet from her, but all she saw was the detective patiently waiting for her suspect's story to begin. "The thing you need to know about Adrian, detective, is that most everything in his life is a show."

Edie heard a man sigh to her left on the other side of the glass. *Is her life that boring*, she thought. The detective either didn't hear her colleague or chose to ignore him. "What do you mean? Are you suggesting Adrian was a con man?"

Edie laughed. "Of course not. Nothing that banal. No, Adrian is all about showing off his superiority. It's why he drives a classic car that rarely runs. Why he smokes only Cuban cigars, drinks whiskey and wine that is not only hard to find but incredibly expensive. And, detective, it's why he insisted on remodeling the kitchen when we bought the house despite the fact that neither one of us can cook to save our lives."

"So you're telling me you never used your chef's knife?"

"What chef's knife. You're the one who says we don't have one."

"You had one. It's missing."

"I guess I might have used it occasionally to butter some toast or to open a jar."

"You don't use a chef's knife to butter bread or open jars, Ms. McEvoy."

"And I didn't use it to murder Adrian as you're so clumsily suggesting I did."

"I'm not suggesting anything. I'm merely trying to ascertain the facts."

Edie sighed as she fell into her chair. She leaned forward on her elbows and clapped her hands together in front of her nose. "Your fascination with a missing knife tells me one of two things. Either the knife isn't missing, and you found it sticking out of Adrian's chest, or it is missing but your medical examiner has told you it would be a potential match for Adrian's wounds. In either case, I am telling you I did not use it — to butter bread or to kill my boyfriend."

The detective leaned in, pointing her pen at Edie to accentuate each word. "You don't find it odd that your boyfriend's possible murder weapon came from your house and is now missing? Wouldn't that make you suspicious if you were in my shoes, Ms. McEvoy?"

"Sure, but as I've told you, the kitchen was for show. Whenever we entertained, which wasn't often, Adrian had food catered in. He controls everything. It is always about ego and image with him, down to the minutest of details. Freud would have loved him."

"Did you love him?"

"Excuse me?"

The detective pursed her lips and squinted as she looked into Edie's eyes. "You heard me. Did you love Adrian, Ms. McEvoy?"

Edie sat in silence. Every muscle tensed. She felt stuck, in both physical motion and metaphysical thought. Just breathing became something she must concentrate on. "Of course I did," she whispered as she slowly exhaled and looked at the floor in the corner of the room.

The detective made more of her retched notes in her pad. Edie studied her face, but it gave nothing away.

"We found his blood in the kitchen. Can you explain that?"

Edie hung her head at the latest neck-breaking change of topic.

THE SILENCE HUNG BETWEEN THEM FOR SEVERAL MINUTES. Weariness clung to Liz. She made a point to periodically move her feet. Otherwise, the soles of her shoes threatened to melt into the icy slab of concrete that formed the floor of the tomb-like interrogation room. As tired as she felt, she knew that exhaustion must be circling around her suspect. She could use that. Most confessions come when suspects are too tired to keep their story straight or just want to make things stop so they can sleep for a few hours. But if this particular subject was on the verge of giving up, Liz couldn't see it. Ms. McEvoy was holding up better than most.

"Look, detective, I know you're just doing your job. I'm sure you even believe you're good at it. But your continued amateurish assumptions, clumsy attempts at traps, and superficial understanding of Adrian's life are wearing thin."

Liz chuckled to herself. Suspects had called her every name in the book, taken swings at her, one even broke her jaw. It had to be wired shut. She couldn't talk for a month. She remembered how her boyfriend at the time had given her shit about that. On the one hand, he said he liked that it shut her up. On the other, he wished she could still use her mouth for other things. But no one had ever come close to the elegance of Ms. McEvoy's verbal assaults. It was definitely going to be a long day.

"Why don't you help me out then. You're obviously smarter than I am. Educate me please."

Her suspect sighed. Her eyes were bloodshot but still looked at Liz with an alertness that made the hairs on the back of her neck stand on end. "Are you suggesting, detective, that if your crack squad of crime scene technicians were to scour your kitchen, they wouldn't find traces of your blood? People bleed in their kitchens, and in their bathrooms. Am I to believe your entire theory of me as the killer hinges on the fact that you found blood in our kitchen?"

Liz sat up. She couldn't help but smile as she set her pen down. She looked at the mirror then back at her suspect. "A kitchen you are on record as stating was just for show."

The laugh bounced off the cinderblock walls and ricocheted from the corners to the mirror and seemed to circle around Liz's head. "Am I guest-starring in a bad legal drama? Are you seriously this incompetent? The very fact that the kitchen was hardly used would seem to indicate that the occupants of that kitchen, Adrian and myself, would be more likely to injure ourselves while trying to keep up domestic appearances."

Liz looked down at her notes. She could feel the eyes on her. One set from across the table. Another from behind the glass. No matter what this wicked woman said, Liz knew she was guilty. After 21 years on the force, nearly 10 as a detective, she could always feel when someone was lying. Evidence or no. She had learned to trust her gut more than her own rational thoughts. She knew this woman was a murderer.

"You have a tidy answer for everything, don't you?" she said while still studying her notes. "I find that most calculated criminals do." She looked up and met her suspect's cold gaze. "They have had a lot of time to get their story straight. To think through all the questions and find neat little answers that show they couldn't possibly be involved. So, I'd very much like to hear your answer to my next question."

EDIE NEEDED TO BLINK, BUT SHE REFUSED TO BE THE FIRST TO look away. She was tired. Of these games. Of this woman. Of her life.

"Can you explain why we found your DNA near Adrian's body? As I've informed you, we found him at a park several miles from your house. And you've already told me you had nothing to do with it. So, please, let's hear your neat little excuse for that troubling fact."

Edie cocked her head. She stared unseeingly into the far corner of the room. Loose Park. How? She hadn't been there for months. The blood from her little session surely would have degraded by now.

A knock on the door startled her from her thoughts.

"What?" the detective called over her shoulder, her eyes still on Edie.

A slight man slunk through the door and whispered something in the detective's ear. They both looked at Edie. "Impossible. We're not done here. It will have to wait."

"What is it?" Edie asked.

"Nothing."

"If it concerns me, I'd appreciate you sharing it with me."

"Ms. McEvoy, this is a police matter. If you hadn't noticed, you're being investigated for murder."

"Am I under arrest?"

"Not technically."

"Is this something concerning me?"

"Ms. McEvoy..."

"I want to call my lawyer."

35

Edie rode quietly in the back of the car she had called from the police station. The detective had offered to have an officer drive her home, but the last thing Edie wanted was to spend more time in the presence of the police. And she had seen a true crime show once about a murderer who was convicted when the police captured a phone call the suspect thought was private while being taken home in the back of a police cruiser equipped with special audio recording equipment. The police, like most people, will do whatever they think they must when they believe they're right.

She closed her eyes and leaned her head against the side window of the car. Its hard, cold surface reminded her of the interrogation room she'd just spent a day in. Her mind replayed the questioning on a loop. The detective. The silly mirrored glass wall. The sounds of the ocean. And blood. So much blood.

She awoke with a start. *Keep it together, Edie*, she whispered to herself. She was starting to feel like one of her patients. Timothy. He was the reason she was no longer enduring that unpleasant detective's interrogation. The interruption in her questioning happened because her receptionist had called with a patient emergency. The police had to take Edie's request for her lawyer seriously. He quickly eviscerated their wafer thin evidence, told them they would embarrass themselves, their department, and the DA if they took what they had to a judge, and walked her out the door thirty minutes after he arrived.

He told her she wasn't out of danger yet as he put her into the car. The police are like a dog with a bone, he warned her. Once they get their teeth around it, they won't let go for anything.

The thought of that smug detective chomping on a bone, her head shaking vigorously from side to side, her eyes wild, made Edie smile as the car pulled into her driveway.

THE HOUSE WAS STILL, BUT EDIE'S MIND RACED AS SHE SHOWERED in the bathroom off the guest bedroom she'd called her own for months. Other than the quietness, the house didn't feel any different. Shouldn't it?

As Edie dressed for her impromptu appointment with Timothy, she felt alone and exhausted but somehow free. Her mind hopped around memories of Adrian. The first time she saw him from her seat in a crowded lecture hall. He was so full of life. Full of himself. But his smugness seemed sexy then. Their first sexual encounter. Forced. Brutal. Unexpected but also exciting. The line between rough and rape was but a thin membrane.

She brewed a cup of coffee while she waited for another car. She wanted to cancel on Timothy. How could she be of any help to him today? No sleep. Accused of murder. Suddenly a...was there an equivalent word for widowed when your boyfriend dies? She drank her coffee and absently stared out the kitchen window.

She'd see Timothy and fake her way through another rambling session. It was the least she could do for the favor he had done for her.

36

The slice was surgical and precise. As always. A wave of pleasure with just a hint of painful undertones rippled across her skin, shivering her spine and scrambling her mind for a brief orgasmic moment. Edie marveled at her one special skill. It was a calling really. It always felt like a higher power guided her hands.

She sat in her private bathroom at the office and patted the blood lightly with an alcohol-soaked wad of toilet paper. Her elation quickly tumbled into fury at the site of the bastardized scars on both thighs. Their ragged edges and inconsistent depths cut large swaths across her uniform rows of cuts on the pleasure zones of her inner thighs. She'd never cut herself like that during a sleepwalking episode.

She blamed Adrian and Timothy. The pressure and anxiety of treating Timothy along with the constant pain of life with Adrian had been too much. Men ruin everything. She hated that Adrian discovered her little secret that way. It was supposed to be just for her. At least he wasn't around to lecture her or to look at her with condescending pity as he often did.

And what of Timothy? She had rushed from the police

station to the office, stopping only quickly to shower away the day-and-a-half of stress stench. She knew the police would be watching, so even though she wanted to cancel their session, she had to keep up appearances.

Everyone wanted to talk as soon as she walked through the door. The receptionist couldn't even get through a hello without breaking down into an ugly sobbing cry that sent her running to the bathroom to compose herself. Edie assumed she was one of many women at the office and around town who would react that way to the news of Adrian's death. Edie herself still hadn't cried. Not for him at least.

After bandaging her fresh cuts, Edie gently pulled up her slacks and put her tools back in their hiding place under the sink at the bottom of a large box of extra heavy menstrual pads.

Out in her office, she sat quietly at her desk. What was she to do about Timothy? She had never felt threatened by him. Not really. She knew she should. And she knew that based on what she and Adrian had discovered about him she should have turned him in to the police a long time ago. Adrian's death and the torturous hours of interrogation she'd just endured had been the perfect opportunity. Perhaps it would have made the conversations with that nasty detective easier.

During her shower and on the drive to the office, she became more and more convinced that Timothy had killed Adrian. But why? He was an admitted killer, but of women. Was she next? Maybe he got Adrian out of the way so he could get to her more easily and take his time with her. She shook her head. She just didn't feel like he was a danger to her. There had been unrelated bad blood between Timothy and Adrian. Maybe Timothy suspected that Adrian was going to alert the police to their suspicions.

She glanced at the phone. If she called the police now, would they wonder why she hadn't told them sooner? Would they consider her an accomplice? She sighed. He would be in her office soon. She didn't have time to call. She needed to know more first, anyway. She gathered her notes and walked over to open the office door. Whatever happened, she needed to know the truth before she did anything.

"Doc!" Timothy spread his arms and went in for the hug he knew she'd reject. As if on cue, his doctor and confidant backed away from him. She seemed to shrink into herself as he approached. Her eyes widened. He could see the red veins winding their way to her dilated pupils. She curled her arms in front of her. Her notepad acting as a shield to his gregarious attack.

He shrugged and took his place on the couch. She slowly unwound her extremities from around her torso and took a seat across from him. She stared unrelentingly at her notepad as if she were expecting all of life's secrets, or maybe just his, to reveal themselves to her there.

"You look tired, doc. They waterboard you in that jail?" She didn't respond. Didn't appear to move, though he could see her chest was moving so at least she was still alive. "I've been there," he said, shaking his head with a laugh that felt too loud and too light for the tension in the room. It threatened to bow the walls outward as the unspoken thoughts between them expanded like so much air in a pressure cooker.

"I'm tired, too," he continued as if she were raptly listening or at least doodling as she would on any other day. "Why you ask? Well, I had a big night. Really big."

His last words hung between them. Content with his intriguing conversation starter, he sank back into the pillows of the couch. He crossed his legs and picked at a random piece of lint as he waited for a sign of life.

Slowly, as if she were fighting to swim to the ocean's surface, the force of the waves pushing on her as the undertow pulled at her feet, she took a breath and looked at him for the first time in days.

"There you are, doc," he said with a smile. "Welcome to the party. It's okay. You'll get used to those feelings soon. Or you'll learn to bury them. Either way, you'll be able to cope as well as I do before you know it."

The doc shook her head, and Timothy swore he could see the ocean's water spraying from her hair as if she were walking up to him out of the surf. Ever since he learned where she came from, he could only ever picture her on the beach. Sometimes she was topless, but mostly she wore modest one-piece bathing suits. Even in his imagination, she was mostly demure with just a hint of the wildfire he knew burned beneath the surface.

He waited for her to speak. To yell at him. To thank him for getting her out of that jail. Anything. But she just stared at him. Daring him to look away. So they sat in silence. Neither wanting to be the first to break the connection. Each searching for answers in each other's eyes. The clock on the wall made the only sound in the room as it measured the seconds and minutes of their silent pleas to one another.

"Adrian is dead." She whispered the words so softly that at first Timothy thought she had placed them in his head through some kind of telepathic connection. He hadn't even seen her lips move. But then her head dropped, and he saw the tears fall like lonely rain drops onto her empty notepad. "I've lost everything."

He wanted to rush to her, to throw the table between them to the side and grab her into his arms so she knew he was there and would always be there for her. Instead, he slowly uncrossed his legs and leaned forward. He waited for her sobbing to slow and her breath to deepen.

She wiped her eyes clumsily with the naked backs of her

hands. She seemed so childlike in that instant that Timothy almost felt sorry for her. He sighed at his own weakness and waited for her to recover.

When she finally raised her head, her eyes were puffy and ringed with red like some kind of demonic raccoon. Those beautiful orbs, those windows into her very soul, pleaded with him. He couldn't hold her gaze. He dropped his head and stared instead at his feet and his newly polished boots.

"Everyone owes nature a death," he whispered to the floor.

THE BREATH STUCK IN EDIE'S THROAT. THE RAPIDLY DEPLETING oxygen in her brain fueled the acceleration of thoughts that threatened to make her head spin. She blinked. She could actually picture her head turning around like some horror movie about demonic possession or an old school Warner Brothers cartoon in the days before concerned mommies complained about the excessive violence their poor children were exposed to.

"What did you just say?"

Timothy yawned. His long arms stretched toward the ceiling causing the hem of his shirt to expose his sculpted abs. In every way he was the antithesis of Adrian, and yet they both had captivated Edie in their own way. "I just meant that none of us are super heroes or gods. We're all going to die. It's just that some of us do the world a favor and do it sooner than others."

He smiled. Edie couldn't tell if he was trying to comfort her or confess to her. That smile, the crooked grin that had once intrigued her, now made her break out in a cold sweat. Her muscles tensed. Her stomach felt like it was in knots. "What did you do?"

Timothy's smile melted into a frown as he cocked his head. He stared at her for a long time. Neither one of them seemed to want to be the next to speak. "Doc, you're tired. I've been there. Up all night. Questioned. Accused. Caged like an animal."

"Tell me what happened and tell me now, Mr. Ridle!"

She was on her feet. Her empty note pad, devoid of even a single doodle, tumbled from her lap to the floor. Her hands flew to her hips like her mother's used to do when she had scolded Edie as a child. Her face felt flushed. Her heart, what was left of it, threatened to beat out of her chest.

Timothy blinked. He shook his head slowly and gently stood. Only a small table stood in his way. She had never felt more exposed. Perhaps sensing her fear, he slowly raised his palms in front of him. "It's okay, Edie. I know it hurts. That's what I'm trying to tell you. I understand you, what you're going through. And you're not alone."

They stood like that for what felt like hours. A silent stand off. Eventually, Edie sat down. Her body ached, and she couldn't stop the flood of tears. It was an ugly cry. A loud one. All she wanted to do was curl up in a ball and sleep. Sleep until this became the dream and her dreams reality.

She knew her question had been a mistake. Maybe even a deadly one. But she had nothing left to lose. She'd been floating along for so long in Adrian's wake she didn't really have a life of her own. Still, if she were to be next, she at least wanted to know why. And such a blunt approach wouldn't work with Mr. Ridle. Whatever else he was, he wasn't stupid.

"I'm sorry, Mr. Ridle. You're right. I'm letting my emotions rule me today."

He seemed to calm down a little as he sat back down on the couch. "I understand, doc. I really do. Probably more than you know. Do you want to call it a day?"

Edie took a slow, calming breath and looked up at the patient who had walked into her life nearly a year ago and had single-handedly destroyed everything she had built as if it were a house of cards and he were a light breeze. She looked into his eyes, but the answers weren't there. She stared at his hands, but they gave no clues either. No sign of the lives they must have taken, the last breaths they might have stolen.

She looked down at her own hands in her lap. Her words pierced the silence in a hushed tone, as if she were talking to herself. "Have you ever been driving in a car, you know like in the passenger seat, and suddenly felt the urge to just open the door and throw yourself out? To end it all? Because you don't deserve to be alive. You've done too much harm, hurt so many people. And you know no matter how deep you bury the hunger you will do it again. And keep on doing it until someone finally figures it out. Figures you out. And by then you'll be so tired and so grateful that you just confess everything because you don't have the strength to keep going but are too weak to stop yourself."

When she looked up at her patient, she saw they were both silently crying.

Timothy set his jaw and bit his tongue. His throat constricted, and his breath threatened to turn to sobs. He looked down at his watch with a tilted head. Trying to focus. To concentrate on anything but what she was saying and how she sounded as she said it. And still the tears came. They started as a light drizzle. Easily swept away by the back of a hand. Barely detectible. Silent. And then the storm broke. He had spent his whole adult life trying to stay in control of his emotions. His ability to bury them and compartmentalize them was like something from a psychologist's dream. And yet here he sat. Blubbering like a schoolboy who had disappointed his mommy.

He felt her silence before his ears registered it. He knew she was looking at him, searching for meaning in his breakdown. She was the only one he would allow to see him vulnerable like this. None of his mother's men ever saw him cry. Not even as they beat him harder trying to get the satisfaction of his tears. He didn't lose it at the sight of dead children blown to bits by the Americans sent to protect them in the godforsaken desert. He shed not a single tear when his best friend took a high-caliber round to the face when they were on a routine patrol that turned out to be a trap set by their Afghan counterparts.

But today, after all she had done for him and he for her, he could no longer hold back his emotions. He took a slow, jagged breath. And looked at her with eyes ringed in red. His voice cracked and his throat burned as he softly spoke. "I did it for you."

Now it was his turn to search her face. Her eyes widened and her jaw went slack. He marveled at her mouth even though he knew this wasn't the time for such thoughts. If he could just kiss the corner of her mouth, nibble lightly on those lips, she would have to feel what he felt.

He blinked the thought away. Still she just sat there. Staring not at him but through him. Her mind seemed to be somewhere else. Maybe she was stuck, unable to process what he'd just confessed.

"I love you, Edie." The words tumbled out of his mouth before he knew he was going to say them. As if they shot directly from his heart, bypassing his brain. He flinched and turned away from her. He glanced at the door as he rang his hands. He shook his head at the thought of running away. He could never outrun his feelings for her. Of all the women he'd known, he'd never felt like this before. He'd never known love before. Not really. Not more than on a superficial level that would fade soon after he recognized it, leaving him searching for another hit.

He turned to face her. "Say something, doc. Please."

EDIE LOOKED AT HER PATIENT, BUT SHE NO LONGER SAW HIM. NOT really. Her eyes blinked slowly over and over. She was aware it was happening but incapable of stopping it. The man in front of her casually blinked on and off before her eyes. He was like a sick mirage. A badly tuned TV channel showing some late night horror fest. The lazily revolving beacon on the top of a lighthouse. Only he wasn't warning her of danger ahead. He was inviting her to jump into the rocky shore.

She wished with all her heart she could close her eyes and make him disappear, like Adrian, forever. She gasped silently at the thought as it looped around her mind. She had despised Adrian, hated the life he had made for her, the way he treated her as if she were some petulant child and sexual plaything rather than an equal, a partner, a loved one to be cherished, respected, and admired. But she had never wished him dead. Not really. Sure, in a fleeting moment or a dream, she would wonder what life would be like without him.

None of those dreams had ever looked like this. On one hand, the cops suspected her of murder, on the other an admitted serial killer and rapist had just casually confessed to Adrian's death and in the same breath exclaimed his love for her.

She felt her stomach clench. Not in pain. Startled, she realized it was a laugh threatening to escape. It would be inappropriate for sure, but no more so than the confessed murderer of her erstwhile lover likewise confessing his love for her.

He sounded just like Adrian. Going on and on about how much he loved her and that everything he did was for her. Like it was really her fault Adrian seduced her then raped her. It was her fault her patient's unabated infatuation with her led him to murder her lover.

She had never asked for their love. And she never went looking for the kind of love that would lead to this. Besides, neither of them deserved her love. They didn't ask for it. They just sought to take it. And they'd certainly never earned it with their sadistic, caveman logic that all men seem to share. I do you a favor; you love me. What a bunch of chauvinistic bullshit. This is the world men have built.

She suddenly understood just how similar Timothy and Adrian were. Particularly their views and treatment of women. Maybe that was why she was so drawn to Timothy. Some weird Stockholm transference. Then, with sadistic irony, it dawned on her. It wasn't just Timothy and Adrian. All men see the world this way. Everything, even women, especially women, is theirs for the taking. It had always been this way and it would never stop.

She looked down at her lap. Her hands were twisted together like the old-world grape vines that made the red wine Adrian had so enjoyed. She thought of Adrian's wine cellar. *My wine cellar now* she reminded herself. Her mouth felt dry. The thought of a glass, hell a bottle, of wine sounded like heaven right now.

"Doc?" With a single word she was sucked back in to the nightmare her life had become. "Doc, are you okay? I didn't mean to blurt that last part out. I'm...I'm sorry. That was unfair of me. But I have been keeping secrets my whole life. From everyone. And I can't do that with you. Not anymore. Not after what has happened."

"What has happened, Mr. Ridle? What exactly did you mean when you said you did it for me? What, exactly, is the 'it' you've supposedly done? And why? Why the hell did you assume I wanted whatever it is done in the first place? I'm not some help-less damsel in distress waiting to be saved. Especially not by you. I didn't ask for any of this. Do you understand me?"

She inhaled deeply. Her thirsty lungs took a long sip of fresh air. Her face felt flushed. Her whole body shook. She was on the verge of more tears, which would likely lead to a full-fledged melt down if she didn't get control of herself.

He didn't answer. He looked as if she'd slapped him, or as if he expected her to at any moment. She thought she should just to get it over with. But regardless of the tears he'd shed, he was an admitted murderer who had shed a lot of innocent blood for less. Her indignation, righteous as it was, had to be tempered for the sake of her own life.

He shook his head. She saw rage flash in his eyes for just a second. Then a deep pain settled in to his gaze. If she hadn't been looking, she might have missed it. A chill shivered down her spine.

"We're the same, doc, you and me." His words came slowly, as if he were measuring the weight of each syllable before letting it cross his lips. "You may not see it yet. But I do. I always have. It's as clear as anything I've ever seen. I know it like I know my own name. Like I know the sun will rise tomorrow. Like I know that fat fuck is dead and will never hurt you again. I'll never let anyone hurt you again."

Edie's breath caught in her throat. She felt her heart pound in her temples. Her whole body felt electric. She recognized the classic fight, flight, or freeze symptoms but was powerless to control them. Just as she was powerless to control her patient. She realized, perhaps for the first time, just how dangerous Timothy really was. Why had she dismissed the danger before? Adrian had seen it. He'd tried to warn her. To force her to stop seeing Timothy. Why hadn't she listened? If she had, Adrian would still be alive. But she was blinded by what Timothy was and by what treating him could mean for her own self loathing and self treatment.

"We're nothing alike, Mr. Ridle," she hissed as she clinched her fists and stood unsteadily to face the cold-blooded killer in the room.

Timothy stood in perfect synchronization with her movements as if they were dance moves they'd practiced before. "Oh, doc," he said, shaking his head with what she assumed was condescending pity. "If only you knew what I knew, you would know we belong together."

She leaned away from his words, as if they were a whip trying to lash out at her. The very thought repulsed her. She wanted nothing more than to kick him out of her office and out of her life for good. But still she had to know. She took a slow, deep breath. Then she bent down to retrieve her pen and notepad, wondering the entire time if he would strike her down while she looked away. Then she sat down and began to doodle.

"Please sit, Mr. Ridle. Our time may be almost up, but we're not even close to finished. I will ask you again. What exactly is it you did for me?"

TIMOTHY EXHALED SLOWLY. HE HADN'T REALIZED HE'D BEEN holding his breath. Her reaction to his confessed love for her wasn't what he expected. He hadn't imagined a deep kiss and effusive thank you, but something more positive for sure. He glanced at the door to his right. He could end all of this now and run. That's what he would normally do. Running from his mother's abusive lovers. Running from the horrors of war. And from love. Especially from love.

At least she was doodling again. Perhaps that wasn't a small thing. Silently he shook his head to clear his thoughts and took his seat. He was ready to face the firing squad he saw in her stare. "What is it you think you need to know, Edie? Because I assure you, you don't want the details. Nobody does really."

She stopped her pen in mid-doodle. Her eyes never left his. "I want to know, Mr. Ridle. You say you did this for me. So prove it. You owe me that much."

Timothy heard the beating of her heart. He heard the ticking of the clock behind her on the wall. His nostrils flared as he cautiously took in her scent. Perfume mixed with adrenaline-soaked sweat. Sweet with just a touch of sourness that didn't turn his stomach like the so many other times the air around him had been filled with the sweaty anticipation of anger, fear, and helplessness.

"After what I've done for you, you still want more? You still think I owe you more? Where would you be right now if I hadn't taken care of things for you, doc? You'd be rotting in the jail you were in all night. A fate, I shouldn't have to remind you, I helped you get out of. So take your righteous indignation and shove it up your, your...."

The words flew from his mouth, from deep within him, fueled by the pent up anger of what he'd done, what he'd become for her. But he couldn't be mad at her. She couldn't help what she was any more than he could help who he was. He collapsed back into the couch. His legs limp. His arms at his sides. His head leaned back against the coldness of the wall behind him. He knew her verbal assault was about to come, but he wouldn't protect himself. He couldn't shield himself from her anger. She knew no better.

He heard her gentle weeping, but he couldn't bring himself to look at her. He thought his actions would bring them closer. Instead, they had torn them apart. He wondered if they were ever as close as he had imagined. Maybe she was playing him this whole time. Maybe she had been playing Adrian, too. *Fuck.* What had he done?

"Mr. Ridle. Timothy." Her voice sounded hoarse. Her words strained. "I know you believe you were helping me. I can even understand why you believe that. And, frankly, you may not be incorrect. But don't you understand why I need to know the details of what happened to Adrian? He's dead. I can't bring him back anymore than you can. And I know that hearing what happened won't change that it happened, but I still have to know."

His neck cracked as he lifted his head to look at her. His soul sank. He knew the truth would not set either of them free. They were captives of a reality neither of them wanted to face. "What do you want to know?"

A smile crossed her tear-soaked face for just a second before drowning back into a frown. "Tell me about the knife. The one from my kitchen."

TIMOTHY STOOD. HIS MOVEMENTS WERE SLOW AND DELIBERATE. Edie thought he must be trying to silently assure her he wasn't about to attack. Although maybe he was just savoring the moment. Prolonging the kill. Playing with his food like some sadistic feral cat in the shadows of a back alley in some dank city far away. She wasn't sure she trusted her instincts any more.

He walked past her without touching her, which didn't stop her from flinching at the slight breeze his movement caused. It might as well have been a gale force wind hitting her in the face as she stood on the edge of an ocean storm. His eyes widened slightly at her reaction, and he increased the distance between them. She shook her head and rolled her eyes as he paced about the office.

"Mr. Ridle, please. I haven't slept. I haven't eaten. My, whatever the hell he was, has just been murdered. The police think I did it. And you, my crazy stalker patient with a history of raping and killing women has just told me that not only did you kill Adrian, but that you did it because you love me. If any situation in this life or any other deserves an explanation, this is the one, pal. So if you don't mind, I'd like to know what happened." She tossed her notepad and pen onto the table. "No notes. No tapes. No proof outside this room."

He stopped pacing and looked at her as he cocked his head and frowned. Edie thought she must have gotten through to him. Serial killers always think they're smarter than the rest of us. And in the end, they all want their story told from their point of view. She felt certain Mr. Ridle needed to explain his brilliant plan and execution, literally she thought with a dark smile, in at least cursory detail.

"What do you think you'll get by knowing?"

She sighed. She wanted to slap him. Instead, she slipped her hands between her thighs and her chair. "I told you. All I want is a shot at closure. I just want to know the ending so I can start anew."

His laugh reverberated off the walls. It boomed between her ears as if it originated inside of her. "There's no such thing, Edie. Not in real life. Hell, it hardly exists in movies or TV. Not really. Everyone thinks knowing the truth about a bad thing will make them feel better about it. That's bullshit. You can't make something bad feel good. Just like you can't undo it. You have to put it in a box and bury it deep. Just forget about it. Otherwise, it will eat at your insides until you wake up one day and realize you've got nothing left. No feelings. No soul. No humanity."

His face turned a dark crimson as his rant intensified. Little specks of spittle flew from his mouth, stressing every angry word. "You need to change the way you're looking at this, and you need to do it right now. Adrian had to lose his life so you could get yours back. Deep down, you know that's true. Deep down, in your subconscious, doc, you already know the truth."

Timothy slumped against the far wall and slid haltingly to the floor. He rested his head in his hands. His breathing came quickly and loudly. Edie thought for a moment he might hyperventilate and pass out.

When it was clear he would remain conscious, she stood and walked to her desk. She leaned against it so she was hovering over him. Talking down to him as a mother would to scold a petulant child. She almost pitied him, and that only made her hate him all the more. This man, this monster, who had been so grotesquely detailed in his descriptions of his sexual depravity and his torturous murders of other women, was silent when it came to details important to her.

"I don't care what you say, and I don't care about the consequences. You and I both know we're far past the time to care about those. All I know is that a man who was a very large part of my life is dead. And another man, who has become a large part of my life in other ways, is doing everything he can to push me away. I don't want to be alone, Mr. Ridle, and I won't let you continue to deny me the closure I've been seeking for most of my life, whether you think it's good for me or not."

"What do you mean you don't want to be alone? Are you saying you feel the same way about me?" He had the look of a hopeful child on the eve of Christmas. One that knows he's been bad but still believes Santa won't forsake him. *Jesus, men are so easy.*

"I don't know what I feel, Timothy," she purred. "I just know I need you to tell me what you did. I'll know you really care about me if you do."

HIS TEARS CAME AGAIN WITHOUT WARNING. AN OUTWARD SIGN OF the storm that had raged within him most of his life. He'd spent so much time compartmentalizing his memories and cutting out the people in his life connected with them. But now here he was. In the presence of the greatest woman he'd ever known. And she demanded that he unlock the doors to those compartments. He was powerless to hold back the decades of repressed emotions. His body shook like it was racked with fever. His mind raced. And his heart ached.

When the storm broke and his breathing had returned to a mostly normal rattle in his chest, he steeled his nerves and looked at her. She looked back with accusing eyes. They didn't match her words, but he didn't care. She was the one. And this was the one thing she demanded of him.

"I've been in your house many times." He looked down quickly so he could avoid the disapproving look he knew would come. "I like to go through your things, to wander, to pretend it's our house. Yours and mine. I sometimes lay on your side of the bed so I can smell you. But I'm never disrespectful with your things. I promise. I just want to feel what it would be like to be with you. To be yours."

He crossed his legs. *Crisscross applesauce*, his mom used to say. He wiped the back of his hand across his soaked cheek and swallowed hard. "I watched you all the time. The both of you. And the other night I couldn't stand to watch what he did to you anymore. You were in some kind of trance. I'd seen it before. Like you were there but not there."

"I sleep walk," she interrupted.

"You aren't safe when you're like that," he blurted without looking up. "I waited as long as I could. Then I took the knife. I took him. I kept you safe. I made sure he couldn't hurt you anymore. Maybe I shouldn't have gotten involved, but I had to, Edie. I didn't know the police would suspect you. You've got to believe me about that. I mean how could they?"

He took a deep breath and let his head fall back against the wall with a dull thud. The pain felt good. It cut through the throbbing dullness of his emotional overload. "It's okay, you know."

"What is, Timothy," he heard her whisper through choked back tears.

"It's okay if you tell the police." He closed his eyes. "I know you have to after everything they put you though. I messed up and led them to you instead of me. I tried. I really did. But do what you have to do. I'm prepared to deal with whatever happens. I'll be okay. You will, too."

They sat in silence awhile before he whispered, "Thank you, doc."

"For what?"

"You helped me find my purpose in this stupid life. You helped me to finally put my skills and personality to work for a good cause. The world is better off without me. That's for sure. So are you, but I am truly thankful for everything you've done for me. For believing me. For being my friend."

A FARAWAY BUZZER RANG, ANNOUNCING THE ARRIVAL OF ANOTHER patient out in the lobby. Edie looked at the clock. Their session should have ended an hour ago. She stood and stretched.

"I think we're done here, Timothy, don't you," she said as she walked over to their seating area and gathered her notebook. "I'm not sure either of us have anything more to share."

He silently got up from his position on the floor and stood awkwardly by the wall. One hand mussing his hair as he looked around the room at every space she didn't occupy. A maternal feeling washed over her once more as she watched him. He was so unsure of himself. It was like he was someone other than the man she'd been treating for months. The man capable of anything. Even murder.

"I guess you're right, doc," he said. "I suppose I don't need to stop at the receptionist's desk to schedule our next appointment?"

"I suppose not, Mr. Ridle."

He seemed to push off the wall to give him the momentum he needed to walk across the room. He stumbled to the couch and retrieved his coat. Then he stopped and turned back to her.

She felt no fear now. She knew he'd never hurt her. Still, his sudden hug surprised her. He buried his head in her neck and bawled like a baby. Slowly, she slid her hands across his shoulders to his back and held him to her while he cried his final tears.

38

A full moon looked down on Edie as she walked to her lonely car at the far corner of the long-deserted parking lot. The brightness of the moon caused her to stop and blink into the darkness. It blinded her for a moment, as if she'd stepped in front of a camera flash. The rustling of the wind and the sounds of the city sent a chill through her body that her coat couldn't fight.

She forced herself to open her eyes and to continue her walk to the car which now felt even longer than it was. The gently swaying trees looked menacing, and even as she could now see that the rustling was simply the leaves, she couldn't help but think they sounded like an impatient hidden army awaiting their orders to advance. Even more fallen leaves skittered across the ground in front of her. She jumped and quickened her pace.

Halfway to her car, she stopped once again. Her hands on her knees, she took slow breaths to calm her fried nerves. A hacking cough racked her tired body before it exploded into dry heaves. Spittle and bile splashed between her shoes onto the cool concrete. Small tendrils of steam rose immediately from the oozing puddle. She dug a tissue from her purse and wiped her spotted brow and dry mouth. After looking around to see if anyone had witnessed her less-than-ladylike display, she shook her head and continued to her car.

She started the engine and immediately locked the doors before collapsing back into the comforting safety of her familiar driver's seat. As much as she wanted to go home, she also dreaded it. It had always felt more like Adrian's house, not hers. *Too bad, sister*, she thought as she put the car in gear. *It's all yours now.*

Her right inner thigh complained quietly as she pressed on the gas. She imagined the freshly sheered skin slowly pulling apart as she moved. She could sense the blood clotting against the bandages. After Timothy's session, she had spent the rest of the day sitting at her desk. Just sitting there. Staring at the wall. Occasionally her hand would act on its own and pick up a pen to doodle on the pages in front of her, but her mind remained elsewhere.

Her eyes saw not dull gray paint but the brilliant deep reds and oranges of the sun as it sank into the Pacific ocean. Seagulls screeched in the near distance as they danced above the waves, occasionally diving into the water with wanton abandon when they spotted a potential snack. The salty air clung to her nostrils and stung her eyes. She knew what she'd see before she even looked down at her hands, but she had to look. The coppery scent contaminated the fresh sea air.

It had taken her a full ten minutes to come out of the haze of the waking dream. And when she did, she headed straight for her tools in the bathroom. Never had she cut herself twice in one day. Doing so twice in one week was even rare. Still the relief came, but it was fleeting. The pain returned as soon as the steel's kiss was over.

What's happening to me, she thought as she turned onto her street, which felt more ominous than inviting? It must be the exhaustion and the shock. Nothing a hot shower, a bottle of wine and perhaps a sleeping pill couldn't fix. *What a plan*, she thought. She felt the tension ease as she turned into her driveway. Until she saw the patrol car and another car sitting in front of her garage.

39

The world went silent but for the ticking of the engine and the high-pitched whisper of a persistent wind that gently rocked the car from side to side. Edie clung to the key chain still in the ignition as she glanced first in the rearview mirror then over her shoulder. Her fingers were slippery, but she found comfort in knowing she could quickly crank the engine and throw it in reverse at the first sign the police were there waiting to arrest her.

Other than the two cars in her drive, there was no sign of the police at all. Were they crouching in the bushes waiting to jump her as she walked to the front steps? She shivered despite the lingering heat in the car. She looked in the rearview mirror again, this time really looking at the narrow strip of neighborhood behind her. Was that hump on the Miller's roof always there? Or did a sniper have his rifle trained on the back of her head right now?

She closed her eyes. Part of her waiting for the kill shot to arrive with the sound of a distant hammer followed by the tinkle of glass onto the backseat. Part of her desperately searching for her center and her sanity. She took several deep breaths then, laughing to herself, opened her eyes.

She wiped the cloud of condensation from a spot on the windshield and strained to find the human shapes in the shadows of the two cars parked between her and the garage. Their engines were still running. Headlights still cutting through the darkness, casting shadows on the aging garage doors that, like her, were beginning to show signs of distress. She sat stiffly. Her muscles felt so tight they gave her a sensation of being paralyzed. Even her teeth hurt as if they too were tensing. Her whole body hummed with pent up stress.

Her mind raced. She tried to regain her reason through the cloud of fear that had descended on her like a cold fog. She shivered. *Why are they here? Where are they?*

Her bladder felt like a fifty-pound weight. She had to pee. Had to pee in her own bathroom, not in a cell with a cold stainless steel toilet attached to a sink out on display for anyone walking by. And not in the driver's seat of her car, too afraid to walk into her own house.

She jumped at the knock on the window just inches from her face.

"I'M SORRY WE STARTLED YOU, MS. McEVOY," LIZ SAID AS SHE cradled a mug of aromatic coffee in the dimly lit kitchen of the woman she had interrogated less than twenty-four hours earlier for murder. She took a cautious sip of the exquisite elixir and thought about what a strange thing it was to be a cop. Doomed always to see the world as a dangerous void occupied by killers and creeps.

"I've gotten used to it, I guess," Ms. McEvoy said as she cast a sideways glance at the two uniformed officers leaning against her counter near the window.

Liz studied the woman carefully. Everyone had a secret. There were no innocents among us. Just degrees of guilt. As a society, hell as a planet, we had decided what degree we were comfortable with. It was up to law enforcement to deal with those who made us uncomfortable and to ignore the rest. Liz had to admit she found it harder and harder to play ignorant.

"I hope you know the things I said, the other night down at the station, that was nothing personal." Liz let the words flow from her mouth without giving them time to process. Otherwise, she might have choked on them. Her antennae rarely failed her. If she gave her apology too much time to bounce around her brain, she'd have to admit that perhaps she had lost a step or two lately.

Ms. McEvoy studied the contents of her cup. The steam of the coffee inside made her look as if she were in a dream state. Liz smiled as she recalled her favorite Saturday Night Live characters Wayne and Garth. They would sometimes make ridiculous noises while making waves with their hands in front of their faces. It always set up a crazy dream sequence. She imagined Ms. McEvoy, too, was in her own dream state. But it probably wouldn't make her laugh. She knew from experience that the woman's dreams would most likely haunt her the rest of her days.

When Ms. McEvoy finally spoke, it was as much to herself as it was to Liz. "I don't agree with your methods, detective, but I know you were just doing your job. That's why I have to tell you something."

"What is it?" Liz's stomached clenched and her skin tingled. She cast a glance at the officers to make sure they were paying attention to the conversation and not the warmth of their drinks.

"My patient, the one who broke up our little interrogation this morning with his emergency, he murdered Adrian." As soon as the words were out of her mouth, the woman exploded into tears and dropped her head into her folded arms on the tabletop.

Interesting that she only now shows an emotional response, Liz thought. Her job would be so much easier if everyone were programmed to react to stress the same way. She waited a moment to let the woman get out some of her grief. She slid her hand across the table, placed it gently on the woman's elbow and whispered, "We already know."

EDIE WIPED HER SLEEVE ACROSS HER EYES AND NOSE. SHE RAN A hand roughly down her face, pulling her skin down with it as if it would slough off onto the table. This was all a dream. She was stuck in a Dali painting, and her body would soon melt onto the chair and the floor under her along with her pain.

Relief mixed with a healthy dose of shock made her words shoot from her mouth without pause or punctuation. "What do you mean? How do you know?"

"I know it probably appeared to you as if we had already presumed your guilt."

Edie laughed. Tears splashed across the table, reaching toward the detective. "Yes, detective. It did appear that way. Very much so."

The detective's eyes widened. She looked toward the lowly uniformed policemen she'd dragged with her. For what? Muscle? In case the wicked widow got out of line and tried to put another kitchen knife to work, this time on the detective?

"You're in shock. That's normal, Ms. McEvoy."

"Nothing about the last several months of my life has been normal, detective. The last couple of days have just been the sour icing on the rancid cake of my life."

The detective shook her head and slumped back in her chair. Edie took secret pleasure in making this difficult for her.

Yesterday this woman was in charge. She knew everything before it was spoken. Knew events with certainty that she'd never witnessed. Now here she was, at Edie's kitchen, with no harsh lights, no filthy cell, and no home court advantage. What a difference a day makes.

"I know you're angry, and that's okay. I deserve as much. There have been some developments in your case. That's why we're here tonight. And it's why these officers will stay after I've left."

"Oh no they won't." The only thing Edie wanted to protect was her night alone with a bottle of wine and a hot bath.

"I'm afraid I have to insist," the detective said. Her voice didn't match the smile on her face. "We found fingerprints and DNA at the crime scene that match your patient, Timothy Ridle. We sent a car to your office as soon as we had the results, but you had both left already. We're having him picked up tonight."

"Great, then you can take these two with you when you leave."

"It doesn't work like that. These officers will stay here until we have Mr. Ridle in custody."

Edie turned in her chair to get a good look at the policemen. One was so young his skin was still broken out with pimples. His Adam's apple protruded so far he couldn't button the top button of his collar. His gangly appearance reminded her of Ichabod Crane. He looked jittery. The other officer, another man, was relatively fit, though he seemed a little long in the tooth to still be out in the streets. Neither of them looked particularly menacing.

"Are there no female officers on the force?"

"I'm not sure what that has to do with anything," the detective argued.

"These two look like they're right out of a horror movie and are playing the parts of the first two to die."

Ichabod stifled a laugh. The older officer just shook his head, his eyes remaining fixed at some object on the wall across the room.

"They can stay, but I don't want them on my property."

"Ms. McEvoy, that's not the way it works."

"I'm not under arrest?"

"No."

"Then that is the way it is going to work. Now if you excuse me, it's been a long couple days, and I need to rest. You can show yourselves out."

40

The ringing of the phone blared through the house. Edie's head throbbed to the beat of the urgent bleating that echoed through the empty hallways. She shook her head, big mistake, and forced her encrusted eyelids to open. Half mast was all they allowed her. Even then the brightness of reality was blinding.

She grunted and grabbed a pillow to put over her head to drown out the intrusion. And still the phone persisted. She sat up on her elbows. Her pillow shield fell to the floor. Even its gentle landing caused new waves of pain behind her now-fully-opened eyes. She grabbed at her cell phone to check the time. Two in the morning? What evil sat on the other end of the line? Why did they still have a house phone, anyway?

"Adrian!" She cringed. A lightning bolt of pain shot from one temple to the next as she cried out his name. "Answer the phone for god's sake!"

She rammed her head into the mattress of her guest room bed. It was still firm from lack of use, and she immediately regretted such an impulsive act. *Adrian.* Her breath caught in her throat at the thought of his name. She knew he wasn't there, but subconsciously she still apparently expected him to answer the phone.

He had been the one who had to have that damn phone. Another one of his brilliantly eccentric ideas to reclaim the original character of their home by recapturing the magic of the home phone line. He had even insisted on finding and restoring period phone receivers. Well, he didn't restore anything. Didn't find anything either, now that she thought about it. He simply paid others to do the work. When she'd chide him about his lack of manliness, he would always tell her his father once told him the measure of a man was not how calloused his hands or dirty his clothes but how large his bank account that he could afford to callous other men's hands and dirty their clothes instead.

The ringing seemed louder now even though Edie knew that was impossible. It felt as if it had burrowed into her brain and now rung from inside her skull, reverberating through her skeleton in rhythm with her speeding heartbeat. Why hadn't the machine picked up? *Oh Jesus Christ*, she thought as she remembered that Adrian, of course, had refused to install an answering machine. *That would ruin the aesthetic appeal*, he'd said.

She swiped at the side table, brushing a bottle of sleeping pills to the floor. They scattered like marbles as she turned on the light. She threw off the comforter that still felt so warm and inviting and carefully tiptoed through the minefield of empty wine bottles between the bed and the door. She laughed as she recalled that in a drunken stupor she had thought they made an impressive alarm system.

"What the hell do you want?" she greeted her unknown phone intruder as she grabbed the nearest phone on the hallway table close to the upper landing of the stairs.

"Hiya, doc."

Edie fell against the wall and slid to the floor. "What the hell are you doing calling me, Mr. Ridle, and at this time of night."

"Technically, doc, it's morning, and this couldn't wait. I'm afraid I don't have much time left, but I couldn't leave without a proper goodbye."

"What? How did you get this number? Timothy, what's going on?" Edie looked around, half expecting him to pop out of a darkened doorway and walk down the hall to where she sat huddled and shivering. The only light shone through the massive window above the front door. The moonlight illuminated the stairs and crept partway down the hall, but Edie and the phone were still shrouded in shadows.

"I'm not sure this is the best time for silly questions, doc, but it wasn't easy. This line is in fatso's name. Your cellphones are both in your name. Weird, huh? Anyway, I figured the police were less likely to be listening in on this line. I mean, who the fuck has a landline these days. I doubt they even know the silly thing exists."

Edie blinked away the last vestiges of wine. She wiped a drop of sweat from her neck. "Is this? Are you calling from jail, Mr. Ridle? Are you actually wasting your one phone call by ringing my home when you knew I'd be sleeping? Why are you terrorizing me like this?"

He didn't answer. The line went silent. So silent Edie feared he might have hung up. She strained against the antique handset. Still she heard nothing. No breathing. No static. No background noises.

She took the handset from her ear, looked at it as if her patient would reach through it and grab her at any moment. As she was about to set it into its antique brass cradle, she heard his voice. He seemed more frantic now.

"What did you say?" she asked as she put the phone back to her ear.

"I said I'm not in jail, doc. And I never intend to be."

"I don't understand. The police have all the evidence they

need. They told me this evening. And, Timothy, they're looking for you. You can't run forever. Trust me, the best thing you can do is turn yourself in."

He laughed. Even over the phone, his laughter gave her goosebumps. She could picture his eyes shining and his face wrinkled. He laughed with his whole body.

"I really did just call to say goodbye. You may not believe it, and I wouldn't blame you what with present circumstances being what they are, but you really have helped me a lot, doc."

Edie's blood ran cold. Her mind raced. "Mr. Ridle. Timothy. This sounds like you're saying a permanent goodbye."

"Oh but I am, doc."

"I don't want you to do anything rash, Timothy. Please don't hurt yourself. If you value our relationship at all, you won't do what I think you're about to."

"Relationship, huh, doc?" He laughed again as he spoke. "I like the sound of that. Is that what we have?"

"Yes, Timothy. I don't care what you've done. I'm your doctor. I want to help you."

"You have. More than you know."

Edie wished she had brought her cellphone with her from her bedroom. She could call the police. Get someone to help him. "Where are you now, Timothy? Let me send someone to help you. Please don't do this."

Again the line went quiet.

"Timothy? Timothy! Answer me, goddamn it!"

"I'm here, doc."

Edie sighed. "Don't do that to me. Now tell me where you are. I'll get dressed and come get you. We can go to the police together. I promise you, you'll be okay."

"I told you I'm here, doc." His voice sounded dead. Edie looked back down the hall. The shadows seemed deeper, darker somehow.

"Where?"

"I'm outside. Under your bedroom window."

The breath stuck in Edie's throat. Thoughts spun around her head. "Hang on a second. I'm going to look."

Without waiting for an answer, Edie set the handset on the hall table and raced to her room. She pulled open the floral curtains and searched the grounds below. Nothing. No Timothy. No sign of movement of any kind. She should have known. Just another one of his sick jokes. As she walked back to the hallway, she grabbed her cellphone and slipped it into the pocket of her nightgown.

"I DON'T KNOW WHY I EVEN BOTHER, MR. RIDLE."

"What do you mean? Come and have another look. I'm here. All I want to do is say goodbye, doc. I promise. I don't want anything else from you. Please."

Something about the tone of her voice sounded off. She seemed colder, harsher more distant than she had been even at the beginning of their relationship. Timothy shook his head. Maybe it was just that he hated to beg for anything.

"I just looked out the window, Mr. Ridle. Don't play me for a fool. I thought we were past that. You say you want nothing from me. How could you? You've already taken all that I had."

Timothy swore under his breath. "Doc, listen, I'm going to throw some pebbles at your window." He ran through the lawn that looked as if it needed a final mowing before it hibernated through the winter. She really did need a man around.

A large evergreen tree grew near the house. It was ringed by a mound of faded red lava rocks. *Who uses those anymore?* Smiling, he grabbed a handful of the light rocks and shook out the largest. *God, could you imagine what she'd think or do if you broke her damn window,* he thought to himself as he pinged a volley of pebbles at her window pane with an accuracy that would have made any teenage Romeo proud.

"Did you hear that? Where are you? I'm here, doc. I swear."

She said nothing, and he saw no movement in the window. No light. No shadow behind the curtain. What if she shut him out? He had to speak with her. He had to make her understand.

"Wait," she said. "Don't hang up. I'm moving to another extension."

He heard the clatter of the receiver hitting a hard surface as she dropped it. He heard the patter of her naked feet on the wooden floor. It grew quieter. Then there was nothing but silence and the sound of his own breathing.

His eyes darted back and forth. He knew the police had left a cruiser to keep watch. He had watched as they left her house. They hadn't looked happy. Especially the one in plain clothes. She had looked familiar. He shrugged deeper into his coat to ward off the wind's chill. *Just a little longer*, he thought. Then it would all be over. He shrank into the shadows under the evergreen and waited.

EDIE NEARLY KNOCKED THE MASTER BEDROOM EXTENSION OFF Adrian's side table as she rushed into the room she hadn't been in since she woke up the morning of his murder. Even then she hadn't looked around and had left as quickly as she could.

The bed was still unmade. Adrian's clothes were strewn about the foot of the bed and the floor.

She heard a tinkling on the glass of the window as she approached. Her breath caught in her throat. The moon cast a soft glow on the yard below. And then she saw him, or at least a shadow of him coming out from under a giant tree.

She paused for a second to slow her breathing and collect her thoughts. The last thing she wanted to do was sound like a breathless teen girl answering the phone for the boy who so obviously had a crush on her. He'd like that too much.

"Well, Mr. Ridle, it seems you are here. What is it you need to tell me?"

He paced on the lawn below. His hand brushed through his hair. He reminded her, not for the first time, of a caged tiger. Her eyes widened as the moon reflected off something in his hand as he moved it across his head. Was he waving it above his head? She couldn't tell from her angle. But she was sure it was a knife. And although she was too far away, and it was too dark, she also knew it was her missing kitchen knife.

She dropped the handset to her shoulder as she reached for her cellphone in her pocket. Never taking her eyes off of the murderer below, she dialed 911.

"Police? This is Edie McVey. The man who murdered my boyfriend is at my house right now. Please send help."

"Edie, Edie, what are you doing?" she heard from the crook of her shoulder. "Dammit, Doc, hang up that phone and talk to me. I don't have a lot of time left."

BETRAYED. THE ONE PERSON HE BELIEVED IN THE MOST IN THIS world had called the police. Not that he hadn't thought it was a possibility. He liked to plan for all contingencies. He could thank Uncle Sam for that training. *Hooah*. But he had hoped. He had thought maybe they'd leave together.

He sighed at his fate. "Well, doc, I guess I misjudged you."

"Me, too, I'm afraid, Mr. Ridle." Her tone made him shiver.

"Oh, no you didn't, doc. I'm exactly what you thought I was." He crept further out of the shadows of the tree so he was standing directly under her window. An easy shot even for a rookie cop. He shook the thought from his mind. "You were just never sure. I wasn't always like this, but you made me realize I was put on this earth to do this. I've been wandering around for so long, floating really, like some big dumb log in the river. I just let the current push me wherever it wanted. I was never in control. Not until I met you."

He sensed the movement before he saw it out of the corner of his eye. Two shapes approaching from his left. His eyes never left her as he continued. "Doc. Edie. I told you. Everything I've done has been for you. To help you."

THE SCREAM ECHOED THROUGH THE BEDROOM. IT REVERBERATED off the glass, threatening to shatter it onto Timothy and the police below. Edie pushed her free hand up to her ear not covered by the phone and shut her eyes to shut out the sound. But it was louder inside of her. It was coming from her.

"No! No!" she screamed. "I don't want any part of this. I want to wake up now. I need to wake up! You didn't do this for me, Timothy. You did it because you're sick. You did it because you're evil and deep down you know you aren't half the man Adrian was on his worst day. You're a killer! I didn't make you. I hope the god who did will damn your soul to hell forever!"

Her forgotten cellphone vibrated in her pocket. She looked at the screen. Blocked caller. She ignored it and looked down on Timothy. Her stomach clenched. Anger boiled up from deep within her. No longer able to contain it, she spat at the window. He never moved. He just stood below her looking up. The hand holding the knife, her knife, limp at his side.

The cellphone buzzed again. A blocked call again. Edie knew who was on the other end before she answered. "Hello, detective. Your cops have done a bang-up job. There's a killer standing in my yard."

"Has he tried to gain access to your house?"

Edie almost laughed. She had an admitted murderer on one

phone who sounded like a man in a love song and a detective on another phone talking like she was reading from some police manual. "No, detective. He is just standing out in the open. He's on the other line."

"What? Right now? Patch me in. I'll record everything from my end. This is great. Anything he says will help us in court."

Edie braced herself. "No. You misunderstand. He's not on this phone line. He's on our house phone."

"What the hell is a house phone? I wasn't given any information on an alternate line. Ms. McEvoy, you should have disclosed this line to us."

"Edie, are you there?" Timothy asked. "What's going on? Is someone up there with you?"

Edie marveled at her reflection in the window. She'd fallen asleep, or more precisely passed out, without taking her makeup off. The smears of mascara around her eyes and her matted hair made her look like a madwoman.

"I'm here," Edie said into her home phone. "Where would I go? The police are probably already surrounding my house thanks to you."

She pushed the mouthpiece into her shoulder so she could speak to the detective without alerting Timothy. "Detective, I don't know how to do this. I'm on two different phones."

"Does your other phone have a speaker?" The detective asked.

"No, it's an antique. Thank Adrian for that."

"Shit. I'm pulling up to the scene now," the detective said. "Let's do this. Put this phone on speaker and set it down somewhere. At least I'll be able to hear and record your side of the conversation. That's better than nothing."

Edie felt more tired than she ever had in her life. As she did what the detective asked, she heard Timothy sigh into the other phone. She looked down on him in a new light. His shoulders slumped. He looked to her like a whipped little puppy dog. "You really are quite beautiful by moonlight, Edie. You're brighter than the jealous moon, really. You're like the sun shining down on me, keeping me warm when the rest of the world is so cold."

He spoke so softly she had to press the phone harder to her ear to hear him. She didn't want to listen. She wanted to slam the phone onto the receiver and turn her back on him as the police took him away. Still, she couldn't make herself move away from the window. Something inside of her wouldn't let her completely shut him out. Not yet.

His sorrowful appearance filled her with hot rage. She scoffed at his weakness, his need for her approval. "What were you planning to do, Timothy? Climb up into my tower bedroom and sweep me off my feet? Or maybe you were going to cut me, kill me completely? Finish the job you started!"

She looked around, rubbing her eyes against the strobe effect of the lights below. Police cars filled the street. She could see some officers cordoning off the road. Others rushed toward her house from every direction. A heavily armed SWAT vehicle sat with one tire up on the sidewalk in front of her house. A sniper in black tactical gear had set up on the roof of the vehicle. The long barrel of his rifle trained unwavering on Timothy.

Despite all the frantic activity around them, Timothy spoke slowly. Like they were the only two in the world, and the police weren't quickly closing in on him. "It's easy for someone to joke about scars if they've never been cut. But we've both been cut. Haven't we, doc?"

"What the hell are you talking about?" She pressed her forehead to the window. The coolness of the glass helped ease the throbbing headache that was just forming behind her eyes. Her vision of Timothy had become blurred by the incessant blue and red flashes of light. And now, the police had set up spotlights in a half circle around their suspect. Just behind the lights,

Edie saw the shadows of several dozen officers. All of them had their guns drawn and pointed at the man in her lawn.

"I had an addiction to pills when we met, doc. I'd spent my entire adult life numbing myself from my fucked up childhood. And you? You did the same thing, didn't you?"

"I've never taken pills to avoid my problems, Mr. Ridle. Don't project your issues onto me."

He laughed, and Edie could sense the police shift around him. "I escaped with pills and by joining the military. You went all the way across the country to school and found relief in the arms of an older man. I wonder if he reminded you of your dear departed dad?"

Edie squeezed her eyes tightly and spoke through clenched teeth. "How dare you bring up my dad. How dare you compare yourself to me. We are nothing alike."

Timothy looked over his shoulder. He seemed to see the police for the first time. Maybe the gravity of the situation was finally sinking in. When he looked back up at Edie, he spoke calmly as if he were a father lecturing his daughter even though he knew she wouldn't understand until much later. "I'm dead inside, doc. I have been for a long time. Then you came along, and you reminded me of the beauty of life. You saved me, so I had to save you. Because you're dead inside, too."

Edie sighed. She wanted this to be over with. She needed to start over, and Timothy kept pulling her back into the darkness. She wished the police would just charge him, tackle him to the ground, and take him away in cuffs. He'd be some institutional psychologist's problem then.

"Mr. Ridle," Edie recognized the detective's voice through the tinny sound of the megaphone. "It's time to put this to an end now, sir. There's nowhere for you to go. You have no more moves, Mr. Ridle. Let's just stop this so we can all go home."

Edie searched the crowd of police, but she couldn't make out the detective's silhouette. When her eyes drifted back to Timothy, she saw he was smiling up at her again. He seemed to enjoy the spotlight. "How's this for an ending, doc?"

As he spoke, he thrust his arms straight out to his sides. His phone in one hand, the knife in the other.

"Don't move, Mr. Ridle!" the detective yelled. "Drop your weapons, kneel on the ground and place your hands behind your head."

Timothy winked up at Edie as he slowly spun toward the officers.

"Stop now! Drop your weapons."

He continued to turn, deaf to the detective's demands. His back to Edie, he shrugged his shoulders, cracked his neck and slowly brought his arms in front of him, pointing them directly at the line of police before him.

Edie flinched as the police opened fire. The sound was deafening. Bullets ricocheted through the trees and ripped into the siding of her house. The force of the onslaught of shots blew Timothy out of his shoes. Edie pounded on the window. Why wouldn't they stop shooting?

"Doc?" The voice was distant. A faint whisper. Edie craned her neck to see him. He laid splayed out on her lawn. One leg oddly bent underneath his torso. A dark shadow slowly puddling around his body. He coughed, and she heard the sputtering of blood in his mouth. "I'm not sorry I did it. I had to. You needed me to."

The tears came before she knew she was crying. As the line of police officers slowly descended on her lawn, crouched and guns still focused on him, Timothy whispered his last words. "Tooth. Fairy. He came. Edie. He loves you."

ACT THREE

"The sexual life of adult women is a 'dark continent' for psychology."

— SIGMUND FREUD

41

The coffee tasted bitter and burnt. But it was hot. Edie cradled it in her hands, willing the warmth of the thick paper cup to seep into her palms and radiate across her body. She took a big gulp. The brackish liquid singed her tongue, cauterizing the taste buds closest to her lips. She cherished the pain. The events of the night before, this morning, she corrected herself, had left her numb.

She set the cup down on the rickety desk and picked up the swizzle stick the detective had brought her when she had apologetically delivered what she called the world's worst cup of coffee. Absentmindedly, she stroked the little piece of red plastic across her wrist. She twirled it between her thumbs. Her mind was a blank. She couldn't be certain she was even awake. Or alive.

"Are you okay?" the detective asked as she sat down at her desk with an arm full of yellow legal pads and battered brown folders.

Edie placed her hands in her lap and stared at the floor. The sound of the detective's voice intruded on her inner silence. She felt off balance. Out of place. "Honestly, I'm not sure, detective. I know I'm in shock. I know eventually, and probably sooner than later, the reality of my situation will come crashing down on me, threatening to crush me. I know it'll be a struggle just to breathe, just to go on living. But right now? Right now I just don't feel anything."

The swizzle stick in her hand impotently sliced at the inner thigh of her jeans. Still, the slight tickle brought faded memories and a familiar, murky sensation that somehow comforted her.

"That's understandable, and actually quite astute," the detective said. "I rarely deal with psychologists. It's nice to have someone who understands what they're going through and what to expect in the coming hours and days."

Edie couldn't bring herself to continue their banal small talk. Her eyes swept the cavernous bullpen of the detective section of Kansas City's downtown police station. It felt dingy. The desk lamps of the few detectives on duty were no match for the darkness of the early morning. The walls were marble and the ceiling two or three stories tall. Edie supposed this must have been an impressive building in its day. But, like her, its best days were far behind it.

"Ms. McEvoy, I want to apologize for the way I treated you the last time you were here. It's an occupational hazard to assume everyone is guilty. You deserved the benefit of the doubt, and for that I'm sorry."

Edie laughed under her breath. "Everybody is guilty of something, detective. You had a job to do. If you were better at it, perhaps two men would still be alive today. Perhaps I wouldn't be sitting here for the second time in a week having lost my boyfriend and my patient in the space of just 48 hours."

Edie studied the detective closely. She seemed nonplussed by Edie's venomous accusation. Angry, self-righteous citizens must be another of the detective's occupational hazards. "I'm sorry," she sighed, no longer able to meet the detective's eyes. "I don't know what came over me. I mean, I do, but that was still uncalled for."

The detective responded with a warm, genuine smile that seemed to shine brighter than the lamp in front of her. It was, Edie realized, the first time she'd seen the woman smile. "Nothing to apologize for, Ms. McEvoy. I'd probably feel the same way if our roles were reversed." She shuffled through the papers on her desk before continuing. "I know you've been through so much lately, and I know how I've acted hasn't helped, but I have just a few questions about your final conversation with your patient."

"I'll do what I can to help, but I'm not sure I understand why it matters. He's dead. Adrian's dead. Nothing can change that. Nothing can change anything that's happened." Edie felt dizzy. She closed her eyes to suppress the spinning sensation.

"I just want to close this case out knowing we've looked at everything," the detective urged.

Edie did her best to answer the detective's questions. Most were benign; some seemed idiotic. But she played along. All the while a nagging thought grew louder in her mind.

"Ms. McEvoy? Ms. McEvoy, are you all right?"

"I'm sorry. What was your question?"

"I asked about your patient's last words to you. Something about the tooth fairy? What did he mean by that?"

Edie looked down at the smashed and twisted swizzle stick in her lap. She closed her eyes, and it all came flooding back. The gunfire. The blood. Timothy crumpling to the ground. "The tooth fairy? I...I wish I understood. It must have just been some gibberish. A memory, perhaps of his childhood, that leapt to the front of his consciousness as he lay dying."

The detective frowned. "You're probably right. Still, it seems rather odd, don't you think?"

"What does, detective?"

"A person's final words are usually personal if not profound. You sure they didn't mean anything to you?"

The thought that had invaded her subconscious grew louder and louder. What if her numbness was more than a reaction to Adrian and Timothy's deaths? As the detective droned on, Edie began to believe her lack of feeling was symptomatic of something else, something deeper. Timothy had said as much, hadn't he? She was already damaged. What if she was completely broken now?

"I'm as puzzled by them as you are, detective, but I must disagree with your premise," Edie sighed. "A dying man's last words are just as likely caused by a jumbled relay of randomly firing synapses as they are from some frantic need for closure. Now if you don't mind, I think I'd like to go home."

THE EVENING WIND SLICED AT EDIE'S NECK AND WRISTS. A familiar chill shivered up her spine. Fall had arrived in full force in Kansas City. And it brought with it more death and decay than usual. Her breath marched in front of her as she walked toward what was once one of her favorite destinations in the city.

A jogger nodded at Edie as she passed her. She looked fit, happy. She didn't seem to be running from anything. Edie wondered what the woman's life was like. Was someone waiting for her when she got home? Would that someone join her in the shower? Ask her about her day? Make her a cup of coffee or tea as they made plans for a romantic Saturday night date. *I bet she's looking forward to the upcoming week*, Edie thought.

In the vast lawn of the park, a father and son played fetch with their black Golden Doodle. The little boy who couldn't have been older than three or four stumbled along gleefully after the dog. The boy's mess of golden hair flopping up and down as he ran. A wide smile pasted to his face, brilliant white teeth surrounded by rosy cheeks and beaming eyes. Edie stopped and watched the action for a moment, wondering about a different life, a different man, an imagined family. But you only get so many building blocks with this life. And you can seldom tear down your creation and start from scratch. Yet here she stood, upon the pile of rubble that had been her life. If only she had the energy to build something new.

She continued on her way. Lost in thought. Lost in general. Luckily her feet knew where she wanted to go. What she needed to see.

She sat down at a bench near the center of Loose Park's rose garden. The city's iconic roses had all been trimmed back. Only bare branches and memories remained. *Not unlike me*, Edie thought. Her life had unexpectedly been cut back to the roots. Would she flourish or whither away?

It seemed fitting somehow that the final resting spot of Dr. Adrian Hillary was filled not with the bouquets of flowers, balloons, stuffed animals, and cards Edie remembered from so many impromptu memorials of crime victims she'd seen on the news from time to time. No, the site of the great doctor's death was instead surrounded by dormant roses. Edie closed her eyes and tried to cry. Everyone deserves to be mourned no matter how badly they lived their life.

She felt the presence before she heard the familiar voice. "Um, Ms. McEvoy? Are you okay?"

Edie inhaled slowly and answered without opening her eyes. "I think you, more than most, should know the answer to that question, detective. How on earth did you find me? Are you still having me followed?"

"No. Not at all. I tried your house. Drove by your office. And then, well, I guess I just asked myself where I'd be if I were in your shoes."

"You really ought to be a detective."

They both laughed unabashedly and unexpectedly at Edie's dry joke. Edie laughed so hard that those elusive tears finally fell from her eyes. She wiped them away as she caught her breath.

"I just came because I wanted you to know something. Something I didn't tell you before."

Edie turned toward the detective. She looked softer in the evening light. Not as harsh or imposing. Human almost. Edie sensed she was embarrassed to have interrupted such a solemn moment. If only she knew. "I thought the case was closed?"

"Almost. I told you I don't like to leave loose ends. I just thought you should know that your patient, Timothy, wasn't a serial killer. In fact, we haven't found one shred of evidence that he was a rapist either. He lived a quiet, ordinary life. I was about to call you last night when you called me to tell me he was at your house. He was still a murder suspect, but your, um, Adrian appears to have been his only victim."

Edie shook her head. "No. That's not right," she said. "He told me, in graphic detail sometimes, about what he did to his victims. He relived his routines as he stalked and studied them."

"I think perhaps he was just a lonely, broken man who wanted to be something more. And maybe he saw the way you looked at him, took an interest in him. I mean nothing by that other than sometimes we all play a part when we're trying to impress someone. I guess all his stories and lives and lies finally did lead him to murder."

"I don't believe it. I would know if he were lying. It's my job, detective."

"I know, Ms. McEvoy. It's my job, too. Nobody is right all the time. As you know," she continued, changing the subject as skillfully as she had in the interrogation room, "the knife he had on him last night was from your kitchen. He hadn't bothered to clean it. It still had spots of Adrian's blood."

Edie's head spun. "I don't understand."

The detective shifted her weight from one foot to the other and looked around as if she were trying to find a reason to leave or perhaps a better topic to end their conversation on. "We believe Adrian's threats to cut Timothy off from you drove him over the edge. You were his obsession, Ms. McEvoy. But you're safe now. I hope this helps to bring you some closure." She nodded curtly and hurried away into the waning night.

Edie watched the detective until she could no longer make out her shape by the soft glow of the park lights. She smiled. It felt strange after the tragedy of the last few days, but she liked the detective. Despite their first encounter.

Isn't it a little crazy how so many people put so much stock into first impressions, she thought to herself. First impressions, in her experience, were awkward, embarrassing, forced, or faked. And in this case, they began with one woman thinking the other was a murderer and the other woman thinking the first was an idiot.

Imagine if her first impression of Timothy had been correct. Just another junkie looking for a fix. A soldier dealing with the deafening reality of PTSD and of a system that refused to acknowledge, let alone treat, his problem even though that same system had sent him to the hellhole that caused his issues.

Her mind flitted from Timothy to Adrian. *Oh, Adrian.* Imagine if she hadn't blown her first impression of the great man himself. A smart, caring, jovial professor dedicated to creating smart, caring psychologists. Nothing more. No coy advances. No rape. No intertwined fates. No middle of the country mid-life crisis. No murder.

As Edie stood to walk away from Adrian's non-memorial, one more thought wandered into her head uninvited, like a wave silently cresting over an unsuspecting ocean tourist out for a swim. Imagine if her first impression of her stepdad had been correct. Just a hardworking, blue collar man who had paid his debt to society and who loved her lonely mom. No sneaking into his stepdaughter's room at night. No doing things no father figure should do.

Edie quickened her step, but she couldn't outrun her past.

THE GOLDEN HUE OF THE LIGHT FIXTURE AT THE FRONT DOOR slowly flickered, vanquishing the shadows on the porch in short bursts. It reminded Edie of a lighthouse warning returning sailors of impending doom ahead.

She stood on the bottom step. Her left foot faltering above the landing. Her right hand in a death grip on the railing.

She closed her eyes. The acrid, bitter scent of seawater blew in with the undulating winds and filled her nostrils. She cocked her head. Was that the far off squawk of a gull? She felt the pounding of the surf against her thighs. It nearly knocked her over, but still her eyes remained clamped shut. Her mind refused to let go of the memory. And then, she heard it. A scream so guttural, so longingly sad. A woman. She was afraid. Hurt. And then a man's angry cry cut short. Finally, the sounds of the ocean returned. Just like the tide erased a footprint in the sand, it was as if the woman and the man never existed. Only Edie knew they did. Once.

She lost her balance as her hand on the bannister slipped free, slick with sweat. Her eyes flew open as she fell against the railing. For a split second she saw the red curl of a wave cresting over the porch, rising above her as if to engulf her and vanish her, too, from this world.

She stood tall. Spread her arms. Threw her head back and waited for nature to take its course. Just as she surrendered to it, the waking dream dissipated like the morning fog along the rocky coastline. The porch light no longer a majestic lighthouse but a paint-chipped, poorly wired memory of Adrian's lack of workmanship in the home repair department.

She looked through the darkened windows. All was still. She felt like a stranger looking up at someone else's house. Nothing about it felt familiar. It was as if she were trespassing on someone else's misery.

This was never her home. Not really. But it suddenly dawned on her it was her house now. All hers. She could redecorate. Remove the Adrian-ness from the place. Still, it seemed rather large for one person, and she had never liked it in the first place.

For the first time since Adrian's death, the weight of her aloneness struck her hard across the chest. A half smile formed on her lips. The second in as many hours. Her new detective friend would find this odd. It wasn't so much that she was alone. Even when Adrian had been around, even when he was at his most attentive, she had felt alone. Isolated behind the invisible, impenetrable walls she had built up around herself over the years. Walls that had grown thicker and higher ever since Adrian had first betrayed her naïve trust as a student.

Those walls that had protected her, kept him from hurting her even deeper than he already had, also kept her in. They held her back from ever really experiencing the world around her. Now that he was gone, she felt the weight of her life with him, under him, lift from her shoulders. She felt like a walking cliché, but the air smelled sweeter and the world seemed more alive now that Adrian was dead.

Her smile turned into a giggle that exploded into an uncontrollable fit of hysterical laughter. She worried for a second that a passerby might think her a madwoman, but that thought just made her laugh even harder. She laughed so hard she doubled over and tumbled onto the porch. Which just set off another round of soul cleansing laughter.

When she finally settled down, she wiped the tears from her cheeks and sat up on her elbows. The world looked different from where she sat. She felt as if she were just awakening from a long sleepwalk. One that was even deeper and lasted even longer than her recurrent beach-filled illusions.

EDIE STOOD UP AND TOOK ANOTHER LOOK AT THE HOUSE. HER house. She felt nothing, no connection, no longing to make the place her own. She wasn't sure why she had expected a sudden change of heart. She had no warm memories from this place. Nothing about it reflected her life.

She walked through the darkened entryway and paused at the stairs. The silence overwhelmed her. The whole idea of staying there one moment more filled her with dread. *I'm not ready for this*, she thought. Losing Adrian, being free of his spell on her, gave her hope. But this house, this cavernous monument to his ego? It was like he was still here. Still haunting her. Still holding her down, ready to do as he pleased. But she had nowhere else to go. No family. No friends. No support system of any kind. Adrian had seen to that. Maybe he was the one laughing now.

A ridiculous thought popped into her head. If she didn't belong there, she didn't have to stay. He could no longer control her movements, make her feel bad for doing something that made her feel good. She had all the power. She was the one who had survived.

She raced up the stairs with a joy she hadn't felt in years. She'd grab a few things and leave. Just go. There were dozens of fabulous hotels in the city. She'd pick the most extravagant and stay in the biggest room she could afford. A bath. A robe. Room service. It all seemed like a dream. She felt giddy as she threw random clothes into a small gym bag. If she didn't have what she needed later, she'd buy it. It was time to start over. Her whole body buzzed with anticipation.

42

The hands on Edie's back pushed down on her with an unexpected force that nearly knocked the wind from her chest. She grunted. The man straddled her hips. The weight of his muscular thighs pinned her arms to her sides.

She gulped for air and was just able to inhale a single deep breath before the next quick thrust of his large hands, now near her neck, as they pushed expertly on either side of her spine. The cracking of her vertebrae reverberating up and down her body with electric force. She grunted again into the face hole of the folding massage table set up in her hotel room.

The sensation of more hot oil being poured over her back made her toes curl. She nearly purred with satisfaction. A very naughty thought occurred to her, and she wondered how he'd react if she were to come on to him.

"How's that?"

She shivered at the sound of his voice. His hands slid easily through the oil, hitting all her sore muscles in long strokes.

"I like it hard," she said to the floor and felt her whole body blush.

"You're very tense."

Her eyes rolled back into her head with every touch. Her skin rippled with pleasure. "I've been pent up for a long time." *God. Did she just say that? Could he sense what she wanted? What she needed?*

His hands slid side to side over her upper back. His fingertips grazed the side of her breasts with each dip over her ribs. He was rubbing deeper. Lingering longer at the apex of his stroke, his fingers spreading over her tender breast tissue. Each fingertip pressing firmly into her.

Her body quivered. Her mind raced. It had been so long since she'd felt the touch of a man that didn't repulse her. What a great idea this had been.

"I like that a lot," she said. "You're great with your hands. Really. So good."

The knock on the door interrupted what could have happened next. *Or*, she thought with a sigh, *it probably saved her from the embarrassment of her clumsy innuendo.*

She didn't dare look at her masseuse as she gently hopped off the table, wrapping the sheet and towel tightly around her body. Though she wished she had the courage to glance slyly at his pants. Just so she could know if the sensuality of the moment had only been one-sided.

"Detective! You found me again." Edie spoke through the crack in the door as she marveled at the detective's appearance. Even on the weekend the detective was all business in her off-white blouse that had seen better days worn under a semi-stylish but natty navy blazer with matching skinny slacks. Her outfit told the world she was a detective or played one on some TV drama.

"As I said last night, you're pretty easy to track, Ms. McEvoy."

"I wasn't trying to hide. I just couldn't...." Her voice trailed off.

"I know. That's how I found you, actually. I wouldn't have

been able to go back to the house either if it had been me in your place. May I come in?"

Edie's cheeks burned crimson. She looked down at her towel and sheet-wrapped body, shining with massage oil and still giving off waves of heat and desire from what might have happened had the detective not been so good at her job. "Of course," she said as she opened the door. "Give me just a second to get dressed."

The detective seemed to take in everything as she crossed the threshold of Edie's hotel room. Her eyes were everywhere at once. Edie took a breath and walked to her purse. She dug out a hundred-dollar bill and thrust it at her masseuse. He had already folded up his table and was waiting patiently in the corner. Edie mustered the courage to look at his pants while she thanked him for his services. *Inconclusive.*

Edie ducked into the bathroom to change. The detective spoke through the door from across the room. "I just wanted to keep you informed as we get more information on Adrian's case. I know I told you last night that Timothy wasn't a serial killer or rapist."

Edie thrust her head through the bathroom door. "Has that changed? Did you find more victims?"

The detective shook her head. "Thankfully no," she said as she looked at the unmade bed then took a seat on one of the two overstuffed chairs in the room. She sat stiffly on the front edge.

"Sorry about the mess," Edie said as she threw a handful of new clothes, many with their price tags still attached, on the floor and sat on the other chair.

"Looks like you're making quite the fresh start."

Edie blushed again. "Just couldn't bear to be in the house even long enough to grab much more than the necessities."

"Your patient Timothy wasn't who he said he was at all," the detective said, making one of her signature abrupt topic changes. "He did do one tour in the army. He was a grunt with a gun. Nothing special in his file, no anomalies about his service other than what you already know."

Edie sank back into her chair and thought about the war stories Timothy had shared with her. It takes a special kind of mind to make up such detail to the level that would pass the scrutiny of a trained psychologist. At least if that psychologist were any good.

"He sought therapy after an incident at work threatened his job. That was years ago. He appears to have developed an appetite for his meds and began hopping from one therapist to another to keep his high going."

"But I didn't prescribe medication," Edie said, as much to herself as to the detective. "I diagnosed his addiction before I even met him. His file was clear. And a call to an army physician confirmed it. So why would he keep coming back? And why make up such a dark story? Why pretend to be a killer when he wasn't?"

The detective looked at Edie for a long time. Edie couldn't match her gaze and looked down at her hands. Her neck and ears grew warm again. Her face flushed. *Why was she having so much trouble controlling her emotions?*

"Maybe he was bored or just curious to see if he could get away with it. But I have another theory based on what I know about his background and what I've found in his house and at his place of work."

Edie looked at the detective from the corner of her eye. "What's that?"

The detective shifted in her seat. "I've spoken to a number of people who knew him. They all described him as an extremely shy man who kept to himself. I believe he couldn't talk to women." Edie felt the detective studying her reaction. She tried to control her breathing and remain nonplussed as the detective continued. "I think that somehow, maybe because your talks were under the auspices of therapy, he felt comfortable talking to you."

"Just not comfortable enough to tell me anything real," Edie said, wishing she could take the words back.

Liz narrowed her eyes as she contemplated the woman in front of her. Erratic behavior. Expensive hotel. Shopping spree. In Liz's experience, most criminals were by nature stupid. Sure, some of them were extremely intelligent, but criminal behavior isn't a natural state of mind. People are creatures of habit. Criminals are impulsive. Even if they believed they'd thought through everything, their subconscious, their impulses eventually tripped them up.

Still, Liz couldn't get a good read on Edie. There's a fine line between grieving and guilt. From the first time she met Edie she assumed she was guilty. Maybe Liz was losing her touch. All the late nights and bad coffee didn't help. Her own life was a wreck; she couldn't even imagine what this woman must be going through.

"One thing is certain." Liz looked intently at Edie as she spoke. "Your patient was obsessed with you."

Edie nearly rolled onto the floor as a fit of laughter overtook her. Liz shook her head. Such an odd woman.

"I spent hundreds of hours with Timothy for nearly a year," Edie said. "I can assure you that there was nothing romantic about our relationship. He expressed no untoward feelings, nor did he act out in a manner that made me feel concerned for myself or others."

"Not even when he punched Adrian in front of an office full of witnesses?" Liz immediately regretted the question. "Look. If we hadn't been at your house the other night, there's no telling what he would have done. He had just killed Adrian. And, according to you, he confessed to you. Why would he leave you alive after that?"

Edie pushed herself out of her chair. Liz thought for a second that the woman intended to attack her. Instead, she began pacing around the room. "I don't know," she said.

"I do," Liz answered. "Whether it was obsession or a crush or whatever you want to call it, he could just as easily have killed you as let you go. Passion makes some people kill and others protective. I don't know which way the wind was blowing with this guy."

Edie sat on the edge of the bed. She looked frazzled. Liz felt bad for interrupting her massage. "What did his mom have to say when you searched their house?" Edie asked.

"Mom? According to our records, she's been deceased for eight years. She died just before Timothy received his discharge from the army. In fact, it looks like the army released him a little early so he could come back and make funeral arrangements. The only house companion we found was a cat."

"Herman!"

Liz flinched at Edie's overly enthusiastic outburst. She tugged at the hem of her jacket to hide her surprise. "Yes. That was the name on his collar. You knew about the cat?"

Edie stood again and beamed down at Liz as she began to pace the room again. Her pace quicker than before. "Yes! Timothy told me he found Herman when he was just a kitten. He thought he was just days old. According to Timothy, he accidentally ran over the kitten's mom one night as he drove home. When he passed the dead cat the next morning, he saw the poor little thing snuggling into its mom. He said he had felt responsible, so he took the orphaned kitten in."

Edie stopped pacing in front of the window. She continued talking as she looked out at the late morning traffic and bustle of shoppers around the Country Club Plaza below. "It was so small that he couldn't tell if it was a boy or a girl, so he named it Herman. 'Her' in case it was a girl and 'man' in case it was a boy."

Liz rubbed her hands up and down her thighs as she thought about Edie's little anecdote. She could use her own massage. She'd been staving off her own loneliness lately by spending more time in the gym. She may be overdoing it, but it kept her mind off the recent end to yet another hopeless relationship that had been doomed from the beginning. Her livelihood made having a life nearly impossible. "That story, as silly as it is, says a lot. Maybe Timothy let you in more than we know."

Edie turned and looked at Liz with a big smile. It lit up her whole face. She might be an attractive woman if the weight of two murders weren't weighing her down. "I doubt it, detective. He told me he ran over Herman's mom when he was racing home to give his own mom her medication. In the persona he created for me, he was a doting son who took in his ailing mother so he could make her comfortable in her final months. He was just manipulating me into caring for him, clouding my professional instincts."

"How so?"

"Because it was that story, actually, that helped create the bond we shared."

Liz sighed. Why couldn't she ever catch a simple case? One where the murderer was caught standing over the victim, gun in hand as he jumps up and down admitting he did it? She smiled at the stupid thought. God she needed to clock out, maybe take a few days off.

She looked at the woman in front of her who had lost everything, including confidence in herself professionally and personally. She liked Edie. Few people could stand up to the kind of interrogation she went through with their dignity intact. On a whim, she shared one final piece of information.

"You know, we found something else. I'm not sure I should tell you."

Edie walked over and fell into the chair next to Liz's. She looked as exhausted as Liz felt. "Jesus, there's more? Might as well get it out there."

Liz felt suddenly unsure. She rarely broke protocol like this. Screw it, she thought. "You may already know that Timothy worked as a security guard at a haunted house."

Edie rested her head on the back of the chair. She looked up at the ceiling for a moment before closing her eyes. "Yes."

"The owner called me this morning. They're getting ready to open for the season and found something disturbing." Liz took a breath. She shouldn't be telling Edie any of this, but it seemed like the right thing to do. "Well, one of the rooms is set up as a zombie brothel. Real weird fetish shit if you ask me. They found pictures of your face taped onto the heads of the female mannequins that are dressed as, um, zombie sex workers."

Edie's giggle startled Liz. It grew into a loud, deep belly laugh. Liz laughed along. It really was a crazy thing she'd just shared. She wiped her eyes. "Funny, huh?"

"You're the one," Edie said.

Liz's laughter dissipated immediately. She cocked her head. "What do you mean, Ms. McEvoy?"

"You're the homicide detective Timothy met at work. He told me he smelled your hair. I thought you would be his next victim."

Liz held her breath. What did this all mean? She didn't believe in coincidences. "It seems like he decided he liked you better than me."

"What can I say," Edie said. "I'm a lucky girl." Edie smiled, but Liz saw the sadness just below the surface. The woman's mouth smiled. Her eyes didn't. Liz wondered how much damage the last few days had done to her.

Liz got up to leave. She hesitated at the door and turned back to Edie. "I have to apologize to you again, Ms. McEvoy. Adrian's history, especially with you, made this seem like an open and shut case of revenge murder. I'll deny this is you ever tell anyone, but as a woman, I wouldn't have blamed you. But I would still have done my job. I just wanted you to know."

Edie hugged Liz. "I don't blame you," Edie spoke into Liz's shoulder. "Hey, can I have the cat?"

Liz pulled back and looked at Edie for a long time. "He's at a shelter. I'll get you the number."

Edie stood at the closed door for several minutes after the detective left. What had she done to deserve such upheaval in her life? The answer whispered to her from the deep shadows of the darkest corner of her mind. She shook her head to silence the malignant voice.

She leaned against the door and slowly slid to the floor. Her head fell into her hands, and she wept silently. She cried for her lost childhood. She cried for the years she'd given to Adrian while receiving nothing in return. Not love, not professional guidance, not even friendship. She cried for how easily she was manipulated professionally by a damaged patient. And she cried for Timothy. She wished she had been good enough to help him. None of the tears that flowed between her fingers and dropped to the floor were spilled on behalf of Adrian.

Edie wiped the tears away and stood up. She hadn't cried so hard since she was a child. Not since her dad had died. She walked past the windows and stepped out onto her narrow balcony. She leaned on the railing and breathed in the crisp early afternoon air.

Timothy's last words came tumbling into her mind. Such a strange thing to say as he lay dying. She thought of one of her favorite movies as a little girl. It had been her dad's favorite, and he had introduced her to it. They'd often watch it in the middle of the night when he'd get home from some twelve-hour shift. He never got mad at her for staying up late to wait for him, even on school nights. He just made them a big bowl of popcorn and their special milkshakes, and they'd sit in the dark living room watching the black and white classic, "Citizen Kane."

Rosebud, she thought. Another strange utterance of a different dying man. In the movie, it was eventually revealed that Rosebud referred to a childhood memory of Charles Foster Kane. Maybe Timothy was trying to tell her something. She could almost see the answer. It was just out of reach, her subconscious mind refusing to give it up yet.

Frustrated and chilled, she went back inside. She looked around at the strange room. She couldn't stay there forever, but she still couldn't stand the thought of returning to the house, to the master bedroom she had shared with Adrian. His house. His room. Nothing was hers even after he was gone.

Edie sat pensively at the foot of the empty kingsize bed in an empty hotel room. The detective's last words floated around in her head. Her hands balled into fists. Her jaw clinched. She could feel every muscle in her back tensing in unison. Her body practically hummed with pent up stress.

She cracked her neck and picked up the phone. "Hi, this is Ms. McEvoy in room 626. I'd like another massage. Would you please send up the same man I had before? Thank you."

43

E die sat alone in the dark. She shook her head and smiled at how comfortable she'd become alone and in the dark. She probably ought to be thankful she'd never been afraid of things hiding in the shadows. Not the physical ones anyway.

Every inch of the reception desk was piled high with breakfast foods. She'd brought donuts of all shapes and sizes, bagels and assorted cream cheeses, fritters, muffins, sausages and bacon, yogurt and granola, and a fruit platter with a honey-sweetened dip the salesperson had told her was to die for, which seemed fitting. She hadn't intended to buy so much, but what does one serve when talking to one's staff for the first time about their boss' murder and the latest news that the man who did it, someone they all had come into contact with, had been gunned down by the police in front of their other boss?

This was the sort of thing most companies would address by bringing in grief counselors. She'd thought of doing the same, but the idea felt insulting. Her staff consisted of counselors, therapists, and psychologists. They could help each other. She planned to offer her own services to the few administrative staff members on the payroll.

Edie had spent most of the night thinking about the practice. She hadn't wanted it. She hadn't been happy there. Most of her colleagues didn't see her as an authority figure. Adrian had seen to that, treating her like a junior associate although she'd financed just as much of their start-up capital as he had. More if you consider the price she paid at school and at home. His blood and sweat might have built the place, but her tears did most of the heavy lifting.

One by one, her associates began to shuffle in from the bitter temperatures that matched Edie's mood. She'd never much cared for Mondays. Even when she could set her own schedule at college and at the office, Mondays always filled her with dread. Then she would think about the people who had tougher jobs, people who put their lives on the line or at least put their bodies through the ringer every day. Those people had a reason for hating Mondays. Such thoughts always made her feel guilty for her privilege, which made her hate Mondays even more.

But today marked a new beginning. She'd come up with a plan for the practice she hoped would both erase Adrian's legacy while erasing her debt to Timothy. She couldn't save him, but maybe she could use her position to help others like him.

Edie felt like the grieving widow at a funeral. It made her want to puke. As people entered the office, they smiled sadly at her, offered unwelcome words of condolence, and hung their heads. She pasted on a smile, offered them food, imploring them to eat as much as they wanted, and told them all to gather in the conference room.

Once everyone had arrived and was seated with plates of food and mugs of coffee in front of them, Edie walked to the head of the table. The conference room was small. They rarely used it. Adrian hadn't believed in company meetings. He preferred to chat one-on-one with his colleagues and employees. *The personal touch is more effective* he had said. Edie had always rolled her eyes. His little personal touch tête-à-têtes seemed to happen more frequently and last much longer with the female members of the staff.

She cleared her throat and looked around the room. She really didn't know the people gathered there. Adrian had insisted he would be in charge of bringing on other psychologists and of personally interviewing the support staff. Now, as they all looked up at her with varying levels of pity, sympathy, and curiosity, she saw a room full of strangers.

"I know Adrian's death has come as a shock to you. To me too, of course," Edie began. She walked around the room as she spoke, telling them the details of how Adrian's body was found and what was done to it, and bringing them up to speed on Timothy's death by police firing squad while she had watched from above. Her story elicited several gasps, which made her smile to herself. A few of the women around the table even wept. For what, Edie didn't know. Nor did she care.

"I know this is a horrific story of death and violence," she continued. "It would be a tragedy if that's where the story ended. But it will not end this way. I won't let it." She paused for dramatic effect. She took the time to make a moment of eye contact with each member of her audience. She felt their tension, their anticipation. It made her feel more powerful than she ever had before. It made her certain she could do this.

"Starting today," she continued, "we are transforming our entire practice. I'm taking over, and together we're going to make a difference in the lives of the people who need it most." She walked back to the head of the table and stood with her hands on her hips, her voice rising in timber and volume as she spoke the words she'd practiced in front of the steamy mirror just hours before. "No longer will we pander to and chase wealthy patients with boring, bourgeois problems that don't matter. No longer will we limit the number of pro bono cases we take each year, doing just the minimum amount of public service to make ourselves feel good while making no real difference. No. Today we start fresh. Today we are not the same practice we were yesterday."

Edie sensed she was losing some in the crowd, but she didn't care. "We will take more pro bono cases. In fact, we will seek them out, specialize in them. And as of today, our focus is on helping women. In particular, we will focus on helping women who have survived abusive relationships."

One of her male colleagues, an older psychologist cut from the same cloth as the late, great Adrain Hillary, scoffed under his breath. Edie sauntered to his chair, put her hands on the man's shoulders and continued speaking to the room. "I know a few of you won't be interested in this kind of work. It's not an easy way to make a living. I understand that. There's little money and even less glory. So for those of you who wish to take your toys and leave, I wish you the best. No hard feelings. No regrets. Come see me after this meeting. You'll find your severance packages to be generous and swift."

She emphasized her last point by patting the man on the shoulders. She smiled as his neck, face, and ears burned a crimson red. "We start today. So let's go. I expect everyone who is staying to get busy finding new patients. And to find new therapists for your current patients who don't match our new focus."

The room filled with the cacophony of shifting chairs, empty dishes, and the hushed whispers of uncertain conversations as she dismissed her team. Edie barely heard the din. Her heart beat so loudly in her chest. The rhythm of its pumping filled her ears. So she had no idea how long the angry voices had been droning on before she finally tuned in.

"Are you even listening to me? Jesus, you're as pigheaded as Adrian was," the doctor whose shoulders Edie had used as a prop said. "Only you're half his age and have half his business acumen."

"Excuse me?" Edie fought back the well-honed impulse to succumb to the opinions of an older man, no matter how chauvinistic and angry his approach.

"Oh. So you are listening," he said as he leaned back in his chair, crossed his arms over his expansive chest and deliberately propped his feet up on the table.

Another male psychologist raised his hand but didn't wait for Edie to acknowledge him before he barreled ahead with his own condescending attack on what he saw as her ill-conceived and naïve plan to drive their practice right into the ground.

Edie slumped against the wall, thankful it was there to hold her up when her own legs betrayed her. Had she bitten off more than she could chew? *Weird*, she thought. That phrase had always bothered her. Every time she heard it as a kid, she imagined a morbidly obese man with a stained white undershirt straining to contain his gluttony. Faded blue suspenders stretched nearly to their breaking point. He sat at a rickety table. His thick, hairy hands holding an overly stuffed sandwich made from an entire loaf of French bread.

Her dad had used the phrase all the time. He loved to watch her squirm every time he did. He knew what she was imagining. He had even helped her to add some of the more horrendous details to her mental picture.

She missed him so much. He always told her she was a strong young lady and he was proud of her. She remembered he used to say nothing could bother you unless you let it. That's why he helped her make her mental image. The more over the top, the better. If you could laugh at the things that bothered you, they couldn't bother you anymore. You'd own them. Not the other way around.

He could always do that. It was his super power. Making her

feel stronger than she thought she was. He made her feel like she could do anything as long as he was there by her side. And then he was gone.

The two men, perhaps sensing they'd found the kink in her armor, continued to berate her. The entire room went silent but for the baritone of their raised voices. Not a single person had left. Though many, particularly the other women, stared at the floor.

Edie pushed off from the wall. She swayed and leaned forward, bracing herself with her knuckles on the table. She hoped it'd look like a power stance.

"Shut up," she said loud enough to bring the men's tirade to an abrupt end. They stared at her as if she were prey. Men always thought they were the hunters. Oh, how little they knew.

"It appears that Frazier and Niles here have a problem with our new reality," she continued, speaking to the crowd and refusing to look the two men in the eyes.

"I'm Thompson and he's Orson," said the man who had made himself comfortable.

Edie glared at him. "I don't care if you're Freud and Jung. I wish you exhibited this much passion for your patients. If I'm not mistaken, you two have the highest turnover rate of the practice. Apparently, you feel talk therapy works best if you talk and your patients listen. I bet you're great with the ladies, too."

The room erupted with laughter. Both men stood and glared at her. Their faces twisted with hatred and spotted red. Edie couldn't tell if it was with rage or embarrassment.

"There is too much testosterone in this place," Edie said before either man could continue their tirade. "The air is thick with it. That's precisely why you both are leaving. I expect your offices to be cleared out by the end of the day."

Someone sniggered under their breath, but neither man spoke. They looked stunned at her sudden assertiveness. "I may not know your names, but I know the kind of men you are," she continued before they regained their voices. "Adrian is dead. This will no longer be a good old boys' club. You don't have to be a woman to work here, but you better at least show that you understand them. Now get the hell out of my practice."

The room erupted into applause. The men looked at each other, then pushed their way through the crowd. Edie took a bow then escaped as quickly as she could to the safety of her office and collapsed onto her couch.

EDIE'S EYES FLUTTERED OPEN. THE LAST THING SHE REMEMBERED was running to the bathroom, hand over her mouth, willing the vomit to hold off, just slow down a little, so she could make it to the toilet. Thank god she'd convinced Adrian she needed a private bathroom. All the stress, the pain, and the loss of the last several days exploded from her with such force that her ribs ached. She had heaved so hard it felt like her sides would crush her internal organs. She felt the capillaries in her eyelids burst just like they used to when she was a kid and got a stomach virus. That hadn't happened in years.

Afterwards, she had sunk to the inviting coolness of the tile floor. She must have fallen asleep. A distant knock brought her mind back to the present. *That must have been what woke me up*, she thought. She glanced at her watch. Oh, no. She had slept the entire day. No wonder whoever was knocking sounded insistent.

She carefully got up and walked through her darkened office. "Hey, Maybelle," she said to the diminutive older woman who had been the only staff member Adrian had allowed her to hire. She was an impressive receptionist. But more than that, she reminded Edie of her grandmother. When Edie had asked her why she was looking for a job at her age, Maybelle had looked her in the eye with such a serious expression Edie thought for a moment she was going to yell at her. But then her sternness melted into the largest smile Edie had ever seen. It was one of those genuine smiles you couldn't fake. The kind that lifts the corners of your eyes and causes your forehead to crease. "Because being a widow with no grandchildren is boring as hell, honey. I'm still alive, and I want to live." Edie hired her on the spot.

"Are you okay, honey?" Maybelle asked as she looked past Edie and around her office. "You've been in here for an awfully long time, and I heard you earlier. Don't worry. I made a lot of noise so nobody else would know what was going on." She winked at Edie with a conspiratorial smile.

"I'm fine, Maybelle. Thank you for checking on me, and for covering for me," Edie said. "It's just been a hard week, you know?"

"I do, honey. I remember when I lost my Eugene. Took me quite some time before I was myself again. You just give yourself some time. Time and wine. That was my secret." Maybelle winked again as she said her goodbyes and left for the evening.

Edie closed the door but didn't move. *Time and wine.* She laughed and shook her head. Maybelle always knew exactly what to say to make things seem better. A thought suddenly came to Edie, and she raced across the office to her filing cabinet. Everyone has secrets. *Of course,* she thought, as Timothy's last words once again came to her. She knew they hadn't been random. They had sounded so oddly familiar. He had sent her a message!

She tore through her files, trying to recall the story that was circling just outside of her conscious memory. "Aha!" she exclaimed to the empty room. She stood in the middle of a pile of papers holding her notes from the session about Timothy's childhood recollection of the tooth fairy. *Okay, so I found it,* she thought. *What now? What are you trying to tell me, Timothy?*

She read her notes over and over, desperate to find a clue. Nothing jumped out at her. No obvious clue or key to unlock the mystery. She slumped down into her chair and stared at the ceiling. The answer was here; she just needed to find it. She pushed off against the leg of her desk then tucked her feet under her as the chair spun around. She closed her eyes and let all thoughts whisk away from her as she twirled.

"Holy shit," she said as she opened her eyes and stomped her feet to the ground to stop the spinning. She smiled, not quite as brightly as Maybelle could, but she could feel it radiating through her whole body. She knew what he was trying to tell her the night he died.

44

Eddie threw open the front door and ran through the foyer. She took the stairs two at a time, using her right hand to push off from the railing with each step. Her shoes flew off halfway up to her bedroom in the tower. At the landing, she doubled over. Her hands, slick with a thin layer of perspiration, slid down her thighs as she tried to catch her breath. Her skin glistened in the moonlight that shone through the window at the end of the hall.

Her legs burned and her lungs screamed at her, but she wouldn't let herself pause for long. The answer was here. She knew it. She was almost there. She bound down the hall and tore open her door. She flipped the light switch and blinked as her eyes adjusted to the brightness.

Her bedroom looked just as it did the last time she had been there. It seemed like a lifetime ago. She paused at the side of her bed. Now that she'd arrived and was so close to getting some answers, she wasn't sure she was ready to open Timothy's pandora's box. As much as she wanted to believe she knew the real man behind the persona he wore as her patient, she had to admit he had fooled her. He had probably sensed her disillusionment about her career and her skills and used it to have a little fun before he moved to his next target.

Her hand hovered above her pillow. She shook her head to drive out the assault of negative thoughts then grabbed her pillow and threw it over her shoulder. Nothing. She leapt onto the bed and knocked the other pillow to the side. Again, nothing.

Edie rolled over and closed her eyes. She wasn't even sure what she had expected to find. A note? A diary? A last will and testament? Maybe a key to a storage unit filled with proof he was a killer. Something. Anything. She sighed as tears welled up in her eyes. The clue was so obvious once she remembered the story Timothy had told her about the tooth fairy. Why wasn't it here?

She was on the cusp of sleep when she shot up onto her elbows. On the night Adrian was killed, Edie had awoken in the master bedroom. *Oh my god*, she thought. *Timothy wouldn't have known she wasn't sleeping with Adrian anymore.* Even if he was watching the house, trees obscured the master bedroom windows, and she always kept the curtains drawn in the guest room.

She rolled out of bed and walked pensively through the hallway and down a flight of stairs to the master bedroom. She didn't run. Didn't take the steps two at a time. Didn't work up a sweat. There was probably nothing there. Still, her skin tingled and her pulse quickened.

She paused at the doorway. She hated this room. *Please*, she thought as she crept into the room and looked down at the pillow on her side of the bed, *please let me be right*. She closed her eyes, bent over the bed, and slowly slid her hand under the pillow. Her fingers bumped into something. She slid her hand farther under the pillow and pulled out a thick manilla envelope.

Her knees buckled beneath her. She knelt at the side of the bed like a child preparing to recite her nightly prayers and cautiously opened the envelope. She pulled out a single sheet of yellow legal paper that had been crumpled but was now neatly folded, a smaller white envelope with her name written on the front in barely legible cursive, and a digital camera.

Edie looked at the crumpled yellow page. As she unfolded it, she could see it was covered front and back with faded writing. She pushed herself up and sat on the bed so she could hold the page close to the lamp on the nightstand. The same words were written over and over in every direction in what looked like a child's handwriting. "I love you," she whispered. She laughed as tears fell on the paper. She pulled it into her chest. Had he given her this to prove his stories were true, that she did know him, or to tell her how he felt about her? Just the act of sharing this sacred artifact of his past was enough to convince her their bond had been real. He had shared with her the real Timothy.

She gently placed the page on the nightstand and picked up the camera. It was a compact model with scratches on the rear viewing screen and a large dent on the front near the lens. She powered it up and navigated to the images folder.

Edie gasped as she flipped through the first few photos. They were taken of Adrian and Ruby Fisher, one of their colleagues. She was bent over the hood of Adrian's car, her skirt bunched around her waist, while he stood between her legs. His pants were on, but Edie could see they were unbuckled and unzipped.

Her finger trembled as it pressed the button to advance to the next photo. She furrowed her brow and brought the camera closer to her face. It was an innocent-looking picture of a young woman sitting on the front stoop of a house. She looked like she was no older than twenty. Edie didn't recognize the woman or the house.

Afraid of what else, and who else, might be on the camera, Edie dropped it on the bed next to her. She picked up the worn yellow page again and ran her fingers lightly over the child's scribbles. She closed her eyes and tried to picture Timothy as a child. Mistreated. Teased. An invisible young man who didn't matter. Not to his mother. Not to his first love.

But instead of shutting down, going inward, and shutting everyone out, with this one piece of paper he tried to let someone in. And she laughed at him for it. No wonder he couldn't talk to women. No wonder he made up the persona of a man who not only had no issues talking to women, but who could make them do whatever he wanted. A man who, unlike the real Timothy Ridle, felt nothing. A man who toyed with his victims, raped for sport, and murdered out of convenience.

Edie hugged his love note to her cheek and breathed in the faint scent of pencil lead. She picked up a slight salty smell. *Dried tears?* How many times had young Timothy held this same note in his hands and cried over a love lost before it could begin? How many times had he crumpled it up and thrown it in the trash can only to run back later to save it before it was lost forever? How many times did he wish his life was different?

Reluctantly, Edie set the paper down. She looked at the bed beside her. A camera with god knows what else on it and an envelope addressed to her. *Quite a pandora's box, indeed,* she thought. She wished Timothy had just left her his tattered middle school love note.

She wanted to put everything back in the manilla envelope and go to bed. So many thoughts filled her head at once she couldn't concentrate on any one of them. Her stomach rumbled, reminding her that she hadn't eaten since breakfast, which surely didn't count because she'd thrown that up. And she was tired. So very tired. But something about the envelope made her pick it up. It was thick but light. What if it was just an updated child's love note with adult scribblings of love over and over, in all directions on several pieces of paper? The last, mad ramblings of a forlorn man who had never learned to express himself, never been taught how to open himself up, to communicate, to love?

She smiled at the thought and wished she was naïve enough to convince herself. She held her breath as she tore the envelope open and unfolded the stack of pages. This was no child's note. It was a letter from Timothy. To her. Each page was neatly typed. She lay back in her bed, holding the letter above her as she used to do when she was a teenager and had received a note from a boy.

Hey, doc, the letter began. Edie could almost hear his voice as she read the familiar greeting.

How you doing? If you're reading this, then I guess you're doing better than I am. Pretty cool clue though, huh? Real cloak and dagger shit. You can't say I don't amuse you, doc, even when I'm dead. I don't know if you started with this letter or my other note or the camera, so I'm not exactly sure how to start this thing. I guess I'll start by explaining what I've left you.

The main thing is the camera. Well, not it so much as what's on it. But I suppose the camera is yours to keep now, too. I got it before I shipped out overseas. It saw a lot of action with me. Lots of GI bars, massage parlors, and marching. So much marching. Nothing as exciting as what it saw ever since I started watching over you though.

Edie rolled over on her side and propped her head on her hand. She wiped a tear from her cheek and shook her head with a smile. She imagined him writing these words, maybe just hours before his death. And yet they sounded so carefree, so

cavalier, so Timothy. She bit her tongue to ward off the water-
works and continued reading.

Now don't think bad of me, doc, but I kind of got into the habit
of watching you. It's what I've always done, I guess, watch the
world go by from a safe distance. But it was different with you.
Ever since I started seeing you, you made me feel seen. Do you
know what I mean? I could sense that we had a connection. I've
always been able to sense another lost soul, a kindred spirit, a fellow
child of suffering. There was Amy, my first girlfriend. We were both
six. Her older brother abused her. Then there was my best friend
Mikey in high school. His dad was a drunk. Beat him real bad.
Brian, my only real friend throughout my illustrious military
career, he killed his uncle when he caught him looking at little kids
on the internet. Well, he was alleged to have killed him, if you know
what I mean.

Finally, there's you. It took awhile for the connection to show
itself, but there it was. I think you could sense it, too, couldn't you?
Took you a bit longer, though, huh? I had to bring you out from
behind that thick-ass wall you've built up around yourself. I know
that wall, doc, just like I know you. We can always spot our own kind,
can't we?

So, anyway, that's why I started following you. And then I started
following that fat fuck you lived with, too. Sorry to speak ill of the
dead, but I figure I'm safe. Takes one to know one and all that. And
boy did he ever make things interesting.

That brings us back to the camera. The first few shots are just a
taste of the extracurricular activities he enjoyed, although how he ever
got any woman to enjoy them with him is beyond me. No offense, doc.
The next several pictures are of a young lady I think you can still help.
She's the daughter of one of the fat fuck's patients. They were sharing
her. If you have a weak constitution, you might want to skip the next
twenty-two images. But they're there in case you want to take them to
the police. Or, and this is what I'd do, take them to the young lady's

father and make him look at them while you pull a Bobbitt on him. Your choice, of course, doc.

EDIE GLANCED SIDEWAYS AT THE CAMERA TO MAKE SURE IT HADN'T moved. As if it were a venomous snake that could strike at any second if she didn't keep her guard up. She'd read less than half of Timothy's letter, and already her stomach was in knots and her mouth dry.

She fanned the pages of the letter out in front of her on the bed. The same bed where Adrian expected her to perform her carnal duties as his loyal girlfriend whenever the mood struck him. And yet she now had proof he wasn't a loyal boyfriend. The revelation itself came as no surprise, but she'd never had actual confirmation. It took a dead patient to prove her dead boyfriend was an asshole. Jesus, what a messed up life she'd been living for the last several years. If her dad could only see her now.

She picked up the camera with her finger and thumb on the wrist strap, holding it as far from her body as she could, and scooped up the letter. She had a feeling things were going to get much darker with Timothy serving as the disembodied host of a fucked up version of "This Is Your Life — The Edie McEvoy Episode."

The one useful lesson she'd learned from Adrian was that one should never face moments such as these sober. Her macabre memorabilia in hand, she descended into the depths of the house in search of a fitting bottle of wine.

Adrian's cellar office seemed dingier than she remembered. She'd never liked this part of the house, which is probably why he claimed it as his own, knowing she'd find it hard to invade his privacy. The wine, however, tasted better than she recalled. She thought about pouring out a dash in honor of the men she'd lost, but then her eyes fell on the camera now hanging from the

ear of Adrian's prized bust of Freud, and she decided she'd probably need every drop to get through Timothy's remaining last
words.

*There's something I never told you, doc. I know this comes as no
surprise. There's really quite a lot I never shared with you, though I
tried to tell you the important stuff. But there's one thing I didn't tell
you, and it's a big one. Forgive me the armchair psychiatry here, but I
think this is the thing that made me the man I am. Was.*

*I half expected you to ask me. I would have told you. I think.
Maybe not. Some things are too hard for a man to admit. Especially
for someone who wasn't much of a man at all. Not where it counted.
Not with women.*

*I wasn't just shy when it came to women, doc. I was practically
comatose. If a woman even looked at me, I froze up. Lose all control of
my muscles. I developed a real bad stutter in middle school, but it
only affected me when I was around girls. Anytime there was a
female of any kind within eyesight, I'd lose the ability to talk
normally.*

*That love note I wrote? The one that ended up being yet another
embarrassing milestone in my stellar career with the ladies? Look at
it? I mean really look at it, doc. What kind of love note is it, really?
Even in writing, all I could do was stutter.*

*In my whole life, there have been two women I could speak to
without stuttering. My mother. And you. Before you get all weepy
that you made the shortlist with my dear old mom, this is where I
have to tell you that big important thing that even in writing, even
when I know you won't see this until I've bid adios to this world, I find
myself stalling.*

*My mom raped me. Holy hell, doc, I said it. Well, I wrote it at
least. I've had that little nugget of Timothy truth locked up so tight
inside of me for half my life.*

The letter slipped out of Edie's hands. Her fingers had gone
numb. She watched the pages flutter to the ground. She reached

for her wineglass, but it was empty. She didn't remember finishing it. She poured another and drank it in one swallow.

One thought raced through her mind, growing louder and louder as it forced all other thoughts to the side. If Timothy had been assigned to a better psychologist, if Adrian hadn't foisted him upon her out of pettiness, he may still be alive. Even the bust of Freud seemed to agree as it glared at her from the side table as she bent and picked up the letter. Reading it was torture, but she felt certain she deserved it.

Remember, I told you my mom never cared too much about me and was always looking for the next man, hoping he'd be the last man? That was all true. She didn't care about me, but she did care about herself. And in between the men, she'd get awful lonely. You know what I mean, doc?

You don't have to answer. I already know your answer. Not the one you would have given me had I asked you in one of our sessions. I'm talking about the true answer. The one about the secret you buried as deep as I buried mine.

We breathe the same air, you and me. Well, we did when I was still breathing. Victims our whole lives. Living make believe characters. We were supporting roles in somebody else's story. Hurt the most by the ones who were supposed to take care of us.

EDIE FLIPPED TO THE FINAL PAGE OF TIMOTHY'S LETTER. TEARS and the effects of the wine magnified then shrank each letter of every word. What had started as neatly typed lines began to float across the page, flipping and circling and chasing one another. She squinted and blinked rapidly. She closed one eye then the other, turning her head slowly from side to side as she moved the page closer and farther from her face.

The words finally swam into precarious focus. She balanced her arms in front of her and was careful not to move. She felt like a kid again, with her dad using her to manipulate the TV antenna to tune in a Giants game.

Her arms seemed unusually heavy, and her eyelids threatened to close. But she dared not move. She had to finish what she started. So far, Timothy had dissected her as cleverly and as carefully as any psychologist could have.

It's hard being two people at once, isn't it, doc? I mean everyone plays different parts depending on the audience. We all choose which pieces of ourselves to share and to whom, don't we? But for you, I had to play the role of serial killer and rapist while also moonlighting as the same boring guy I've been staring at in the mirror my whole life.

I knew you would tire of the real me quicker than most because you're smarter than most. But I also knew my charade couldn't last forever. You'd see through me, eventually. We can always spot our own. I had to do something, you know? Some grand romantic gesture to prove to you, to myself really if I'm honest, that I was worthy of your love.

So the ball, as they say, is in your court now, doc. Although I don't know who says that, and frankly I've never understood it. If you're playing a game with someone, you're on the same court, aren't you? You're both there, so why is it your court? I should have asked you this during one of our sessions. It would have driven you crazy, and I like the look you get in your eye when you're slightly annoyed but also a little amused.

Anyway, my one regret is that I am not around to see that look anymore or to see what you thought of my gesture. And as for which life was worth more, yours or his, or mine or yours? I'll always bet on you, doc.

In the end, we both killed the one responsible for our sorrow. I by police. And you...well you know. And I want you to know it's okay. You're not evil. Far from it. In fact, Edie, I honestly believe you saved us both. And for that I thank you.

Edie's elbow slipped off the armrest of the couch, sending all three wine bottles crashing to the ground in a symphony of broken glass. The wine from the half-full third bottle splashed across the cellar floor. She flung herself over the side of the couch, trying to save it. She landed on her shoulder, but the force of the fall caused her head to bounce off the concrete. The last thing she saw was a sea of red. Her eyes widened as remembered pools of blood splattered across her last few moments of consciousness.

45

E die awoke in the darkness of the dungeon. She shivered against the cold concrete. Her head felt like it was being squeezed in a vice. She slowly pulled herself onto her hands and knees. She was covered in something sticky. Her eyelids fought against a thin layer of crust as she squinted into the darkness.

"What the hell," Edie whispered, then immediately winced at the sound of her own voice. It felt like someone had stuffed cotton in her mouth. The insides of her cheeks stuck to her gums. Her tongue seemed to have inflated to four times its normal size. Her brain threatened to pound its way out of her skull every time she moved her head. So she tenderly lowered it back to the soothing coldness of the floor. What happened to the lights?

She had never spent much time in the cellar, but she did finally remember why she'd woken up in the dark. Adrian had spent a fortune to renovate the house in meticulous period detail, except for his damn man cave. Everything here was connected through a wi-fi hub that controlled the lighting and the temperature, which he had explained to her many times must remain precise for both his wine and his cigars.

She turned her head and pressed her cheek to the floor. Her stomach bubbled and churned. She knew she was about to either burp or throw up if she didn't move. She couldn't predict which, so she struggled to lift herself to the couch. As she fell into the warmth of the cushions, her hand brushed against Timothy's camera. Through the fog of her hangover, she remembered nearly finishing his letter, which seemed longer than her college thesis and more insightful into the human condition.

She set the camera on her lap. She'd already seen the evidence of Adrian's depravity. Why bother looking at the rest of the contents? But, she reasoned, she was over the shock of the first images so she might as well objectively view the rest. She wanted to laugh at the insanity of silently arguing with herself, but she dared not jostle her head.

The screen glowed a soft green as she powered the camera on. She toggled to the first photo, the one of her colleague and Adrian. She stared at it for several minutes, feeling nothing but allowing her eyes to adjust. They seemed to focus independently of each other and took a while to synchronize. She didn't hate Alison. She barely knew her. Nothing had stood out about her as particularly memorable. Average intelligence. Average looks. What did that say about Edie if this was Adrian's type? *Fuck her*, she thought, and chuckled because that's precisely what Adrian must have thought, too.

She scrolled to the photo of the twenty-something daughter of one of Adrian's patients. Heeding Timothy's warning, she squeezed her eyes half shut while she advanced through what must have been two dozen photos of the girl and two men. She nearly retched all over herself and the camera even as she intentionally kept her eyes out of focus while the photos scrolled across the screen.

Just knowing that the man she lived with was capable of such a thing filled her with anger. Not with him, but with herself. She was mad she had stayed for so long with someone she knew, better than most, was a monster. How weak must she have been to have let him take over her life?

She squeezed the camera tightly in her hands. Image after image continued to scroll across its tiny screen. How long had he been involved with these people? It was like he was an alcoholic with an unquenchable thirst.

The camera's screen finally went black. *Thank god*, she thought, grateful she could bring her eyes into focus again. Her body felt numb, but her mind raced. Her pulse throbbed in her temple, echoing through her head like a jackhammer.

This photographic proof seemed a step too far, even for Timothy. His final act, his final letter, they would have been more than enough to convince her he was telling the truth about Adrian's infidelity. Why, then had Timothy thrown in the camera, like some added bonus with an order from a late night infomercial. It was the cruelest thing he'd ever done to her. Even worse than convincing her he was a rapist and serial killer.

Her grip hardened around the camera. She willed all of her strength into her hands so she could smash the cursed thing. Her fingers turned white, and her nails made superficial scratches along the surface, but it refused to bend to her will. Just as she decided to throw the camera across the room, she noticed that its screen wasn't completely black. A small white triangle flashed in the middle. Without thinking, she pressed play.

Little flashes of light appeared at the top edges of the screen. A man's voice streamed quietly through the camera's tiny speaker. Edie turned up the volume. Chills ran down her spine and a shiver jolted through her body, shaking her so intensely she almost dropped the camera.

It was Adrian. "We're done. Tomorrow I'll move into a hotel until we can sort out our affairs."

As he spoke, the camera, which must have been pointed down at the ground, tilted up. There he was. Alive, and more agitated than Edie ever remembered seeing him. His image kept bouncing around as if the cameraman, Timothy, was across the street with the lens zoomed in as far as it could go.

It was nighttime. Adrian was facing away from the camera talking to someone at the large tree in their front yard. When the hell did Timothy shoot this? And why?

"You can leave, but I won't make it easy for you. I won't be the victim. Not this time. Not ever again." Edie's disembodied voice floated up from the speaker. She threw the camera to the other side of the couch. *What the hell?* She knew it was her, but at the same time she refused to believe it.

Her sleepwalking episodes began shortly after she and her mom moved in with her stepdad. She was just a naïve teenager then. Her mom, who was even more naïve, had been convinced they were caused by the onslaught of her periods. And they did start around the same time. Blood played a big role in some of the most pivotal moments of Edie's life. But in all the years she had been a sleepwalker, nobody, not her mom nor roommates nor even Adrian, had ever said anything about her being able to hold lucid conversations in her sleep.

"Jesus, Edie, what did you do?"

Timothy's voice shook her back to the present. She picked up the camera. Blood was pooled and splattered across the light dew that covered the ground. The image shook violently. Edie held the camera tighter, but she wasn't the cause of the vibration. Timothy, who must have crossed the road once she and Adrian had gone inside the house, now stood over the bloody area where she had been sitting.

His breath sounded ragged and rapid. He made retching sounds but never threw up. *Good thing*, Edie thought. In her current state, just hearing him retch was enough to turn her already sour stomach.

Small beads of sweat popped up along her neck and forehead. Her inner thighs radiated with an uncomfortable heat. It felt as though each individual cut had been lit on fire. So this must be the night her beautifully neat rows of scars had been obliterated. How could she have done so much damage to herself and held what appeared to be a heated argument all while asleep?

Edie rubbed her arms against her thighs while still holding onto the camera as if it were a lifeline. It was in a sense. It was a peek into a side of her life she'd only ever heard about from others. Her entire life, she'd endured countless stories of her sleepwalking adventures. Some had been funny, others just weird, but none of them had been like this. It scared her to look, but her eyes remained glued to the screen.

The camera jerked to the left. Timothy started walking toward the front door. *Oh my god*, she thought. *He came into our house. Oh no. Timothy, why? And why did you film it?* She thought back to her first impressions of the man. Meek. Boring even. She knew first impressions were a lazy way to categorize a person, but she'd never been so wrong about someone in her life. She held her breath as he paused on the steps to the porch.

The camera jerked again. Timothy pointed it at the ground. She saw only his feet as he ran back into the yard. His breathing came in heavy gulps as the camera settled on the side of the house. The bottom of the kitchen window just visible at the top of the frame. Edie held her breath. The hairs on the back of her neck stood up. Her skin tingled and every muscle tensed. The rhythm of her heartbeat pulsed through her whole body.

"Go home, Timothy," she pleaded to the camera.

But he didn't go home. The screen didn't go black. After a moment, it tilted up. He was filming into her kitchen.

Adrian stood at the island. He was making a sandwich. Slamming cold cuts, lettuce and cheese onto his bread. Edie stood a few feet from him. She leaned against the island. Her eyes were open, but nothing about this moment was familiar to her now as she watched the events unfold.

She and Adrian were clearly continuing their argument. She couldn't make out what was being said, but their manic hand gestures and fiery looks made it clear neither of them was backing down. Edie closed her eyes and tried to will the memories from the darkness of her brain. Nothing. It was as if the moment didn't exist except on film.

When she opened her eyes, Adrian was walking back to the island from the knife block on the other counter. He cut his sandwich and took a bite before using it as a prop, jabbing it towards her to punctuate whatever hateful words were coming out of his mouth. She hated it when he talked with his mouthful. Such a disgusting habit for someone who claimed to be so refined.

The Edie on the screen smacked the sandwich out of Adrian's hands. He raised his hand above his head as if he were about to strike her. But before he could, she picked up the knife and jabbed it into his chest. His arm fell to his side and his face went slack. He looked down at the knife she still held. Blood slowly seeped into his shirt. He blinked emptily. He started to say something, but she pulled the knife out and casually slit his throat.

The picture on the camera jerked, then showed a closeup of the base of one of the bushes under the window. She heard Timothy retching in the background. When the camera moved again, she saw herself bending over Adrian, his pants around his legs as she cut into him again before the screen went black.

Edie sat motionless for a long time. Then she rewound the footage and watched herself murder Adrian over and over. Each time she watched it, it felt more and more right. Like she was seeing her true self for the first time. She wasn't weak. She wasn't a damsel in need of a white knight. She was a warrior.

She hoped with each new viewing that her memory would fill in the blanks. But, like the screen at the end of the footage, her mind was just blackness. She turned the camera off and wept into the darkness.

Timothy had video evidence that she murdered Adrian. He could have taken it to the police, but instead he took it to his grave. No man had ever done something so noble, so romantic for her.

EPILOGUE

"Unexpressed emotions will never die. They are buried alive and will come forth later in uglier ways."

— SIGMOND FREUD

SIX MONTHS LATER

Eddie slices through the flesh slowly, meticulously. Straight, razor thin lines. Her hand is practiced, her mind on autopilot. The knife makes a satisfying sound with each cut. She closes her eyes and listens. The scent is intoxicating. It mingles with the fresh spring breeze that's making the kitchen curtains dance lightly behind her.

She licks her knife and sets it down while she examines her handy work. *Perfect*, she thinks to herself. She sprinkles a healthy dose of cinnamon on each slice of the apple as she neatly stacks them on a small dish. Satisfied with her creation, she grabs the knife and turns to the sink to rinse it off. The late morning sun sparkles across the water and the blade, and she's reminded that this knife is new to her collection. It replaced the blade that felled the mighty Dr. Adrian Hillary some six months ago.

Life is strange sometimes, she thinks as she dries her hands on a bright yellow kitchen towel. If someone had asked her a year ago if she would be running a successful psychology practice devoted to the treatment of abused and battered young women, she would have laughed. It was the sort of thing she never would have even entertained when Adrian was around. He ran things, not her. Especially not by herself. She, well, she just existed. What was it Timothy said about his own life? Oh yes, she just floated along, content to be taken wherever Adrian's rapids led her.

She picks up her plate of apples and carries it carefully to the table. Then she sets about making herself a cup of tea. As the water boils, she heaps four tablespoons of green tea leaves into the infuser of her teapot. It's a beautiful antique ceramic pot. The lid looks like the lantern room of a lighthouse. Its yellow windows are so bright they appear to glow, and she just loves the little red roof on the top. The pot itself serves as a canvas for a whimsical hand-painted lighthouse on the shores of a quaint little seaside village.

The first time Edie saw the teapot, she felt like she could walk into it and disappear into the sunset. It had felt like home. She discovered it just a few weeks ago at a garage sale while she walked around her neighborhood. She walks a lot these days, but she's always fully awake.

She uses her knife once more to cut a lemon. She shivers as she makes each wafer thin slice. She thinks about rinsing the knife again but stops herself, admiring the thick lemon residue across its blade. *That would sting*, she thinks with a smile. She sets the knife down on the cutting board.

She pours boiling water into the pot and grabs an old coffee mug. It's nothing special. Its Columbia University crest is fading into obscurity, much like the memory and legacy of the late Adrian Hillary. He's been on her mind a lot the past few days. As she nibbles on a cinnamon apple slice, she thinks about his impact on her life.

She killed him because, even in an unconscious state, she had known that she needed to end his hold over her. She had needed to avenge her rape, to punish him for the pain he had caused her. And the worst thing anyone could do to Adrian was to forget him.

She takes a sip of tea and smiles at the logo of their alma mater. Adrian isn't even a footnote in its vaunted history. None of his old colleagues sent cards or called with their condolences. It is as if he never existed at all. Edie smiles over the lip of her mug.

Oh how he must be rolling over in his grave. Even it doesn't serve as a reminder. Edie had seen to that. No gravestone. Just a numbered plaque corresponding with his name in a large and dusty ledger the cemetery keeps of all of its occupants. The caretaker had assured her that no one ever asks about random graves. Nevertheless, she had promised to pay him well to make sure nobody ever learns the identity of the corpse at marker SW1130.

She pops an entire apple slice in her mouth and holds it on her tongue, savoring the tangy sweetness of the cinnamon. It wasn't until after the fat fuck was dead that she had realized the extent and depth of the damage he'd done to her. He must have sensed something in her. She knew from research that predators could sense when their prey was weak, damaged somehow.

Hell, she thinks, her entire life has been primary research for this particular area of psychological study. Maybe she had given off some battered woman pheromone that Adrian couldn't resist. *There's a lovely thought.* What if the "she made me do it" defense is real? What if she and all other abused women truly are responsible for their attacks, at least biologically, because they give off some stupid victim-scented invitation to their attackers? Wow, she is starting to sound like Adrian. Still, she wonders if she has a different scent these days. She will have to ask. Something floral, she hopes and laughs at the absurdity of her own thoughts.

She dabs the corners of her eyes and mouth with an orange

cloth napkin. She sighs as she thinks, not for the first time today, of the sacrifice Timothy made for her. If she had witnessed a murder, she doesn't think she'd have the wherewithal to keep herself together. And yet he not only cleaned up the crime scene and dumped Adrian's body, but he also cleaned her up and tucked her into bed before making sure all the evidence pointed to him.

She smiles as she takes her dishes to the sink and dons her white rubber gloves with pink polka dots and lacy ruffles. She looks out the window as she scrubs her plate. This is her favorite time of year. Not so long ago, she didn't think she'd see another spring.

Funny how time changes things, she thinks. We're all just tiny pebbles in a stream. And time is the relentless water. It has a way of moving us around, smoothing out our edges, sometimes even beating us down or changing us completely. We're helpless, all of us, captive to this relentless flow of time.

Once, Edie had believed the world was filled with liars, and that love was the greatest lie mankind had ever invented. She still believes everyone lies. She, more than most, knows everyone has secrets. Some are innocent, silly even. But then there are the darker lies, which ironically often reveal the truth about someone you thought you knew. Adrian had thought he knew her, but he hadn't. It was Timothy who saw through her lies. Who saw her true self. And he loved her anyway.

The truth, she now knows, is that time is cyclical. She doesn't believe in karma so much as she understands that time catches up to all of us. It comes back around eventually. Just like the seasons. Adrian represented the dismal transition from fall to winter. All death and decay. And Timothy? He was her spring. A ray of warmth that had convinced her life is worth living. And that she should no longer be afraid to live as she wants.

The hot water washes over her hands, and she feels

cleansed. She flicks her gloves and hangs them neatly next to the drying rack. On her way out of the kitchen she picks up the lemon juice encrusted knife and heads to her cellar. She smiles as she sings her favorite song, "Love is a Battlefield," under her breath.

EDIE STOKES THE FIRE IN THE LIVING ROOM FIREPLACE. THE thought that this might be the last fire of the season makes her a little sad. Nothing is more relaxing, more hypnotic and meditative than staring into a blazing fire. She loves this fireplace. In fact, the living room has recently become her favorite room in her house. It had been neglected when Adrian was alive. The two of them never just sat together. He'd lumber down to his cellar, and she'd go to bed hoping to be asleep by the time he joined her. But now she looks around the room with its fresh coat of autumn orange paint and its rustic wood accents, and it fills her with peace.

Music fills the air and her heart. She chose a record by Bessie Smith for tonight's soundtrack, and the beautiful, bluesy number, "Outside of That," wafts up from the record player in the cellar with the occasional muffled baritone moaning accompanying the late great singer.

Well, I better get down to business, she thinks to herself as she pours her first glass of wine of the day. Adrian may have been a world-class asshole, but the man sure knew how to pick a great wine. She sinks back into the leather couch she'd brought up from the cellar months ago and looks at the stack of papers she trudged up earlier. The last of Adrian's scholarly works.

One by one, Edie reads each page. She's been cleaning out Adrian's papers for three months. Reading them has really helped her understand the man. Although, like most men, Adrian wasn't overly complex. And she actually enjoys reading his treatises on various psychoses. After she reads each page, she tosses it on the fire and watches as the flames burn holes in it, melting the ink before devouring the entire page.

She picks a crinkled envelope from the box. It's sealed with her name on it in Adrian's heavy, pointed handwriting. She rips it open wondering why he'd never given it to her. The envelope holds a single, sloppily written note.

My dearest Edie. I know I'm not perfect. I know you and I see the world differently and that it might seem to you that I never listen, never agree with you, never heed your counsel. But, my darling, I do. It might take me some time. I have to internalize your opposing viewpoints, your unique way of interpreting situations. I have to battle with my own stubbornness and desire to always be right. But I, more than anyone, know that I'm not always right. It's necessary to hide my uncertainty, to veil it in an attitude of hubris that befits my stature. Still, I think even you'd agree that I eventually come around, despite my worst instincts. Because I respect you. I trust you. And I love you. All I ask is that we leave the past behind us, let old wounds heal, and old mistakes die. I'm not a perfect man. But I do love you. I hope, I wish, that is enough for you.

Edie stares at the limp piece of paper in her hand. Uncertainty pushes its way into her thoughts. She blinks, and it's gone. *Too little too late as always*, she thinks. She shreds the page and envelope into long strips and slowly drops them one by one into the fireplace.

The pop and hiss of the fire move her mind from Adrian and back to a much larger blaze. Like her sleepwalking spells, her nightmares about the burning lighthouse have all but disappeared. Excised with Adrian's ghost, she supposes. Or perhaps her new calling in life and all the good works she has done in the six short months since Adrian died have relieved her conscience.

Still, sitting here admiring the fire brings back the faint

whispers of her past. She could almost hear her step daddy's breathing as he panted above her on her tiny twin bed, its rusty box springs squeaking in time to his assault. She smells his whiskey tainted breath, the warmth of it makes her shoulder twitch and her head shudder at the memory. His hand is on her throat. He makes her look at him.

Ever since he had started dating her mom, he would surreptitiously find reasons to touch Edie. Even when her mom was in the room. But the woman was blinded by love, or maybe she was just happy to have a respite from the loneliness after having lost her husband. Still, hadn't she seen this man was nothing like Edie's dad? Didn't she notice her bright, beautiful daughter had withdrawn into herself? If she did, she chose the man over the daughter.

Edie crouches forward on the couch as she stares into the fire. It's pulling her in, inviting her to relive that day when she became a woman. She looks into his eyes. She sees the fire there, too. He doesn't notice as her hand slowly reaches for the knife she stashed under her mattress after dinner. He barely slows down at first after she slices at his throat. She can smell the copper scent of his blood as it pours from him. His hand recoils from her as he desperately tries to clasp the wound shut, to stem the bleeding. Then slowly, she sees the realization in his eyes. She's killed him.

She pushes him to the floor and runs to the front door of the lighthouse. Her mom meets her at the front steps. She'd just gone out for her evening walk. She screams at Edie, but she can't understand a word she's saying. Then her mom pushes past her into the house. Edie climbs the long staircase to the top. The ocean crashes in rhythm to her heartbeat on the rocks below. She throws the knife into the sea. She steps over the railing. She just wants the pain to end. She closes her eyes. Before she can jump her mother's screams tear through the air, first from behind her then down to the rocks below. Her mom let a man rob Edie of her childhood, and then she robbed her of her final escape.

EDIE THROWS ANOTHER PIECE OF PAPER ON THE FIRE. SHE HAD left Adrian's latest work for last, and now that she's reading it, she is glad she saved it. She intends to burn all of his research notes, letters, and other papers of little consequence. There's plenty of that minutia. The man hoarded everything he wrote, even grocery lists. Not that he ever did any of the shopping on his own.

She shakes her head as she reads about herself from Adrian's perspective. He got a lot of things wrong, but his theories and diagnoses weren't all together wrong. Not bad, she thinks, for research that excluded any subject interviews and relied solely on biased secondhand observations. He wasn't so much dating her as studying her. The man was a born romantic.

He knew she was looking for a daddy figure. The bastard wrote how he pegged her the first time she had visited him in his office with a question about one of his lectures. He might have been a genius, but his flaws outweighed his gifts. She sighs and takes another sip of her wine. She enjoys this little drinking game she's invented. Read. Burn. Drink.

A few drops of wine slosh onto her hand. She should slow down. As she looks at the crimson droplets sliding across her skin, her thoughts turn to blood. The police had eventually come around after Edie hadn't shown up to school for a couple days. They found her sitting against the railing at the top of the lighthouse. Her bare feet dangling over the waves. She was barely conscious. According to their crack investigation, it had been a clear-cut case of murder suicide. Edie, they surmised, had walked in on her mom in the act and chased her up the lighthouse. But she had been too late to save her mom.

It's a good thing she never told Adrian everything about her childhood. He would have had a field day with that new data. While other boyfriends might have tried to console her or even runaway as fast as they could, she imagines Adrian would have probed her for the most minute details so he could more accurately describe her particular psychological issues.

Herman leaps into Edie's lap. He purrs loudly as he paws at the fuzzy blanket she'd thrown over herself, knowing he'd come for a visit, eventually. She rubs behind his ear. He rewards her by nuzzling against her hand. She tosses the final few pages of Adrian's opus into the fire and smiles as she watches them disappear in the flames. *Just like that*, she thinks, *all traces of the monster have been erased from this earth.*

She absentmindedly scratches Herman's head. "Just one more thing to burn," she says to him, but he ignores her. Typical man. Her laugh spooks him, and he jumps down to find a quieter place for his sixtieth nap of the day. "Your loss," she yells after him, eliciting renewed moans from the cellar.

She gingerly picks up the worn pages of Timothy's letter. Read. Burn. Drink. Tears drop unfettered onto the last page as she clutches it in her hand, rereading his last words.

You know that woman I told you I was chasing, doc? The one in my dreams? The one I hoped I deserved but knew I didn't? Well, I finally caught up to her. To you. I even think I saved her in the end. At least I hope I did. Even though my armor was all tarnished and dented, I hope I finally helped you rediscover the warmth and the light of the day. Because nobody as beautiful as you should be locked in the darkness.

I guess this is it. Thank you, doc. Thank you for helping me finally step out of the shadows. You helped me discover my life's meaning.

Better late than never, right? I hope you find yours, too. Love, Timothy.

Edie smiles and holds the last page, the last vestiges of Timothy's confession, over the fire. She lets it drop. The fire crackles and pops and grows brighter. So does her heart. She's finally comfortable with who she is and has always been.

She looks around. Nothing more to burn tonight. She pours the last of Adrian's expensive wine into her glass and lights one of Adrian's prized cigars. Maybe you can't outrun your past anymore than you can pretend not to be the person you were born to be. At least not forever. The lies always catch up to you. For some, they end badly. She thinks of Adrian as she puffs on the cigar.

She stands up and heads to her man cave. She smiles around the cigar as she walks closer to the man's screams below the house. *Man cave is still a fitting name for the repurposed cellar*, she thinks. Adrian's last patient, and her newest, waits for her there. His daughter is safe now, but he isn't.

It's refreshing to know your true self. To not have to lie to the reflection in the mirror like you do to everyone else you meet. Since Adrian's death, Edie has found a renewed passion for her life's work. She hasn't cut in months. Not herself anyway. She's found a way to cut without drawing her own blood. Remarkably, the euphoria and the release are just as powerful without the nasty scarring. And there seems to be no end to those in need of a little cutting.

She reaches for the door to the cellar just as someone knocks on the front door.

"Hɪ, Ms. McEvoy," the detective says through the crack in the door. "It's been awhile."

Edie pastes on a smile. "Detective! What a pleasant

surprise," she says without moving to open the door wider or offering to let the detective in. "To what do I owe the honor?"

The detective looks past Edie, who wonders if she can hear her patient over the music. "I just thought I'd check in. I've been keeping an eye on you ever since everything went down. It's funny, you know? How some cases stick with you even when they're closed."

"I can imagine."

"I bet you can. I've even thought maybe I could come and see you at your office. You know, like as a patient."

Edie cocks her head, her eyes squinting as she examines the detective more closely. "Oh. Well, that might be a little unorthodox, but I guess we could give it a try. I don't have my schedule on me though. Why don't you call my office on Monday, and we'll see if we can work something out?"

"Sure, doc."

Edie freezes. "You okay, Ms. McEvoy? You look like you've seen a ghost?"

"I...I'm fine, detective. Thank you for stopping by." She tries to close the door, but the detective wedges her foot between the door and the frame.

The detective is still smiling as if nothing out of the ordinary has happened, but Edie sees something dark in her eyes. "May I come in?"

Edie's mind races. "I don't think that'd be a good idea right now. I'm in the middle of something. Let's talk Monday."

The detective pushes past Edie with ease. She stops in the foyer and looks around. Then she turns to Edie. Her smile has widened, but her eyelids are at half mast. They stare at each other. Then the detective winks at her.

"If there's nothing else, detective, I really think you should go now."

"Just one more thing, actually." The detective wanders over

to the cellar door. Edie holds her breath and hopes her patient remains quiet. "I have a confession to make, Ms. McEvoy. I know it was you. I know what you did, and I know what you're doing now."

Edie's blood runs cold. She tries to remember where she left her knife. If she could lure the detective into the kitchen, she could distract her with an offer for tea or coffee and then grab a knife or hit her with the kettle full of boiling water.

"I have just one question," the detective said, pulling Edie from her half-formed plan. "Do they all deserve it?"

Edie wonders at the trap such a simple question hides, but she can't help herself. "Yes," she confides.

The detective strides over to her. Edie flinches, readying herself for the blow. Instead, the detective grabs her cigar and puts it in her own mouth. After a few puffs, she blows the smoke from the side of her mouth with a flourish.

"Then I want in."

BOOK EXTRAS

If you enjoyed this book and aren't ready to let these characters go, sign up for my free newsletter at jeffberney.com/killer-extras-signup.

I'll only visit your inbox about twice a month. Sign up now for an instant behind-the-scenes experience only available to my readers...

Get tons of exclusive book extras, including:

- The news article that inspired the novel
- Book Club discussion guide
- The original three-act synopsis
- Character worksheets (see how the characters changed from initial idea to final book)
- One-page story writeup (it definitely changed once the characters took over and started doing what they wanted)
- Advanced notice on upcoming books

- Chances to win signed books and other prizes
- Chance to become a beta reader
- A behind-the-scenes look at the life of a novelist
- And more fun stuff we haven't even thought of yet

REVIEWS

I hope you enjoyed this story. Your honest review would mean a great deal to me. You can review this book at any online book retailer or at Goodreads.com.

This is my debut novel, so I really want to know what you enjoyed about it. Every review helps. I appreciate your support and look forward to seeing you in the pages of my upcoming books!

ACKNOWLEDGMENTS

This is actually my second debut novel. The first is enjoying a long run in the dark recesses of my hard drive and in the cloud. And there it shall stay until I'm gone from this earth or too senile to stop my progeny from selling it to the highest bidder where it will be published in a limited run and rightly scorned, perhaps irreparably tarnishing my stellar image as one of the greatest novelists to ever live. Most likely, though, it will be forgotten. As it should be. But I learned a lot from that process. I'd like to think this story you just read is better for it. You'll just have to take my word on that.

Writing a book is mostly a solo journey filled with much introspection and navel gazing. You make up these characters then mess with their lives. All while trying to make an imaginary world seem real for yourself and the reader. It's a lot of fun. And heartache. And worry. Much like real life. But that's writing. On the other hand, editing and publishing a book is a team sport. And as a new author, an independent one at that, I'm lucky to have a talented team of family and friends who helped me shape my story.

This book would not be what it is without my wife, alpha reader, editor, harshest critic, and loudest cheerleader. Thank you, Christy, for believing in me even in my darkest moments. You are my best friend, my rock, my confidant, my savior. I love you so damn much. My kids and parents were also enthusiastic cheerleaders throughout the whole process. I'm sure there were several times you thought I wouldn't finish, but it was your excitement, energy and endless questions that kept me going.

The brilliant cover was designed by a great art director and first-time cover designer, Jake Campbell. Jake, thank you for your friendship and for bringing my vision to life in a way that far exceeds even my imagination. If people judge a book by its cover, your work will make sure they judge mine positively. I hope this won't be our last literary collaboration. I should also add that his young daughter, Bristol, helped her dad by flicking the red paint that became the blood splatters on the cover.

And to my beta readers, a huge thanks for your enthusiasm and honesty. I didn't choose you because I hoped for pats on the back and easy critiques. I knew that although you are family, friends, and colleagues, you would give me honest, constructive criticism that would only make my book better. And that's exactly what you provided. Many thanks to Dave Altis, Brittany Berney, Rich Berney, Vicki Berney, Laura Harrity, Brandi Parsons, Chelsie McCullough, Adam Seitz, Missy Simms, Monica Swearingen, Mike Yardley. I hope you enjoyed your preview as much as I enjoyed your feedback. I am forever in your debt.

A big thank you to Kenny Johnson for my brilliant headshots that make me look better in print and on screen than in real life. Kenny is an amazing Kansas City based photographer. If you know me and think I look a bit different, well that's because we did the photo shoot for my original debut novel a few years ago. At least I finally got to put these great shots to use.

And last but not least, thank you to the city of Kansas City, Missouri, for being an interesting place to live and grow. Most of the KC locations I mention in this book are real, though I might have taken a bit of creative license with the details.

Made in the USA
Middletown, DE
11 August 2021

45844835R10210